Indecisions

Nelda Jo,
The trilogy
ends!
Mary c. Drechsel

Sissy Marilyn
3/06

Also available by **SISSY MARLYN**:

Intimacies

Illusions

Details at www.sissymarlyn.com

Indecisions

SISSY MARLYN

Copyediting by Robert Ritchie

BEARHEAD PUBLISHING
- BhP -

Louisville, Kentucky

BEARHEAD PUBLISHING
- BhP -

Louisville, Kentucky
www.sissymarlyn.com

Indecisions
By Sissy Marlyn
Copyediting by Robert Ritchie

Cover Photography Licensed to Bearhead Publishing
Front Cover Design by Bearhead Publishing
First Printing – November 2005
ISBN: 0-9776260-0-8

Printed in the USA

To my husband, Gary, a.k.a. *Bearhead*,
who has supported my writing 110%.
I couldn't have done it without you!
Love ya' bunches!

- Baby

Acknowledgements

I would like to thank the following Individuals, Places, and Organizations for your help in making this book come to life:

David Letterman and *The Late Show with David Letterman* –
   for having the most amazing nighttime show.
   Sissy Marlyn hopes to visit the set soon.
House of Blues, Myrtle Beach, SC and HOB Entertainment –
   a great venue for concerts. **Sissy Marlyn** peeped
   inside once.
Gaylord Entertainment Center, Nashville, TN –
   an awesome venue for concerts. Neil Diamond,
   October 2005 – **Sissy Marlyn** was there!
United Center, Chicago, IL –
   a mega venue for concerts. **Sissy Marlyn** loves Chicago
   and everything associated with it.
National Street Rod Association –
   for putting on great shows, of which **Sissy Marlyn**
   was privileged to be a vendor at in their Women's World
   in Louisville, KY, August 2005.
Holiday Inn Anaheim Resort Area, Anaheim, CA –
   Sissy Marlyn enjoyed her stay there, May 2005.

I would also like to acknowledge all of the hard work, talent, time and effort that my copyeditor, Robert Ritchie, put into *Indecisions*. Thank you also for your skills on the second printing of *Intimacies* and the first printing of *Illusions*. I look forward to working with you on many more novels. *Hint: Jury Pool – 2006.*

This is a young man to be proud of. He teaches at the University of Louisville. He is finishing up his Masters, and he is also an aspiring published author. Bearhead Publishing would be honored to publish this fine young gentleman's first book. Kudos, Robbie!

Readers are Happy People!
- *Sissy Marlyn*

Chapter 1

Death

The day was warm; there was not a cloud in the picturesque blue sky; the sun was shining brilliantly. Regardless, all was cold, dark and gloomy in sixty-seven-year-old Jackie Lynn Greathouse and her children's world. Abraham 'Long Wolf' Greathouse had passed away earlier that day. Now, the remaining family members were all sitting together in a bleak funeral parlor, about to begin making arrangements for Long Wolf's memorial service and burial. The wafting sweet smell of too many flowers was about to turn all of their stomachs. They were devastated by Long Wolf's death. They had all loved him a great deal.

Long Wolf died from a fatal heart attack. It was not the first attack he had ever suffered. He had encountered the first one five years ago, when he was sixty-three. Even though it had done a fair amount of damage to his heart, a triple bypass saved his life. Since then, Long Wolf changed his diet, began eating healthier and cut down significantly on his stress. He began working less and less at Greathouse Construction, the company he had been President of since his own father's passing many years before. Long Wolf's children, Mason and Katie Rose, took a much more active role in working at the company. He had been doing well. This fatal heart attack came as quite a shock to them all.

The entire family was all encumbered by grief. They were all centered on doing whatever it took to fully support one another at this heart-wrenching time. Jackie Lynn and her children made all of the arrangements for a memorial service for Long Wolf at the funeral home. They chose the food that would be catered, the music played, and what this magnificent, loving man would be dressed in for this special, sad occasion. They also made arrangements to have Long Wolf's body flown to his family's Indian Reservation, where he would be buried. Everything was precisely planned.

The casket they picked out was made of dark cherry. They had chosen this particular wood because it was known for its beauty, strength and richness. The casket was specifically crafted by Jackie Lynn, intending to signify what her beloved husband would have wanted. The elegant creation had an outset cross upon the top of the large casket door. An old Indian prayer was carved on each side of the outside walls. It read: 'Do not stand at my grave and weep...I am not there, I do not sleep. I am a thousand winds that blow; I am the diamond glint on snow. I am the sunlight on ripened grain'.

Heavy brass handles were attached on both sides and at both ends for the pallbearers. Eight of them would carry this exquisite casket from the funeral home, place it into the hearse, and carry it to the plane. When the plane landed at the Reservation, eight Indian tribesmen would take charge of it. They would have this honor until it was laid into the dark soil on the Reservation burial grounds.

* * * *

After they finished making all of the arrangements at the funeral home, Mason took his mom and Katie Rose home. He stayed with them for a short while before he left to return to his apartment. After he left, Katie Rose called BJ, her boyfriend of several years.

They only talked for a few moments, because he told Katie Rose he was coming over. BJ's visit was fine with her. She wanted to see him. He would comfort her, and Katie Rose needed all the comfort she could get.

Katie Rose had convinced herself she was in love with BJ, even though the two of them had always seemed to make an odd couple. She was tall, beautiful and smart. Katie Rose looked like a younger version of her mother. She had long black hair and the most alluring, emerald green eyes. She also had a very attractive body, with a slim waist and nice bust line. In contrast, BJ was only average in everything – in height, in looks and in intelligence. BJ stood barely as tall as Katie Rose. He was shorter than her if she was wearing heels. He had sandy brown hair and grayish blue eyes.

Since his eyesight was bad, he wore glasses. BJ was happily content working as a mechanic at a nearby muffler shop.

Regardless of their physical differences, things had recently turned intimate between Katie Rose and BJ. Katie Rose was attracted to BJ for his caring nature and close friendship, rather than his appearance or intellect.

BJ did not live far from Katie Rose, so he was there within ten minutes. When Katie Rose opened the door, BJ pulled her into a snug, loving embrace. Katie Rose began to cry. She thought she had already cried all of the tears she could and was amazed to discover she could find more.

BJ cradled Katie Rose in his arms and whispered comforting words in her ear. He was trying to convince her everything would be okay. His heart was breaking for her. BJ loved Katie Rose deeply, so her pain was his pain. He wanted to remove it whatever way he could.

"I'm here, sweetie. I'm so sorry about your dad. But I'll be here for you. I'll do anything you need me to."

Katie Rose eventually pulled back from BJ. She gave him a strained smile, and she kissed his lips with affection. Katie Rose's heart swelled with love for BJ. He was always there whenever she needed him.

"I should invite you in," she said. She stepped backwards a few steps. Katie Rose pulled BJ forward through the doorway. BJ reached to shut the door. He followed Katie Rose down the hall and into the living room. They had a seat side by side on the couch.

"How are your mom and Mason?" BJ asked with concern. He liked Katie Rose's family a great deal; this had included her dad.

"Mason is still numb. He hasn't cried yet. He's just been there to support my mom and me. My mom is crushed." Her mom had taken a sedative and gone to bed. "Mom and dad had an everlasting love for one another. I want the kind of love they had to be a part of our life."

"I'll sure do my best to give it to you," BJ said with a caring smile. He gave Katie Rose another kiss, this one more moving. Katie Rose earnestly returned his affection.

They had become lovers only a few months ago, but it had all come so naturally between them, like their whole relationship. *We must surely belong together.* Some day Katie Rose hoped to marry BJ. She dreamed of living happily ever after with him, as her mom and dad had lived.

"Katie Rose, why don't you come back to my apartment with me and spend the night," BJ proposed in a husky voice. "I don't want you to be alone tonight. Let me comfort you."

She had yet to spend the night with BJ, because she was still living at home. She had not wanted her parents to know what she and BJ were doing. The offer was tempting tonight.

However, she did not want to leave her mom there alone to dwell on the wretchedness of this whole situation. Her mom and dad had rarely been parted. She could not imagine what it might be like for her to be left alone.

"I can't," Katie Rose told BJ with noted disappointment. "I want to be here for my mom tonight. Can you understand?"

"Of course," BJ told her, putting his own selfish desires aside. "Do you want me to stay here too? I can sleep on the couch. Then if you need me, I'll be here for you."

"You are so sweet," Katie Rose cooed. She gave him several more fleeting kisses on his lips. "I love you, BJ."

BJ never tired of hearing Katie Rose say these words to him. "I love you too, Katie Rose. With all my heart. Tell me what you need, and I'll do it."

"I need some time alone with my mom tonight. But I'll call you if I need you."

"Deal," BJ agreed.

He hugged Katie Rose, kissing the side of her neck. "I'll be here in a flash if you call."

Katie Rose felt cozy and loved in BJ's arms. She took a second to thank God for allowing her to have him in her life. Katie Rose could still not comprehend why God had so cruelly taken her father away from her or her family. She remained cuddling with BJ for quite some time, gathering strength from his immense love for her.

* * * *

Callie Roberts was sitting on a sofa by the door in her and Mason's small apartment. There was a television a few feet in front of her and a stereo on the other side of the room, but she did not have either of these turned on. The bright sunshine from the beautiful day outside was streaming through the front window. It warmed the room, lit up the tan Berber carpet, and caused the glass in the pictures on the white walls to glisten, but Callie was not aware of the illumination. The room seemed dark and cold to her. She was sitting in silence, crying, and waiting for Mason to return home.

Callie hopped up when she heard a key in the lock and sprinted toward Mason. Mason was a staggeringly handsome, twenty-six-year-old man. Mason was tall and well built – years of working construction and being an avid athlete had paid off to build muscles in all the right places. Mason looked much like his father had looked when he was younger. He had jet-black hair and handsome, golden brown eyes.

Callie enfolded him in her arms as soon as he cleared the doorway. "Mason, honey, I am *so* sorry," Callie emphasized and began to sob. Callie's heart was breaking for the whole family. She had known all of them her entire life. They had always been there for her, so Callie felt as if she had lost a family member as well.

Callie held Mason and tried her best to comfort him. "Are you okay?" she asked him. Callie pulled back from him and stared into Mason's hard, somber eyes. *He hasn't been crying. He almost looks angry.*

"I don't know how I feel right now," he confessed. "It hasn't all sunk in yet. It's hard for me to believe he's gone…dead. I feel…I feel…actually, I don't feel anything. I'm numb. I keep expecting to wake up and find out my dad's death has all been a terrible nightmare."

"I truly wish it were," Callie commiserated. She stifled another sob and wiped a few remaining tears from her cheeks. "Are you hungry? Do you want me to fix you some dinner?"

"I'm not hungry," Mason answered after several moments of pensive silence. "But thanks for offering to fix me something. Have you eaten?"

"No. I wasn't hungry either. I've been waiting for you."

"I'm glad you're here," Mason professed. He gave Callie a loving, grateful kiss.

"I wouldn't want to be anywhere else," she told him, gazing into his eyes with overwhelming love. "What can I do for you?"

"Just come to bed with me, and let's hold one another. I need to feel you next to me. To know you are there. Your love will help me make it through," Mason told her in a soft voice, an extreme sadness overtaking him. He did not even realize he had started crying until Callie started to tenderly kiss his tears away.

"Come on, honey. Let's go to bed. I'll be there for you. I'll hold you all through the night. It will be okay. You'll see," she said. Callie took Mason's hand. She led him across the living room and down the short hallway to their bedroom.

* * * *

The memorial service for Long Wolf was held the evening before they left on an early morning flight to the Reservation. The room was packed with friends, business associates, and acquaintances. Photographs of Long Wolf sat on stands by his casket and on tables all around the parlor.

In his open casket, he looked as if he was serenely sleeping. He was dressed in a black suit, white shirt, and solid maroon tie. His hands were peacefully folded at his waist. A large, beautiful spray of yellow roses sat atop his casket with wide maroon ribbons that read 'Beloved Husband' and 'Beloved Father'. A CD player lay on the floor, obscured by an overabundance of plants and flowers beside the casket. Some of Long Wolf's favorite songs were softly being played. A near forest of plants and flowers had been sat all around the room. The room smelled like a garden in springtime.

Mason and Callie were talking to his old college roommate, Josh. Mason had not seen him since he had graduated from college. He was touched that Josh had come to the funeral home. Regardless of the sad occasion, Josh and Mason had been happily reminiscing about their college days and catching up on Mason's current life.

"So you guys have really been together for five years? How'd all this come about?" Josh asked Mason. Mason had volunteered this tidbit of information right after he introduced Josh to Callie.

"That's a very long story, my friend. Let's just say that when we were growing up together, no one would have ever convinced me that Callie would have become the love of my life," Mason responded, giving Callie an affectionate squeeze.

Both were living at home with their parents when their deep friendship blossomed into romance. Callie had been a ravishing teenager, with long, shimmering, naturally curly, blond locks; the most beautiful sapphire blue eyes; and a very attractive and well-rounded figure. However, she had been extremely wild, a put-off to the well-mannered Mason.

13

She came on to Mason at every turn, but he refused all of her well-planned advances. She was his sister's best friend and his mother's best friend's daughter. Callie was Katie Rose's age – three years younger than him. Mason watched these girls grow up together. Since their birthdays were only a day apart, he even witnessed them celebrating most of their birthdays together. At first, Callie's flirtations troubled Mason. He considered Callie to be like another little sister.

Mason even decided to go away to college to get away from Callie's constant tormenting. While he had been at college, Callie's family fell apart, and she ran away from home. She turned to drugs, alcohol and prostitution to survive. When Mason returned from college, he discovered Callie had come home too. He also discovered she had grown up. Her harsh life, going through rehab and learning to forgive her parents had changed Callie a great deal. She was no longer the unruly girl he had known.

Instead, a wise, mature, lovely woman had returned. She and Mason became good friends, using one another as constant sounding boards. The intense romance that followed took them both by surprise. At first, they attempted to hide the fact that they had become lovers. They were not sure how their families would react, particularly Callie's mom. She had always threatened to harm Mason if he ever laid a hand on her daughter. Of course, Callie had only been a teenager – the years she spent chasing and seducing Mason.

"Well, it's good to see that a woman finally settled this guy down," Josh remarked with a devilish smile. "So I take it you guys live together?"

"Yeah. We moved into our own apartment about six months ago. But for the last four and a half years, we've practically been living together anyway. My mom and dad let me convert the garage into my bedroom. This was after my sister caught Callie coming out of my bedroom in the house naked..."

"Mason!" Callie chastised him, slapping his arm.

"Well, it's the truth," he defended with a chuckle. "We would have moved into an apartment sooner, but it took awhile to save up money for furniture and the lease. It wasn't so hard coming clean with my family. They were pretty cool about Callie and me. But Callie's mom was a different story. She's come to accept the two of us as a couple though."

As expected, Callie's mother, Mary Julia, had been more upset about their 'affair'. She had not wanted Callie to be used by Mason 'just for sex'. Mary Julia believed Callie's love for Mason was true, but she was not as convinced Mason felt the same way.

Mary Julia had been molested and sexually abused as a child. She had been hospitalized for this abuse twice, once before Callie was born and once right before her daughter had run away. A basic mistrust of men kept her from seeing Mason's honest intentions – Mason intended to marry Callie. He envisioned a family with this woman. Mary Julia's mistrust of men is what finally ended her marriage to Jonathan, Callie's father.

Mary Julia did not take a stand against Callie's love for Mason. She had received enough therapy that she realized acting in such a manor would not work to her advantage. Her disapproval would only drive her daughter farther into Mason's arms. So in the end, Mary Julia reluctantly gave their relationship her blessing.

"I'm glad he's got you, Callie," Josh said. "He was a slow starter, but once he got started, he was quite the playboy in college. A different girl each week…or was it each day? I was actually surprised with all the playing around he did that he actually earned a degree. So are you using that Business Admin degree, Mas? Or did your band finally take front stage?"

Mason was an excellent songwriter; he enjoyed organizing bands and playing nightly to cheering crowds. His true passion rested in his musical talent. Long Wolf had come to terms with the fact that running Greathouse Construction was not Mason's dream, but his own, and he had begun supporting his son in his musical endeavors. Long Wolf had merely been grateful that Mason had continued to have some small role in the construction business. His son had always loved working construction jobs, so moving up the ladder to supervise the crews had been a natural, and pleasant, progression for Mason. Mason had never felt closer to his dad than right before his death.

"Actually, I'm a Head Supervisor at Greathouse now. But my musical career is about to take front and center. A talent scout has expressed an interest in making a studio recording of one of my songs."

"Man, that's great!" Josh commented. "I'm happy for you, buddy. I'm really sorry about your dad."

"Thanks. I appreciate you coming out," Mason told him, giving him a tense smile.

His younger sister, Katie Rose, was standing across the room, also talking to an old friend. She and Maria had gone to high school and graduated together. They had gone to separate colleges, so they had lost touch with one another. Katie Rose had been surprised and happy to see Maria again.

After Maria expressed her sympathy to Katie Rose about her father, she asked Katie Rose about her life. "I graduated from Moore University with a degree in Business Administration last year," Katie Rose filled her in. "I'm going for my Masters now."

"So you can run your dad's company?" Maria asked. "That's what you always wanted. Right?"

"Yeah," Katie Rose admitted a little sadly. She had never anticipated taking over the company this soon. She had thought her dad would be President for many more years.

But Katie Rose *had* always dreamed of someday taking over the reign of management at Greathouse Construction. Her dad resisted this desire most of her life. Yet, when Long Wolf suffered his first heart attack, he came to the realization that he had been grooming the wrong child to take over for him. Her father had supported Katie Rose in her career choice, and she was quickly climbing the ladder at Greathouse Construction. Right now, this achievement felt bittersweet.

"Well, it's great seeing you again, Katie Rose. I'm sorry it has to be under such sad circumstances."

"Me too, Maria," Katie Rose said. Her old high school friend gave her a comforting hug then. Death always seemed to bring people, not seen in ages, out of the woodwork, and Long Wolf's memorial service was no exception.

Jackie Lynn and her children were all very relieved when the service came to an end at 9:00 p.m. They were in for a very long day tomorrow, when they would finally lay Long Wolf to rest.

Chapter 2

The Burial

Long Wolf's wish was to be buried beside his mother, who had lived and died at the Reservation. Side by side they would lie beneath a beautiful, old, weeping willow tree. It had been his mother's favorite place to go and deal with her thoughts as a young woman.

The family arranged to have his body flown with them to the Reservation. Jackie Lynn, Mason and Callie, Katie Rose and BJ, Mary Julia and Flora – two of Jackie Lynn's oldest and dearest friends – would be attending the burial ceremony. In making their reservations along with the immediate family, Mary Julia and Flora would be seated in the same area of the smooth 747 aircraft. It would be a huge comfort for Jackie Lynn to have her children, their loved ones, and her dearest friends close at hand. Their casual conversation helped to ease her misery during the long flight.

* * * *

Jackie Lynn had always found the Reservation grounds to be lovely and peaceful, but today, as they arrived for Long Wolf's burial, she could not see the beauty or the serenity. The miles of endless trails, among deeply wooded acres, only seemed to lead to dead ends and darkness. The wind blowing through the leaves in the massive trees, the running waters of the unspoiled stream to the west, the soft noises of the birds, all of these noises brought only pain to the hearts of this mourning family. It especially brought irrepressible heart ache for Jackie Lynn, as she remembered delightful days, so many years ago, when she and Long Wolf had spent hours walking hand-in-hand by this body of water, under these same brilliant skies. The miles of mammoth mountains, to the east, only seemed to be there to block out the ardent rays of sunshine and cast depressing, ugly shadows all across the land.

Today, there was no tranquility at the Reservation. Long Wolf's casket was being removed from the hearse by eight Indian braves. Long Wolf was being taken to Big Rock, where the burial services would be held at sunset. Big Rock was so named because a huge, raised stone platform stood in the middle of this clearing in the woods. Jackie Lynn and Long Wolf had been married at this sacred grove. Both Mason and Katie Rose had been given their Indian names – Running Wolf and Emerald Sea – at this same awesome place. But today, Big Rock, like the rest of the Reservation, was a site of sorrow.

As Chief Ironhorse approached the Greathouse family and their friends, he went to Jackie Lynn first. Taking both of her hands into his and looking deeply into her sad eyes, he spoke with an Indian accent, "Beautiful squaw, bride and lifelong partner to Long Wolf, I am sorry our brother has had to leave us. His body will now be prepared for the burial rite. Our tribe's medicine man will perform the ceremony. Follow me, and my people will help you and your children – Emerald Sea and Running Wolf – dress appropriately for the ritual."

He turned and faced the others. "Friends of Long Wolf, you are also welcome. You will be taken to a separate place and my people will help to prepare you as well. Once my people have helped you prepare for the ceremony, you will wait. A tribesman will come get you when the sun has begun to set behind the mammoth mountains. At that time, the medicine man will begin the traditional ritual."

Jackie Lynn barely made eye contact with the chief. She nodded her agreement to his requests. Then she stared off into space once more. She seemed to be lost in some trance. Mason came up on one side of her and placed his arm around her waist. Katie Rose followed suit on the other side.

Tears slowly began to stream down Jackie Lynn's flushed cheeks. Three members of the tribe walked over to lead the three of them into the lovely wooded countryside. Another of the tribe's members walked over to guide Callie, BJ, Mary Julia and Flora, who had all begun to follow in slow deliberate steps behind their dear friends.

But before Jackie Lynn and her children could be guided away, the chief caught sight of the tears running down her face. He rudely stepped into her path. His harsh words cut into Jackie Lynn's heart like a knife, "You, white woman, chosen partner of our departed Long Wolf, do not cry. Your tears will keep his spirit from the sacred Spirit World!"

The urgent look in his cold eyes only made Jackie Lynn want to cry all the more. Regardless, she fought to contain her emotions as best she could. Looking Chief Ironhorse directly in his eyes, she spoke in a soft but earnest voice, "I am not crying for my beloved husband to return." This proclamation was not exactly true. Jackie Lynn would have given anything to have Long Wolf back, but this was not possible. "I am crying because there is emptiness in my life now. My tears show my love and my emptiness."

In a protective gesture, Mason stepped between the chief and his mother. He further justified, "Her tears are not meant to hold back my father's spirit, but only to show how much she loved him and how desperately she will miss him." Mason returned to his mother's side and defiantly led her past the chief, without giving him time to respond.

Jackie Lynn and her children were eventually led to one teepee, and the others were directed a short distance away to another. Before they were completely separated, Callie scurried over to Mason and gave him a gentle kiss on his cheek. She held him close for a brief moment and whispered in his ear, "I am so proud of you. I will see you soon, very soon."

BJ, looking uncertain of what he should do, swiftly gave Katie Rose a peck on her forehead. Then he turned and walked away with the others. Both Callie and BJ hated that they could not stay with Mason and Katie Rose, but they did not wish to disrupt any sacred rituals. Flora and Mary Julia looked on sadly as Jackie Lynn disappeared inside the darkness of the large teepee.

As if he had something to prove, Chief Ironhorse, once again spoke in a coarse voice. He matter-of-factly instructed Callie, BJ, Mary Julia and Flora to continue with the tribe members to their appointed teepee, where they would be shown what to do next. Callie hated the way Chief Ironhorse was presenting himself. *These Indian people seem as if they have no heart at all, as if they feel no loss.* Regardless, she was here to support Mason and his family, so she would do what was asked of her. She started away with her

19

mother, BJ, and Flora, following the tribe member to their assigned teepee to await further instructions.

* * * *

Hours later, Chief Ironhorse instructed the same tribal members that had led them to their appointed teepees to go, gather the family and friends, and bring them to Big Rock. Jackie Lynn was dressed in a formfitting, long, buffalo skin smock, which fell to rest at her ankles. On her feet was a pair of traditional moccasins. On the front of her smock in white, were painted shadowed faces – symbols of the Great Spirit. A black band was around Jackie Lynn's forehead, with a single, dark green peacock feather falling at her left temple. Her nose and chin were painted with black charcoal. Her cheeks had two single lines of white smeared across them.

Katie Rose also donned a buffalo skin, formfitting smock, moccasins and a black headband. However, she had no feather in her headband, her smock had no color or design on it. The clothing she wore was completely plain. Her face was painted similar to her mother's.

Mason had on an unadorned, buffalo skin kilt and a stole. He also wore the traditional moccasins on his feet. His entire face was painted black. The contrasting, bright white stripes on each of his cheeks were a bit shocking. He had on a black headband with three brown feathers sticking out of it.

Callie, BJ, Mary Julia and Flora were not dressed in Indian garments. However, the Indians had painted their faces with the black charcoal and white paint. Once they had all gathered at the base of the clearing, Chief Ironhorse began to lead them all toward the ritual site.

They zigzagged along the well-worn path through the forest toward Big Rock. A few feet ahead of them were eight of the Indian tribesmen. Their faces were painted completely black. They carried the handsome wood casket that held Long Wolf.

Katie Rose looked around at her surroundings. She could not help but recall running this same path with excitement as a little girl. It had been the night she had been given her Indian name. Her heart had been light and full of such happiness.

Now, she was walking the same path but not to a rapid, jubilant drumbeat as in the past. Instead, the drums were pounding out a slow steady beat and horns were sounding out a mournful, haunting melody. Katie Rose hated being here. She felt vulnerable and unprotected. These feelings were not something her father would have wanted, but she could not control the fear within her heart. Never would her life be the same without the strength of her father to protect her.

As they came into the clearing and upon Big Rock, the drums and horns were silenced. The eight tribesmen, using extreme caution, sat the heavy casket onto the ground. They opened the top and lifted Long Wolf's body from it. They ascended the raised rock platform to place Long Wolf's body atop a scaffold that had been constructed on Big Rock.

Long Wolf's large framed body was placed on a bison hide rug, which covered the four post scaffold. His walking stick was placed beside him. He was covered in a buffalo skin blanket from his neck to his ankles. Shadowy pictures of the Great Spirit had been sketched in white paint onto the blanket.

Long Wolf's face was painted with white stripes along his cheeks, chin and nose. His forehead was adorned with a shiny golden band, which secured the vibrant red, blue, orange and black feathers protruding from it. There were several torches lit behind his body. In front of his body, on the ground, lay a pile of the favorite clothes he had worn, and a few items he had cherished. Jackie Lynn had been instructed to bring these things.

All of Long Wolf's people stood stoically, looking toward where his body was laid. They gazed at him and bid his spirit farewell into the free world. Upon first sight of Long Wolf, Jackie Lynn's heart leapt. He looked so peaceful that he appeared only to be sleeping. But her heart sank as the cruel reality of why she was really here set in – this was the funeral of the only man she had ever truly loved. Long Wolf was dead and about to be buried.

Her legs grew weak and her entire body began to tremble, and without her consent, a horrifying wail escaped her throat. She dropped to her knees in front of the pile of Long Wolf's belongings, his scent engulfing her soul. Without thinking, she began to clutch some of his things into her hands. She buried her face in them and was sobbing uncontrollably.

Mason dashed forward, dropped to his knees beside his mother, and cradled her in his arms, in a futile attempt to try and comfort her. Katie Rose could not help but begin to cry as well. BJ moved to stand behind her, encircled her waist with his arms, and held her shaking body against his. He was trying in the only way he knew how to give her comfort and strength. Callie, Mary Julia and Flora all began to shed tears as well. Mary Julia hugged Flora on one side and Callie on the other. She could tell her daughter felt helpless because she could not be near Mason to comfort him.

The medicine man and Chief Ironhorse approached Jackie Lynn. The medicine man laid a hand upon the top of her head and softly spoke some foreign words. Chief Ironhorse interpreted them, "Beautiful Squaw, who weeps for Long Wolf, mourn him for he is no longer amongst us. But know that his spirit will soon be released and will travel the long road to dwell with the Great Spirit. You should weep no more, for he is in Autumn – the final harvest – the end of Life's Cycle. For him there is no death, only a change in worlds. Allow us to release Long Wolf's spirit so he may be one with the Great Spirit."

Chief Ironhorse extended a hand to Jackie Lynn and helped her to her feet. Mason stood and supported her trembling body against his. Chief Ironhorse moved them back several paces. He nodded at the medicine man to begin the burial ritual.

The medicine man raised his head and hand towards the sky. The drums began to beat again and the women of the tribe began to chant the "Death Song". Their voices were loud and piecing. Jackie Lynn could not understand the words, but the chilling, sorrowful rhythm of their voices coursed through her very soul. Each note cut into her like a rifle being fired for a twenty-one gun salute. Mason was trying his hardest to remain strong, but even so, he could not keep the tears from rolling down his cheeks and wetting his chest as they dripped off his chin.

When the song ended, the drums were again silenced. The medicine man looked toward Jackie Lynn and the children, and once again began to speak. Chief Ironhorse again interpreted, "Wife of Long Wolf, mother of his offspring, his son and heir Running Wolf, his daughter and treasure Emerald Sea, friends and people of the tribe, our brother Long Wolf has been prepared for his spirit's travel along the Spirit Road. His body was cleansed with water and oil. He was wrapped in bison cloth with the Great Spirit's image, and he was placed on this scaffold. His face was painted white – the color of peace and happiness. Let us proceed in releasing his spirit. Braves, please bring Long Wolf's wife and children each a torch."

Three tribesmen stepped forward from the crowd. Their faces were painted an awful black and their headdresses comprised of a black band adorned with brown feathers – no colorful feathers like they wore for joyful ceremonies. They went around behind Long Wolf and retrieved one torch apiece. They walked over to Jackie Lynn, Mason and Katie Rose and handed them each a torch. Chief Ironhorse directed Katie Rose to step forward with the torch beside her mother and brother. BJ reluctantly released her.

"Take these torches, hold them together, and light the pile of clothing in front of your father," Chief Ironhorse instructed.

All three of them stepped forward and did as instructed. They were amazed when the fire from their torches spontaneously combusted the clothing. *They must have poured something very flammable on the clothes*, Mason concluded.

Chief Ironhorse led them all back a safe distance from the leaping fire, and the braves came and took the torches out of their hands. The braves walked around the body again and placed the torches back in the holders behind Long Wolf. Another brave joined the other three, and in pairs, they picked up two, large, thick, stout white pieces of material. They all came back around to the front of the fire. The braves began fanning this material, directing the smoke toward Long Wolf's body. After a few moments, it appeared as if the smoke was rising from Long Wolf's body instead of the pile of his clothing.

"As the smoke arises about our brother Long Wolf, so his spirit arises with it. Go to the Spirit Road…on to the Great Spirit," Chief Ironhorse commanded in a loud voice, mimicking what had just been ordered by the medicine man.

The drums began again, but this time it was to a brisk and joyful beat. It sounded like the day Jackie Lynn and Long Wolf had married and on the days their children had received their Indian names. Chief Ironhorse could see the confusion on all of their faces, so he explained, "The drums are meant to sound happy and upbeat now. Autumn – the end of the life cycle – has gone away. In the smoke that rises and swirls toward the sky is Long Wolf's spirit. The joyful drums signify the joy of the Great Spirit that another spirit has come to be one with him. Sorrow should be no more. Your hearts should no longer feel weighted down and somber."

Some of the Indian women approached them. They had buckets in one hand and a cloth in another. They began to wash the black charcoal from all of their faces, including Callie, BJ, Mary Julia and Flora. They were careful to leave the white paint – representing peace and happiness. Children from the tribe handed out white headbands, with small colorful feathers in them to replace the black ones.

Jackie Lynn was so moved by all of the symbolism, that she genuinely had a better feeling in her heart, a warm and safe feeling. She was pleased with the fact that she had brought Long Wolf here to be buried. She said a silent prayer that his spirit was indeed happy and at peace sharing this glorious land with the Great Spirit. Her shoulders shook as she shed still more tears, especially as she beheld the braves removing Long Wolf's body from the scaffold.

"We will place his body back into the elegant, strong, wood box you have chosen for Long Wolf. This box will rest the being which held his soul while he spent his time in this world with his family, his people and his friends," the chief told her, as the tribesman placed Long Wolf's body back inside the casket. As he looked intensely into Jackie Lynn's sad eyes, she no longer saw the coldness in Chief Ironhorse's eyes. She saw sorrow. Together, they took hold of the casket lid and closed it shut.

The eight tribesmen, who had carried the casket to Big Rock, came and placed it onto a large cart. The medicine man motioned for Jackie Lynn, the children, BJ, Callie, Mary Julia and Flora to follow him. The rest of the tribe slowly fell in behind them. They all walked in a measured gait a quarter of a mile into the forest. The tribesmen pushed the cart with Long Wolf's casket along in front of the assemblage. At the gravesite, they connected six ropes to the handles of the casket. They slowly lowered the casket into the grave that had been dug.

The grave had been dug to rest under a large, old, willow tree. Standing underneath its sad branches, they faced the most incredible sunset. It was the perfect ending. The sky was changing before their eyes; the orange glow of the sun turned to a bright yellow, then to red, then to a deep violet. It was a taste of heaven without leaving this world.

Jackie Lynn shuddered as the final sense of loss took over her body. She used every ounce of strength she had to fight the impulse to lunge forward and throw herself into the grave with Long Wolf. Her heart was shattered into a thousand broken pieces. *I don't know how I am going to survive without Long Wolf.*

Mason, sensing something terribly wrong, wrapped his arms around his mother and pulled her to him. A feeling that he was saving her from a worse fate than he could imagine came over him. Katie Rose felt it too. She clung tightly to her mother as well.

Jackie Lynn was suddenly given the answer to her question. She would survive because of the love for her children. This was as Long Wolf would have wanted it. She would still have parts of Long Wolf through Mason and Katie Rose.

After the ropes were removed from the casket, the family was each directed to pick up a soft handful of soil and drop it into the grave. Mason walked Jackie Lynn up to the opening of the grave, so she could be the first to take part in this final part of the burial ceremony. Jackie Lynn glanced up at her son; then she looked down into Long Wolf's grave. Her hand shook as she dropped the dirt down onto the dark box at the bottom of this hole. She heard it hit the wooden box that held her beloved's body with a thud. She secretly promised him, *Long Wolf, you were, and will forever be, the love of my life. I will miss you always and love you until I die. I will go on because of the love we share for our children. I will do this for you. Goodbye my love.*

The burial ritual was over, and so was Jackie Lynn's life with Long Wolf. As the silent tears again began to fall from her desolate eyes, she thought again to herself, *my only hope of surviving this great loss will be our children and the love we have for one another.*

Chapter 3

Green-Eyed Monster

In the months following her father's funeral, Katie Rose began spending more and more time at home with her mom. She was very worried about her mother, because Jackie Lynn seemed so lost without Long Wolf. Katie Rose frequently found her mother sitting alone, with tears running down her pale cheeks.

Her mother was suffering from a broken heart. There was nothing Katie Rose could do to make the pain go away. Extreme sadness tore at Katie's Rose heart as well. It took every ounce of strength she had to keep her own emotions under control.

One evening, Katie Rose and Jackie Lynn were sitting together at the dinner table. Jackie Lynn confided to her daughter, "Katie Rose, honey, I'm a burden to you. Your father's death is hard on you as well. But I can't seem to help myself. Even at work during the day, I find myself waiting for the phone to ring."

Long Wolf had always, for no specific reason, phoned Jackie Lynn each day. Often, it was only to tell Jackie Lynn he loved her. Other times, it was to share that he was thinking about her. He would ask how her day was going. He always ended their conversation with, "I love you". Jackie Lynn told Katie Rose she found herself wondering during the day, 'Why haven't I heard from Long Wolf?' and then the awful reality that he is dead would hit her all over again.

"I miss those calls from your daddy," Jackie Lynn declared. Then she broke down and cried. Katie Rose moved to her mother's side. She wrapped her arms around her mom's shaking shoulders. Katie Rose was overcome by grief as well, and the two women held each other and cried.

Katie Rose did indeed miss her dad very much as well. She shared with her mom that she too had these types of moments. "I expect to see him walking down the hall at work or into my office, as dad has done so many times in the past. Then I remember he's gone, and a sickening feeling hits me like a ton of bricks."

It was hard not having her father watching over her at work. Katie Rose had shared her thoughts for the day with him. Long Wolf had guided her decisions. He had also encouraged her to grow more and more in her knowledge of Greathouse Construction.

As expected, Long Wolf had willed the company to Katie Rose. Katie Rose did not believe she was experienced enough to run the company yet, so she put Samuel Lewis in charge. Samuel had been Vice President of Greathouse Construction for over thirty five years. He was also one of her father's oldest and dearest friends. Katie Rose could trust him to make the right decisions in the company's best interest.

With Samuel's help, Katie Rose was striving to learn everything she needed to know about the company. Then she would become active President of Greathouse Construction. Samuel was training Katie Rose without any regrets. This was what Long Wolf would have wanted.

Samuel had no desire to be President. It had been Long Wolf's wish that Katie Rose take over as President of the company. Samuel intended to see his friend's wish fulfilled. He assured Katie Rose, on a daily basis, he would soon be handing the company over to her capable hands.

Mason stayed on with Greathouse as Head Supervisor of Construction. His father had left a sizable amount of money to Jackie Lynn and to him. It was in a trust fund, and Jackie Lynn was the administer of the trust. Even though Mason was a grown man, he still had to go through his mother to take money out of the trust. Long Wolf had wanted his children to make their own way in the world, and Mason was. He did not intend to touch a penny in the trust unless there was some emergency.

BJ came over and visited for a few hours each evening with Katie Rose, but he missed their alone time at his apartment a great deal. He had waited a long while to become intimate with Katie Rose, so having to abstain once more was even more difficult for him. However, BJ was trying very hard to be sympathetic of Katie Rose's situation. He prayed things would soon return to some degree of normalcy.

* * * *

Mason and Callie came over to visit with his mom and Katie Rose at least one night a week. Jackie Lynn was always grateful to see Mason; yet part of her wanted to cry each time she looked into his face. Mason reminded Jackie Lynn a lot of his father. Not only did Mason's looks favor Long Wolf, but he also had many of his father's same endearing mannerisms. Jackie Lynn had not observed this until now.

Jackie Lynn's two dearest friends, Mary Julia and Flora, were also coming over to the house to see her on a regular basis. Each time someone would visit, it would raise Jackie Lynn's spirits. It was such a comfort talking about everything under the sun with these friends. It helped Jackie Lynn to forget she had lost Long Wolf for a short while.

However, after they would leave, Jackie Lynn was again engulfed by loneliness. Nights were the worst times. She sat in the dark and cried. At least during the day, Jackie Lynn was at work, so she did not think of Long Wolf as much. Jackie Lynn had never been so miserable in her entire life. Her world had come to an excruciating, crashing halt. Hard as she tried, Jackie Lynn could not seem to get her life back in order.

Mason would be flying to Santa Monica in a few days for his band to audition for Epic Records. If Epic liked Mason's band's live performance, they were supposed to record one of the songs he had written in the studio. Mason was delighted, and Jackie Lynn was very proud of him. Her only other wish was that Long Wolf was still alive to see what Mason was accomplishing.

* * * *

Callie flew to Santa Monica with Mason and the band. Callie was excited to be traveling with Mason and to be there to see him audition in person with Epic. However, when they arrived at the studio, they both got their first bitter taste of what it would be like dealing with a big record company. Callie was not part of the band, so they would not allow her to go into the studio with them. She had to stay in a tiny waiting room in the lobby.

Callie picked up and read every magazine in the waiting room from cover to cover – a McCall's, two Rolling Stones, and one People. She glared at the receptionist from time to time, as if it was this young girl's fault she could not be with Mason. Callie moved from chair to chair – all five of them – waiting with anxiousness for Mason to reappear. She paced and examined all the gold records that lined the walls. She beheld the door across from her – through which Mason and his band had disappeared eons ago – open and close and open and close.

Many strangers came and went through this door, but no Mason. Before long, she thought she would lose her mind. Callie was beginning to panic – *Could something have happened to them?* The calm baby blue the room was painted was not even helping. Mason and his band had been behind closed doors for over two hours.

When Mason opened the door at last and came back into the waiting room, Callie sprang to her feet, raced toward him and leapt into his arms. The other three band members came through the door behind him. They all, including Mason, wore glorious smiles.

"I take it things went well," Callie speculated.

"Did things go well? Let's just say you are now hugging one of the newest recording artists for Epic Records," Mason cooed in utmost delight. "What do you think of that?"

"Mason, that is so wonderful!" Callie exclaimed and began to shower his face with little, excited, fluttering kisses. Mason lifted Callie off the ground and spun her around in the air.

"Did they already record your song?" Callie asked as he placed her feet back on the ground.

"Yes, they have. And the band and I signed a contract with them today. That is what took so long. It was pages and pages and pages long, and we all wanted to take a good long look at it before we signed off on anything."

"Shouldn't you have taken the contract to an attorney before you signed it?" Callie asked with some concern.

She had seen stories where recording stars had been ripped off by recording companies, and she was unhappy with this particular company right now anyway. Callie still could not understand what it could have hurt for her to have sat in the studio. Even though she was elated that Sony had recorded Mason's first song, it was still disappointing to Callie that she had missed witnessing the actual taping.

"No. Our agent negotiated everything for us," Mason explained with a jovial chuckle.

"Agent? What agent?" Callie questioned. She wondered if Mason was teasing her.

About that time, the door to the waiting room opened again. A tall woman, with short, shiny, auburn hair and the prettiest, alluring, greenish blue eyes, sashayed into the room. Callie could not help but notice that this lady was dressed in an attractive, rather formfitting, teal suit, which perfectly complimented her beautiful eyes and all the attractive curves of her body. Her perfume was also very appealing.

"Speak of the devil," Mason said with an amused grin. "Callie, this is Fawn Donovan. Fawn has signed on to be the band's agent. She has some very good credentials. She represents bands like Seventh Sign and Full Sail. You recognize those names."

Callie did recognize those names. Both of those bands were doing well, with several hits playing on the radio. She was impressed that this woman had agreed to sign with Mason's band.

Regardless, Callie could not help but feel threatened. This woman was pretty, and Fawn looked a little older than they were. *Mason's first love was an older woman.* Plus, if things went well, Mason and Fawn would be spending a lot of time together. *Stop, Callie! Don't start thinking like that. Fawn's only going to be his agent. That's all!*

Callie wished she had fixed herself up more. Her long, naturally curly, blond hair was hanging loose around her face. She had not put on much eye makeup to bring out the alluring blue of her eyes. Plus, Callie was dressed in a loose fitting T-shirt and some jeans.

"It's nice to meet you, Fawn," Callie attempted to be cordial. She also reached to shake her hand. "I'm Mason's girlfriend, Callie." *I love him very much!*

"Nice to meet you, Callie. You have a very talented boyfriend," Fawn said.

As if I didn't already know that. Callie also observed this woman spoke with a soft, sexy voice. She watched the way the other members of the band were studying her with obvious interest.

"Yes, he is very talented," Callie swiftly agreed. She tightly clutched Mason's arm, planting a kiss on the side of the mouth.

"She's one of my biggest fans. Has been ever since I first started playing," Mason shared with Fawn. He turned his head and gave Callie a full, grateful kiss on her lips and another heartwarming smile.

He's so happy! You need to pull it together, Callie. Mason loves you. This other woman isn't going to be a problem.

"It's good to have the support of those you love," Fawn said. "This is a tough business, Mason, and you will need all the support you can get. I wish you all the luck in the world. Rest assured that I will be doing everything I can to see that you and your band become a raging success."

"Thank you so much, Fawn," Mason gushed. Then much to Callie's dismay, he pulled Fawn into a tight embrace.

He's grateful. That's all! Mason is always affectionate…Okay, that's enough. Let her go! Callie ground her teeth. She had to suck in a deep breath, as Mason released Fawn.

"I'll be talking with you guys again soon," Fawn said and proceeded toward the front door.

"Okay, thanks," they all chimed almost in unison. As Fawn vacated the office, Callie beheld all the men, *including Mason*, poring over Fawn's shapely, swaying hips.

Callie could not help but wish a different agent – *preferably a man* – were representing Mason and his band. But Fawn must be good if she represented those other *big name* bands. *I'll have to learn to live with it.*

Callie gave Mason another kiss on the lips, this time longer and with more heat. The guys in the band began to cheer. *I'll have to make sure Mason remembers he already has a woman to love him. Then he won't even be tempted to wander.*

Chapter 4

First Encounter

Members of the negotiations' committee for Gates Towers filed into Greathouse Construction's boardroom one by one. They had a seat around the rectangular, twelve foot, shiny, walnut, conference room table. Samuel, as acting President of Greathouse Construction, was seated at the head of the table, in the high, plush, black leather armchair that had belonged to Abraham Greathouse. Mason and Katie Rose were seated in their usual low-back leather armchairs, on the left and right of the table. Their father's chair was bigger than the other thirteen chairs in the room to symbolize his leadership role. Katie Rose would be honored when she could occupy this larger chair.

She was seated facing the door. Katie Rose was rather absentmindedly watching the last few men and women enter the room. The young man coming through the door caught her attention. He looked familiar to her for some unbeknownst reason.

Katie Rose scrutinized this individual with curiosity as he walked along the wood-paneled wall. The wall sconce lighting illuminated his face more as he walked past. Katie Rose remembered his handsome, sparkling, blue eyes from somewhere, but she could not pinpoint where.

This man took a seat in the last chair on the opposite side from Katie Rose. It was then that he happened to look in her direction. His eyes met Katie Rose's and locked for several moments. Katie Rose noted she and this stranger were staring at one another, so she averted her eyes in embarrassment.

Good gosh! This guy might think I am interested in him in a romantic nature if I keep staring. But he looks familiar for some reason. He looks to be around Mason's age; could he be a friend of Mason's? Where have I seen him before, or whom does he resemble?

Katie Rose dared to glance in his direction again. His eyes met hers once more. Katie Rose looked away, picked up one of her pens, and pretended to be writing something on the steno pad lying on the table in front of her.

She was relieved when Samuel stood and started the meeting a moment later. Now, Katie Rose's entire focus was centered on taking note of what was transpiring during the contract negotiations. She no longer had any time to evaluate the mysterious young man across the room.

The meeting went well. Greathouse Construction was awarded the building contract. When the meeting ended, Katie Rose, Samuel and Mason remained standing outside the doorway, as the conference room slowly cleared.

This way they made themselves readily available to everyone who had been in the meeting. Anyone could stop and speak with Samuel, Katie Rose or Mason if they wished to. The young man, who Katie Rose had been so preoccupied with at the start of the meeting, approached the three of them.

"Hi, I'm Garrison Parker," he introduced himself and offered Samuel a hand to shake.

Samuel shook his hand and said with a smile, "Nice to meet you, Mr. Parker. What is your capacity with this project?"

"I'm with Parker Architecture," he disclosed. "I'll be drawing up most of the plans for the building you are about to construct."

"Oh, well great! Great!" Samuel recognized with enthusiasm. "So is there something I can help you with? Other than constructing the building for you," he joked with lightheartedness.

"Um…this is going to sound strange," the young man told him, seeming hesitant to continue. "It's just…well…I think I recognize the young lady, who is standing beside you, from somewhere else."

"Man, what a bad line!" Mason instantly chimed in with a mischievous grin. "The young lady you are referring to is my sister, and I won't allow you to use a dumb line like that on her," he teased some more.

"No, that was *not* a pick-up line," Garrison hastened to correct him. He gave an amused chuckle, looking embarrassed.

Although, I wouldn't mind 'picking-up' your sister. She is a very *appealing young woman.* Garrison was giving Katie Rose another perusal. Katie Rose glanced away. For some reason, he was making her uncomfortable with his intense stares.

"It's just…I'm part Indian, and when I was a boy, I met a couple of other kids on my father's Reservation that looked like you and your sister. I especially remember your sister. I recognize her green eyes. Her Indian name has something to do with them. Emerald… something."

"Emerald Sea," Mason shared with a wide, accepting grin. "I am Running Wolf. What is your Indian name?"

"I am Soars Like An Eagle. My father was Fighting Bear. He passed away a few years ago. I was sorry to hear of your father's recent passing. I had been looking forward to meeting him, since I had heard high praises about him and Greathouse Construction," Garrison revealed with compassion.

"Thanks. I'm sorry to hear about your father's passing as well," Mason replied. He added with a friendly smile, "I do remember you. You showed me some of the ropes of being on a Reservation the first time my father took us there. My sister hated you! She thought you were a bossy know-it-all."

"Mason!" Katie Rose protested, speaking up for the first time. "That's not so!"

As Garrison glanced in her direction again, she noted, *He's very handsome.* Garrison had short, shiny, thick black hair and a darker complexion, like her and Mason. *He's such a* big *man.* Garrison was not only tall, but he had large arms, muscular legs and a robust chest. He worked out regularly at least three days a week. *He must take after his dad and that's why his father was called Fighting 'Bear'.* In deep contrast to all of the traits he had clearly inherited from his Indian father, Garrison's eyes were deep sapphire blue. *He has nice eyes and a kind smile.*

Garrison was pleased Katie Rose was appraising him. He pretended not to notice, directing his attention back to Mason. "I probably was a bossy know-it-all. There weren't many visitors who came there, so I was enjoying showing off." With a reminiscent grin, he continued, "So did the two of you get to spend much time there?"

"Yes" Mason shared, "My dad took us back to visit the Reservation often after that first trip. I guess we just never ran into you again. Maybe our timing was off. Do you live here in the city? I'm surprised we didn't run into one another away from the Reservation until now."

"No, my stepfather recently moved Parker Architecture here. I didn't grow up here. I grew up in the west, closer to the Reservation. But regardless, I didn't visit there again until I was a man. That was three years ago when my father died. My dad had no money for child support, so my mother saw fit to deny him any further visitation with me. My dad wrote to me once and tried to explain that it was in my best interest that I remain with my mother and stepfather. After that, my mother tried to contact him, and the courts also tried. After a long period of time passed and they got no response back, my stepfather and mother took legal action, and he adopted me. That is why I bear his last name – Parker. I never forgot about the Reservation or my real father though," Garrison clarified.

He sounded bitter about his parent's battles and his estrangement from his dad. Catching a glimpse of the pity Emerald Sea's eyes held, Garrison apologized, "I'm sorry I've been going on and on. Please forgive me; I just feel so comfortable around the two of you. Must be our Indian spirits," Garrison finished with a hearty laugh.

Mason observed another man had stepped out of the conference room and appeared to be waiting to talk with him. "Well…it was great seeing you again, buddy," Mason concluded his conversation with Garrison.

Garrison saw Mason looking over his shoulder. He glanced behind him and glimpsed another man standing there. "It was nice making your acquaintance, again… Mason," Garrison offered his hand for a departing handshake. The two shook hands, and Garrison stepped aside.

He directed his full attention to Mason's sister. "It's nice to be able to reconnect a little with my Indian roots. Emerald Sea, I am sorry I was such a bossy know-it-all when you last met me. Don't blame the man for the way the boy behaved all those years ago. If you got to know me better, I'm quite certain you would see I am nothing like that deplorable little boy."

Katie Rose studied Garrison for a few seconds, letting what he said sink in. *Good gosh, he apologized to me for something that occurred years and years ago and that I barely remember. Does he think I'm still angry with him? I can't let this guy walk out of here thinking I obsess over such silly little things. It makes me seem like a shallow nitwit. I need to set the record straight.*

"Your apology is accepted, Garrison," Katie Rose assured him. She added with a smile, "Obviously, you are nothing like that little boy, because it takes a big man to apologize to a woman. Not that I was holding something that happened when we were mere children against you anyway."

She remembered my name, and I got a smile out of her. Progress has been made, Garrison concluded with pleasure.

Garrison returned Emerald Sea's smile and replied, "Good. I'm glad you aren't angry at me, Emerald Sea."

More people had stepped out of the conference room and were trying to talk with Samuel and Mason, so Katie Rose stepped a few more paces off to the side of them. "Um…my name is actually Katharine Rose. I don't get called Emerald Sea except when we are at the Reservation. Actually I'm only called that name by my dad…or at least he used to call me by that name," she admitted a little sadly. "It sounds especially odd coming from someone at the office."

"Oh, I'm sorry," Garrison apologized again. "I didn't remember you by any other name and your brother did not volunteer another one. As a matter of fact, he didn't volunteer his own name, only his Indian name. I just picked it up, because you called it out when you reprimanded him for telling me how you felt about me as a boy. Katherine is a lovely name by the way. Do you go by Katherine or has it been shortened to Kate? I like both. I also like your Indian name. Emerald Sea suits you well. All of these names are excellent names for a beautiful young lady."

"Thank you." Katie Rose acknowledged his flattering comments with a self-conscious grin.

She did not answer Garrison's question about how she was addressed. For the first time in her life, Katie Rose did not want to be called 'Katie' because it sounded like a child's name to her. She was surprised to realize she did not want this man to address her in such a manor. Katie Rose wanted Garrison to call her by a woman's name instead.

How odd! She found herself concluding.

"Well…" Garrison bridged the silence. "I should let you get back to work…Um…Kate. It will be nice doing business with *you*."

'Kate'…I like the way that sounds coming from his mouth. I also like the way Garrison's voice sounds. He has a deep voice; yet he speaks soft but stern…very sexy. Stop it!! Katie Rose was shocked to realize she was having such wayward thoughts. *What is wrong with me today?*

Garrison took Katie Rose's hand in his and could not help but think, *My, how soft her skin feels.* As Garrison caught himself staring at Kate, a wave of embarrassment washed over him, and he corrected his last words, "I mean it will be nice doing business with *all* of you at Greathouse Construction." With that said, Garrison released Katie Rose's hand.

Garrison's handshake was firm yet gentle. She liked the feel of his big, strong hand. *I must be hormonal. Back to work, Katie Rose! Enough of this nonsense!*

"So…will I be seeing you at the groundbreaking ceremony? Do you attend those types of things? Or is this merely a boring, summer, clerical, office job at daddy's company for you?"

Katie Rose was offended. "What gives you the right to assume I only have some boring, summer, clerical job my daddy has given me out of the kindness of his heart? Did you also assume that about Mason? I bet you didn't! You only assume it about me because I'm a woman. Isn't that right?!"

Garrison was stunned to hear Kate snapping at him. He had not meant to offend her. Yet, it was obvious he had done so. *Boy, I'm batting a thousand with this pretty, young lady today! Open mouth; insert foot!*

"Kate, I ask your forgiveness yet again. You are absolutely right. I should not be making any sort of assumptions about what your job at this company might be. I didn't mean to suggest your dad had only given you a job because he's your dad and not because you are qualified for whatever position you are in. You are right. I did not automatically make assumptions about Mason, and I should not be doing so with you. I'm quite certain you are as smart as you are pretty."

For the second time that day, Katie Rose felt awkward around this guy. *Why did I go off on him like that? Garrison is a virtual stranger and I'm standing here chastising him. What difference does it make what he thinks about me?*

"No, I'm the one who is sorry. I overreacted to what you said," Katie Rose backed down with haste. "In answer to your original question, I will be at the groundbreaking ceremony. I am trying to learn everything I can about the business as quickly as possible. I will soon be running Greathouse Construction. My father willed the company to me. He understood it was my dream to someday be President. I have a lot to learn from Samuel before this can be possible. But I promise you, when I become President, I plan to do my father proud. You can rest assured Greathouse Construction will still have the same esteemed reputation with me at the helm."

Why did I tell him all that? This information was not something she normally relayed to a near stranger.

"Ah…that's great! I hope to someday take over the reins at my stepfather's company, Parker Architecture. So, we'll be running companies that go hand-in-hand with one another. I've heard nothing but good about Greathouse Construction, so I don't expect this current deal to be anything but a huge success. Let's hope this project is the beginning of a plentiful, long-lasting relationship between our two companies," Garrison peddled.

"Yes, that would be nice," Katie Rose halfheartedly agreed.

For whatever reason, she had begun to feel uneasy talking to this man. *I, all at once, have a runaway mouth with this guy.* Katie Rose was unnerved she was so freely sharing company plans with this stranger from her past.

Garrison sensed it was time to end this conversation. *I'm on good footing with this young lady. I need to get out of here before I screw up and say something stupid again.*

"Kate, it was nice seeing you again. You guys take care. I will see you at the groundbreaking ceremony. I can't wait to see what you do with my building designs."

"We will do your designs proud," Katie Rose pledged. "It was nice seeing you again too, Garrison."

Garrison turned and began making his way down the long hallway toward the elevators. Katie Rose stepped back over beside Samuel and Mason and started greeting others again. *I need to get back to work.*

In spite of her attempts to squelch her thoughts of Garrison, in the back of Katie Rose's mind, there were these odd thoughts. She could not still her brain from reflecting on the encounter she had just had with Garrison.

While approaching the elevator down the hall, Garrison was still contemplating his unexpected reunion with the Greathouse children as well – Mason – and particularly the lovely Kate. *I'd like to get to know Emerald Sea on a more personal level*, he concluded with a slight smile. Entering the elevator, Garrison pressed the button for the ground floor.

Chapter 5

Letting Go

Katie Rose and BJ had just made love – hot passionate love. He had even left the lights on in the bedroom, because he wanted to plainly see Katie Rose. She was lying with her head on his shoulder and her hand over his heart. His heart, beating beneath her fingertips, left Katie Rose feeling content. Her physical reconnection with BJ had somewhat alleviated the terrible stress she had endured over the last few months. She needed this intimacy in her life a great deal, and BJ did too.

BJ was such a caring, patient man. He had raised the subject of the two of them stowing away to his apartment, as they had tonight, on several other occasions. But never had he pushed this issue.

"Katie Rose, why don't you spend the night?" BJ proposed. He was making light, pleasurable contact up and down her spine with his fingertips. "I want to wake up with you in my arms in the morning. I love you so much."

"I love you too, BJ," she uttered with a pleasant sigh.

Katie Rose pulled her head off of BJ's shoulder and gazed with devotion into his eyes. "I'm so glad I let you talk me into coming to your apartment and being together like this tonight. But I can't spend the night. The nights are still very, very hard for my mother. I still hear her up walking around the house during the night. Often, I will catch her sitting in the kitchen crying in the early morning hours. She needs me there."

"The person she needs there is your dad," BJ pointed out. "But he can't be there, and he never will be again…" BJ abruptly stopped when he saw Katie Rose flinch and look away from him. He realized how inconsiderate he was being, and how selfish he sounded. "I'm sorry, sweetie. I know you miss him too. But your mom, and especially *you*, need to start getting on with your lives. Tonight was an excellent start. But I want more. I want so much more."

"Like what?" Katie Rose dared to ask. She did not want to disappoint BJ. "What more do you want, BJ...other than me spending the night? You have wanted that for a long time."

"I don't *only* want you to spend the night with me, Katie Rose. It's so much more than that. I want...oh...I wasn't going to do this like this, but...."

BJ slid to a sitting position and climbed out of bed. Katie Rose also rose to a sitting position, propping her back up against the headboard. She reached to pull up the sheet to cover her nakedness. She was self-conscious about her body. If it had not been for the heat of the moment earlier, Katie Rose would not have allowed BJ leave the lights on while they made love.

She stared at BJ's skinny, nude behind as he walked across the room to his Chest of Drawers. Other than a small nightstand by the bed, which held BJ's alarm clock, the Chest of Drawers was the only other furniture in the room. BJ's bedroom was rather sparsely furnished, as was his whole apartment. You could tell be was a bachelor. His apartment was outfitted for necessity, not for style. There was no feminine touch.

Katie Rose saw him open one of the small top drawers, extract something, and close it. BJ turned to make his way back to the bed. He had his right hand behind his back. "What exactly have you got in your hand?" Katie Rose questioned with a blossoming smile and exceedingly inquisitive eyes.

She giggled for a moment when, instead of climbing back into bed with her, BJ walked around to her side of the bed and dropped down on one knee. She was all set to tease BJ about how his naked body looked lowered on one knee. But before Katie Rose could speak, BJ swept a ring box out in front of him. He held it up to her and popped it open. Katie Rose was awestruck. She and BJ had discussed marriage in the abstract many times, but she was not expecting him to propose, at least not now.

"Katie Rose, will you make me the happiest man alive and agree to become my wife?"

Is this really happening? Or am I only dreaming? "Um…BJ," Katie Rose stuttered. She was having an awful time forming a coherent sentence. Her eyes were spellbound by the modest, but beautiful, sparkling, diamond ring that was being held out in front of her.

"I know…I shouldn't have sprang this on you like this, Katie Rose," BJ half apologized.

He rose from the floor, sat on the bed beside her and pulled Katie Rose into a tight embrace. "This is not at all the way I had planned for this proposal to unfold. Not with us both naked in the bedroom. I wanted to take you out for a romantic, candlelit dinner at an expensive restaurant, give you flowers, wine and dine you, and propose. But I couldn't stand to wait any longer. I've waited so long for you to be in my life like this already, Katie Rose. I don't want to waste another day. Please say yes. Say you'll become my wife, and I promise you I'll spend the rest of my life trying to do everything in my power to make you the happiest woman in the world. Tell me yes, Katie Rose. Let me slide this ring on your finger. I promise you won't be sorry."

"BJ…" Katie Rose began to formulate a response. "We have discussed marriage. Of course I am not going to say 'no' to your proposal. You know my answer is, 'yes'. But…I'm not sure now is the right time," she professed with noted hesitation.

Katie Rose did not want to hurt BJ's feelings. However, accepting his proposal would demand all her attention be placed on her relationship with him. She was not at all certain she could give this much to BJ right now. In fact, the little bit of energy she had was already used up. She was still too worried about her mom. Katie Rose had to find a way to help lift her mother's deep despair over her father's death. Then she would not feel guilty about going on with her own life.

"It's the perfect time for us to become engaged! Don't you see? Your mom feels lost without your dad. She needs something totally out of the ordinary to focus on. Your mom likes me a great deal, sweetie. Of this, I'm positive. She will be thrilled to find out we are getting married. And we won't plan to have a long engagement. But we will plan to have a nice, big wedding. Your mom will have to help you take care of all the details. It will give her little time to think about your dad. It will be good for her. Your mom needs…no…she deserves…to have something wonderful come about in her life. It will raise her spirits, Katie Rose. It will be the start of her getting out of the depression she has been in since your dad's passing. So see…if you say yes, you won't only be making me the happiest man alive, you'll also be helping your mother. Wouldn't you like to kill two birds with one stone? It's all so simple and so perfect! All you have to do is say...yes."

Katie Rose had not thought about his proposal in this light at all. She had merely been thinking she needed to be by her mother's side as much as possible. But, what BJ said was true. Her mother did like him a lot, and her mom wished for the two of them to marry.

It would make her extremely happy if I were to marry BJ. Could my engagement be exactly what my mom needs to help her start getting over dad and getting on with her life?

BJ lifted Katie Rose's left hand. "So what will it be, Katie Rose?" he asked with a hopeful, expectant smile. He took the ring from the box and held it to the tip of her finger.

Maybe it is *time to move on with my life. Maybe me getting engaged will help both me and my mother deal with our grief.*

"Benjamin James, I would be honored to become Mrs. Katherine Rose Rafferty. So that means my answer is, 'Yes'! I will marry you! I accept your proposal!" she declared in a loud, animated voice. Katie Rose threw her arms around BJ's neck and gave him a series of devoted, excited, playful kisses all over his face.

BJ hastily slid the ring the rest of the way onto her finger. The ring fit – *as Katie Rose and I fit* – perfectly. "You'll see…you will not be sorry, Katie Rose!" BJ pledged once more.

With gentle hands, he began to slide them both back down onto the mattress. BJ kissed Katie Rose with unbridled passion. "We'll make love once more. Then I'll take you home and we'll give your mom the good news. I can't wait to see her reaction!"

"Sounds like a plan to me," Katie Rose purred. She kicked the sheet back off her body and wrapped her legs around the slim lower half of BJ's body. She returned his kisses with equal fervor. The sizzle they shared made all their worries go away.

Katie Rose began to fantasize, *the kisses from my future husband.* This thought was rather comforting to her. If nothing else fit well in this relationship, their sexual pleasures made the difference. Katie Rose loved the way BJ always took her fast and hungrily.

* * * *

As expected, Jackie Lynn was thrilled to learn of Katie Rose's engagement to BJ. BJ was not the most handsome man in the world, nor did he have much material worth, but BJ was a good man. He was more than capable of giving her daughter the most essential thing – deep, lasting love. She hoped BJ and Katie Rose's devotion would rival what she had shared with Long Wolf. She did not want, in any way, her daughter's newfound happiness to be overshadowed by her continuing grief over her beloved husband's death.

Jackie Lynn needed to push her pervasive sorrow over Long Wolf aside. Katie Rose was worried about her and had been putting her life on hold to help her though this difficult mourning period. Jackie Lynn was determined her daughter not behave this way any longer. She wanted Katie Rose to focus solely on BJ and her future with him.

I've got to pull it together, she told herself. *Long Wolf, putting Katie Rose first is what you would want me to do. I'll do this for you as well. My primary focus needs to be on planning Katie Rose's wedding and helping her begin her new life with BJ.*

* * * *

At dinner, the next evening, Jackie Lynn decided she should talk to her daughter about the future. Katie Rose had just sat down at the table with her mother when Jackie Lynn raised this crucial issue with her daughter.

"You should be eating dinner with BJ," Jackie Lynn said with a somewhat forced smile.

"I could have invited him over for dinner. He'll be over a little later though," Katie Rose rather absently replied. She was focusing more on cutting up her chicken breast.

"You should go to his apartment instead," Jackie Lynn dared to suggest. She folded her hands and rested her chin on them. Jackie Lynn still had not touched her food. Her focus was on Katie Rose and not on eating.

Katie Rose took a bite of her dinner and looked up at her mom with slight confusion. She asked, "Why should I go to BJ's apartment? He's fine coming here. Then he can visit with you as well."

"It is nice BJ has taken so much time to visit with me over the past few months, since your father's death. You have been a wonderful daughter to me, Katie Rose. But it's well past time the two of you have the privacy you deserve. The privacy I'm sure BJ would like for you to have. I love you very much, and I want you to stop focusing on me and move on with your life."

"I love you too, mom, and I *am* focusing on moving on with my life," Katie Rose began to argue, giving her mother a hard stare. "I'm engaged, aren't I? I'd say getting married is definitely moving on with my life. Besides, BJ likes you and enjoys seeing you. We still have our private time too."

"I wasn't talking about the two of you going down in the basement, watching television, and sneaking a few kisses. I was talking about the two of you having time alone so you can be intimate. You are bound to want to spend the night with BJ, Katie Rose, and you should be free to do so."

Katie Rose almost choked on the mashed potatoes she had just placed in her mouth. She grabbed her iced tea and took a huge swig. She had not expected to hear these words coming from her mother. She was more than a little embarrassed.

"You don't need to be embarrassed, darling," Jackie Lynn continued, seeing her daughter's cheeks color to a soft pink. "You are twenty-four years old. You are a grown woman, who is in love and engaged to be married to a great guy. It's only natural for the two of you to want to be together in this manor. In fact, I would understand if you wanted to move in with him."

"Mom! Where is all this coming from?! Are you having some kind of breakdown?" Katie Rose demanded to know. *Has BJ been talking to my mom about these things?*

"No, I am not having a breakdown, dear," Jackie Lynn assured her. She cut up and took her first bite of chicken. She chewed it up and took a drink of iced tea before she added, "I was forty when I met your father. Do you think he was the first man I ever slept with?"

"Um…I don't know, and frankly, I don't want to know," Katie Rose admitted with a nervous chuckle, looking down at her plate again. She almost felt as if she should be covering her ears. This was a weird conversation. Katie Rose had always felt comfortable talking to her mom about almost anything. But talking about her parent's sex life and her own was flat out awkward.

"Well, I'll tell you your father was *not* the first man I ever slept with. In fact, when I was your age...well...let's just say I didn't value love or did not know what making love was...I only knew what sex was. I'm proud you have valued yourself and your virginity more than I did. I'd like to think the way you were raised by your father and I had something to do with that."

"It had *a lot* to do with it," Katie Rose hastened to confirm, making grateful, steady eye contact with her mother. She played with her mashed potatoes, stirring them with her fork, before finally admitting, "I'm not a virgin, mom. Is that what you are getting at? BJ and I thought at one point we might wait until we were married, but...together we decided a loving commitment was enough. Just because we have become intimate doesn't mean I have to move in with him. BJ understands you need me here. Besides, what would daddy think if I did something like that? He may not still be here, but I still feel him watching over me."

"That's part of the problem. You worry too much about what other people think! Your father loved you enough to trust you in making your own decisions. He is gone now, and I am left to look after the family."

Jackie Lynn paused a moment to control the tears that were threatening to ruin this important talk with her daughter. She took another long drink of tea to wash away the sob that threatened to choke her. "I trust you enough too, Katie Rose. You will make the right decision. I don't want you to have BJ come over every evening. Nor should he have to bring you home after the two of you have made love. I don't need you to baby-sit me at night. I'm a grown woman. You have been very worried about me, but this is the time you should be focusing *all* of your energy on your relationship with BJ and sharing your love. I am going to be fine. In fact, I've decided to focus all of my free time and energy on planning your wedding. I may still have periods of grief; I may still cry on occasion; I still miss your dad terribly, but I'm going to be okay. If you want to do something to make me happy, you will stop feeling obligated to me. I want you to start spending as much time as possible with BJ. If you don't want to move in with him until after you are married, I can respect that. But I expect you to be over at his apartment the majority of the time, and not here watching over me. Can you do this for me, Katie Rose?"

"BJ will love you even more," Katie Rose said with a rather devilish smile. "He's been wanting me to spend the night with him for a long time. But I didn't want to be disrespectful to you and…and dad."

Katie Rose paused for a second. It dawned on her that her last statement revealed she and BJ had been sleeping together for quite awhile – before her father had died. Her mother did not look shocked or horrified to learn this fact either.

"Long Wolf and I raised an amazing daughter in you, Katie Rose. It's time you started thinking about yourself…and BJ…and not everyone else. I am so proud of you, and all I want is your happiness."

"Okay, mom," Katie Rose agreed, and rose from the table to engulf her in an embrace. "If me spending more time with BJ will make you happy, I'm willing to make the sacrifice," she half teased. "I'm sure he will be too."

"I love you," Jackie Lynn whispered in her daughter's ear, and gave Katie Rose a peck on the lips.

"I love you too, mom," Katie Rose replied. She continued to hold her for several more moments, delighted to be able to claim having such a fantastic, loving parent.

* * * *

Katie Rose, as promised, began spending more and more time with BJ – including spending the night with him on occasion. She was grateful to her mother for encouraging her to move forward with their relationship. It was much more natural for her to stay with BJ after they had shared intimacy. It felt marvelous to fall asleep in his arms.

Jackie Lynn wanted to further encourage Katie Rose's new independence, so she enlisted the help of Mary Julia and Flora. The three women began taking turns, different evenings during the week, hosting dinner at their homes. Sometimes, they also picked a favorite restaurant and all went out together. Still other times, they all went and saw a movie, or spent an afternoon shopping. On other occasions they would take in a concert or a play.

They had been Jackie Lynn's friends for many years – Flora, longer than Mary Julia. Jackie Lynn and Flora had been the best of friends ever since they roomed together in college many, many years ago. Theirs had seemed an odd friendship. Jackie Lynn had been tall, slim and beautiful, with long shimmering black hair and enticing green eyes. She always had a man on her arm. Flora, on the other hand, could have only been described as cute – short, a little on the heavy side, with mousy brown hair. She had been shy and awkward around men. Flora's most attractive feature had been – and still was – her large, warm, deep chocolate eyes. Regardless of their physical differences, the ladies had become fast friends and their friendship had endured.

At sixty-eight, Jackie Lynn was still very pretty. Her waist, hips and belly were fuller since bearing two children late in life – at forty-one and forty-four – and going through menopause. Her hair was mid-length and kept colored a light brown. She had some wrinkles around her eyes and mouth, but most people guessed she was much younger than what she was.

Flora was the same age as Jackie Lynn, but she looked much older. She had stopped coloring her hair, so it was totally gray. She kept it cut short, and curly permed. Since Kenny's death, Flora had taken comfort in food. She had put on significant weight as a result. She had a chubby, full face and a body that jiggled when she laughed. She wore size sixteen clothes.

Since all three ladies were attorneys, they had met and befriended Mary Julia at work. Mary Julia was three years younger than Jackie Lynn and Flora. She had been a tall, blond-haired, blue-eyed ravishing young woman. Years of mental torment, over the sexual abuse she had suffered as a child, had taken its toll on Mary Julia's looks. At sixty-four, there were deep wrinkles in her forehead, to the sides and under her eyes, and around her mouth. Her hair was kept cut shoulder length. More white than blond, her hair still had nice body to it due to the natural curl Mary Julia had always had. She had also put on some weight around her hips and middle.

The ladies made it a point now to spend much of their time together comforting each other in their own special ways. After all, each of them had lost someone. Flora's husband, Kenny, had passed away many years ago, and Mary Julia was still adjusting to being divorced, after a long and turbulent marriage to Jonathan.

The nights were still very hard for Jackie Lynn – coming home to a big empty house to sleep alone. But at least most of her evenings were not being spent alone anymore. She was chasing away her sad thoughts of Long Wolf by sharing her free time with her friends. They allowed her to talk, or to shed tears, as she needed. Overall, Jackie Lynn was crying less and less these days.

Mary Julia and Flora were making things much easier for her. As always, Jackie Lynn had been able to turn to them in her time of need. Jackie Lynn thanked God she had these special ladies in her life. The three of them had a lifelong friendship.

Chapter 6

Groundbreaking

The day of the groundbreaking ceremony and celebration for Greathouse Construction's Gates Towers' project had arrived. The event was held downtown, at the new construction site. Fortunately, it was a pristine, sunny day. Long Wolf's custom had always been to have a large paper banner, announcing the beginning of a project, strung along the front of the new construction site. Samuel continued his friend's tradition – the banner was in place for this new project.

Mason, wearing hardhat and goggles, took the honors of jack hammering the first several pieces of asphalt from the new site, even though he was wearing a suit. He reached to pick up some of the pieces. He began to pass them out to Samuel, Katie Rose, their many financial backers and the architect – in this case, Garrison Parker.

"Katie Rose, why don't you do the honors?" Samuel said to her with a welcoming smile.

Katie Rose looked unsure for a few moments, as if this was not her place. Mason nodded to her to proceed. "It's your company now, little sister. This is your role."

Katie Rose stepped forward meekly, feeling overshadowed by her father's strong spirit. She directed everyone there to gather in a compact circle, hold their piece of asphalt up in the air, and touch them together.

Katie Rose had a knot in her throat as she began to speak the words that had always been spoken by her father, "Today we break ground for Gates Towers. Let these small pieces of broken asphalt, being held joined together again, serve as a sign. Let them be a sign of our solid commitment to this project; a sign we will work with diligence; a sign we will work with respect and integrity for one another; a sign we will strive to accomplish important goals. The most important of these goals being to raise out of this broken ground, Gates Towers. Gates Towers will be another magnificent building for our city to take pride in, and for individuals of our community to flourish in. Greathouse Construction takes immense pride and feels blessed to be allowed to erect this important building. Thanks to all of you, in advance, for your hard work and dedication."

With that, they all slightly rubbed their pieces of stone together. They almost appeared as if they were trying to light a fire. Then Katie Rose instructed them, "Place this piece of stone where you can see it each day. It is intended to remind you of your dedication to Gates Towers, and to all of the individuals who will be involved in working with you on this project."

She, Samuel and Mason all stepped forward, picked up a huge pair of scissors, and cut through the enormous banner that stood at the front of the construction project.

"Let the project proceed!" Katie Rose announced with tremendous enthusiasm. All in the small group of people cheered. "Please everyone join us now at Greathouse Construction for a celebration luncheon. We'll celebrate our combined efforts to create this city's newest, architectural wonder!"

As they walked toward their cars, Mason came up beside his sister and placed an arm around her shoulder, "Good job, sis. I'm sure dad is very proud of you. You are going to make this company an excellent president. I am proud of you too."

"Thanks, Mason."

As they walked together the rest of the way to their cars, Katie Rose thanked her brother by in turn placing one of her arms around his waist. She was suddenly fighting tears. Gates Towers was Greathouse's first major project since her father's death. Her brother's unwavering support meant more than he could ever imagine. Without knowing it, Mason was also stepping into one of their father's roles – staunch mentor and supporter.

* * * *

A delicious catered luncheon was being held in the imposing assembly hall at Greathouse Construction. This room was on the twenty-sixth floor and had windows all around that looked out over the city. The serving tables were set up on the east side where everyone could look out on the waterfront, which was only a few miles away. The radiant sun sparkling on the water today gave it a dazzling bluish cast.

In the middle of the room, upon the marble floor, many round tables had been set up. The tables were adorned with white tablecloths and napkins, silverware and crystal goblets. A full bar had been set up at the other end of the room. There was a jazz band playing soft tunes at the opposite end of the floor.

Instead of eating, Katie Rose had been milling around in the crowd, shaking hands and making friendly conversation, for nearly an hour. She all at once came face-to-face with Garrison Parker. He had come from the bar. He had a glass of white wine in his hand.

"Hello, Kate," he addressed her. He noted that her green knit sweater brought out the vibrant green in her eyes. He also checked out her attractive long legs. He was glad she had on a skirt and not a pantsuit.

Katie Rose once again liked the sound of her *new* name reverberating from this man's deep, baritone voice. Garrison looked very handsome in his tailored, black suit. She also became aware of his inquisitive, sweeping eyes and his moist lips, as they curved into a smile. This awareness troubled her.

"You did a magnificent job with the speech at the groundbreaking ceremony today. It had a very Indian feel to it. Another reason I'm pleased to be associated with Greathouse Construction on this project. You will do your father proud running his company. You seem to be as business savvy as you are lovely."

Why did he comment on my looks? Katie Rose found herself contemplating with unrest. *For one thing, I have my hands folded in front of me and I'm holding my right hand over my left. Garrison hasn't seen my engagement ring. I need to make sure he does. He needs to understand that this is a business relationship, nothing more. Comments about my physical appearance are inappropriate.*

Katie Rose hurried to refold her hands. She placed her left hand on top of her right, and she wiggled her fingers to draw even more attention to it. She saw Garrison's eyes glance at the ring.

Good! He's seen it.

His eyes grew serious and he inquired, "You are having quite a wonderful month aren't you, Kate? First, Greathouse Construction lands the Gates Tower project, and now you've gone off and gotten yourself engaged."

Garrison reached with tenderness to lift her hand. *Why is he touching me?* Katie Rose wondered, feeling herself tense. She liked the touch of his large, strong, yet gentle hand.

"The ring is very pretty. So when did this come about? You weren't wearing this ring the last time I saw you."

He looked to see if I was wearing a ring the last time we met. I'm not imagining that Garrison is attracted to me. I need to nip this attraction in the bud now.

"I got engaged about three weeks ago, but I've been in a committed relationship for several years. My fiancé and I met while we were in high school," Katie Rose shared. "So what about you? If I remember correctly, you are my brother's age, or maybe even a bit older. Isn't there some special lady in your life?" *Why did I ask him that?*

"I'm twenty-eight, and no, there is no special lady in my life right now. I have too much fondness for playing the field for that," Garrison confessed with a carefree smile and mischievous dancing eyes.

"Mason used to feel the same way. It must be a guy thing. But he's head over heels in love now. It all comes down to meeting the right person."

"As you obviously have. I couldn't imagine meeting someone in high school and spending the rest of my life with only that person."

Katie Rose was dismayed to see the smile disappear from Garrison's face. He also took a drink of his wine. *Why does he look disappointed? Garrison doesn't even know me. What would he care if I'm taken or not?*

Garrison also released Katie Rose's hand. "Well, Kate, as before, it was nice talking with you. We should be seeing much more of one another. I have more building plans to bring in on Monday."

"Great," she remarked. "I hope you enjoy the rest of the afternoon. I will most likely see you Monday."

"Okay. Congratulations on today's successful groundbreaking, a most exquisite luncheon…and…on your impending nuptials. I hope your young man realizes how lucky he is."

"We *both* know how lucky we are," Katie Rose corrected. She continued to be unnerved by Garrison's repeated personal comments.

"That's exactly the response I would expect from someone like you."

"Someone like me?" she questioned in bewilderment.

"Yes. You have an air of grace about you. It will be my pleasure to work with you, and I'm glad I got to make your re-acquaintance."

"Thank you," Katie Rose replied, touched by his nice comments. It was exactly the way she hoped strangers would regard her. "I'm sure I will enjoy working with you as well, Garrison. You've come a long way from being that rude, know-it-all boy I met all those years ago on the Reservation," she teased with an amiable smile.

"I'm glad you feel that way," he said with a chuckle.

As Garrison was getting ready to turn and walk away, he reached to touch Katie Rose one final time – on the side of her arm. He had not been able to resist one last feel of her silky skin. Something about Kate drew him like a magnet. Garrison trailed his fingertips along her arm as he was leaving. With a sexy smile and an appreciative lingering gaze, his last words came out ever so slowly, "Take care, Kate."

"You do the same, Garrison," Katie Rose replied, returning his glorious smile. She was trying to ignore the pleasurable tingle Garrison's final touch had caused.

Katie Rose was relieved to watch Garrison leave her side and begin to make his way through the crowd. *I like this guy*, she concluded. *The fact that he was initially attracted to me or that I find him handsome should not be a problem. I'm fully committed to BJ, and now Garrison understands I'm taken. So we should have a good work relationship.*

Katie Rose turned and began to walk toward others still remaining in the crowd. Putting Garrison out of her mind and getting on with the business at hand proved more difficult than it should have been.

Chapter 7

The Proposal

In only a matter of months, Mason and his band were moving at nearly the speed of light from being virtual unknowns to being overnight sensations. "So is the way with the music business," Fawn had rather flippantly told them.

Mason's first single was number ten on the Billboards Top 40 Rock chart, and he and his band were getting requests from talk shows and late night shows to start making some appearances. Behind the scenes, Fawn was also busy, setting up concerts in different states for them.

The urgent thrust of his musical career had Mason's head spinning. To say he was excited would have been the understatement of the century. Mason was euphoric. Callie was right by his side sharing, with elation, in his newfound success. They felt closer than ever.

Mason's family was thrilled about his success. His extended family was as well. Flora called to congratulation him and tell Mason how proud she was of him.

"Aunt Flora," he addressed her with affection. Mason and Katie Rose had always called her Aunt Flora, even though she was not their biological aunt. Since Flora had no children, she had always been actively involved in Mason and Katie Rose's lives. She was family to them, even if she was not blood kin. "You were one of the first people to encourage my love of music. My first band job was at your Fourth of July party when I was sixteen. I feel like, in some ways, I owe my success to you. Thanks for always believing in me, Aunt Flora. It meant…um means…a lot."

"You are an extremely talented musician, Mason. You always were. It just took a while longer for your parents...or I guess we could say your father in particular...to recognize your gift. Your father is looking down at you now and is very proud of you."

"Thanks," Mason said, a wave of despair washing over him. He wished his dad was still alive to see what he had accomplished. "I love you, Aunt Flora. I've got to get going. Thanks for calling."

"I love you too, Mason," she professed. They talked for a few moments longer and they ended their conversation. Both Mason and Flora's hearts were warmed by their discourse. Mason was glad Flora was in all of their lives. She was kindhearted, loving, and an essential support to them all.

* * * *

Katie Rose was delighted by Mason's musical success as well. Mason's dreams were at long last coming true. Mason came into her office one morning – the office which had belonged to Samuel. It was one of the largest offices at Greathouse – only Long Wolf's was larger. Pictures of buildings they had constructed over the years still hung upon the walls on one side of the office. Along the other side, a row of windows looked out over the city toward the waterfront. Since the executive offices were on the twenty-eighth floor, Katie Rose had an exquisite view of the city. Samuel resided in her father's office now, which was next to Katie Rose's.

Mason took a seat in the cloth armchair in front of his sister's massive cherry desk. It came as no shock to Katie Rose when he sheepishly told her he would be quitting his job at Greathouse Construction soon.

"I knew this was coming," Katie Rose admitted with dejection. She pushed aside the papers she had been looking at and gave her brother her full attention.

"I'm sorry, Katie Rose. I don't want to let you down. I know you don't think you are qualified enough yet to run this company alone," he confessed, his eyes relaying guilt. He rushed on to justify, "But Samuel is still here. I'm only the construction supervisor, and I have the perfect replacement for me in mind – Gregory Thompson. He knows all the safety rules and the guys like and respect him. He is dedicated to Greathouse Construction and will do a fine job."

Without delay, Katie Rose attempted to placate her brother. "You aren't letting me down in any way, Mason. Your dream has never been to work at Greathouse. Your dream has been to sell the songs you write and become a famous recording artist. It looks as if you are well on your way to doing that. I'm proud and happy for you. But one thing is for sure – I'm going to miss you, and that's a fact."

"How can you possibly miss me? If you want to hear me, all you'll need to do is turn on a radio. That should be a huge comfort. Or maybe, in time, if you are missing my pretty boy face, you'll have to turn on the television, and there I'll be on MTV. You do have that, don't you?" he braggingly teased.

"Okay, big shot!" Katie Rose laughed. She proceeded to pick up a piece of scrap paper from her desk, wad it up, and hurl it toward her brother's *inflated* head.

Mason, his reflexes fast from years of playing baseball, reached out and caught the ball of paper before it struck him. He gave Katie Rose a mischievous grin and was plainly considering sending the paper projectile back at his sister.

"Don't you dare!" Katie Rose warned with a knowing smile.

She snatched up her trashcan from under her desk, and she held it up over the desk for Mason to dispose of the paper he held. After another few moments of hesitant temptation, Mason seemed as if he was going to toss the paper in the waste receptacle. However, at the last minute, instead, he fired it over the wastebasket. With perfect aim, he beamed Katie Rose in the side of the head.

As if they were back at home playing as they did when they were children, Katie Rose was determined her big brother would not get the best of her. She sprang from her high back leather chair. She charged around the desk with the trash container still in hand. Her thought was to dump the whole contents over Mason's head. In turn, Mason's first reaction was to elude her feeble attempt. Mason leapt out of his chair, overturning it. His hand automatically flew out, catching the wastebasket and sending trash spraying everywhere except onto his head.

Katie Rose accidentally dropped the waste can. She put on her best serious face, stooped down, as gracefully as she could in her skirt, set the wastebasket up, and pretended to be picking up pieces of paper from the floor. Then suddenly, without any uncertainty, she began tossing everything she had in her hands at Mason. Of course, being the young mischievous man he was, Mason ducked, stooped, and gathered the paper around him, retaliating and tossing it back at Katie Rose.

They bombarded one another for several more minutes. They were slow to return to their senses. A second later, they glanced around at the disorder they had created. There were wads of paper strewn all across the carpet in the spacious, professionally decorated office. The two could not contain their laughter. Delightful memories of their childhood, and the times they would tease and chase each other around the house, came to mind.

"I'll help you clean this mess up," Mason offered. He bent down to pick up the discarded wastebasket that lay in the middle of the floor, with paper and other debris all around it.

Katie Rose and Mason took a few moments to walk around the room, gather the scattered trash, and deposit it back in the waste container. They were still giggling over their foolishness as they cleaned up the office. It had felt good to act like children again for a few brief moments. Katie Rose was glad she and Mason could still be so carefree with one another. She was going to miss her big brother a great deal.

Gingerly turning their interaction serious again, her tone changed completely as she inquired, "So when do you leave for New York?" Mason and his band were supposed to be flying to New York for an appearance on *The Late Show with David Letterman.*

"Early tomorrow morning. Callie is coming with me. Neither of us can wait to see New York."

"Oh, shut up! I'll be stuck in this office and you and Callie will be off trotting around the Big Apple. Something doesn't seem right here," she joked some more.

"What's sad is you'll be happy stuck in this office wheeling and dealing. You love it, and you know you do!" Mason pointed out the truth, with a wide, knowing grin.

"I do," Katie Rose admitted with a content smile. "I feel like we are both so blessed, Mason. The only thing I wish is that dad could be here to witness it all. I miss him so much."

"I know," Mason concurred with a degree of sadness. "I still miss him too, Katie Rose. Mom seems to be doing much better though. Your engagement to BJ has helped her a lot. He's a great guy. I'm happy for the both of you."

"Well, Callie is a great woman too. So when are the two of you going to bite the bullet and get engaged? I'm sure that would thrill mom as well," Katie Rose dared to suggest.

Katie Rose did not understand why Mason and Callie had not already gotten married, instead of only living together. The two of them had an unwavering love and were totally committed to one another. She wanted to see them get married and start having children. Then all of the aspirations she had for her brother would be fulfilled.

With a lopsided grin, Mason confessed, "You...and mom...won't have to wait too much longer."

"What's that supposed to mean?" Katie Rose questioned, dying of curiosity now.

"It means I do intend to propose to Callie very soon. You're the first to know. If you breathe a word to Callie, I will have to kill you, little sister or not."

"Details! I need details!" Katie Rose demanded. She jerked on Mason's arm with persistence, threatening to spill the contents of the waste container again. "When do you plan to propose? Where do you plan to propose? How do you plan to do it? Have you gotten the ring yet? Can I see it? I need to know! You need to share everything with me!"

"No can do," Mason rather meanly maintained. He walked away from her a few paces to sit the trashcan down by the side of the desk. "You can get the details from Callie *after* I propose. All I will tell you, once again, is you and mom won't have to wait much longer."

"Are you going to do it while you guys are in New York?" Katie Rose persevered for answers, examining her brother's eyes for clues. "Come on Mason, I won't tell Callie anything."

"Maybe...maybe not," Mason continued to be vague with his sister, a wide devilish smile on his handsome face. "You will find out soon enough. All you need to know is I *do* intend to propose. I want very much for Callie and me to get married."

"Oh, Mason, that is so wonderful!" Katie Rose purred, engulfing him in a delighted bear hug. "I'm so happy for you both. You make the perfect couple."

"Thank you. I'm inclined to agree with you."

Before they had finished their show of affection, there was a knock on the door, and Katie Rose could see Samuel standing in the partially opened doorway.

"Katie Rose, I'm sorry to interrupt, but Garrison Parker is here with more of the plans for Gates Towers. I'd like for you to meet with him. That is, if you haven't already made other plans." Samuel was looking between the two of them.

"Of course, I don't have any other plans. Mason and I have concluded our little get-together," she acknowledged, becoming serious all at once. "He was on his way out."

"Okay, I guess I'm through here," Mason told him. He was still grinning as Katie Rose released him from her embrace.

"For now," Katie Rose was forced to relent.

They started to walk toward the door, and Katie Rose whispered in Mason's ear, "Don't think I'm letting you off the hook, Mason. Callie had better be calling me soon with very happy news to share."

"She will be," Mason promised her with a cheery smile.

Katie Rose was overjoyed. She felt as if she were walking on air as she strolled out of the office to follow Samuel. Not only were things going excessively well in both her and Mason's professional lives but things were also richly progressing in their private lives as well. Katie Rose was, all at once, looking forward to her meeting with Garrison Parker. They would be finalizing some more plans for Gates Towers. It would be one more exhilarating thing accomplished that day.

* * * *

Katie Rose entered one of the small conference rooms with a glorious ear-to-ear smile on her face. Garrison was already seated at the small rectangular table. He gave her a wide grin in return and greeted, "Hello, Kate. It's nice to see you again. It's especially nice to see such a pretty smile on your face. It must be a good day for you."

"It's a magnificent day!" she chirped with noted enthusiasm, taking a bouncing seat in the fabric weaved armchair across from Garrison. "It's nice to see you again too, Mr. Parker."

"Please not so formal," he protested. "It's Garrison. We are going to be working together for quite some time on this project. I would think that qualifies us to be on a first name basis. That is, unless you would prefer I call you Ms. Greathouse."

"No, because soon, you would have to change that to Mrs. Rafferty. I wouldn't want to confuse you," she teased, feeling carefree. She was still wound up from her good-humored escapade with Mason and from the awesome news he had shared with her. "Kate is fine," she stated.

Katie Rose very much liked it when this man called her Kate. She liked the sound of it when it so naturally rolled off of his tongue. The name also made her feel so much more like a grown woman, because it was a woman's name, unlike Katie Rose.

"So when exactly is this wedding of yours scheduled to take place?" Garrison dared to ask. He was still smiling, but his cheerful expression looked more forced.

"April fifteenth," she relayed without hesitation. "We decided to get married in April to overshadow my dad's death this April – something joyful to replace the sad, especially for my mom. Plus, as I shared with you the last time we spoke, I have known my fiancé, BJ, since high school. So our marriage is hardly sudden."

"And when did you fall in love?" Garrison surprised her by questioning.

This guy can ask some of the darnest questions. Why does he care so much about my personal life anyway?

"Well…let's see…I turned twenty-four in May. I was sixteen when we met. I'd say I've been in love with BJ for about five years; that's only on my part. BJ has confessed more than once that, for him, it was love at first sight," Katie Rose bragged with good humor.

I can certainly see why, Garrison ascertained, but did not share. He found Katie Rose to be very appealing, not only to his sight but also to his sense of smell.

"BJ and I developed a close friendship that blossomed into something much more serious," Katie Rose also shared on a more serious note.

The smile on her face was somewhat strained, and she was examining Garrison with serious eyes. Katie Rose was wondering if she should steer this conversation in a different direction. Her personal life was none of Garrison's business.

"Friendship growing into love. That sounds like a winner to me," Garrison commented. He seemed a little preoccupied now. "If this young man makes you happy, that's all that counts. In turn, I should have a contented partner to do business with. You looked on top of the world when you came in here today. Did that have something to do with BJ?"

It sounded odd to hear Garrison using BJ's name almost like he knew him. For some reason, it unsettled Katie Rose. "I *was* on top of the world. And my great mood did have something to do with BJ. I'm happy being engaged to him," Katie Rose acknowledged. She continued in haste, with a grim expression on her face, "Let's get one thing straight, Garrison. You do not need to worry about my happiness. Everything in my life is going wonderfully. Regardless, I would never let my personal life interfere with business affairs."

"Affairs? Who said anything about an affair?" he insinuated. A suggestive grin was spread across his face, and his eyes were dancing with mischief.

Katie Rose was not amused. Quite the opposite, in a stern voice, as she lost what measure of control she had, she snapped, "Look…I don't know why you feel you need to get personal with me. Perhaps you feel some weird connection because we briefly met as children, but we are only business associates. That's all I'm interested in. I have a fiancé. I am taken! That may be hard for a playboy like you to accept, but it is necessary if we are going to work together. Either that, or maybe you are not going to be the right architect for Greathouse to do business with."

"I got that loud and clear," Garrison stated. However, Katie Rose was bemused to see that he was laughing.

"What's so funny?" she inquired. Her eyes were giving him a hard, disapproving stare.

"I'm not laughing at what you said," he was quick to confirm. Garrison had to force himself to be serious once more. "Okay, perhaps I am laughing at part of what you said. Or maybe it's merely the way you said it. You are very spirited. I like that. I like that a lot! This *playboy* is on warning. The woman of my dreams has been taken off the market. Can my ego deal with it? It will have to, because this project with Greathouse

Construction is extremely important to me. More important to me than putting the moves on a woman that is obviously not available."

The way he had informed her of this knowledge made Katie Rose feel belittled. "Are you making fun of me?" Katie Rose demanded to know. Her eyes challenged, burning with anger. Garrison's half-grin seemed to mock.

"Not hardly!" he hastened to declare. *I find you adorable when you are angry,* he observed, but wisely kept this fact to himself.

Garrison was attracted to this lovely young lady. Any normal, red-blooded man would be. I need to make sure Kate knows I respect the fact that she is already taken. "I would never make fun of you, Kate. I respect you a great deal. You are a beautiful, smart, ethical, determined woman. I've said it before and I'll say it again. I'm looking exceedingly forward to working with you. But there is something you need to understand about me, Kate. I am a very good architect, and I enjoy what I do tremendously. However, I also have a lighthearted side. I was teasing about the affair thing. I respect that you are off the market. Though I would like it if we could be friends as well as business associates. That's all I was trying to do...be friendly. I find that interjecting some humor sometimes puts things on more relaxed level. I was not in any way trying to be a player with you." *Although...if you were not taken...Don't go there, Garrison.*

Why am I always so quick to try and snap this guy's head off? Katie Rose found herself wondering. Garrison had only been teasing her. Katie Rose had been teased by Mason her entire life, so she should have been more than accustomed to this sort of relationship with a member of the opposite sex.

"I overreacted. I'm sorry," Katie Rose apologized in a much calmer voice. *I have to apologize to this guy on a regular basis for my behavior. If I'd relax when I'm around him, we probably* could *become friends as well as business associates and develop a mature work relationship.*

"No apology necessary. Maybe it *is* because we met as children all those years ago. I don't know for certain. All I know is I feel as if I've known you forever. I'm probably more comfortable with you than I should be. It's no wonder I am putting you on the defense. Can we start over again, and try to be friends, as well as an outstanding team of business associates?"

"I would like that," Katie Rose proclaimed, giving him a heartwarming smile once again.

Garrison could honestly see forgiveness in her eyes. *Those beautiful emerald eyes.* "Good. Here's to friendship and an outstanding business partnership," Garrison proposed with enthusiasm. He offered his hand to Katie Rose for a confirming handshake.

Katie Rose slid her petite hand into Garrison's large, smooth, extended one. Garrison gave Katie Rose a firm, yet tender, handshake. As they stood there facing one another, a friendly and inviting smile came across Garrison's face. Their eyes met and held; it seemed like the minutes were slowly passing by. Katie Rose was alarmed to discover that, once she looked him in the eye and he held her hand, she was somehow drawn to this man.

Okay, so I find Garrison handsome. He's a very good-looking man. Any normal female would find him attractive. In fact, I'm certain most do and aren't shy about sharing this attraction with him. That's no doubt why Garrison is still enjoying being a bachelor so much. Unlike a man, I will not let the fact that I am attracted to him pose any sort of problem between us. I'm taken. I'll be married soon. I'm fully committed to BJ. I can handle Garrison and me merely being friends and business associates. Even as she was trying to convince herself of this fact, a heated feeling was moving over her body and butterflies were unsettling her stomach.

"We should get to work," Katie Rose proposed. She freed her hand from Garrison's uncomfortable, spine tingling touch. She glanced down at the shiny wooden tabletop, to break the alluring eye contact between them.

"Yes we should," Garrison agreed. *Kate, fighting my attraction to you is not going to be easy. But working with you is certainly going to be a pleasure!* Garrison was careful to rein in his forbidden desires.

* * * *

The Late Show with David Letterman was a total adrenaline rush for Mason. To Callie's dismay, Fawn met them there. She was there to make sure all went according to plan. This was Savage Pride's first television appearance, and Fawn wanted to make sure it was flawless.

Callie was once again separated from them all. She was given a seat in the first row of the audience. She sulked as she sat alone in the theatre, until David Letterman came out and personally greeted her. Then, even though she missed Mason and wished she could be by his side, she still felt privileged to be there.

Mason and the other band members were whisked off to the wardrobe department. They were given matching white T-shirts, with Savage Pride embroidered in red across them. They had all been instructed to wear blue jeans. Their footwear was left to their discretion.

After they finished dressing, they were led to the hair and makeup department. It was odd to have women combing his hair and setting it just so-so with hairspray and even putting makeup on his face. For the first time, Mason felt like a star. When they were deemed ready by the David Letterman staff – and Fawn – they were taken onstage for a brief rehearsal.

They remained on this stage, concealed behind a stage wall, and watched the first part of the taping on television monitors. They all laughed amongst themselves at David Letterman's jokes.

"He's funny, isn't he?" the cameraman asked.

"He sure is," Mason and everyone else agreed.

As it got closer to their performance time, the cameraman told them. "Guys, I need you to watch me. I'll give you a countdown from ten. Then it's Showtime! You launch right into your song. Have you got that?"

They all assured him that they did. "Good. I'm looking forward to hearing you guys. I love your first single."

"Thanks," Mason said with pride.

When it came time for them to perform, as they had been told, they were cued by the cameraman with a countdown from ten…nine….eight... As soon as he said, "action!", the stage door slid open and Mason and Savage Pride were starring into a multitude of bright lights and cameras. Even though it was hard for them to see the studio audience because of the glare, they could hear them cheering wildly. They launched into their song. They were the last act, so the taping was over after their act. They bowed as the audience cheered and clapped for everyone – David Letterman, Savage Pride, and all his other guests.

The taping was officially over at 5:30 p.m., but they stayed in the studio until about 6:00 p.m., since the studio allowed them to talk with David Letterman, take photos with him and get his autograph.

"You guys were terrific!" David told them all.

"Thanks!" they all chimed almost in unison.

"You're on your way," he professed.

"Thanks for having us on your show," Mason relayed his gratitude, shaking his hand. The other guys were all nodding their thankfulness as well.

"The pleasure was all mine."

They all got his autograph, and they were amazed and gratified when David asked for their autographs as well. They took turns having photos made with him. Even Callie got in on the action. She was thrilled to have her picture taken with David Letterman.

Callie looked very pretty. She had on a turquoise, long-sleeved blouse which brought out the dazzling blue in her eyes. Her thick, long, naturally curly, blond hair glistened as it framed her face. Her formfitting, black, dress slacks accentuated her lower half perfectly, making her legs look longer and even slimmer than they already were.

When Fawn came out to congratulate Mason and Savage Pride on a "Job well done!", Callie darted to Mason's side, grasping his arm to remind him she was still there. He turned and gathered her in his arms and gave her an excited kiss. He did not notice the jealously in her eyes.

Mason had their VCR set up to record the show that night. He could not wait to see the tape of the show. When they left, the other band members went off together to have some dinner, drinks and to celebrate. Mason parted from them. He wanted to be alone with Callie. Since it was October, it was already dark when they left the studio. Regardless, there were still crowds of people moving to and fro along the sidewalks.

He and Callie enjoyed a quiet dinner at a small diner on one of the side streets. Since it was a nice evening – the temperature in the fifties – they took a stroll to the Empire State Building, several blocks away. Mason was always cozy to snuggle against, and he had his arm around Callie's waist as they walked. She was still glad she had brought along a jacket to put on – especially when they got to the observation deck at the Empire State Building. It was very windy there, and Callie was thankful for the extra warmth her mid-weight jacket provided, even though it only came to rest at her small waist.

New York was a glorious, lighted masterpiece from high above. The only thing Callie did not like was the way the building swayed – even though Mason assured her it was supposed to sway. He explained to her that the Empire State Building was built to move gradually back and forth, with the wind, so the windows and such would not be broken.

They walked to Times Square next. They were both awed from the extreme brightness of all the millions of lights and animation all around them. When Callie first walked out into the middle of this magnificent place, she spun around in a circle, pointing to everything. "Take a picture of that, Mason! Take a picture of that! Did you get a picture of that?" Mason enjoyed taking in her reaction almost as much as he enjoyed the sights and sounds all around him. Television did no justice to seeing the wondrous Times Square with their own eyes.

Now, Mason and Callie were strolling, hand in hand, along Broadway in the middle of Times Square. Because of the fun and exhilaration they were having, they were not aware of how late it had become; it was already midnight. Yet, the sidewalks were still crowded with hundreds of people. The streets were also still bustling with traffic, especially taxis, which honked their horns repeatedly. They had been walking along Times Square for a few hours. They had made frequent stops along the way to check out stores and pick up souvenirs from sidewalk vendors.

"I still can't believe we are in New York, walking in Times Square and that we got to meet, talk to, and have our pictures taken with David Letterman, and you were on television," Callie was chattering. She was bouncing along beside Mason through the crowd with energetic animation.

"I know. It's almost too good to be true," Mason agreed with a wide, jovial smile.

All at once, he pulled Callie out of the crowd. He had spied a rare unoccupied entranceway. It led to one of the stores that had closed for the night. Mason took a second to give Callie an appreciative kiss on the lips. She put her arms around Mason's neck and deepened the kiss, rousing Mason with her eager tongue.

Many people walked and rushed past them, paying them little or no heed. Hundreds of private conversations were going on all around Callie and Mason, but they were oblivious to them all. They were fixated on one another.

"Hmm…maybe we should go back to the hotel," Mason suggested. Desire glowed in his eyes and increased within his groin, as he continued to hold Callie against his body. The inviting scent of her perfume hungered him.

"That might be a good idea," Callie shared his enthusiasm, a devilish grin playing at the corners of her mouth. She stepped back and teased, trailing her fingers down to his belt buckle, "Do you think we should wait a few moments, so you can compose yourself?" At that, Callie and Mason both lost themselves in laughter; they were so in love and happy.

They were fortunate their hotel was only a few blocks away. Of course, even at that, it took a while to get there, because Mason and Callie were forced to amble along with the multitudes of people strolling along the sidewalks. New York was a city alive. You could almost feel the energy all around you.

Mason and Callie finally arrived at their hotel. They took an elevator to their room on the tenth floor. In the elevator, Callie sneaked another yearning kiss. Mason placed his arm around Callie's waist as they strolled down the hallway toward their room.

Arriving at the room, Mason slid his keycard into the slot on the door, unlocking it. He turned the polished brass handle and opened the door. Mason stepped back to let Callie enter first. This was strange, but Callie was anxious to get inside. She slipped past Mason into the room.

When she switched on the light, lovely red and pink rose petals were the first things she noted, scattered all across the floor. As the two walked through the room hand in hand, Callie was greeted with more of these beautiful rose petals. They led past the entrance to the bathroom and down the short hall. They were also scattered all over the floor by their king-sized bed. "Mason... what...?" she began to question.

Callie's attention was diverted as she noticed their cushy, red, velvet bedspread had been turned back. There was a small teddy bear, holding a large Hershey's kiss, sitting on the middle pillow. The soft aroma of the rose petals was making her mind wander; the entire room had this enticing fragrance about it. As she turned to face Mason, the last thing she took note of was a bottle of sparkling cider chilling in a bucket on the nightstand. Two crystal long-stemmed glasses were sitting beside it.

"Is this the norm for this hotel?" she asked with confusion. They were staying in a nice hotel – a Hilton – so Callie was not certain what their standard protocol was. The rooms cost over two hundred dollars a night. Fortunately, the studio was paying, and not them.

"Not hardly," Mason confessed in delight, with a conniving smile. "I requested a few extra services from the hotel staff. I wanted tonight to be very special."

"As if it hasn't been already," Callie declared with a beautiful, enormous grin. Her lovely sapphire eyes were sparkling with enchantment.

What you've seen so far is only the beginning, Callie. He sat the bags from their city purchases down on the desk. He took Callie's hand and walked her over by the bed. "Sit beside me on the bed," Mason requested.

He took a seat on the side of the bed, turned her hand up, and kissed the palm, to give her added encouragement. He also reached to pull the bottle of cider out of the bucket. As Callie sat, hip to hip with him, Mason proceeded to open the bottle and poured them both a glass. He handed one of the glasses to her.

"Thank you," she said. He realized her gratitude was for more than the glass of cider. Callie's devoted eyes said it all.

"Callie, I love you with all my heart," Mason began.

"As I do you," Callie professed, taking a second to place a lengthy heated kiss on his lips.

"Good. I'm glad," Mason said with a nervous chuckle.

He drank a little of his cider. Mason wished it was alcohol to help calm his nerves. He had gotten cider instead, since Callie was an alcoholic and could not drink liquor.

Callie sipped a little of her cider as well. Mason placed his glass back on the nightstand. He stood up, and took Callie's glass and sat it on the nightstand as well. Callie wondered for a second where Mason might be going. However, instead of walking away, Mason unexpectedly dropped down on one knee in front of Callie.

Callie's heart raced in anticipation. *Is he doing what I think he is doing?*

She only had to wonder for a second. Mason started speaking in a soft voice, and Callie knew at once he was, indeed, proposing to her. Her heart felt as if it might burst. It was overflowing with abundant love for this special man.

"Callie, as I said, I love you with all my heart. These last few years with you by my side have been some of the best of my life. I want you by my side always. I want to spend the rest of my life with you. I'm asking you to marry me, Callie. Will you say you'll be my wife?"

Mason reached to pull a ring from his pocket. Callie's eyes were wide with wonder, as they transfixed on the giant diamond ring he held out in front of her. Tears of joy slowly formed, and she could not speak for several moments she was so shocked by what Mason had done.

"So are you going to answer me?" Mason asked with apprehension. A few seconds of awkward silence had passed; yet they seemed like an eternity to Mason.

"I…oh my God, Mason! I love you so much!! You know what my answer is! Yes! Yes!! Yes!!!" Callie screeched. She thrust her left hand forward, so Mason could slide the ring on her finger.

Callie's hand was trembling as Mason placed the ring on her finger. He sprang off the floor and threw his arms around Callie. He engulfed her in a secure embrace.

When Mason released her, Callie gazed with joy at the ring that glistened on her finger. Tears trickled down her pink cheeks. She was so touched and filled by consuming love for this amazing man.

"Now where were we before all of this commotion took place?" Mason teased, trying to lighten the mood. "Oh, yeah. I remember." He bent to kiss the bend of her neck.

"They've already turned the bed back for us," Callie pointed out with a euphoric grin. She began to pull up his T-shirt. She ran her lips along every inch of exposed skin.

"We'll have to tip the hotel staff tremendously well," Mason commented. He pulled Callie to her feet, continued to kiss her, and began to unbutton her blouse.

Callie whipped Mason's shirt over his head. Her frantic need to make love to this man – this love of her life – was enormous. They were made for each other. They would always be together – now, tomorrow, and forever.

Chapter 8

Temptations

Greathouse Construction landed another large construction deal. Garrison Parker and Parker Architecture were also involved with this project. The negotiations meeting had ended, and Garrison once again stepped forward to talk with Samuel and Katie Rose – or as Garrison liked to call her, *Kate*. Mason was no longer working at Greathouse Construction. He was solely pursuing success with his career as a musician now.

"Congratulations, Samuel…Kate," Garrison said, flashing his usual arresting smile. He reached to shake each of their hands, lingering, as always, when he took Kate's hand.

"Thank you," Both Katie Rose and Samuel replied in unison.

As usual, Garrison looked stunning. He had on a dark gray, Armani suit; a pale gray, long-sleeved shirt; and a vibrant red tie with small silver diamonds. His thick black hair was shorter.

A month had passed since Katie Rose laid eyes on this attractive and creative man. *Why is it I always have to notice how perfect this guy looks – the way his suit fits his body, the way his hair lays, the way he never stops smiling with those soft, full, tempting lips?* Crossing her arms, she pinched the inside of her forearm to bring herself back to her senses. *Stop!* she mentally scolded herself. *Back to business!* "It looks as if the two of us will be working together on another project, Garrison. *We* are exceedingly pleased with the work you've done on the Gates Tower project thus far. It goes without saying *we* are looking forward to working with you again on this new project," Katie Rose told him.

"It's been a pleasure to work with *you* as well, Kate," he commented. His eyes held with hers longer than necessary. "In fact, why don't *we* start right now," she was surprised to hear Garrison add. She noted that he too had emphasized words. He was making certain she knew he was referring to her and *only* her.

"Right now?" she questioned.

"Yeah. It's lunchtime. Why don't *we* make it a working lunch?" he suggested. Garrison raised the briefcase he held in his right hand and tapped it. "We, as in you and I, can go out, or we can call someplace and have lunch brought in. That is, unless you have previous plans for this afternoon that can not be changed?"

"Actually she doesn't," Samuel spoke for Katie Rose, much to her chagrin. He thought it was best, since for some strange reason, Katie Rose was standing there mute.

Katie Rose had been deliberating stalling, trying to think of an excuse to get out of going to lunch with Garrison. "Would you like to join us?" she asked Samuel. There was a hint of panic in her eyes.

"No. I don't think that will be necessary. You can handle the details fine on your own," Samuel assured Katie Rose.

Garrison was studying Kate's attractive profile – her face as well as her shapely body. Her V-neck, dark burgundy blouse, with just the top two buttons left open, and short, fitted, grey, blazer were a compliment to her bust line and small waist. Her tailored skirt, which came to rest just above the knees, showcased her sexy, long legs.

Katie Rose was still looking at Samuel, so she was not aware of Garrison's eyes poring over her. His mind continued to wander. *Kate also smells nice. I wonder what the scent of that perfume she always wears is. Whatever it is...it suits her. Business, Garrison! You need to focus on business. This young lady already has a fiancé to appreciate her beauty and her mouthwatering scent!*

Garrison hastened to avert his admiring eyes and stepped back from Kate a few paces. He was trying to escape the pleasant aroma she was emanating. Kate was making him hungry for things other than food, and nothing physical was going to take place. They were destined to be on a professional basis only.

"We might as well go back into the boardroom and have lunch brought in," Katie Rose suggested with reluctance, giving Samuel one last, disapproving look.

"That's fine by me," Garrison agreed.

He turned and made his way back into the room to put even more distance between him and Kate. Garrison had a seat in the chair that had been occupied by Katie Rose. Her scent still hung in it. *Smart, Garrison! Really smart, sitting in Kate's chair!* he reprimanded himself, as he fought all over again not to notice the pleasing fragrance.

"You two enjoy your lunch," Samuel said and started down the hall.

Katie Rose hesitated for only a second longer. Then she re-entered the boardroom. She closed the door behind her, and she walked over to the phone. Katie Rose called her secretary and instructed her to order some box lunches for her and Garrison.

"What kind of sandwich would you like?" Katie Rose asked Garrison.

"A club sandwich. Pepsi to drink. Regular potato chips, if they give a choice of that," he told her.

Katie Rose gave her secretary Garrison's order as well as her own. She hung up the phone and made her way over to the table. Since Garrison was in her seat, she sat down in the big chair at the end of the table – now Samuel's, previously her father's. She felt dwarfed by this chair, but she was also proud to occupy it. It was the beginning of her occupying this chair for good.

"We can get started if you'd like. Carla will bring our lunches to us when they are delivered, which should not be long," Katie Rose shared.

"Okay," Garrison concurred.

Garrison reached down and lifted his briefcase off the floor where he had sat it. He pulled some plans out of the case, and he spread them out on the table between Kate and him. Katie Rose gave Garrison's plans all of her attention as he began to discuss them with her. Garrison was a gifted architect, so Katie Rose never tired of looking at his drawings. She was delighted to have the opportunity to work with him on another important project.

* * * *

About twenty minutes later, there was a soft knock on the door. Carla opened the door and crept into the room with their lunches and drinks. She sat the boxes on the table in front of each of them.

"Should I have them bill us, or would you like to pay for the food right now?" she asked Katie Rose.

"Oh...I hadn't thought about that," Katie Rose replied. She sounded dazed. She had been so engrossed in studying Garrison flawless drawings it was taking her a few moments to switch gears.

"I'll take care of the bill," Garrison volunteered before Kate had a chance to continue. He reached into the inside pocket of his suit jacket, which was hanging on the back on his chair. He whipped out his wallet, opened it, and handed Carla a twenty-dollar bill. "Here you go. Will that cover it? Is that enough to give the delivery guy a tip?"

Carla glanced at the receipt she held in her hand. "That will give the delivery guy almost a five dollar tip," she advised Garrison.

"That's fine," he consented

Carla glanced towards Katie Rose, "Okay with you, Ms. Greathouse?" she asked.

"Yes, that's fine," Katie Rose replied as she turned to look Garrison in the eye.

After Carla had vacated the room with his money, Katie Rose protested, "Garrison, you didn't need to buy lunch for us."

"It's not a problem. I appreciate you taking time to work with me on such short notice, Kate. You hadn't planned on it today, but I was eager to get the ball rolling. So at least you can let lunch be my treat. Okay?"

"Alright, but I should be treating you instead. Going over your drawings at lunch today was a terrific suggestion. It will give us a bit of a jump on the project. You make a splendid partner. I'm very impressed with your drawings," Katie Rose flattered, with noted enthusiasm.

"Good! That's what I like to hear," Garrison declared with a pleased smile. "How about we switch gears? Why don't we put work aside for a short while, relax and enjoy a friendly lunch. Can we do that?"

"This warden will grant you free time for your good behavior," Katie Rose began to tease. Oddly enough, for the first time, she was comfortable being with Garrison. Of course, they had been focusing completely on business. But the nervous feeling she usually felt in the pit of her stomach was gone.

"Thank you oh so much," Garrison replied with a silly grin. He opened up the box in front of him and started sitting the items from within the box out onto the table – a club sandwich, a bag of chips, a pasta salad and a cookie.

Katie Rose did the same with her lunch – a roasted chicken sandwich and a small side salad.

"Your lunch looks much healthier than mine," Garrison commented, as he took his first bite of his piled-high sandwich. "Trying to keep that slim figure for a sexy wedding gown, perhaps?"

"I don't know about sexy," Katie Rose contradicted with a nervous giggle. "But I would like to look pretty."

"You have a lovely figure, Kate. You'll look breathtaking in a wedding gown. You look extraordinary in business attire," Garrison disclosed before he could stop himself. *I shouldn't have said this, but Kate doesn't have a clue how captivating she is.*

Katie Rose chuckled again. *Garrison should* not *be noticing my body.* She was staring at Garrison's mouth. She was watching him chew and lick his lips. *Is he doing that on purpose? Is he flirting with me? So much for feeling comfortable with this guy. Garrison makes that impossible. Why does he always have to get so personal with me?*

Katie Rose looked away from him. She began concentrating on preparing her salad. *I need to finish eating. It's time we called this meeting to a close. We have concluded our business for the day.*

"Did I make you uncomfortable?" Garrison inquired, after a few moments of silence.

"Not really," Katie Rose lied, meeting his eyes again.

Garrison's eyes locked with hers once more, and Katie Rose tried to ignore the strange aroused sensation she was experiencing. *I'm merely responding to all the nice comments Garrison made about me. He's an attractive man, but I can't be drawn to him in a sexual manor. I'm in love with BJ. It isn't possible for me to be physically attracted to another man.*

Katie Rose informed him, "You shouldn't be making personal comments about me, Garrison. I have mentioned this before. It's not appropriate."

"Sorry. You're right, Kate," Garrison agreed. "I'll be honest with you. I'm not used to working this closely one-on-one with such a..." He paused. He was searching for an appropriate word other than the one lingering in his mind...*sensual.* Finally, with a confident smile, he completed his sentence, "intriguing woman. You're very attractive, and I'm a normal male. If you flaunted your beauty, it would be easier to fight my attraction to you. But you don't even seem to recognize how engaging you are, how gorgeous you are, and this quality draws me to you like a magnet. Sorry...I commented on your looks again. It's hard not to."

"So are you telling me you are going to have a problem with the two of us working together?" Katie Rose asked him with concerned eyes.

"No. I won't let my attraction to you compromise our work relationship," Garrison pledged. "Going forward, I will make every effort to keep my personal comments, in regard to you, to myself. I may slip up every now and then, but I'm certain you will keep us on track." *I can't believe I've run off at the mouth as much as I have today. What was I thinking? I shouldn't be telling Kate I'm attracted to her. As she said, it's not appropriate.*

"I will keep us on track," Katie Rose guaranteed with assurance, as much for herself as for Garrison. *Garrison is a brilliant architect. I need to keep my head on straight and keep things all business between the two of us. I can't allow foolishness to screw up a beneficial working relationship.* Katie Rose broke eye contact with Garrison once again and went back to eating her lunch.

Garrison began eating again as well. *It's about time I finished eating and concluded this meeting, before I say anything else unwise,* he concluded. He was struggling to rein in his sexual attraction for this alluring woman. He and Kate had engaged in a good meeting on the business end of things. He should have left it at all business, but it was too late for him to take back anything he had said. All Garrison could do was finish eating and make a graceful exit.

* * * *

Mason and Savage Pride's first single had been top of the charts for the past few weeks. Fawn had set up a concert tour for them that would take them to several states in just four short weeks. Mason was excited about the tour, but he also was ambivalent about going on the road. He would be gone a month, and Callie was unable to go with him.

Callie had recently started a new job, so she had no vacation time earned as of yet. Mason hated to leave her behind, but she had landed an office job, for a well-known company, and it meant Callie would no longer have to work as a waitress. He would have loved for her to go with him, to be there when he came off stage, but he did not want her to risk losing this job. Callie was burned out on being a waitress, dealing with rude and ungrateful people, trying to grin and bear it, and make it on the small wages and tips she received. Mason was thankful Callie was able to leave the job at the restaurant. Callie had been unhappy there for some time.

"Soon, you won't have to work at all," Mason declared with pride. His first single was doing incredible, so he had reason to believe he would be successful with his recording career. "Then you can come on the road with me, and we won't have to be separated anymore."

"I'm going to miss you something awful," Callie assured him with eyes full of despair.

"I know. I'll miss you too. I'll call every day," Mason promised, giving her another cozy, extended kiss.

They were lying in bed, holding one another. They had made love, had given themselves to each other with a passion only true love makes possible. Callie wanted Mason to hold her in his arms until she fell asleep. She could not help but dwell on the knowledge that Mason would be leaving on a tour bus, with the rest of his band, early the next morning.

"You better call me every day, or else!" Callie playfully warned. She kissed Mason again and gazed into his eyes in adoration.

"Do I need to show you once more how much I'm going to miss you," Mason teased, desire showing in his eyes.

"Mason, it's getting late. You need to get up early tomorrow," Callie reminded him with concern, glancing at the clock on the bedside table. It was nearly 1:00 a.m. They had been wrapped in each other's warmth for hours.

"I can sleep on the bus," Mason reminded her. He began to kiss her neck and trail his hot, eager tongue down over her breast.

Callie was not going to argue with Mason. She wanted him as greatly as he wanted her. She did not know how she was going to stand being separated from Mason for four weeks. *How will I be able to sleep alone in this bed, the bed we make love in almost every night?* She laid her head back on the pillow, closed her eyes, and submitted to the splendid pleasure Mason was so capable of providing.

* * * *

The screaming females were almost deafening. Mason and Savage Pride were leaving the stage for a final time after their sixth concert opening in two weeks. Savage Pride had been booked as the opening act for Full Sail, a band that was very popular and had many hit songs. The two groups had been whisked, by tour bus, from state to state. Fawn had scheduled a show for Full Sail and Savage Pride in a different state or city every two days. The exposure Savage Pride was getting from this first tour would have people everywhere recognizing them, not just by the name of their band, but their faces as well.

After two weeks of being on the road, Mason was at long last beginning to get used to the exaggerated response of concertgoers to him and Savage Pride. Women everywhere seemed to have formed an instant love affair with him and all of the members of the band. It was unsettling, but it was also extremely flattering. The guys were all very much taking advantage of this situation.

After the shows, a lot of the guys went to nearby bars, some topless, and had some drinks to celebrate. Mason also, unfortunately, noted that some of the guys in the Full Sail band smoked some weed from time to time. Mason was the loner of the two groups. He only wanted to get through this tour and go home to Callie. So, after each show, instead of following his buddies to the nightclubs, he would go back to the tour bus, play a little guitar to help him relax, and place a call to Callie.

As Mason promised, he called Callie each day. In fact, sometimes, he called Callie more than once each day. Mason had just ended a call with Callie, after he realized it was after midnight. Callie had to get up early the next morning to go to work. Yet, she had still been waiting up for Mason's call. She never said a word about how late it had gotten or how tired she would be when the alarm rang in only a few hours. Callie loved Mason immensely and was willing to give up a few hours of sleep to listen to his voice – to hear him relay a few details of his evening.

Fawn climbed the steps of the tour bus and came onboard with Mason. She was not traveling with the group, but she was meeting them periodically along their path. She primarily showed up before the shows to make sure everything was set up and ready to go. It was late, and Mason was surprised to see she was still here. He thought she had already left.

"So you are here all alone again?" Fawn asked him. She had a blue beret atop her short auburn hair and she was wearing a long leather jacket. Still, she crossed her arms to ward off the chill. It was November, and even though the bus had a heating system, it was still chilly onboard.

"I'm the only guy who has a special lady in his life," Mason said with a bittersweet smile.

"The other guys have special *ladies*. They pick a new one in each city we stop in," Fawn said with a chuckle. The fiber optic bus lighting caused her unique, greenish blue eyes to sparkle like glitter.

"That's for sure," Mason agreed, sharing her laugh. "I've given up a few of them myself. Some of these women will throw themselves at your feet. They don't know me from Adam, but they are ready to sleep with me. It's a little overwhelming sometimes."

"You might as well get used to this, Mason. It will only get worse the more popular Savage Pride gets," Fawn shared with knowledge. *Especially since you are such a nice looking young man.* Mason was the perfect poster boy – tall, dark and handsome. Fawn could not help noticing his engaging golden brown eyes as well. *He'll have to fight them off with a stick!*

"It's a terrible life, isn't it?" Mason teased with a silly smile.

"There are a lot of temptations. It's why musicians have come up with their own cardinal rule – 'whatever happens on the road stays on the road'. Most men do not resist the temptations. So far, you are the exception to the rule, my friend."

"I intend to remain the exception," Mason said with conviction.

He could not imagine cheating on Callie. Some of the women, who were making themselves so readily available, were very pretty, but Mason loved Callie tremendously. He did not want to do anything to jeopardize his relationship with her. He would never intentionally betray or hurt Callie.

"Would you like to get out of this chilly bus for awhile?" Fawn offered.

"And go where exactly?" he questioned. "I'm not into the drinking scene either. I'm not your typical musician."

"You don't have to sound apologetic. That's a good thing," Fawn complimented with a pretty smile. "I wasn't proposing we go to a bar. I'm restless and not ready to go back to my hotel and go to bed yet. I could use some company, and it looks as if you could as well. I bet we could find some all-night diner. We could have a late, greasy meal, some pie, or just a soft drink. What do you say? My car is right outside. I don't want to go wandering all over the city by myself. If you aren't game, I'll have to force myself to go back to the hotel and order some room service."

Mason could hear the loneliness in Fawn's voice. *She's an attractive lady. Surely she has a special man somewhere. I'm surprised she isn't going back to her hotel room to call him. But didn't I just get off the phone with Callie?* Yet, Mason still had to admit he was still lonely as well. It sounded good to be able to get away from the bus for a short while. Other than going into the concert halls, Mason had been pinned up in this bus for the past two weeks.

"You're on!" he said with enthusiasm.

"Great!" Fawn replied with equal fervor.

Mason vacated his seat, grabbed his jacket, and followed Fawn out of the bus. They hopped into her neon blue, turbo-charged, all-wheel drive, five speed, Mazda WRX sports car. As Fawn turned the key in the ignition, the engine purred.

"Wow! Really nice car," Mason commented with admiration.

Fawn smiled in response. They raced off into the darkness, in search of a roadside diner. Tonight, they would provide some much needed companionship to one another.

Chapter 9

Appraisals

It was Sunday afternoon. BJ and Katie Rose were hiking across the mostly full parking lot at Berkley's Mall. Fortunately, even though it was late November, it was a nice day – sunny, with the temperature in the upper fifties.

Thanksgiving had come and gone, so Christmas was just around the corner – about three weeks away. Katie Rose had talked BJ into coming to Berkley's Mall to Christmas shop. BJ had already bought Katie Rose a present. He had gotten her a pair of small diamond earrings. BJ was still paying on Katie Rose's engagement ring, but he wanted to get her something extra special for Christmas this year. After all, they were engaged.

BJ had worked overtime at the garage on a few occasions, and he planned to put in even more hours. Katie Rose was worth every dime. BJ wanted her to feel special.

As they stepped onto the curb in front of Macy's, Katie Rose heard the bell from a Salvation Army worker. She approached this woman, extracted her wallet from her purse, and dropped a few dollars into her bucket.

"Thank you. God bless you. Have a wonderful Christmas," the woman said to Katie Rose.

"Same to you," she said and stepped away.

They walked over to the double doors and pulled them open to enter the store. Their eyes were at once met with Christmas decorations in every direction. Frumpy green garland with red ribbons and slow blinking lights hung from the ceiling all throughout the store. A mechanical Santa rotated, waving at people as they entered. Christmas music softly played over the PA system.

There were also SALE signs everywhere. Each and every rack of clothes had one sitting atop it. BJ took Katie Rose's hand and the two began to stroll through the women's department. The store was crowded. Shoppers bustled by on both sides of them looking for that special Christmas bargain.

All at once, Katie Rose was surprised to hear a familiar voice call, "Kate." She ignored it, because she thought it was someone else talking in the throng of people all around them. BJ did not pay any attention, because he did not know Katie Rose by this foreign name.

"Kate," Garrison called again. He came up behind her and tapped her on the shoulder. BJ was puzzled when Katie Rose stopped and turned her head to look behind them.

Katie Rose released BJ's hand and turned to face this other man. "Garrison...hello," Katie Rose replied, sounding rattled. She had not expected to encounter this man here. "What brings you to Macy's?"

"I'm shopping for a special lady's Christmas gift," Katie Rose was disturbed to hear him reply.

"A...special lady?" she stuttered. *Why does this bother me?*

"Yes," Garrison answered, confused by Kate's facial expression. She looked flustered by his statement. *Is she jealous because she thinks I'm buying something for a lady friend?* "My mother," he clarified.

"Oh...it's for your mother," Katie Rose responded, sounding even stranger.

BJ was examining her oddly. Katie Rose became aware he was staring at her. She had been conversing with Garrison as if he was not even there. *What was I thinking?*

"BJ, this is Garrison Parker. He's an architect. His firm, Parker Architecture, has been working on a few projects with Greathouse Construction. Garrison, this is my fiancé, BJ."

Garrison took a second to appraise BJ. Then he replied, "It's nice to meet you, BJ." "I've heard a great deal about you." *You're not anything like I imagined you would be.* Garrison offered his hand.

BJ linked his small hand to Garrison's large one, and the two men shook hands. He scrutinized this other man with intensity. BJ even adjusted his glasses as if to get a better look. *I wish I could say I had heard a great deal about you. But Katie Rose has never even mentioned you. Wonder why?*

Katie Rose found herself comparing the two men. BJ's short, slim body was dwarfed by Garrison's tall, immense, encompassing one. Garrison did not have a hair out of place. *He must use hair gel or mousse.* He was also dressed impeccably in a bright red, short-sleeved polo shirt, belted khaki slacks and tan casual loafers. *The red in his shirt makes his black hair glisten all the more and his blue eyes sparkle.* He had a light jacket thrown over his arm.

BJ's sandy brown hair, on the other hand, was wind tousled. He was wearing a tattered denim jacket, an old concert T-shirt, faded jeans, and dirty, worn, tennis shoes. They were without question two very different men.

"Kate says you are a great guy, and you must be. You allow yourself to be drug to the Mall for a shopping spree. It's obvious you are very much in love with this lady," Garrison half teased, as the two men released hands. *What an odd couple they make. Kate is so beautiful, and BJ is so plain. And she dresses so immaculate and he looks as if he bought his clothes at a thrift store.* Katie Rose was wearing a short, black, London Fog jacket; a light green, cashmere sweater; Liz Claiborne jeans; and clean, leather, Reebok tennis shoes.

"I *am* very much in love with her," BJ stated with certainty. He also placed his arm around Katie Rose's shoulders and pulled her tightly to his body. *Why does this guy address Katie Rose as Kate? It sounds weird. Wonder why she lets him call her this?*

Katie Rose squirmed to free BJ's grip a bit. *Why is he squeezing me so hard? Surely he doesn't feel threatened by Garrison. He has no reason to be.*

"*Ka..tie Rose,* has not drug me to the Mall," BJ enlightened Garrison. He had stressed each syllable of her name on purpose. "I enjoy spending time with her anywhere. Besides, we are Christmas shopping."

"'Tis the season," Garrison said with a grin. He had not failed to notice how BJ had stressed Kate's name. *He doesn't like me calling her Kate. Kate has never protested, so this is what I intend to keep on calling her. It suits her much better than that little girl's name BJ used.*

Katie Rose was giving BJ a weird look. *Why'd BJ say that to Garrison about me* not *dragging him to the Mall? He hates to shop. I did have to drag him here today.*

BJ was still looking at Garrison, and there was not a smile on his face. Katie Rose was anxious to get back to shopping. She did not like that BJ appeared to be tense around Garrison. *He's acting strange.* They were also somewhat blocking the aisle. Several shoppers had already pushed past them.

"Well…are you ready to mosey on?" she asked BJ. She tugged on his arm to relay her impatience.

"Okay," he agreed. "Garrison, it was nice to meet you," BJ said, being polite.

"Great to meet you too, BJ. You guys have a terrific day. Kate, I will see you Monday. I have more plans to bring in. I'll call Monday morning to find out what time is good for us to meet."

"Alright," Katie Rose conceded. "You enjoy the rest of your day too. I hope you find a nice present for your mom."

"I'm sure I will," he replied. Garrison could not help but observe BJ's hard stare.

"Bye," BJ dismissed him without a smile. He and Katie Rose began to walk away in the other direction. *I want to find out more about this guy. I'll talk to Katie Rose about him later. Right now, I want to go back to enjoying our day.*

BJ took his arm from around Katie Rose's shoulders. It was hard for him to walk in this position, because he was a bit shorter than her. Instead, BJ slipped Katie Rose's hand back into his and began to lead her farther away – *away from* him.

* * * *

After the first night, Fawn invited Mason on a fairly consistent basis to spend time with her. The guys in both bands teased Mason. They believed he and Fawn were having an affair. Mason did not care what they thought. He knew the truth. He and Fawn were all they would ever be – friends. It was not that Mason was blind. He recognized Fawn was a pretty woman, but he was not interested in her in that way. He was madly in love with Callie.

Mason merely enjoyed Fawn's companionship, liked escaping the bus, and appreciated getting away from the other guys.

Through their many conversations, Mason discovered many things about Fawn. She was five years older than him and very eclectic. She liked wearing only certain clothes – over-the-head, knit ponchos with white T-shirts; tan or black Capri pants; clog shoes; red, blue or black berets; and long sweater coats or leather coats. Her jewelry was also different – nothing with diamonds. Her beaded necklaces, stone rings, and earrings – most of them turquoise – were handmade. Even Fawn's watchband had been crafted out of colored stones by an artist. Mason was also shocked to discover Fawn's lovely eyes were not naturally, effervescent bluish-green. Fawn revealed her eyes were actually a lackluster grayish color. Contact lenses provided the stunning shade they were now. These lenses were only to color Fawn's eyes. She did not need them for corrective action. Fawn's eyesight was perfect. Fawn liked Mason a great deal. Even though he was extremely good-looking, she was not at all interested in anything romantic with him.

Mason and Savage Pride were due on stage in a little over an hour. Mason was sitting in Fawn's car. They had gone to dinner at a nearby restaurant. He shared with Fawn that he intended to call Callie before the show.

"Where do you go to call her?" Fawn inquired, giving him a glance.

After a big meal and relaxing conversation, Mason looked comfortable and satisfied. He was dressed in a nylon, Cincinnati Reds, baseball jacket; a T-shirt; jeans and tennis shoes. True to form, Fawn had on a black beret; a long, black, sweater coat; a blue poncho with a white T-shirt underneath; black Capri pants; and her infamous clog shoes. She was speeding along the highway, driving Mason back to the tour bus.

"Where else would I call Callie from, but the bus? I call her on my cell phone," Mason replied.

"You don't get much privacy that way, do you?"

"No. I usually end up walking around outside, so I can have some privacy. Even then, sometimes the guys still butt in. They love to tease me about Callie. They want me to run around with a different woman all the time like they do."

"As I've said before, Mason, I'm glad you are different," Fawn told him. There was an amiable, approving smile on her face. "Would you like more privacy to talk to Callie?" she questioned.

"Sure. But where?"

"How about my hotel room?" she offered.

"Your *hotel* room?" Mason repeated.

Fawn had seemed okay with associating with him on a friendship basis. However, Mason could not help but suspect her motives, since she mentioned a hotel room. Fawn heard the inference in Mason's question and saw he was eyeballing her strangely.

I need to clarify things. "Mason, let's get one thing straight, okay?" she began with hardened eyes. The smile had been replaced by a frown. "You are a handsome man. But I do *not* sleep with the people who I manage. I made this a principle of mine a long time ago. All I want from you is friendship and occasional companionship. I offered you my hotel room to make a call to your fiancé. I was only offering the phone. Nothing else! You need to stop thinking with a typical male mind. I realize this is difficult, but I'm asking you not to read anything into my offer – other than a telephone and some much needed privacy. Alright?"

"Okay," Mason consented. "I'm glad we are on the same page, Fawn. All I want from you is friendship and occasional companionship as well. As far as your offer of using the phone in your hotel room goes, that would be awesome!"

"Okay. Let's head to the hotel," Fawn agreed, focusing all of her attentions on the road again and letting the other subject drop.

Mason was looking forward to having some much needed privacy to talk to Callie.

* * * *

Fawn's hotel room turned out to be a suite. It was almost as large as Mason and Callie's apartment. It had a living room area, with a coffee table, two end tables and lamps, a recliner, and a twenty-inch television. There was a small, full kitchen, with a counter to eat at, a refrigerator, stove, cabinets and a microwave. In the hallway, there was a bathroom with only a toilet and a sink. Behind another door were the bedroom and another bathroom. This bathroom had a shower/Jacuzzi tub in it. Mason was impressed by all of the perks Fawn's career afforded her. He could not wait until he was making enough money to have the same advantages.

Fawn directed Mason to the phone in the living room. She went into the bedroom and closed the door so he would have the room all to himself. Then she turned on the television in the bedroom, so as not to overhear Mason's private conversation.

Mason enjoyed relaxing on the comfortable leather sofa as he conversed with Callie. It certainly beat the hard, high backed, bus seats. *Thank God I only have to be on the road for one more week.* The days seemed to pass much too slowly without Callie by his side.

Time slipped away and before Mason realized it, he had been talking to Callie for over thirty minutes. Fawn came back out of her bedroom and softly called Mason's name to gain his attention. When Mason looked up, she told him, "We need to be leaving. You and Savage Pride are due on stage soon."

Callie was surprised to hear a women's voice. She normally only heard the voices of other men, usually one of the other band members. "Who's calling you?" she asked Mason.

"Huh? Oh…It's only Fawn. I need to go. Savage Pride is due on stage soon. We're only about five minutes from the theatre. But the band will need a little time to warm up before the concert."

"Where are you?" Callie asked. She sounded concerned. *What's Mason mean he's five minutes from the theatre? Usually the bus is right outside. Where is he? Why is Fawn there with him?*

"Do you mean what city am I in?" Mason asked.

He was being evasive on purpose. He did not want to tell Callie he was in Fawn's hotel room. His purpose for being here was innocent, but Mason did not want to raise suspicion in Callie's mind. She appeared to be jealous of Fawn.

"No," Callie said in aggravation. "I know what city you are in. I was wondering why you are five minutes from the theatre. You and Fawn aren't at the bus?"

"Mason," Fawn called again and pointed to her watch. She hated to cut his conversation with Callie short, but business was business. Fawn needed to get Mason out of the hotel and over to the concert hall, so the band would not be late going on stage.

"Listen…I'll have to talk to you after the concert. I need to get off the phone. I don't want to be late for the show. I love you, and I miss you, Callie. I'm counting the days until we are together again."

"I love you too, Mason. I miss you so much it hurts, and I can't wait to see you again either. Have a fantastic show," Callie said. She did not like that Mason had not answered her last question, but Callie did not want to hold him up and make him late for a concert. "Bye. Talk to you soon."

"I'll call you right after the concert," Mason promised. He hung up the phone, much to Fawn's relief.

Fawn was fast to usher him from her suite. She was glad Mason had a special lady in his life. Callie would keep him grounded, and in the music industry, being grounded was a very good thing. Too many musicians got lost in worlds of loose women, drugs and alcohol. So far, having Callie in his life was helping Mason to forego these tempting traps. Fawn was delighted to encourage such a relationship. She wanted to see Mason and Savage Pride go far.

Chapter 10

The Gift

Katie Rose had not moved in with BJ, but she might as well have. She was spending more and more of her time there. She had a key to his place, and little by little she was changing things at his apartment. Katie Rose bought blue towels, a ceramic soap dish, a toothbrush holder and a cover for the tissue box; these all matched the powder blue tile in the bathroom. These items were a charming enhancement from the hodgepodge of colors BJ had.

Katie Rose hung matching pictures on the typically bare living room walls. She replaced the old gray and brown comforter in BJ's bedroom with an antique looking, floral bedspread. Heavy Chantilly lace trimmed this new comforter. Katie Rose also added extra pillows to the bed. She bought solid color shams to coordinate with the colors in the comforter. The colors in the comforter, burgundy and gold, brought a since of style to the bedroom, especially since the walls were painted a deep gold. She also replaced the ugly curtains with matching, louver blinds. A bottle of Katie Rose's perfume sat on BJ's Chest of Drawers. Beside it was a small jewelry box she had brought over on one of her earlier visits.

Katie Rose's makeup took up space on one side of BJ's bathroom vanity. Some of her personal toiletries were on shelves in the shower and in his bathroom closet. Katie Rose was spending most of her nights sleeping in BJ's queen-sized bed. She felt comfortable about these small changes and was looking forward to the day she would live with him for good.

Jackie Lynn, Mary Julia and Flora were all heavily involved in planning Katie Rose's wedding. Mason's engagement to Callie delighted

Jackie Lynn as well. Mason and Callie had decided to wait until after Katie Rose's wedding to set a date for their nuptials, not wanting to take away any of the limelight BJ and Katie Rose deserved. Besides, Mason's life was too crazy to try and pin down a date for a wedding. When Savage Pride began doing stand-alone tours, his schedule was supposed to be more manageable.

Mary Julia was also very pleased Mason had proposed to Callie. She had come to accept that Mason and Callie were genuinely in love and fully committed to one another. Mason brought Callie joy, so Mary Julia at last welcomed him with open arms. All Mary Julia ever dreamed was for her daughter to be truly happy. She was thrilled to see this dream coming true.

Flora was delighted to be included in the planning of Katie Rose's wedding. She also looked forward to helping with Mason and Callie's wedding. The unions of these special children gave Flora immense pleasure. They were her extended family, and she loved them as if they were her own flesh and blood.

* * * *

Katie Rose received an unexpected visit from Garrison. When her secretary showed him to her office, Katie Rose flashed him a radiant smile and asked, "More plans to go over? I thought we covered everything Monday."

"We did," Garrison assured her. He tried to ignore the fact Kate had almost taken his breath away when she looked up at him and smiled. She had on a red suit with a sheer, cream-colored blouse. The color of the suit gave Kate's face a beautifully healthy glow. She also had her hair swept up in a French braid – also incredibly becoming. *She looks even more lovely than usual. If that's possible.*

Several moments of silence passed before Katie Rose realized she was staring at Garrison. He was wearing a black, pinstriped suit, a pale yellow shirt, and yet another vibrant tie. This tie had a splattering of bold colors – red, orange and yellow – all throughout it. He had a long trench coat, folded over his arm, and a small black umbrella in the other hand. His short hair was unruffled, even though it was a rainy, blustery Wednesday.

"You can hang your coat on the rack by the door. There is also a place at the bottom for umbrellas," Katie Rose told him. She pointed to the coat rack. "So if you don't have more plans for me, what are you doing here?" she inquired.

Garrison turned and walked over to the rack. "The reason I came by is personal rather than business," he shared. He hung his coat on a peg beside Kate's raincoat and placed his umbrella in a slot at the bottom. Then he turned to face Kate again.

Garrison knew better than to share his personal observations about Kate's appearance. Their meeting Monday had gone well, because they had stuck strictly to business. Garrison had not shared with Kate that he had been unable to get her off his mind after their chance encounter Sunday at the Mall.

He also had not brought up his observations about BJ. Kate and BJ made a very odd couple. Her devastating beauty made BJ's small-framed homeliness even more obvious. Garrison could picture BJ being a best friend to Kate, but never her lover. *Regardless, BJ somehow got the girl. So what does it matter what others think – including me?*

"The reason you came by is personal?" Garrison heard Kate ask. "Are you going to share with me what makes it personal?" Kate was smiling at him again, and Garrison's legs all the sudden felt weak. He was not used to this reaction. He made his way farther into her office and took a safe seat in the armchair in front of her desk. Then he pushed it back a safe distance.

"Um…I wanted to give you something," Garrison announced with a coy grin. The gift had arrived yesterday, and Garrison had intended to wait until closer to Christmas to give it to Kate. But his curiosity to see her reaction was killing him.

"You want to give me something? And it's personal? Is it a gift?" Katie Rose probed, studying him with suspicious eyes.

"Yes," Garrison answered with some hesitation. He could not recall being this nervous since his first date.

"Well, how about you give me this gift then," Katie Rose coaxed. She loved surprises. They brought out the girl in her.

"Of course," Garrison replied.

He reached in the pocket of his suit jacket and pulled forth a small package. It was wrapped in Christmas paper. Garrison held it out to Kate, and she took it from him with eagerness. Her eyes were sparkling and there was a wide smile on her face. *She looks like an excited little girl*, Garrison could not help but muse. He liked it.

"Can I unwrap this gift now? It's wrapped in Christmas paper," Katie Rose asked Garrison's permission.

"I'd like it if you would. I found it much too difficult to wait until the holidays had arrived."

"Okay," Katie Rose responded with a bubbly chuckle.

She stuck a long fingernail, painted red to match her suit, under the crease in the wrapping paper. Katie Rose peeled the paper from the small box with ease. She glanced up at Garrison once more. Her eyes were full of cheerful anticipation. Then she lifted the top of the box. Katie Rose pulled forth the contents. She stared at the present, and then she looked into Garrison's eyes in astonishment. A pair of Dream Catcher earrings rested in her hand. Each earring had a stunning, pear shaped, emerald stone in the center.

"May all of your dreams be sweet, Emerald Sea," Garrison shared his wish.

"Where…where did these come from? They are beautiful," Katie Rose uttered.

This gift touched her heart in a way she had not anticipated. It reminded her of her Indian heritage. It also made her think of her dad and made Katie Rose a little melancholy. Garrison could see the emotion come to Kate's eyes; those bright, dazzling eyes were now deep emerald pools of watery sadness. Katie Rose desperately struggled to control her emotions, choking back the tears. Christmas was going to be hard this year with her dad not being there to celebrate with all of them.

"They came from the Reservation," Katie Rose was amazed to hear.

"The Reservation? You're teasing me, right?"

"No. I had them make these for you and send them to me. The emeralds are real by the way. It's nice to have someone with Indian heritage to share this gift with. You understand its significance. I need to go back to the Reservation sometimes."

"Yes, you do," Kate told him. "I need to visit again as well. Thank you, Garrison. These earrings are a very nice and thoughtful gift. You shouldn't have done this."

"I wanted to. Consider this present not only an early Christmas gift, but also a thank you gift. It is wonderful being able to work hand-in-hand with Greathouse Construction to erect new buildings in the community."

Katie Rose stood up from her desk chair. She came around to the other side of the desk and bent to offer Garrison a slight, grateful embrace. Garrison had not anticipated Kate hugging him. Her arms felt incredible, and the alluring scent of her perfume caused his head to swim.

Garrison slid his burly arms around Kate. He pulled her tightly against his robust body. He inhaled deeply and allowed himself to enjoy her delectable scent up close. Kate was driving his senses wild.

Katie Rose had only meant to give Garrison a small, loose hug. She had not expected to be squeezed to his body. She also could not help but notice how fantastic he smelled. *I love his cologne!* She was even less prepared for the rush of sensation that being held against Garrison's muscular body created in her.

Several moments later, Garrison reluctantly released her. Katie Rose was slow to pull away. She had enjoyed being held by him. As she drew back from Garrison, their eyes met and Katie Rose was shaken by the desire she saw in his eyes. What she did not realize was a mirror of this same desire shown plainly in her own eyes. Katie Rose stumbled back behind her desk. She nearly fell into the chair.

It was not until she sat down that she became aware of how hard her heart was beating. Since neither of them was speaking, Katie Rose worried Garrison might be able to hear how loudly her heart was beating. Picking up a glass of water from a marble coaster on her desk, her hand trembled.

I should give the earrings back to Garrison. He didn't give them to me as a sign of friendship. He wants more from me. I could see it in his eyes. Why am I feeling so lightheaded? Must be because Garrison was holding me so tightly. He must have cut off my oxygen supply.

Garrison was also shaken. *I've got to get out of here! I never should have held Kate like that. She only meant to give me an innocent thank you hug.*

Garrison rose to his feet before he reconsidered his actions. "Well, Kate. I don't want to tie up your time. I only meant to drop in for a few minutes to give you your gift. I hope the rest of your day goes well," he rattled. He turned and made long strides toward the door. The coat rack shook as he snatched his coat from the hook.

"Th…thank you, Garrison," Katie Rose managed to stutter. She was trying to catch her breath and still her pounding heart.

"You're very welcomed, Kate," he said, trying to keep the huskiness out of his voice.

He reached to grab his umbrella. With his back still mostly to Kate, he waved goodbye. Garrison did not dare turn and look back toward her. He needed to make his escape while he still had the strength. His yearning to take Kate back into his arms and let nature take its course was too overwhelming.

After Garrison left, Katie Rose picked up the earrings and gaped at them in wonder. *Why didn't I give them back to him?* she questioned herself. *Because I didn't want too. And because they are beautiful and they remind me of him,* her mind betrayed.

Katie Rose took out her gold posts and placed Garrison's earrings in her ears. She opened the bottom drawer of her desk and pulled forth her purse. She rummaged in a zippered compartment inside, extracting a small mirror. She took a second to admire the earrings, as her mind wandered to the man who had given them to her. The shrill ring of the telephone ceased her silent approval. *Back to work, Katie Rose!* she ordered. She sat the mirror on her desk and reached for the phone.

* * * *

Katie Rose was at BJ's apartment, and the two of them were eating dinner. She was discussing her workday at Greathouse, as was the norm. Out of the blue, BJ brought up Garrison. He asked Katie Rose if she and Garrison had met Monday, as Garrison had mentioned at the Mall.

"Yes," she replied. She glanced at BJ and then sunk her fork into her salad. *Why is he bringing up Garrison and something that occurred two days ago?*

"How'd the meeting go?"

"Fine," she answered, chewing up her lettuce and cucumbers.

Katie Rose was thinking about Garrison's visit earlier that day. As she did, she realized she was still wearing the earrings Garrison had given her. She had forgotten to take them out. She absently fingered the one in her left earlobe for a few seconds. Her mind briefly wandered back to the heated moment between her and Garrison earlier today.

BJ waited a few moments for Katie Rose to elaborate on her meeting with Garrison. When she said nothing else, he further questioned, "Why is it you never mentioned this guy before? He acted like you talked a great deal about me, and it sounded like the two of you meet on a regular basis. I was kind of surprised I had never heard about him. You never even mentioned your meeting with him Monday." He picked up his knife and fork and sawed into a pork chop on his plate.

"I don't know why I never mentioned Garrison to you," Katie Rose responded. She lowered her eyes from BJ's intense scrutiny. She also picked up her knife and started concentrating on cutting up a pork chop.

As she put a bite of the meat into her mouth, Katie Rose tried to determine why she had not talked about Garrison with BJ. She talked about everything else that happened in her life with him. BJ had heard about every deal Greathouse had ever landed or lost. *Maybe it's because Garrison makes me uncomfortable most of the time? Garrison is attracted to me and that sure isn't something I would want to share with BJ. That's what any man would want to hear – that another man is attracted to his fiancé. That he brings her Christmas gifts. I would not want to give BJ the impression I am attracted to another man either. Because I'm not. Garrison is handsome. He has a certain appeal. But I need to make sure BJ understands that he has nothing to worry about when it comes to Garrison.*

Katie Rose's silence was too long and was making BJ even more distraught. He laid down his knife and fork and focused his entire attention on Katie Rose. *Katie Rose is not comfortable talking to me about this guy. Why?* "Katie Rose, is there something about this guy you don't want me to know?" BJ questioned, nervous. He had his hands one on top of the other and he was fidgeting with them.

"No," she was quick to answer. She gave him a fleeting look, then hurried on, "I met Garrison a long, long time ago when I was just a girl...I believe I was about...oh...six years old. Anyway, because of this brief encounter, he acts like we've known each other forever, even though we only met that one other time. Garrison makes me uncomfortable a lot of times. I guess that's why I haven't talked about him. Most of the time, I'm glad when my meetings with Garrison have ended. I usually tune him out of my mind afterwards. I don't want to talk about him after I'm away from work."

"What has he done to make you so uncomfortable? I noticed he calls you Kate. Is that one of the things?"

"No. The place we first met was on the Indian Reservation. It was the time I was given my Indian name – Emerald Sea. So when we first met again, Garrison was calling me by my Indian name, Emerald Sea. I told him my real name was Katherine Rose, and he took it upon himself to shorten it to Kate. I didn't correct him. I don't care what he calls me," Katie Rose added.

She took another bite of salad. She was attempting to appear indifferent about this whole issue. *I'm pretending I hardly noticed that Garrison gave me a special name.* Instant remorse washed over Katie Rose, as it dawned on her that she was lying to BJ. *What on earth is wrong with me? I don't tell BJ lies.* Katie Rose knew the answer to her own question. *I can't share with BJ I like the sound of this new name. That I like the way it rolls off of Garrison's tongue, each time I hear him say it. That I not only met with Garrison on Monday, but also today. That today's meeting wasn't even on a professional basis – that it was purely personal because Garrison gave me a special gift. Worse yet, that I couldn't bring myself to return this man's gift today.*

BJ was meticulously scrutinizing Katie Rose. He knew her well. He could tell Katie Rose was giving careful thought to every word she uttered about Garrison. *She's hiding something from me.* This conclusion disconcerted BJ. He and Katie Rose had no secrets.

Katie Rose looked into BJ's eyes and saw grave concern. *I have to find some way to put BJ's mind at ease over Garrison. I don't know why I'm having all of these strange thoughts. This is ridiculous!* "Look, BJ, you have nothing to worry about when it comes to Garrison. He's merely another business associate. I don't mention every single business associate I interact with. Why don't we forget about Garrison and focus on the two of us instead? Evening is *our* time. I don't want to talk about Garrison or anyone else."

Katie Rose scooted her chair over closer to BJ. She took BJ's glasses off and laid them on the table. She proceeded to draw in close for a kiss. BJ took the bait and kissed Katie Rose. They continued to kiss with fervor for several more moments. As Katie Rose began to rub the inside of BJ's upper thighs, it suddenly dawned on her that Garrison's arms were almost as big as BJ's upper thighs. *Why am I having these thoughts? Go away! I don't want to think about Garrison. I want to solely focus on BJ.*

"When I come home from work, all I want to focus on is the love of my life. And that is you, BJ," Katie Rose professed. "Do I need to show you again how much I love you? How entirely devoted I am to *only* you?" She was panting in his face in breathless anticipation.

"Oh yes. You do," BJ encouraged. His voice was hoarse and his eyes burned with desire.

Katie Rose stood, and she took BJ's *small* hand into hers. "Maybe we should go in the bedroom where we would be much more comfortable. We can always microwave what's left of our dinner and eat it later. How's that sound?"

"Sounds great!" he proclaimed with excitement.

BJ leaped to his feet, and he and Katie Rose rushed from the room.

I'll make him forget all about Garrison. I'll make myself forget all about Garrison as well. BJ is the only man for me. He always has been, and he always will be.

Chapter 11

Separation Anxiety

Mason's suitcases were still sitting just inside the door. His bags had been discarded as soon as he walked through the entranceway. Callie made a running beeline into his arms. They began kissing in reckless abandonment. Callie kicked the door shut as she pulled Mason farther into the apartment. In fevered impatience, they began undressing one another. Their want for each other was immense. Neither had any need to tell the other how much they had been missed. Their only wish was to express their all-consuming love, to share their passion for one another. They only made it a few feet before they tumbled onto the couch. They made love right there, in a famished rush.

Callie and Mason were lying naked now, entangled in an afghan on the living room sofa. They were content to be able to hold one another. He had not been home much more than an hour, and they had already made love twice. "What are you trying to do, baby? Kill me?" Mason asked with a pleased smile. He was still gasping for breath.

"I haven't even begun to quench the need inside my body for you or to wear you out," Callie murmured in a soft, seductive voice. The yearning in her eyes was unmistakable. "You've been gone for four weeks. You need to make up for lost time."

"Is that the way it works?" Mason asked with a chuckle. He kissed Callie again on the lips and then on each of her nipples. "Well, I'll have to give it my all. Won't I?"

"You better believe it," Callie proclaimed, kissing him yet again.

"I love you, Callie," Mason declared in adoration.

"You show it well," she complimented. There was a pretty, contented smile spread all across Callie's face.

"So do you. I've been riding for hours on end on a smelly bus. You didn't even give me a chance to take a shower before you jumped my bones. You *must* love me."

"I do," she acknowledged, gazing into his eyes with devotion. "You're right though. You do need a shower. So do I. Why don't we go and take one now – *together*."

"As long as you'll grab me if my legs buckle," Mason instructed with a playful snicker.

"I'll be glad to grab you," Callie said with a wicked chuckle.

Callie scrambled from the couch, and she held out a hand to Mason. He took Callie's hand, and Mason eagerly allowed himself to be led toward the bathroom. *It's great to be home!*

* * * *

Hours later, Callie and Mason were still lying in bed. They were snuggling and snoozing when the phone rang, disturbing their peacefulness. Mason reached to grab the phone on the bedside table.

"Hi. How are you?" Callie heard Mason ask. There was a pause, and Mason said, "I'm fantastic! It's great to be home."

There was another, longer pause, and Callie watched as Mason rose to a sitting position on the side of the bed. Mason exclaimed, "You're kidding me! That soon? That long? Yeah, I know it's important that we are seen and heard from, but I thought my time at home would be longer."

Callie rose to a sitting position in the bed. She did not like the way this conversation was sounding. *Who's on the phone? Are they telling Mason he is going to have to go away again?*

"Okay. I need to talk with Callie. Can I call you back in a little while?" Mason asked. The person on the other end of the connection obviously said yes, because Mason said, "Alright. Thanks. I'll call you back."

Mason hung up the phone. He turned to face Callie. The somber expression on his face told Callie he was not at all pleased about the chat he had just had.

"Who was that?" she asked.

"It was Fawn," he answered. She's set up another tour with us opening for another band. We're supposed to leave Monday."

"Monday?! Th..this Monday?!! Two days away?!" Callie asked in disbelief.

"Yes," Mason confirmed with an unhappy frown.

"How long will you be gone?"

"Six weeks," Mason answered with some hesitation.

"You're kidding!" Callie exclaimed, even though she knew Mason was serious.

"I wish I was," he sighed.

"Mason, call Fawn back and tell her no," Callie insisted.

"How can I do that?" Mason inquired in a defeated voice.

His eyes were pleading with Callie for understanding. Mason was caught between a rock and a hard place. He did not want to leave again so soon, but it was important to his recording career he do so.

Unfortunately, Callie was not in an understanding mood. Being parted from Mason had been unbearable for her. She was in no way ready for him to leave again so soon.

She began instructing him in a harsh, imposing voice. "Pick up the phone. Dial Fawn's number. And tell her *no*! Seems pretty simple to me. Would you like for me to make the call for you? I'd be happy to help."

"Callie, I can't do that," Mason argued with her.

"Why not?" she demanded to know. Her face was locked in an angry scowl, and she had crossed her arms across her chest. Mason could tell Callie was settling in for a good fight. She did not like it when she did not get her way. She had been this way since she was a child. Callie had been a very strong willed child, and she was now a headstrong woman.

"Fawn already has everything all arranged. I can't just call and tell her I can't do it. It doesn't work that way, Callie. This is big business. You either play by their rules, or you don't play."

"So Fawn calls, and you put our life on hold. That's the way things are going to be from now on? Is that what you are telling me?" Callie questioned. Her eyes were burning with fury.

"Basically…yeah," Mason confessed. "I didn't make the rules, Callie. I do have to play by them though. At least for a while. Once we get our feet under us, I should have some control. But not right now. I don't want to leave anymore than you want me to go, but I have to. You need to try and understand. Can you do that for me? Don't make things any worse than they already are. Okay?"

Callie tossed the covers from the bottom half of her body and sprang from the bed. She scurried across the room, flung open the closet, jerked a pink silk robe loose from a plastic hanger and covered her body with it. She dashed from the room.

Mason also arose from the bed. He slid on some boxers, and he too vacated the room. He could hear Callie's sobs as he made his way down the short hallway toward the living room.

Callie was sitting on the end of the couch. Her knees were doubled up under her chin. She was rocking back and forth and crying. *How many times did I see Callie act this way as a little girl when she didn't get her way?* Mason recalled with pity. Callie's emotional tirade was both real and show. She was in despair that he would be leaving again, but she was going overboard to make sure Mason realized this fact.

Regardless of her charade, her tears still tore at Mason's heart. He sat down on the sofa beside her and endeavored to pull Callie into his arms. "Callie, it will all be okay," he tried to reassure her in a quiet voice.

Mason kissed the side of her temple. He hugged Callie to his side. He waited with practiced patience for the worse of Callie's angry, perturbed outburst to pass. Several moments later, Callie pulled her emotions under control. She said nothing to Mason for several more minutes. Mason did not utter a word either.

I'll wait for Callie to say something else. Mason did not want to risk throwing her back into another tearful escapade.

"Mason." Callie called his name. He looked over at her. Callie looked as if she had been in a catfight and lost. Her eyes were watery and bloodshot. Her cheeks were bright red. Her hair was a tangled, frazzled mess.

They had climbed into bed right after their shower together. Callie's long blond hair had still been wet. Mason's hair had been wet as well, but because it was so short, his was not as disheveled.

"Yes," he responded. Mason planted a gentle kiss just to the side of Callie's mouth. "Are you okay, baby?"

"No," she answered in a small voice.

A few more tears escaped. Callie swiped them away in frustration. She did not want to spend the rest of the night crying. She and Mason needed to talk.

Mason wanted to ask Callie what he could do to make everything okay. *She'll say cancel the tour*, he recognized. Canceling the tour was the one thing he could not do, so Mason remained quiet and waited for Callie to say something more.

"Mason, I don't want you to go," Callie professed again, fighting more tears.

"I know. I don't want to go either. But don't you see I have to?"

"So how do we – you and I as a couple – survive if you are gone all the time. I've seen movies and documentaries about rock stars, Mason. I know women are constantly throwing themselves at you guys. You'll end up with some groupie."

"Fawn and I have talked about this very thing," Mason said.

No sooner were the words out of his mouth then he realized he had made a mistake. *Dumb, dumb, dumb, Mason! That's exactly what Callie needs to hear...that you were talking to another woman about other women coming on to you. Do you have a brain?!*

"How often do you and Fawn hang out? The two of you were off together somewhere that one time when you called me. You never did tell me where the two of you were. You always conveniently changed the subject."

"Fawn and I have gone out to dinner a few times. It's no big deal. She is becoming a friend to me. She believes my relationship with you is a good thing. She says it keeps me grounded. I'm not running around with bunches of other women like the other guys."

"So there are bunches of women throwing themselves at you guys?" Callie questioned in alarm.

This conversation keeps getting worse and worse! Mason was thinking with apprehension. *How do I steer this discussion in a different direction?*

"Yes. There are some wild women we encounter. But, Callie, that doesn't need to concern you. You're the only woman I want to be with. These other women don't exist for me. I love you. I'm not going to do something stupid and screw up what we have. I want to spend the rest of my life with one special woman. And that special woman is you."

"Mason, you are a man. I know how men's minds work. Your brains, which control your bodies, are powered by sex. The more we are apart the greater the temptations are going to become. What's to keep you from eventually giving in to these temptations? Especially if we spend less and less time together and our time apart keeps growing longer and longer? I don't like you going to dinner with Fawn either. You do remember that you and I started out as only friends, don't you? And don't even try to tell me you haven't noticed Fawn is an attractive woman. The first day I met her all of you guys had your tongues hanging out as she walked past. You have a thing for redheads anyway."

"For redheads?" Mason questioned, looking confused.

"Rebecca. Your first girlfriend, remember?"

"Oh…barely," Mason answered, shaking his head and rolling his eyes. "What I remember more than Rebecca was how jealous you were of her. You locked her in a small changing room in the summer heat to keep her away from me. Don't deny it. I know it's true, even though you denied it then. You aren't going to go after Fawn, are you?" he half teased.

"I would if I have to," Callie said. Her eyes were very serious as she stated this truth.

Mason did not doubt her word. He had no doubt this jealous mean streak still existed somewhere in Callie. Mason did not want to find out if he was correct.

"That's even more reason for me not to give you an excuse to then," Mason said. He smiled for the first time in several minutes. "Besides, I happen to have a major thing for blonds now. One blond in particular." Mason massaged Callie's shoulders as he relayed this information. "But I'm glad you brought up Rebecca and my teenage years. Let's talk about that."

Callie was at a loss as to why he would want to pursue this subject. "What do you want to talk about from all those years ago? You're twenty-seven and I'm twenty-four. What's that got to do with anything now?"

"A lot. You were talking about temptations, and men's bodies being controlled by their sexual urges. Do you have any idea how much you tormented me from the time I was sixteen to the time I left for college?

Those walking boner years when a young man's body really is controlled, for the most part, by sexual urges."

"I don't know. I only know you pushed me away all the time and most of the times you were nasty to me. What's the past got to do with you going away now?" Callie questioned in annoyance. *Mason is trying to change the subject. I'm not going to allow that.*

"I pushed you away because we grew up together, and I still looked at you like you were a little girl. But boy, did you have the body of a woman. And you flaunted that relentlessly in my face every time I turned around. I spent a lot of time alone in the bathroom because of you, relieving stresses you caused – if you know what I mean – and taking cold showers. You made my blood boil I was so attracted to you."

"Now you tell me. I would have died if you had only been honest then."

"No, you probably would have wound up pregnant if I had not been able to control my desires. The point I'm trying to make, Callie, is I did control those desires. I controlled them at a time when it was much harder for me to do so than now. So why, when I'm so in love with you I can't see straight, do you believe I won't be able to control my desires now? You still make my blood boil, and you always will. I mean it when I say I want only you. What have I done that you feel you can't trust me? Haven't my past actions proven anything to you?"

Callie did have to admit what Mason was saying did make sense. She had admired him a great deal when she had grown older, because he had not taken advantage of her. She had indeed given him every opportunity in the world to do this very thing.

"We'll find a way to make it all work, Callie. You have to believe me. I'm asking you to trust me, and I'm asking you to trust in *us*. Can you do that for me?" Mason almost pleaded.

"I'm going to miss you so much, Mason. We won't even get to celebrate Christmas together," Callie stated, tears welling in her eyes again.

"Maybe we can work something out for Christmas. Surely there won't be any concerts on Christmas day. We'll find a way to celebrate together," Mason promised. *I'll take some money out of savings and fly home if I have to.* "Believe me, Callie, I'll miss you too. We'll talk every day. And if today's homecoming was any sign of what the next one might be like, I better take lots of vitamins while I'm gone," he kidded her, chuckling. "We have tonight, and the rest of the weekend to spend together, before I have to leave again. Can we make the best of the time we do have?"

Mason's right. We can spend the weekend sad and miserable because he is going to leave again, or we can make the best of the time we have together. I need to make our time together happy and not sad. I want to send a clear message with him when he leaves that he has someone wonderful waiting for him. Then maybe he can forgo all of the temptations he'll face. I have to believe Mason can. I love him too much to take the chance of driving him away.

Callie put her arms around Mason's neck, and they shared a long, loving kiss.

"We have to make it work," she said to Mason, and to herself.

"We will," Mason declared with assurance. *I intend to have it all. A career in music and the love of my life beside me. I'll see to it that we make it work, Callie.*

Chapter 12

Decisions

Katie Rose's second groundbreaking ceremony was held on December eleventh. Artic air had moved into the area and made the day very cold – thirty degrees with a wind chill in the teens. Big snowflakes were also falling. Some of them were sticking to the ground even though the local weather station swore they were merely flurries.

This new project, McMann Tower, was one of the biggest Greathouse Construction had ever landed. Greathouse Construction would be building the tallest office building in the city. Katie Rose was bursting at the seams with pride over this success. So much so she invited BJ and her whole family to the groundbreaking festivities. She was accustomed to sharing her successes with her family. Once again, her heart ached that her father was not alive to see the incredible thing Greathouse Construction had accomplished.

The customary ceremony was held at the new building site. Gregory Thompson, Mason's replacement, did the honors of jack hammering the concrete. The brutal wind was battering all of them, cutting at all exposed skin. Fortunately, most everyone was dressed for winter – coats, scarves, gloves and earmuffs.

Katie Rose still hurried everything along. Her words and the practice of holding the broken stones together touched Jackie Lynn. She could hear Long Wolf speaking through their daughter. She stifled a sob. This was the first time she had felt like crying in a long while.

BJ was very proud of Katie Rose's success, but he found the whole groundbreaking ceremony strange. It all sounded like a bunch of hocus-pocus to him. He would be glad when this part of the day was over. For one thing, he did not own a long coat. He had on a polyester jacket, which was keeping the top half of him isolated from the wind. But the steady, bitter breeze was slicing through his dress slacks as if they were not even there and freezing his uncovered head, ears and face. He stood shivering beside Jackie Lynn, with his ungloved, grease stained hands sunk deep in the pockets of his jacket. He counted the long minutes.

After cutting the banner, as usual, Katie Rose invited everyone to a celebratory, catered cocktail luncheon at Greathouse Construction. Katie Rose and BJ, Mason and Callie, and Jackie Lynn all headed there as well.

The assembly hall at Greathouse Construction, on the twenty-sixth floor, was festively decorated for this event. The falling snow, which could be seen through the windows all around, seemed to fit in perfectly with the Christmas theme. The serving tables were covered by red and green tablecloths and lined all around with garland.

Each round table, in the center of the room, was also covered by either a red or green tablecloth and had a small poinsettia as the centerpiece. There were white cloth napkins, embroidered around the edges with holly, Santa and snowmen upon each table. The glasses also had a Christmas scene on each one. A small, twinkling Christmas tree sat behind the full bar at the other end of the room. Naturally, the featured drink was eggnog. A small orchestra played soft Christmas carols at the other end of the floor. There was a ten-foot tall, Christmas tree on each side of the room. These were decorated with wide, red and gold ribbons, huge red, green and gold balls and hundreds of clear white lights.

BJ meandered at Katie Rose's side as she made her way through the crowd, meeting and greeting many of the invited guests. Occasionally, BJ fought to keep from pulling off his tie. Katie Rose had bought him a nice, navy suit; a light blue, oxford cloth shirt; a tie; and dress shoes and socks for this party. BJ hated dressing up, but Katie Rose had asked him to be here today. For her, he had compliantly donned the clothes and uncomfortable shoes she had bought him.

Katie Rose, as usual, was dressed in a suit. Her blazer and skirt were emerald green. In contrast, her long-sleeved blouse was a shimmering, royal blue. She loved wearing blues and greens because these colors brought out the vivid color of her eyes. She had curled her long hair with hot rollers, so soft, luminous, feathery curls cascaded around her face. She looked adorable. BJ was proud to be her escort and her fiancé.

Eventually, BJ and Katie Rose came upon Garrison. He was standing over by one of the windows nursing a drink. Occasionally he would glance out the window and watch the snow quietly fall on the city. BJ examined Katie Rose with assiduousness as this other man approached them.

"Hello, Garrison," Katie Rose greeted when she saw him coming their way.

BJ noted that Katie Rose averted her eyes. She seemed unsure of what to do with her hands. Most of the other guests, she had shaken their hand. With Garrison, she crossed her hands conservatively in front of her. *Garrison makes Katie Rose uncomfortable. That's obvious in her posture. Why?* BJ wondered.

"You're wearing the earrings I gave you," Garrison commented with a pleased smile.

Katie Rose felt her face begin to burn as she looked up at Garrison and reached to touch the bottom of each of the earrings. *I shouldn't have worn these.*

"Yes. Thank you," she rather curtly replied. She looked over at BJ. He was giving her a hard stare. *He's probably wondering why I didn't mention Garrison had given me a gift. Why did I wear these today?*

"They look very becoming on you, as I knew they would," Garrison commented.

"That's one opinion," BJ mumbled under his breath.

Garrison only heard part of the comment. "Excuse me?" he questioned, giving BJ a perusal for the first time. His concentration had been on Kate. As usual, she looked extraordinary, and Garrison was thrilled to see she was wearing his earrings.

"I was wondering where those *odd* looking earrings came from," BJ spoke up. He had an ugly scowl on his face. "They are weird. Not something you usually see Katie Rose wearing."

"BJ!" Katie Rose said his name with a chastising tone, her eyes relaying her displeasure. Her face had really colored now. Katie Rose could not believe BJ was being so rude. It was out of character for him.

"They are Dream Catchers," Garrison informed BJ, giving him a smug look. "They came from *our* Indian Reservation. I'm part Indian too.

Custom has it they filter out bad dreams and keep only the good ones. I gave them to Kate about a week ago as an early Christmas/thank you present. As I told Kate, it's a privilege to be able to work with Greathouse Construction. *She* appreciates the significance of the earrings. You have to have some Indian blood to fully understand. I'm glad you are proud to wear them, Kate."

Katie Rose wanted to open up a hole in the floor and drop out of sight. *First, BJ insulted Garrison's gift. Now, Garrison talked down to BJ.* She felt caught between these two men. They were glaring at each other like two male dogs about to fight over a bitch in heat.

"I do appreciate the gift, Garrison," Katie Rose forced herself to speak. She also made fleeting eye contact with him for the first time. She averted her eyes again as she lied, "I hope we will have many more opportunities to work together."

Katie Rose hoped they did *not* work together on any more projects. She wanted to dismiss Garrison and walk away with BJ by her side. Katie Rose was still questioning her intelligence over wearing Garrison's earrings today. She had known he would be here.

What had I hoped to accomplish? I certainly never meant to pit these two men against one another. "We should mill around some more," Katie Rose said to BJ and linked her arm to his to pull him along. "Garrison, it was nice seeing you. Enjoy the rest of the party."

"I will. Have a nice day, Kate," he told her. *I should be polite and tell BJ it was nice seeing him again,* Garrison concluded. However, he did not make the effort to do so. Instead, he forced himself to turn and walk away. *What a clod! What does Kate see in that man? She deserves so much better!* Garrison headed toward the bar. He needed another, stiffer, drink to curb his fury. He had been drinking eggnog.

BJ was also seething. Out of the corner of his eye, with relief, he watched Garrison disappear into the crowd. BJ allowed himself to be led away by Katie Rose. *Who does this guy think he is? He talked to me like I was a moron. Why didn't Katie Rose tell me he had given her those earrings?* A thousand questions were running through BJ's mind.

Katie Rose could tell by BJ's demeanor that he was angry, and she understood why. She felt terrible about their confrontation. She had no one to blame but herself. *I'll have to talk to BJ about this later. Now is not the time.*

BJ was having similar conclusions. *Katie Rose and I will have to talk about this guy after we leave this party. Right now, I'll stay by her side and help her host this party. But later, she is going to talk to me about Garrison. She put me off the other day, but not today. I need to know what is going on with this guy.*

* * * *

Callie and Mason did not stay long at the cocktail luncheon. Mason had to leave Monday morning at 6:00 a.m. The two of them wanted to go home. They wanted all the private time they could squeeze in before Mason left again.

Mason offered to give Jackie Lynn a ride home. She had come with Katie Rose and BJ. Jackie Lynn declined Mason's offer. She said she would wait and ride home with Katie Rose and BJ. She was sitting at a table talking with Samuel. The table sat eight, and it was full, so there were several other conversations going on at the same time. In fact, the whole room was quite noisy. It was jam-packed with people, either sitting at the tables or dawdling about. Jackie Lynn and Samuel were able to tune out the other noise, because they were focused on their own private conversation. Samuel was telling her how well Katie Rose was doing.

The fact that Jackie Lynn was an attractive woman had not escaped Samuel's observation. Her green eyes, outlined by long black eyelashes, still shone with vitality. Her choice of clothing, jewelry, and the style of her hair also helped emphasize this point. Jackie Lynn was wearing a fully lined, scooped neck, mid-length, black satin gown. A matching, long-sleeved, black satin jacket hung to the fitted waist of the dress. There was a string of pearls around her neck, and diamond earrings in her ears. Her permed, light brown hair showcased flawless, loose curls.

Samuel was a nice looking, seventy-two-year-old gentleman. He was normally taller than Jackie Lynn. But Jackie Lynn's high heel pumps stood her at equal height with him today. He had a full head of snow-white hair and striking, dancing, blue eyes. The black suit, white shirt and pale blue, silk tie he had on brought emphasis to his kind eyes.

Samuel's heart ached for Jackie Lynn, because she and Long Wolf had shared an extraordinary love. He and his wife, Amanda, had as well. Samuel had lost Amanda three years ago to cancer. So he could fully understand Jackie Lynn's grief.

"It won't be long now until I can retire. Katie Rose will make an excellent president. She will do Abraham proud," he told Jackie Lynn with a smile.

"I still miss him a great deal, Samuel," Jackie Lynn relayed. This was the second time today she had felt like crying over Long Wolf. Being at his company today rekindled all kinds of memories of her beloved husband.

"I do too, Jackie Lynn. It's still hard for me sometimes to accept he is gone. He was a treasured friend. He loved you and your kids deeply. He was always bragging on one, or all, of you," Samuel said with a reminiscent grin.

"He thought very highly of you, Samuel. You were a treasured friend to him as well."

"I'll never forget that day all those years ago when we both thought we had lost him in that construction accident. You were devastated. I felt so badly for you."

"You were wonderful to me that day, Samuel. You escorted me home and offered to stay. Do you know that was the first time I ever told Long Wolf I loved him. That incident at long last woke me up. The rest, as they say, is history."

"The rest is an incredible love story that brought about two outstanding kids. I see Abraham in both of them. You must be proud of them. It must help to have kids."

"It definitely does make things easier. In fact, they were my reason for putting my grief aside," Jackie Lynn acknowledged. She gave Samuel a pretty smile.

"I wish Amanda and I had had children," he said with a sad expression. "It's been lonely since she's been gone."

"I'm sorry to hear that," Jackie Lynn sympathized. She reached to give Samuel's hand a tender, reassuring squeeze. "Do you get out much? Planning Katie Rose's wedding is tying up much of my time right now. But before that, I started going out on a regular basis with two very dear friends."

"It's harder for a man to do that. We don't keep close friends like you women do. Abraham...um...Long Wolf was my closest friend."

"Well, you can call and talk to me anytime, Samuel," Jackie Lynn offered.

"Thank you, Jackie Lynn. Along those same lines, would you ever consider going to dinner with me sometimes? As you said, it would be nice to get out."

Jackie Lynn was rather taken aback by this proposal. Going out with her girlfriends was one thing, but going out with a man was quite another. She was not ready to start dating again. In fact, Jackie Lynn could not imagine ever dating another man. Long Wolf would always have her heart.

Samuel saw the bewildered expression on Jackie Lynn's face. *I've frightened her. That wasn't my intention.*

"Jackie Lynn, I'm not suggesting we date. I only meant the two of us could go out as friends. But if you aren't comfortable with this idea, that's okay. I would never want to do anything to make you feel uncomfortable around me," Samuel explained.

He's lonely, Jackie Lynn. He was Long Wolf's best friend. What could it hurt to go out to dinner with him occasionally? She reconsidered.

"Of course we could go to dinner, Samuel," she told him with a reassuring smile. "Call me, and we'll set up a time. Okay?"

"Good. Very good," he agreed. Samuel flashed Jackie Lynn a happy grin.

I've done the right thing by agreeing to spend some time with him. After all, we have both lost someone we dearly loved. We can help one another with our bereavement.

Jackie Lynn and Samuel continued to converse for quite some time more. Their conversation was interrupted from time to time as business associates came by to say a few words to Samuel before making their departure. As the crowd slowly thinned out, Katie Rose and BJ came over to check on Jackie Lynn and see if she was ready to go. Jackie Lynn said goodbye to Samuel. She also reiterated he could call her.

Katie Rose was surprised, but pleased, to overhear this part of their conversation. She liked Samuel a lot. Spending some time with a member of the opposite sex might make her mom miss her father even less. The three of them left the party.

* * * *

BJ and Katie Rose went to his apartment after they dropped Jackie Lynn off. As soon as they walked in the door, BJ discarded his suit jacket and pulled off the tie. He tossed both these items across the arm of the sofa. He also unfastened the first button of his shirt and kicked off the dress shoes by the coffee table. He had been quiet ever since the bizarre encounter with Garrison. "We need to talk," BJ said.

Katie Rose was not looking forward to this discussion, but it was something that needed to take place.

"Yes. We do," she agreed. She had a seat on the couch and waited for BJ to join her.

BJ chose to pace the living room instead. He also unbuttoned his sleeves and rolled them up. *He's agitated,* Katie Rose realized. BJ always paced when he was nervous or upset. Once again, guilt washed over her.

I shouldn't have worn these damn earrings! Katie Rose toyed with one of them. However, when she saw BJ was glaring at where her hand rested, she dropped both hands in her lap.

"Do you like the earrings Garrison gave you?" BJ began his interrogation. His face was set in granite and his voice was gruff.

"Yes...I...I suppose I do," Katie Rose admitted with hesitation. Her head was bowed as if she was ashamed. Glancing up at BJ again she admitted, "I like them because they remind me of my Indian heritage, which of course reminds me of my dad. It seems to bother you that Garrison gave me a gift."

"The fact he gave you a gift isn't what bothers me," BJ half lied, a sneer on his face. *I don't like another man giving you gifts.* "What bothers me is the fact you didn't tell me about Garrison giving you the earrings. You've evidently had a week to mention them. All of the sudden, when it comes to this guy, you are keeping secrets from me. Why?"

"It's not like that, BJ," Katie Rose tried to reassure him. *But isn't it?*

"So how exactly is it? First, you have all kinds of meetings with this guy. You talk to him about me, but you never bother to mention Garrison to me. Then he gives you a Christmas gift, which you already admitted has some meaning. Yet, you never even made the slightest mention of the gift to me. This is not like you, Katie Rose. I need to know what is going on with you and this guy."

"Nothing is going on between me and Garrison," Katie Rose stated with conviction, making full eye contact with him again. "You have no reason to be jealous of Garrison Parker, BJ. As I told you, Garrison is *only* a business associate. As he said, the gift was also a thank you for allowing him to work with Greathouse Construction."

"If he is *only* a business associate, like all other business associates, why have you allowed him to give you a pet name? Why are you so uncomfortable around him? You were fidgeting with your hands when he approached us, and you didn't seem to want to make eye contact with him. What are you afraid of?"

"I'm not afraid of anything," Katie Rose said with more assurance than she felt. She averted her eyes again as her thoughts ran wild. *I'm afraid Garrison is attracted to me. I'm afraid he gave me these earrings because of this. I'm afraid I find him attractive as well.* Katie Rose's last contemplation flustered her. *How could I possibly be attracted to another man? A woman isn't supposed to be attracted to other men when she is in love, and engaged. What is wrong with me?!* Katie Rose was staring forlornly at her engagement ring.

"Katie Rose, are you attracted to him?" BJ dared to ask. He feared what her answer might be. Regardless, BJ needed to know. "I need an honest answer."

Katie Rose's head sprang up. She had a stunned expression on her face. *How could BJ possibly know?*

"I...I don't know," she confessed forthrightly. BJ asked her for an honest answer, and he deserved as much.

"Well, we are getting somewhere now," BJ uttered. He had a downhearted expression on his face. BJ looked as if someone had punched him in the stomach. Katie Rose did not want to hurt him.

"BJ, even if I was attracted to Garrison, it wouldn't matter," she hastened to reassure him. "I would never act on this attraction. I love you. I'm engaged to you. You are going to be my husband in a few short months. That's all that matters. Can't we focus on *us* like we always have?"

Katie Rose reached up and slipped each of the Dream Catcher earrings out of her earlobes. She placed them on the table in front of her. "I won't wear *his* earrings anymore. I'll give them back to Garrison if you want. I'll do whatever you want. Can we forget all about Garrison Parker?"

I wish it was that simple, BJ was thinking. *Katie Rose is attracted to another man,* he pondered again. BJ felt sick to his stomach. *She's loyal. If I tell her to give the earrings back and fire Garrison, she would.* BJ considered this option. "Do you think it is wise for you to work so closely with a man you might be attracted to?" BJ inquired. He was giving Katie Rose an unwavering stare.

"What other option do I have? Parker Architecture has been chosen as the architect on this project. I'm sure they will be chosen on many others. Garrison is very good at what he does. I can't fire him from this project, and I'd be shooting Greathouse Construction in the foot if I decline to use Parker Architecture on future projects," Katie Rose told BJ, almost as if she had read his thoughts.

I could still ask her to fire Garrison regardless, BJ mused. *But Greathouse Construction means the world to Katie Rose. I can't ask her to do something that might harm her business. That would end up hurting Katie Rose as well. What should I do?*

"You should give the earrings back to Garrison. You also need to ask him *not* to call you Kate. You need to send a crystal clear message that you and him are business associates and nothing more. Garrison is a handsome man, so it's only natural for you to feel some attraction to him. Being in love and engaged doesn't mean you are blind and dead. But this guy is playing with you, Katie Rose. He's noticed your attraction, and he is trying to seduce you. Take away all of his ammo – his pet names and gifts. If you can wound his ego a little, Garrison may back off. If he doesn't, we'll cross that bridge when we come to it. I trust you, Katie Rose. I know you love me and would never do anything to hurt me."

"I do love you, BJ," she responded with honesty. Her caring eyes locked with his gave veneration to her words.

"Thank you for being honest with me," BJ said.

He walked over to the sofa. He sat down beside Katie Rose and pulled her into a demonstrative embrace. "If we are honest with one another, we can work through anything, Katie Rose. Okay?"

"Okay," she agreed, giving him a smile and a kiss.

Katie Rose glanced over BJ's shoulder at the earrings lying on the table. *I'll give those back to Garrison the next time I see him. Neither these earrings, nor Garrison, will cause me any more trouble in my relationship with BJ. I love BJ, and that's the most important thing.*

Chapter 13

The Kiss

The next morning, Katie Rose called Parker Architecture and asked the receptionist to put her through to Garrison.

"This is Garrison Parker," she heard his deep voice say.

He has such a sexy voice, Katie Rose's thoughts betrayed her. *Oh, God! It is true! I am attracted to Garrison*, Katie Rose concluded with repulsion. *How could I have allowed this to come about?*

"Hello?" Garrison said after a few moments of silence had passed.

Start talking! "Hello, Garrison, it's Kate." *It's Katie Rose! Why did I call myself Kate?*

"Hello, Kate," Garrison said in a chipper voice.

Katie Rose imagined his rousing smile. It made her heart speed up a few beats. *Make the appointment. Get Garrison over here, and set things straight between the two of you!* she directed herself. "Garrison, I need to meet with you today. Have you got some time available this morning?"

"Um…sure," he agreed. "How about 10:00? Will that work with your schedule?"

"Yes, that's fine," she swiftly agreed. "Thanks. I'll see you then."

"Okay," he said. *Kate sounds rattled. Wonder what's up?*

"Bye," she said. Katie Rose did not even listen for Garrison's reply before she abruptly hung up the phone. *There. That's done. Now all I have to do is give him back his earrings and tell him not to call me Kate anymore. I can do this. I need to do this. I don't know what's wrong with me, but I won't allow myself to be attracted to this other man. It isn't right, and it stops today.*

She looked down at her watch. It was only 8:15 a.m. She picked up some papers from her desk and tried to concentrate on them. She could not wait for 10:00 a.m. to come, so she could do what she must with Garrison.

* * * *

Katie Rose's phone rang at 9:50 a.m. It was Carla, announcing Garrison was there to meet with her. "Send him in," Katie Rose instructed. She sat up straight in her desk chair and tried to brace herself for his appearance.

Garrison came into Katie Rose's office with a smile on his face. He discarded his coat, hanging it on the coat rack. He had on a black suit, a white shirt and a red tie, with cartoon characters mingled into it. His nonconforming ties always captured, and held, Katie Rose's attention. However, today it was Garrison's hair that drew her. It was another windy day, and Garrison's hair had actually been tousled on top. Katie Rose felt her heartbeat quicken. *Messy hair is so out of character for him, but he looks adorable.* She had to fight the urge to leap from her chair and run her fingers through Garrison's disheveled hair.

"Well, should I have a seat? Or are we going to one of the conference rooms? You didn't say what you needed to meet with me about," Garrison pointed out. He noted that Kate had a strange expression on her face. He drew closer to her desk.

Katie Rose inhaled the heady scent of Garrison's cologne. Butterflies began to flutter in her stomach. She wanted to run and hide. She had never felt so intoxicated by a man in her life.

"Kate, is everything alright?" Garrison asked, after several more moments of silence. He was scrutinizing her with critical eyes.

Stop staring! What am I going to do?! Katie Rose tried to decide. She felt miserable.

Still eyeballing Kate, Garrison sat down in the chair in front of her desk. He was waiting for her to say something. He was beginning to get worried. Kate was not at all herself. *What's taken place?*

"Garrison," she slowly began. Katie Rose forced herself to look away from him. She stared down at the top of her desk. "We need to talk."

"Did I screw up on some of the drawings or something?" Garrison asked.

"The…drawings?…oh…no," she clarified. She raised her eyes again and gave him a fleeting look. "Your plans are great. This meeting has nothing to do with that."

If Kate doesn't have a problem with my drawings, then what? She's upset about something. It's written all over her face.

Katie Rose opened her top desk drawer. She pulled forth the small box that held the earrings Garrison had given her. She slid the box across the desk toward him. "Garrison, I need to give these back to you," she informed him. Her eyes looked remorseful.

Katie Rose loved the earrings and hated to return them. However, now more than ever, it was essential she did. She did not need any extra reminders of him when he was out of her presence.

Garrison reached for and picked up the box. He opened it and looked inside at the earrings. When he looked back up at Katie Rose, he had an annoyed grimace on his face.

"Can I at least ask why?" he questioned.

"It's not proper for me to keep them," Katie Rose began to explain. She squirmed in her seat.

"Not proper?" Garrison echoed. "Why is it not proper?" He was becoming exasperated.

"Because you should not have given me a Christmas gift," Katie Rose pointed out. She gave him a pained glance and looked down at her desk again. *Because I'm engaged to another man and should* not *be attracted to you.* "We are business associates, not close friends, Garrison. Business associates don't give one another personal gifts."

"I told you it was more of a thank you gift, Kate," Garrison argued. "You were pleased with the earrings…even delighted by them. You're returning them because BJ does not like them; aren't you? He doesn't like that I gave you a gift. That's what this is all about, isn't it? Do you always bow to his commands, Kate?" *I can't imagine that little wimp bossing this amazing woman around. The thought of it makes me sick.*

"Let's leave BJ out of this, Garrison," Katie Rose strongly suggested. She forced herself to make eye contact with him.

"Fine by me. That means you can keep the earrings. We don't have a problem if we leave *BJ* out of this. Am I wrong, Kate?" he quizzed.

Garrison stubbornly laid the box with the earrings in it back on Katie Rose's desk. He even shoved them toward her.

"Yes, you are wrong, Garrison," Katie Rose contradicted him. She was frowning at him in disapproval. "The decision to return your earrings was made at my discretion. It has nothing to do with BJ."

"Then why did you wear them, Kate? If you decided the gift was inappropriate and you should return them to me, why didn't you return them right away? Why'd you wait until now? Might it have something to do with BJ and me coming to heads over them yesterday? Don't try and tell me you returning these earrings has nothing to do with BJ, Kate. At least be honest with me about your reason for returning them." Garrison crossed his arms across his chest. His eyes were looking daggers at her. He was angry now.

"Alright," Katie Rose conceded with irritation. She slid back her desk chair and stood up. Her throat was so dry; she desperately needed something to drink. Luckily, there were some glasses, a water pitcher, and an ice bucket on the small table in her office. *I wish it was alcohol. I could use a strong drink to settle my nerves.*

Garrison beheld Katie Rose's long, *sexy* legs and swaying hips as she made long strides over to the conference table. Her royal blue suit and cream V-neck blouse were very becoming on her. *She is so pretty. She takes my breath away every time I see her. I wonder if BJ appreciates her beauty.*

Katie Rose put some ice in a glass. She picked up the pitcher and filled her glass with water. She took a drink of the cool, refreshing liquid before she continued. Turning back toward Garrison, Katie Rose admitted with a scowl, "You're right, Garrison. BJ does not like that you gave me the earrings, gift or no gift. He also doesn't like it that you call me Kate. He thinks both are inappropriate for an office relationship. I agree with him. So I have returned your earrings, and I'd like for you to address me as Katie Rose from now on. Is that honest enough for you?"

Garrison stood up from his seat as well. He approached Kate. As she took a deep breath to steady herself, she caught the sensual scent of his cologne. Katie Rose stepped back until she was suddenly stopped. She had backed herself up against the table. She could not escape an encounter with Garrison. He drew even closer to her. *Too close!* She felt trapped. *What does he want?*

Desire crept inside of her and made her want to touch Garrison, to feel the heat from his skin against hers. Her mind was betraying her; her control was beginning to weaken. Katie Rose stood frozen by fear.

She watched Garrison's lips move as he asked in a husky voice, "Why is BJ so threatened by me, *Kate*?" Garrison had no intention of starting to call her Katie Rose. Katie Rose was a little girl's name, and Kate was all woman. He reached and took Kate's left hand in his, holding it tight so she could not remove it from his grip. He looked down at her engagement ring. "After all, you are BJ's fiancé. You *are* head over heels *in love* with him. He's the man of your dreams. Right? What would it matter if I gave you a small gift or called you by a special name? That is, unless BJ perceives you are attracted to me. Is that the real problem, Kate? Are you attracted to me?"

Katie Rose had not expected this interrogation from Garrison. She was having problems breathing, and she could not think straight. His questions were echoing in her head. *Is the attraction that obvious? Does it show on my face? Oh, dear Lord, what do I say now? I need time to think. I need to get rid of him! Space...I need space! He needs to give me some room to breathe! He needs to let go of my hand!*

"Garrison," she spoke his name. Katie Rose's voice sounded funny – almost hoarse.

She took another large gulp of water. She noticed she was short of breath and her legs felt weak. She jerked her hand loose from Garrison's rousing touch. She sat the glass of water down on the table. Katie Rose placed both her hands on the table in back of her to try and lend herself some extra support.

"I...I think I need to sit down," she told him. She was feeling lightheaded.

"Or maybe you need a man's *big* strong arms to hold you," Garrison suggested. Without any reserve, he scooped Kate into his arms. "Feels quite different being in my arms than it does in BJ's, doesn't it?" Garrison dared to ask.

"Garr...Garrison, you need to stop," Katie Rose protested in a small voice. She was trying to ignore the pleasurable sensations raging through her body. *This can't be happening!*

Garrison felt Kate's body tremble, and he could see her want of him in her eyes. *It is true! Kate is drawn to me as much as I am to her. Sorry about your luck, BJ!* Garrison brought his face very close to hers. *God, she smells incredible!* He could feel Kate's warm breath as she panted in anticipation. *I can't stand it any longer. I've got to feel her lips on mine!*

Garrison brought his mouth to Kate's. He was impatient to feel her magnificent full lips. He had wanted to do this from the first day he set eyes upon her. As their lips touched, Katie Rose became senseless with desire. She opened her mouth to draw Garrison in for an even deeper kiss. She began to further tease him with her eager tongue, and he reciprocated with his. Katie Rose released the table and tossed her arms around Garrison's neck. She pulled herself even closer. It was as if she could not get close enough to him.

They continued to kiss for several more, sweltering, mind-blowing moments. A basic survival need – breathing – ultimately interrupted their passionate exchange. Their lips parted at last. They stood staring at one another in astonishment. Both of them were gasping. Yet they still held one another, not wanting to give up the closeness or coziness their bodies shared.

Oh, my God! What just happened?! Katie Rose was attempting to ascertain. She was completely disoriented. It was impossible for her to comprehend what was developing between the two of them. It was past the stage of denial. She had wanted this as much as Garrison had. She and BJ had kissed millions of times. Not once had their kisses ever had the intensity she and Garrison had just shared. *Not even when BJ and I make love do I feel this heat, this desire from so deep within my soul. How can this possibly be? What is going on?*

Guilt began to gnaw at her. *It never should have happened. Why did I allow it to take place? I'm engaged. I'm supposed to be in love with another man. How is it possible for me to be so drawn to Garrison?* "Oh, my God!" Katie Rose spoke out loud without meaning to. She was agonizing over her wayward actions.

She pushed herself out of Garrison's arms. Her legs wobbled as she began to make her way back toward her desk. *I have got to sit down before I fall down. I feel so drained.* Katie Rose had not gotten far when Garrison came up behind her and slipped his arms around her waist. "Garrison, leave me alone!" she pleaded in a panicked voice.

Katie Rose balled her hands into defiant fists. Tears of distress formed in her eyes. A sob caught in her throat.

"Kate, you can't run from what just happened," Garrison told her. Then he began to speak more softly, in a rasping voice, as the fierce desire he felt for her began to consume him again. "You want me as greatly as I want you. You can't fight that. Why should you?"

"Why should I?" she repeated, turning in his arms and looking directly into his striking blue eyes.

There were hot tears running down Katie Rose's cheeks. She used what strength she had left to shove herself out of Garrison's arms. Katie Rose did not trust herself to be held by him. In just that short moment, she could feel the passion taking her over again.

"*This* is why I *should*!" she proclaimed. Katie Rose thrust her left hand into Garrison's face and wiggled her ring finger. "Because I'm engaged! Because I have another man who loves me with all his heart! Because I have no right to...to br...break his heart! Do you understand now?" Katie Rose was sobbing. She almost felt like she was going to have a complete meltdown. Her head was spinning; her heart ached; her stomach churned.

"I understand only too well," Garrison responded. "You are a very caring and loyal person, Kate. You would never do anything on purpose to hurt someone you love. And you *love* BJ. You love all of your family and *friends*. You told me you and BJ were only friends. Then that friendship grew into love. I don't doubt you love BJ. But are you *in love* with him? Have the two of you ever shared as much passion as we did in one single kiss?"

"That is none of your business, Garrison," Katie Rose spat. Defiance flickered in her teary eyes. Katie Rose turned her back on Garrison. She stomped the other few feet to her desk. She grabbed the back of her desk chair and stood behind it, as if it were a shield. "You need to leave, Garrison. Take the earrings with you." Her voice sounded stern and unfeeling.

"You can send me away, Kate. You can return my gifts. But it won't change the fact you want me. It won't change the fact that I want you or that the kiss we shared was filled with intense passion. And it won't make you fall *in love* with BJ," Garrison noted.

"Leave! Now!" Katie Rose demanded in desperation. She gnashed her teeth at him.

Katie Rose pushed the chair out of her way, bent to pick up the box of earrings from the desk, and propelled the box through the air toward Garrison. It dropped and hit the floor hard, bouncing a few feet shy of him. The box lid popped off, and the earrings spilled out on the floor. Garrison walked over to the box. He stooped down, retrieved the earrings, and placed them safely back in the box. He stood and placed the box in his pocket.

"I'll take these with me for now. But you'll take them back from me one day," he enlightened Kate with assurance. "I'll leave. You need some time alone. I never meant to upset you, Kate. Call me after you've thought everything through, and we'll talk about everything."

Oh sure! Like I'm just going to think all that's taken place through, and we'll talk. Then everything will be okay, Katie Rose was pondering, in despair. *How can everything ever be alright again?*

"Goodbye," Garrison said in a quiet, almost repentant voice. He ultimately started for the door.

Katie Rose did not say anything back. She merely watched Garrison gather his coat and leave. Immense relief washed over her when he disappeared from her line of sight.

* * * *

Katie Rose was glad when the workday ended. She had an awful time concentrating the rest of the day, after Garrison left. He and 'the kiss' consumed her mind the rest of the day. When the time came to go home, Katie Rose did not go to BJ's apartment. She could not bear to face him. She needed to pull her head together first.

Katie Rose went home instead. Her mom had gone to dinner with Samuel, so Katie Rose would have the house all to herself. She was so grateful her mother would not be there. She needed the solitude. She wanted to think everything over and decide how she needed to proceed.

The first thing I need to do is call BJ, and let him know I'm not coming over tonight. What am I going to tell BJ as to why I'm staying home tonight? Katie Rose attempted to decide, as her mind kept wandering back to the 'kiss'. *I don't want to lie to him. But I can't tell him the real reason I don't want to see him tonight. How could I have allowed things to get so out of hand? I've got to find a resolution to this nonsense. And soon!*

Katie Rose picked up the telephone and dialed BJ's number. He answered the phone on the second ring. As Katie Rose heard his voice, her breath nervously caught in her throat. She could not speak.

"Hello," she heard him say a second time.

You have to say something! Katie Rose told herself. "Hi," she uttered at last.

"Katie Rose? Where are you? Are you working late?" BJ inquired.

He sounded so relaxed and lighthearted. Katie Rose's heart ached. *I don't want to hurt him.* "No. I'm at mom's," she informed him. "Tonight is the night she is going to dinner with Samuel. I got to thinking, and I decided I'd like to be here when she gets home. She may want to talk to someone about the date. So...I won't be coming over tonight."

"Do you think your mom will be out late with Samuel? If not, you can always come over after she gets home, and you guys have your talk. It will be bad enough not having dinner together. But I've gotten used to having you in my arms at night. I don't know if I can sleep without you here."

BJ sounds so sweet. He loves me unconditionally! How could I have betrayed him? Katie Rose's heart was breaking. She was fighting to keep from crying. *Pull it together! You can't break down, Katie Rose!*

"Um...I'll miss you too," she said in a soft voice, choking back her emotions. *I will* miss *BJ. How can I not be* in love *with him? Garrison has to be wrong!*

"You seem to have decided you aren't coming over," BJ said with notable disappointment. "Why would you need to spend the night at your mom's? Do you think this date with Samuel is going to upset her?"

"I don't know. That's the thing. I want to be here just in case. Mom and Samuel going out is a good thing. I want to be here to support her. She has always been there for me. Can you understand? It's only one night. Then everything will go back to normal." *It has to. I'll find a way to get past what happened today with Garrison. He isn't going to destroy my relationship with BJ.*

"It's going to be *one*, very lonely night. But, you obviously feel like you need to spend the night at your mom's. So, I'll have to struggle through the night alone. I'll miss you. I love you."

"I love you too, BJ," Katie Rose told him. Despite her resolve, tears formed in her eyes and a sob caught in her throat.

"So how was your day?" he asked her. They normally talked about their day over dinner.

I can't talk about my day. I need to end this conversation. Before I lose it!

Katie Rose took a few more minutes to pull herself back together. She cleared her throat, and she simply said, "My day was fine." *I shared a passionate kiss with another man. That's all! It was a grand day!* "How was your day?"

"Your day was fine? That's it? No excited news to share about the Greathouse business world? Are you sure everything is alright?" BJ asked with a carefree chuckle. Katie Rose always had some grandiose story to tell him about her day.

BJ's much too perceptive. Now tell me he doesn't know me well, Garrison. How well do you know me? How well do I know you? Some stupid kiss cannot replace history! And BJ and I have history. We know one another. With BJ is where I belong.

"Katie Rose," she heard BJ call. "Are you there?"

"I'm here," she spoke. "I'm preoccupied. That's all."

"Are you that worried about your mom? I'm sure this date with Samuel will turn out fine."

"I'm afraid it might bring up a lot of feelings for my dad again," Katie Rose relayed. She honestly was fearful that this might occur.

"Your mom will be fine," BJ tried to reassure her.

"I'm sure you are right," she agreed. "You never did tell me how your day went," she changed the subject.

BJ still found it odd Katie Rose was not talking about Greathouse. *She seems to want to change the subject. Something doesn't seem right. Maybe she's just concerned about her mom. I'll talk about my day, and try and give her something else to concentrate on.*

"My day was a usual day in the auto industry." As BJ began to converse about his day, Katie Rose relaxed. She heard BJ talking, and she attempted to listen. *It will all be okay. I'll find a way to make everything okay,* she attempted to convince herself. *At least I don't have to face BJ tonight.*

Chapter 14

The Confession

Samuel took Jackie Lynn to Cornucopia Restaurant. This restaurant had been around for many, many years. Cornucopia provided casual dining in a sophisticated environment. Like most everywhere else, it was decked out for Christmas. One, small, live, pine tree piled full with gleaming white lights stood on each side of the doorway. Two enormous wreathes hung in the frosted windows of the double wooden doors. The foyer was strung with garland, and gigantic red Christmas bows lined the walls. A roaring fire was burning in the cultured stone fireplace. A stationary, lighted, musical, Christmas train sat atop the mantel. The Christmas carols it was chiming out could barely be heard over the extensive din of people lingering around, waiting to be seated.

The restaurant was dimly lit. The tables were all covered by burgundy linen tablecloths, and the silverware was wrapped in cloth napkins. The plates were china and the beverage glasses crystal. There was a small tea lamp candle, in beveled glass, burning in the center of each table. A live jazz band was playing by the small dance floor. They were playing a mixture of traditional jazz and some Christmas songs.

Cornucopia was always crowded. Fortunately, Samuel had made a reservation, so he and Jackie Lynn only had to wait about fifteen minutes to be seated. Their waiter took their drink orders right away – a tall Makers and coke for Samuel and iced tea for Jackie Lynn. He rushed away to procure their drinks.

This restaurant brought back a wealth of memories to Jackie Lynn – both happy and sad. The first time Flora and Mary Julia had met Long Wolf had been at Cornucopia. Jackie Lynn had been trying to deny her love for him then. She had lied to Long Wolf and told him she had a business dinner. She had gone out with her two very dear friends instead.

Jackie Lynn recalled that Long Wolf had followed her to the restaurant and uncovered her deception. She had been furious with him. However, when Long Wolf had gotten her alone, her fury had catapulted into passion. They had left Cornucopia in a heated rush. Their unquenchable hunger for one another had been much too overwhelming to deny – as had Jackie Lynn's love for him.

As usual, Jackie Lynn looked very becoming this evening. Her red, crew neck sweater made her brown hair and green eyes shine all the more. Her black slacks hid her small belly. Her loosely curled hair was pulled back on each side with sparkling, gold, butterfly clips. She had been nervous when she was getting ready. It had taken her quite some time to decide what she should wear, how she wanted to fix her hair, and how much makeup she should apply. Jackie Lynn wanted to look nice, but she did not want to appear as if she was going on a date. She did not want to give Samuel the impression she wanted anything more than friendship from him. Right now, however, she was more bothered by being at Cornucopia than anything else.

Samuel observed Jackie Lynn looked uneasy. He saw her looking all about the restaurant a few times, and Jackie Lynn had also grown quiet ever since they had arrived. Samuel finally asked her, "Jackie Lynn, is everything alright?"

"Everything is fine, Samuel" she said and gave him a coerced smile. "This place has a lot of memories for me. That's all."

"Memories of Long Wolf?" he guessed.

"Yes."

"I'm sorry. You should have told me. We can leave if you'd like. There are lots of other restaurants in town."

"No," Jackie Lynn objected. "There are memories of Long Wolf everywhere. I can't run from all of the places that hold memories of him. If fact, I wouldn't want to. Memories are all I have left."

Samuel reached across the table and encircled Jackie Lynn's hand in a tender grasp. The stripped polo shirt he was wearing – eye-catching, wide, red, blue and yellow strips – brought even more attention to his kind blue eyes and snow white hair. "I know what you mean, Jackie Lynn. It still hurts when I visit a place where Amanda and I made memories. But I hold on to our happy memories. They become like a treasure chest over time. The happy memories help lessen the pain."

"Yes, they do," Jackie Lynn agreed. Samuel's warm hand on hers felt nice and comforting. "It's hard for me to believe Long Wolf has been dead for eight months."

"I know. Time marches on. Amanda has been dead for over three years. Sometimes I still expect to see her when I walk in the door of my house," Samuel confessed.

The waiter returned and sat their drinks on the table in front of them. He told them he would be back in a moment to take their orders. Samuel was still focusing on Jackie Lynn. She had a somber expression on her face, so he said, "Enough with all this sad talk. I didn't bring you to dinner to depress you, Jackie Lynn. Let's talk about something much more joyful. How are the plans for Katie Rose's wedding coming?"

This subject brought an easy smile to Jackie Lynn's face. "They are going well!" she told Samuel with confidence. "Katie Rose is going to make a beautiful bride. She and BJ will have a wonderful life together. The next thing I'll have to look forward to will be Mason's wedding – If he and Callie ever set a date. Then I look forward to having one of my children give me some grandchildren to occupy my time."

"Wouldn't that be great?" Samuel said, sharing in Jackie Lynn's happy wishes.

He loved to see her smile. Samuel intended to do everything in his power tonight to see that Jackie Lynn smiled often. He wanted to help her continue to conquer her grief over Long Wolf. They both picked up their menus to try and decipher what they might like to eat before their waiter returned.

* * * *

Since it was dark outside, and she had forgotten to turn the porch light on, Samuel walked Jackie Lynn up to her front door. It was a clear night, so they at least had the moonlight to illuminate their path. "I had a nice time tonight, Jackie Lynn," Samuel divulged.

"I had a nice time too, Samuel," she confessed.

She and Samuel had dined, talked, and even shared a dance. Jackie Lynn liked the way the evening had unfolded. It had been a relaxing time. In fact, she was feeling guilty, because she had enjoyed the evening very much.

"I hope we can get together for dinner again soon," Samuel proposed with boldness.

Samuel liked Jackie Lynn a great deal. He enjoyed sharing her company. They were friends. That's all he was looking for from her at this time. Jackie Lynn was not ready for anything other than friendship with him, and he understood.

"You are a good friend, Jackie Lynn," Samuel added. "How about I call you, and if you have a free night, we'll have dinner again. How would that be?" Samuel suggested.

"That sounds fine," Jackie Lynn agreed. She gave Samuel a warm smile. *He's such a sweet man! I'll have to agree to have dinner with him again. Samuel could use the companionship. He isn't asking for anything more from you, Jackie Lynn.*

"Well, I better let you get in for the night. It's a bit chilly out here," Samuel said.

He placed his arm around Jackie Lynn's shoulder and gave her in a loose, unthreatening squeeze. However, Jackie Lynn was alarmed to discover she liked the feel of Samuel's arm around her. She did not allow him to hold her for long.

Jackie Lynn had experienced the same reaction when they had danced earlier. It was not because Samuel was, in any way, fresh. If anything, Samuel went out of his way to keep things circumspect between the two of them. Regardless, Jackie Lynn was careful to limit their dance to *one*. Jackie Lynn appreciated Samuel's prudence. He seemed to respect her feelings. He wanted companionship and friendship from her.

Companionship and friendship is something I can provide. "Goodnight, Samuel. Thank you for everything. Call me, and we'll set up another time," Jackie Lynn said and gave his arm a grateful pat.

"Have a good night, Jackie Lynn," Samuel said. He reached to touch her hand before he started down her porch steps.

Jackie Lynn unlocked her door, but she did not enter the house. Instead, she turned and watched Samuel walk down the walk. *I want to make sure he gets to his car okay.*

When Samuel got to the car, he observed Jackie Lynn was still standing on the front porch. He gave her a wide smile and waved to her. *It's nice to have a woman watching me leave.*

Jackie Lynn waved back to Samuel. Then she disappeared into the house and closed the door behind her. As she stood just inside the door, she realized, *I feel happy. I made the right decision to go out with Samuel tonight. I'll have to go out with him again. It's good for the both of us.*

* * * *

Jackie Lynn rounded the corner into the living room. She spied Katie Rose sitting on the sofa. She was not surprised to find her daughter there, because she had seen Katie Rose's Mustang in the driveway.

She had expected her daughter to be in her room, retrieving some more of her belongings. Katie Rose was slowly moving all of her things to BJ's apartment. Jackie Lynn encouraged this move.

"Hi, mom," Katie Rose greeted with a sheepish expression on her face.

"Hello. What brings you to the house?" Jackie Lynn asked with a smile. She approached the couch.

"I stopped by to see how your dinner date went," Katie Rose told Jackie Lynn.

"It wasn't a date, Katie Rose," Jackie Lynn corrected her. She had a seat beside her daughter. "Samuel and I are friends. Tonight was merely two old friends getting together for awhile."

"So did you have a good time with your *old friend*?" Katie Rose dared to inquire.

"As a matter of fact, I did," Jackie Lynn confessed with reluctance. *Does it bother Katie Rose that I went out with Samuel?* Jackie Lynn sensed something was troubling Katie Rose. Her eyes looked disconcerted, and she wore an uncharacteristic frown.

"Mom, how did you know dad was the *one*?" Katie Rose questioned.

Where is this strange question coming from? Jackie Lynn wondered. "Why do you ask? Look, if me going out with Samuel bothers you, then...."

"What?" Katie Rose interrupted. "No, mom. It's doesn't bother me at all that you and Samuel went out. In fact, it is great," Katie Rose tried to assure her.

"Then why are you questioning my love for your father all of the sudden?"

"I'm not questioning the love you and dad had. It was obvious. What I'm wondering is how did you and dad know you were truly in love? Did you always know you and dad belonged together?"

Something's definitely up, Jackie Lynn concluded with concern. "Katie Rose, did you and BJ have a fight or something? Are you questioning your love for him?"

"No, we didn't have a fight." *At least not yet.* "But...yes...I am questioning my love for BJ," Katie Rose acknowledged with hesitance.

"What?! Why?!" Jackie Lynn asked in alarm.

"It's more like...*who,*" Katie Rose shared. Her heart began to beat very briskly, and her stomach rolled. "I...I kissed another man today, mom."

"You...you what?!" Jackie Lynn grilled. Her eyes were wide in astonishment.

"I'm attracted to another man, mom. Were you ever attracted to another man after you and dad fell in love? I'm supposed to be in love with BJ, but...this other man got under my skin. How could this have taken place?"

Oh, Lord! Does Katie Rose really have feelings for another man.?! The tears forming in Katie Rose's eyes answered Jackie Lynn's question. *It is true!*

"You think I'm an awful person now. Don't you, mom?" Katie Rose said as tears began to run down her cheeks. She choked back a sob and added, "It's okay. I feel the same way about myself. I can't believe I kissed another man. I don't want to hurt BJ, mom. I love him. So how can I be attracted to another man? How could I have kissed another man?"

Jackie Lynn placed her arms around Katie Rose and pulled her into a secure hug. Her heart was breaking for her daughter. Jackie Lynn could not believe this turmoil was happening to Katie Rose. *Who is this other man? How could he have gotten into Katie Rose's heart? I need more details.*

Jackie Lynn held Katie Rose and stroked her back for several moments. She allowed her daughter to cry in anguish. Katie Rose eventually managed to contain her emotions once more. She pulled back and looked Jackie Lynn in the eyes. "I'm sorry, mom," she acknowledged with clear remorse.

She was amazed to hear her mom say, "Katie Rose, you don't need to apologize to me. We can't help who we develop feelings for. I need for you to tell me more about this other man? Who is he? How did this all come about?"

"His name is Garrison Parker. You probably don't remember him. But the first time we met was at the Reservation. He was the only other child who spoke English. It was the first time you and dad took me there. The time I was given my Indian name."

"The boy who approached Mason. Yes, I do vaguely remember this child," Jackie Lynn revealed. "Did you have some sort of childhood crush on this boy?"

"Not hardly," Katie Rose was quick to rectify. "In fact, I almost hated him. He was a bossy, know-it-all."

"Hate and love are very close emotions, Katie Rose. Especially in children," Jackie Lynn pointed out.

Katie Rose had never thought about it in this manor. *Did I have a crush on Garrison when we were children? Is this why I was so mad, because he wouldn't have anything to do with me?*

"So when did you run into him again?" Jackie Lynn further interrogated.

"He's an architect now. Garrison has been the architect for the last two projects Greathouse has taken on. We've been working closely together. Garrison made personal comments about me every now and then. So I knew he was attracted to me. What I didn't know was I was attracted to him as well. I don't understand how I can be attracted to another man. How can I be in love with one man and be attracted to another? It makes no sense, mom."

"Emotions do not always make *sense*, Katie Rose," Jackie Lynn shared her wisdom.

"So what do I do, mom?" Katie Rose asked. Her eyes seemed to be pleading for an answer.

"I'm not sure I can answer that," Jackie Lynn replied with honesty. "Are you here tonight to hide from BJ?"

"Yes," Katie Rose confessed. "I couldn't face him tonight. In fact, I told him I needed to stay here tonight."

"That will solve things for one night, but what about tomorrow? You can't run from BJ forever. You know, Katie Rose, love between two people is very important. But so is trust."

"I know, mom," Katie Rose agreed. "What are you suggesting? That I go to BJ's apartment tonight and tell him what went down with Garrison today?"

"I don't know about that. I wouldn't want to see BJ do something stupid and go after Garrison. But you do owe it to BJ to be honest about your feelings. He needs to know you might have feelings for another man."

"BJ already guessed I was attracted to Garrison," Katie Rose said. "Telling him I actually may have feelings for Garrison as well would crush BJ, mom." She looked as if she might start crying again.

"What do you suppose it will do to BJ if you marry him and not be able to love him like you should? You asked me earlier how I knew your dad was the *one*. That's not a difficult question to answer. I knew it because I thought about him constantly; because my desire for him physically was inexhaustible; because I would have died for him. And most importantly, because all other men ceased to exist. I never was attracted to another man after I fell in love with your father. Oh, sure, I noticed when a man was nice looking. I wasn't dead. But I had no desire to be with another man...kissing or otherwise. You obviously can't say the same. You need to find out why this is, Katie Rose."

"How?!" she demanded to know. There was desperation in her voice and eyes.

"Start with honesty. Hopefully, BJ can help you sort out this mess. He loves you a great deal...."

"And I believed I loved him a great deal too. Now you are saying I don't love BJ as I should...."

"Yes, honey, I am," Jackie Lynn hated to admit. "Something is clearly wrong in your relationship with BJ."

"Oh, God, how has it come to this?!" Katie Rose lamented.

Jackie Lynn was wondering the same thing. Katie Rose's revelations were all coming as such a shock to her. She had thought BJ and Katie Rose belonged together. But perhaps she had been wrong. *Did I cause this mayhem? I'm the one that advised Katie Rose to explore a romantic relationship with BJ in the first place. She only considered him a friend up until then. What if that is still the only way she loves BJ – as a friend?*

Katie Rose was also lost in her own pervasive thoughts. She could not imagine telling BJ she had feelings for Garrison. He had taken her attraction to him hard enough. *There has to be another way.* However, Katie Rose could not think of a better solution. *I'll have to talk to BJ. But not tonight. I need to have my thoughts together better first. I'll do it tomorrow.*

Jackie Lynn could see how distraught Katie Rose was, and she could understand why. She reached out to her daughter and enfolded her in another embrace. *This will all work out one way or another. I like BJ a lot, but Katie Rose's happiness is what's most important. I can't let Katie Rose marry a man she may not love the way she should.* Jackie Lynn was extremely concerned for her daughter.

Chapter 15

The Standoff

BJ called Katie Rose before she left for work the next morning. He asked her how her mother was. It took Katie Rose several seconds to recall her lie...*I stayed here last night to allow my mother to talk about her date with Samuel. The date that supposedly upset her so much I had to spend the night. Mom's right. I can't keep lying to BJ.*

Katie Rose assured BJ that Jackie Lynn was fine. She told him she would see him that evening after work. When BJ told Katie Rose he loved her and she responded in kind, her heart ached. *Mom thinks I don't love BJ as I should*, Katie Rose mused, in anguish.

Now, Katie Rose was having a horrible time focusing at work. She had gotten little sleep the night before. Her mind was too burdened by thoughts of BJ and Garrison. Katie Rose also had been thinking over all she and her mom had discussed.

Katie Rose was engrossed in thought, attempting to give attention to some paperwork. Garrison strolled into her office. The first thing that alerted Katie Rose of *his* presence was that alluring cologne. She looked up with apprehension, thinking her nose must be deceiving her. Katie Rose jumped in alarm when she viewed Garrison standing in front of her desk. *What's he doing here!*

"I'm sorry. I didn't mean to startle you," he apologized, giving her a concerned stare. "It's almost lunchtime. We need to go to lunch and talk about what happened yesterday."

Katie Rose sprang from her chair. She practically ran across the room to the door. She wanted to bolt. *Maybe I should!* She gave this notion serious consideration for a few, panicked seconds. Then she mustered her courage. Katie Rose closed the door and turned to face Garrison.

Their eyes met, and Katie Rose's heart leapt in excitement. *Mom is right! There's a major problem in my relationship with BJ. I've never felt this urgent pull toward BJ.* Katie Rose almost felt like crying again.

"Those stunning eyes of yours look a bit tired, Kate," Garrison told her.

Katie Rose observed Garrison had not shaved. He had the slight shadow of a beard and mustache. It made him that much more appealing. *Why can't I stop having these thoughts?* she agonized. She forced her eyes to look away from him.

Garrison began to ramble, "I didn't sleep well last night either. I kept seeing your magnificent emerald eyes every time I closed mine. I kept thinking about what your scrumptious lips felt like on mine. I thought I'd go mad. I've been biding my time all day waiting to come and see you. I wanted to call, but I was afraid you wouldn't talk to me. I snuck past Carla, because I did not want her to announce I was here."

Garrison raked his fingers through his hair. He was nervous. This conversation with Kate was extremely important. He had to convince her to give him a chance. *I know I'm the better man for her. She and BJ do not belong together.*

"Garrison, what happened yesterday never should have," Katie Rose reiterated; her eyes were solemn. Her heart was beating in her mouth. She was standing with her back against the door. Katie Rose was still thinking about bolting.

"Why shouldn't it have happened?" Garrison dared to question anew. His eyes were burning holes through her.

"You know the answer to that," Katie Rose staunchly maintained, fighting not to look away. *I can't allow him to think he has the upper hand. Stare him down!*

"No, I don't know why it *shouldn't* have happened, Kate. And neither do you. In fact, if you were honest, you'd admit you want it to happen again. Again and again and again," Garrison taunted. He took a step forward.

Katie Rose gripped the doorknob. She also held up the palm of her other hand, signaling him to stop. "I'm not going to let you put me in another compromising position, Garrison. I'll open this door and yell for security. I'll have you escorted out of this building, and that will be the end of any relationship we have," she threatened.

Garrison could see the fear and determination in Kate's lovely eyes. It would not take much to push her to the limit. *Kate is desperate to keep anything physical from transpiring between us again. Watch your step, Garrison.* He did not advance any closer. He stood frozen in place. They were at a standoff with one another.

"This is ridiculous, Kate. You were so free with me yesterday. Now you are threatening to have me thrown out. You need to stop hiding behind BJ and be honest with your feelings."

Be honest with my feelings? Isn't that what mom said too? "You want me to be honest with you, Garrison?" A flicker of fury was in her eyes.

"Yes."

"Okay…here goes. I feel…trapped by you. I'm disgusted with myself for what I let take place yesterday. I don't want to hurt BJ. He deserves better. He's a terrific guy, and he's done nothing to deserve being hurt. You see, I actually *know* BJ. I've known him for years. I can't say the same about you, Garrison. All I know about you is there is some sort of strong physical attraction between us. So basically, I have only *lust* with you. I have *love* with BJ. Why would I throw that all away to be with *you*?"

The urge to step forward and take Kate in his arms was so overwhelming Garrison thought he would lose his mind. Nonetheless, he stayed where he was. *Look, but don't touch.*

"You're right, Kate. You don't know me well. You do basically only know me physically. But if you stay with BJ, you will always wonder what might have been between the two of us. That wonder in your mind is enough of a reason for you to give *us* a chance. You would soon learn I'm a terrific guy too, and you'd have the physical attraction as well. You might even fall in love for the first time in your life. Don't tell me you are *in love* with BJ, Kate. Because you are *not*! BJ's only a close male friend, who you love. You know it, Kate. You won't be happy in a marriage without a little *lust* in it. You need an overpowering attraction like we have."

"You don't know anything about my relationship with BJ! I may have as much passion or *more* with him," she argued, sounding infuriated.

"There is no way, Kate. You've tried to convince yourself there is passion between the two of you. You even believed this untruth, until I came along. You couldn't have kissed me, like you did last yesterday, if your relationship with BJ was filled with the passion it should be."

Again, Garrison is telling me the same thing my mother did, Katie Rose noted with trepidation, aggravated. "Well, I have a solution," Katie Rose informed Garrison. She laced her hands and held them over her heart. She was tapping her thumbs, and she was glaring at Garrison with unveiled hostility.

"What might that be?" Garrison challenged.

"The solution is…we stay apart. My relationship with BJ was fine before you came along. If I avoid seeing you, things will be fine again…."

"You are sadly mistaken, Kate…." Garrison began to argue.

"I don't think so," she contested. "And if I am, I'm only hurting myself…."

"Wrong again! You will also be hurting BJ, and…you'll be hurting me. You say you love BJ, Kate. If you love BJ, you will be honest with him. If he's this terrific guy, he deserves more than to be caught in some loveless…passionless marriage. You are not being fair to him, Kate."

"You let me be concerned about BJ, Garrison. You aren't concerned about him anyway. You're only concerned about yourself. I'm just another female conquest to you, and you are only upset you can't capture me. You'll have to get over that. Once you had me, you wouldn't want me anyway. You would want to find your next conquest."

"Is that really the impression you have of me, Kate?"

"Yes, it is," she resoundingly replied. Her face had an ugly grimace on it. "I remember what you were like as a boy. You left quite an impression…not a good one. You were a showoff, who liked having all the attention. You liked having your own way. You're upset, because you aren't getting your way with me. And you never will. You thought you had captured me with some…some…*meaningless*…kiss yesterday. You're the one who is sadly mistaken, Garrison."

Kate's acidic words caught Garrison off guard. They tore at his heart a bit. *Kate thinks I'm just some worthless, egotistical playboy. Is this really how she feels or is she only saying these things to push me away?* "Is this how you actually feel, Kate?" he asked.

Katie Rose glimpsed a trace of pain in Garrison's eyes. *I'm being harsh.* She hated to hurt Garrison. Regardless, Katie Rose could not back down. *If I back off, Garrison will pull me in again. I can't allow that to come about. I have to put some distance between us.*

"Yes, it's how I actually feel," she maintained with conviction. She gave him an unsympathetic stare and rocked back on her heel.

"You say we need to 'stay apart'. Does that mean you intend to fire my firm from the projects we are associated with Greathouse on?" Garrison interrogated.

"No. You are a very talented architect. I am not going to shoot Greathouse in the foot, because things got out of hand with us personally."

"How are we going to stay apart?"

"I'll see to it that someone else meets with you. I have several individuals I can depend on to work with you," Katie Rose explained with confidence.

"So you don't want anything else to do with me? Is that what you are saying, Kate?" Garrison inquired once more. His eyes seemed to be pleading with her to recant.

"That's right," she insisted with stubbornness. "I want you to move on to your next lady candidate, Garrison. As you say, I'm attracted to you, so obviously you are a very nice looking man. You will have no trouble at all finding someone else to spend your time chasing. Maybe you can even find another engaged woman to try and capture."

Kate's vicious words were knifes in the gut to Garrison. He wanted to defend his honor, but Garrison understood how Kate might have drawn these conclusions. He had given her a bad first impression when Kate had met him as a boy. And now, he *was* vying for her while she was engaged. And he had admitted to having no, one, special lady in his life. Kate's conclusions were logical.

No wonder she would chose BJ over me. Even though their relationship must certainly lack passion. Kate believes our relationship would only be some flash in the pan lust fest. Could she be right? Garrison suddenly felt he needed some time alone to think. "Okay. I'll leave," he agreed in a quiet voice. His facial expression was despondent.

"Good," Katie Rose snapped, putting the final nail in the coffin.

She stepped sideways, away from the door. Katie Rose was closely watching Garrison the whole time. She wanted to make certain he did not try to spring forward toward her. *He might try to pull me into his arms. I won't allow Garrison to touch me again. I need to break things off with him.*

Garrison moved in a disheartened gait toward the doorway. He opened the door. He turned back toward Kate. He was silent for a few moments, as if he expected her to say something more. *Tell me not to go.* His eyes were beseeching. "Goodbye, Kate," Garrison said at last. His face was strained.

"Bye, Garrison," she replied with inflexibility. *I'm doing the right thing*, Katie Rose attempted to convince herself. However, she found it hard to stop looking at the empty doorway after Garrison had gone. All of the sudden, this bizarre, forlorn yearning was clutching at her heart.

Chapter 16

Trust

Mason had been away from home for almost two weeks. He called Callie every night, whenever possible. The tour was going awesome, but Mason did miss Callie very much. Fortunately, he was due to come home Christmas day. Unfortunately, he would only he home the one day. He had to leave the next day, but at least he and Callie would be able to celebrate Christmas together.

Fawn had continued to take an active interest in Mason's free time. She often invited him to accompany her to dinner, and Mason did not turn her down. Callie was uncomfortable with him spending time with Fawn. Regardless, Mason saw no real reason to turn down Fawn's kind offers. Mason did not share with Callie that he and Fawn were still spending time together. He saw no reason to worry her. *It would only make Callie jealous to tell her I am spending time with Fawn. Fawn and I are only friends. That's all we will ever be.*

* * * *

Callie was out at a department store. She was fighting the massive crowds to do some last minute Christmas shopping with Katie Rose. Christmas was only three days away. Long lines of people stood in all the checkout lanes. Callie and Katie Rose wheeled their bask cart into the shortest line they could find – there were seven people in front of them. A picture of Mason caught Callie's eye. Rudely, she pushed past a few people and reached in front of one stranger to jerk forth the tabloid paper she had spied.

Katie Rose saw the angered expressions on the tired shoppers' faces. She tried to communicate a speedy apology for her friend. She mouthed an 'I'm sorry' to these strangers. Callie rejoined her side. She was perusing the giant, bold headline on the paper with a perturbed look on her face.

When Katie Rose saw Mason's picture on the front of the paper, she exclaimed, "Oh no! Don't tell me Mason has made the tabloids! He must be getting popular! Don't read that garbage, Callie. It's all lies! You know that."

"So how'd they get the picture of Mason with Fawn if they weren't together?" Callie demanded to know. Her eyes were burning with anger.

"Callie, they doctor those pictures sometimes," Katie Rose argued. She refused to believe Mason and his agent were an item. This was the first time Katie Rose had seen a picture of Fawn. Callie had told Katie Rose that Fawn was pretty, and Katie Rose did have to concede this was true. She could understand why Callie might be jealous about Mason spending time with this woman.

"Callie, that picture was probably taken at one of the concerts. Fawn would be there with the band. She is their agent, after all. Then these rag sheets print a headline like that, 'Mason Greathouse, lead singer of Savage Pride, and his agent, Fawn Donovan. Are these two a hot item?'. You know the answer to that, Callie. N-O! Because you and Mason are the *hot item*. You can't let all this garbage bother you, because there will be plenty more, I'm sure."

Regardless of Katie Rose's reassurances about Mason, Callie could not resist thumbing to the next page of the article. On the next page were a few more pictures. These were obviously taken at other places. Mason and Fawn had on different clothing in the assorted pictures. The backgrounds had also changed.

The article read that Mason and Fawn had been sighted at several restaurants together in different cities. This article also hypothesized they most certainly must be a couple. In every single photograph, they were either smiling or laughing. Their bodies were also in close proximity to one another.

Katie Rose had hastily perused the article on her brother. She looked at Callie's face, and she could tell her friend was seething. Katie Rose could not help but feel sorry for Callie. Her friend greatly missed Mason, and these insinuating pictures were not helping matters any.

"Callie, I'm telling you, don't let these photos upset you. Mason has called you every night, right? So how can he be spending all his time with Fawn? The answer is…he isn't. Right?"

"No, he isn't spending *all* his time with *her*," Callie hissed. "But he is spending some of his time with Fawn. I asked Mason not to. If he'll go behind my back and do this, what else is he hiding?"

"Callie, don't go there!" Katie Rose cautioned. "If you let yourself, you can start imagining all kinds of things. You have to remember that imagination does not make things true. You need to trust Mason, Callie. Don't let some rag newspaper cause problems between the two of you."

Katie Rose confiscated the paper from Callie. She excused herself to the people in front of them and stretched to place the paper backwards on the stand. The picture of Mason was hidden from Callie's view. "Forget about that, Callie. Don't let it upset you," Katie Rose begged.

However, she feared it was too late. Katie Rose and Callie had been friends their entire lives. Katie Rose knew when Callie was upset about something. It was obvious Callie was livid over these pictures. *Mason, you are in for it when you call Callie tonight*, Katie Rose ascertained. There was nothing she could do. Katie Rose hoped Mason could help Callie put her fears and jealousies aside.

* * * *

Callie's telephone rang about 11:20 p.m. She had been waiting for Mason's call. Normally, Callie was joyous about his calls, but tonight, Callie was anything but happy.

"Hi, baby, how was your day?" Mason asked when he heard Callie's voice say hello.

Callie gave the odd response, "Eye-opening."

"Eye-opening?" Mason repeated with a chuckle. "What does that mean?" He was curious.

"Before I answer that, I'd like to ask you a few questions," Callie disclosed.

"Callie, is everything okay?" Mason inquired. Her voice sounded funny. Usually, Callie's voice sounded light and cheerful. Tonight, she sounded much too serious. *She almost sounds like she's pissed about something.*

"That's what I'm trying to determine…if everything is okay," Callie replied.

"Everything…like…*what*?" Mason asked. "I'm fine. The band tour is going fantastic. The only thing that would make life more perfect is if you were here with me. But at least I'm due home in three days for Christmas."

"So you're lonely without me?" Callie interrogated.

"Of course," he agreed. "What kind of a question is that? I miss you like crazy, Callie. I'm counting the next few days by the hours…even by the minutes…so I can have you back in my arms, where you belong."

"Isn't that sweet," she mocked.

Mason was taken aback by the condescending tone of Callie's voice. *Something's definitely wrong.*

"Callie, what's up?" Mason dared to ask.

"How much of your *lonely* time have you been spending with Fawn, Mason? Why don't you enlighten me?"

"*Fawn*?" Mason questioned, sounding stumped.

"Don't pretend you don't know what I'm talking about, Mason!" Callie warned. She also raised her voice an octave.

She is good and pissed! Mason ascertained. *How does Callie know I've been spending some of my time with Fawn?* "We've gone out to dinner a few times," he allowed Callie to pull forth the truth. "It helps pass the time, but it still does not mean I don't miss you, Callie. Fawn is *only* a friend. You are the *only* woman I love."

"Why exactly should I believe this?" Callie challenged with noted antagonism.

"Why would you not?"

"Well, let's try because you have been lying to me. If you'll lie to me about one thing, who's to say you aren't lying to me about other things as well?" Callie accused.

"When have I lied to you?" Mason inquired in bewilderment.

"We talked about you and Fawn *hanging out* together when you were home last time. I specially told you I did not like you spending time with her. I asked you not to do it. But you did it anyway, and you were going to keep it secret from me. Weren't you, Mason? Omission is a lie too. Don't even try to deny it! You've been going out with Fawn several times over the last two weeks. You've called me almost every night since you've been gone. You haven't mentioned a single one of your dinners with Fawn. If they are so innocent, why have you kept your time with *her* secret?! Can you explain this to me?"

"Because I was afraid of the very thing that is taking place," Mason tried to defend. "You are jealous of Fawn, Callie. You have no reason to be, but you are. I didn't want you to go ballistic. You have absolutely no reason to. How'd you find out I was spending time with Fawn anyway?"

"There were several pictures of you with Fawn in the Star Inquirer," Callie revealed. "The reporters know more about your life than I do. Imagine how that makes me feel?"

There are pictures of me in the tabloids? Mason took a second to accept. He was both shocked and excited by this detail. "I'm sorry, Callie. I didn't mean to hurt your feelings," Mason apologized.

"Are you really sorry?"

"Of course. Why?"

"Because if you are, you will prove it to me," Callie goaded.

"How so?"

"If Fawn means nothing to you, you will stop spending time with her. This shouldn't be a hard thing for you to do. Right?"

"It would *not* be a hard thing for me to do," Mason agreed. "But I don't like you giving me ultimatums, Callie. I need to know you trust me. If we don't have trust, we don't have anything."

"How true!" Callie concurred. "You are the one messing with *our* trust. Not me!"

Both Callie and Mason were silent for a few moments. Both were letting the others words sink in. Mason almost felt as if Callie was pushing him into a corner. He did not appreciate her saying 'do this, or else!'. However, on the other hand, he understood Callie's words were coming from a sense of jealousy and loneliness. She missed him immensely when he was gone, as he did her.

"So what will it be, Mason?!" Callie demanded to know.

"I'm not going to do something that threatens our relationship, Callie. I don't like that you don't trust me with Fawn. But if it bothers you that much for me to be with her, I won't hang out with Fawn anymore."

"Do you promise me, Mason?" Callie probed.

"Yes, I promise I won't go out with Fawn anymore," he assured her.

Callie was enormously relieved. Mason would keep his word to her. Callie *did* trust Mason. She did *not* trust Fawn. *Not with my fiancé! I've done what I needed to. Fawn is a much too attractive woman. Maybe she and Mason are* just *friends. But I can't chance they might become more.* "Thank you, Mason," she said.

Mason could almost hear the stress leaving Callie's voice. *I'm doing the right thing. Callie is the most important thing to me. I like Fawn, and I like getting away from the bus and the guys for awhile. But Callie's feelings are much more important. I only have to stick out being on the road for three more days; then I'll be home for a day.* "I love you from the bottom of my heart, Callie. You have to realize I would do anything for you," Mason declared.

I love you from the bottom of my heart too, Mason. I won't allow some other woman to waltz in and steal you away from me. "I do realize this," Callie confirmed. "I love you more than I can put into words, Mason. I can't imagine if I ever lost you…."

"You don't ever have to imagine that, Callie. Because it's never going to happen. Put that out of your mind!" Mason demanded.

"I will," she promised him. "Let's put all this all aside, and pretend it never occurred. Why don't you tell me about your day?" Callie was sounding much more lighthearted.

"Never mind about my day," Mason said with a laugh. "Was I really in the Star Inquirer? That's really something! I must be hitting the big time! Did you buy a paper for the scrapbook?" he teased.

"What do you think?" Callie asked, pretending annoyance.

"Um…I'd guess…*no*. Well…that's okay. I'm sure there will be all kinds of *nice* articles about me to come out soon."

"For sure!" Callie agreed.

She was glad to be conversing with Mason on a cheerful basis again. She felt much better. Callie would be counting the minutes until Mason was home again. She would never want for Christmas day to end. *Mason is still all* mine. *He'll be home soon, even if it is only for a day. I'll make him very glad that's he's decided to put me first!*

* * * *

147

Katie Rose and BJ were making love. Katie Rose had her eyes closed and was lost in the moment. Her body was fully relaxed. An intoxicating sensation began to rock her body. Katie Rose was in the midst of a rip-roaring orgasm.

All at once, Garrison's face floated into her consciousness. *No!* she rejected. However, as hard as Katie Rose tried, she could not erase the image. BJ joined with Katie Rose, and the two rocked together, but Katie Rose was still visualizing Garrison.

She could not help picturing she was with Garrison. Katie Rose clung to BJ, and the two climaxed together with dizzying intensity. BJ was slow to separate his body from Katie Rose's. He rolled onto his side, facing her. "Wow!" BJ exclaimed. "That…that was awesome! That was the best it's ever been between us."

BJ's words were jarringly true. She had been with BJ physically, but mentally, she had been making love to Garrison. *How could this happen?!* Katie Rose agonized with self-reproach. *I've been keeping my distance from Garrison. I haven't seen him in almost two weeks. Why am I having thoughts…or fantasies…about him? It doesn't make sense!*

However, even though Katie Rose had not seen Garrison in almost two weeks, she had still been unable to force him from her thoughts. In fact, she thought about him, on and off, a great deal. These wayward thoughts eventually would end, but tonight's incident deeply concerned her.

"So what brought about all that passion?" BJ asked. He reached to lightly run his fingers through Katie Rose's hair.

"Wh…what?" she asked in slight alarm.

"Sorry…I interrupted your thoughts, didn't I? Were you still thinking about it?" BJ further questioned. "It was incredible!"

No, I'm thinking about another man, Katie Rose accepted, guilt stricken. "I'm just very relaxed right now, BJ," Katie Rose lied. She was anything but relaxed.

"Me too, sweetie," he said with a blissful smile.

BJ gathered Katie Rose in his arms, and he gave her a kiss on her lips. He continued to hold her. Soon, BJ fell into a light slumber.

Katie Rose carefully slipped out of his arms. BJ felt her move and stirred. "Where are you going?" he asked, drowsy.

"To the bathroom. I'll be back," Katie Rose promised.

"Okay. Hurry back," he murmured.

Katie Rose watched as BJ rolled over on his other side. He was back asleep within a few moments. She stood, went over to the closet and pulled out a robe. She slid it on and crept from the room.

What happened in there? She was asking herself in disgust. Katie Rose made her way down the hallway and into the living room. Dejectedly, she had a seat on the couch. *What am I going to do?*

Katie Rose wanted to talk to someone about what had transpired. *It can't be mom. She has already told me I should be honest with BJ about my feelings for Garrison. But I haven't told him, and I don't intend to. I only want to erase Garrison from my mind. This process has to come about in time, if we stay apart. But why did I fantasize about Garrison tonight while I was making love to BJ? And why did it bring about so much passion in me? This madness has got to stop. I'll lose my mind if it doesn't.*

Katie Rose found herself picking up the phone. She dialed Callie's number. Callie answered on the first ring.

"Hi," Katie Rose said. "Did I wake you?" It was almost midnight.

"No. I just hung up from talking to Mason," Callie admitted. "What's up?" she asked with concern. It was not like Katie Rose to call this late.

"How did your conversation with Mason go?" Katie Rose changed the subject for a few moments. *Maybe if I concentrate on something else, Garrison will totally leave my thoughts.*

"F-i-n-e," Callie slowly uttered. "You did not call me at midnight to talk about my conversation with your brother. What's wrong?"

"Um...." Katie Rose stuttered. She was reconsidering having this discussion with Callie. *I can trust Callie, but is talking about it going to help?*

"Okay...I need a bit more than that," Callie teased.

This comment caused Katie Rose to laugh and relax. "It's late. You were probably headed to bed. I shouldn't have called...."

"Why don't you let me worry about when I go to bed. If you need to talk to me about something, I'm here. Okay?"

"Thanks," Katie Rose said. "I...I don't even know how to start."

"Why don't you try one word at a time?" Callie suggested.

"Okay...." Katie Rose agreed. "Here goes," she said. Then she rushed on, "Garrison and I kissed in my office almost two weeks ago, and now I can't get him out of my head. In fact, he popped into my mind while BJ and I were making love a little while ago."

"You...did you say you and Garrison have kissed?!" Callie questioned, incredulous. Katie Rose had mentioned Garrison to Callie. Callie knew he was an architect and was working with Greathouse Construction. But her friend had not mentioned any attraction to this man.

"Yes, I did," Katie Rose confirmed.

"Was this a...'Garrison kissed you and you slapped his face' sort of thing, or did you reciprocate his kiss?"

"I reciprocated," Katie Rose confessed in shame.

"Oh my God! How did this happen?" Callie demanded to know. She was awestruck.

"I don't know," Katie Rose admitted. "It wasn't something I planned. I felt terrible when it happened. I feel terrible tonight about fantasizing about Garrison while I was in bed with BJ. I don't know what to do, Callie!"

"Are you still working with Garrison?"

"No. I told him I wanted nothing more to do with him. Garrison is still working with Greathouse, and I've seen him in the building a few times. But I haven't talked to him in almost two weeks. I don't want to hurt BJ. But I don't know how to get this guy out of my head."

"Does BJ know about 'the kiss'?"

"No."

"So do you intend to keep this whole thing a secret from him? What about trust? I just had a conversation with Mason about this very thing. You can't keep secrets between the two of you, Katie Rose."

"But, Callie, if I tell BJ, it will hurt him. I don't want to do hurt him."

"And if it comes out somewhere down the road, what do you think it will do to BJ? Look at how upset I was about Mason being with Fawn and his not telling me."

"What was that all about?" Katie Rose changed the subject again for a few seconds.

"Nothing major, but the problem was Mason was keeping secrets from me. You need to talk to BJ, Katie Rose."

Another person telling me to confess all.   First, mom.   Then, Garrison.   Now, Callie.

"You're right," Katie Rose conceded.

"I know I am," Callie said with conviction. "You need to keep things honest between you and BJ. Unless you intend to break your engagement to BJ and run off with Garrison. Trust is as important as love."

Didn't my mom tell me this too? "I know," Katie Rose agreed again. "Thanks for talking with me, Callie. I needed an ear."

"I can understand," Callie empathized. "You know you can call me anytime; don't you? I love you, Katie Rose. We've been best friends all our lives. That's what best friends are for."

"I know. I love you too, Callie. Thanks for everything."

"Let me know what happens," Callie told her.

"I will," Katie Rose promised. "Good night."

"Good night," Callie said.

Katie Rose hung up. She stood, and she trudged back down the hallway. Katie Rose slid into bed beside BJ. She slid her arms around him and pulled her body in close to his.

I need to talk to BJ about Garrison, she tried to resign herself. However, Katie Rose was still besieged by grave doubts.

Chapter 17

Christmas

It was Christmas Eve. But nothing was normal about today. The weather was not right. There were no swirling snowflakes falling outside. Quite the opposite, the day was sunny, and it was downright warm for Christmas – forty-five degrees.

Mason was still not home. He would not be back in town until tomorrow at 8:00 a.m. – at least this was when his plane was supposed to land. Jackie Lynn realized she would see little of her son. He and Callie only had the one day to spend together, and then Mason would be out of town for four more weeks.

The worse thing missing from Christmas this year, of course, was Long Wolf. Jackie Lynn found her heart aching as she awoke the morning of Christmas Eve. She felt a vast sense of loss. She and Long Wolf and the children always celebrated Christmas together on Christmas Eve. They shared an enormous dinner – with turkey, dressing, cranberries, green beans, mashed potatoes, and yams. Then they all settled in the living room around the big Christmas tree and exchanged gifts. It was always a heartwarming time for all of them.

This year, however, Flora would be hosting dinner at her house. She was baking the turkey and making the dressing. Each of the others – Jackie Lynn, Katie Rose and BJ, Callie and Mary Julia would be bringing a dish to round out the dinner. This would be who Jackie Lynn would celebrate Christmas as a family with this year. She anguished over Long Wolf's absence.

As usual, Flora and Mary Julia were attuned to her feelings. Each of them called to talk with her during the day. Katie Rose also called. *Mom must be thinking about daddy, because I've been thinking about him all day.* She was saddened he would not be there sharing Christmas with them this year. However, she did not share this depressing thought with her mom. She merely called to check on her.

An unexpected visit from Samuel caught Jackie Lynn off guard. "Hi, Jackie Lynn, how are you?" he asked when she opened the door.

"Hi, Samuel, Merry Christmas," she greeted him with more enthusiasm than she felt. All of the calls from friends and family had helped, but Jackie Lynn could not seem to shake her melancholy.

"I'd say the same to you, but I know it's not merry," Jackie Lynn was surprised to hear Samuel say with sympathetic eyes. "I remember only too well how hard my first Christmas was without Amanda. That's why I decided to stop by."

"That's sweet," Jackie Lynn replied with a bittersweet smile. "Come in."

She stepped back and ushered him into the house. She led him down the hallway and into the living room. "Can I take your coat? Would you like something to drink?"

Samuel discarded the short jacket he was wearing. He handed it to Jackie Lynn. He was wearing a bright red polo shirt with a small Santa crest. "I just came from having lunch, so I'm not thirsty. But thanks for the offer."

Jackie Lynn took his coat, and Samuel made his way into the living room. Jackie Lynn left the room to hang Samuel's jacket in a closet in the hallway. He took a seat on the sofa and waited for her return. When she came back into the living room, she sat in the recliner across from him.

"So how are you doing today, Jackie Lynn?" Samuel asked. His hands were folded across his waist and he was studying her intently.

"Actually, today is very hard. I haven't felt this sad about Long Wolf in a long while," she admitted with mournful eyes.

Samuel was the first person she had been honest with regarding her feelings. No one else had asked. They merely called and talked with her awhile. They tried to keep her mind occupied – to prevent her from thinking about Long Wolf – but none of them actually broached the subject. Jackie

Lynn did her level best to put on a happy facade for Flora, Mary Julia and Katie Rose.

"Yes, today is hard. We're all more sentimental around the holidays – especially Christmas. I wanted to be an ear in case you need one. I've even got a strong shoulder if you need a good cry."

Samuel's kind words touched Jackie Lynn more than she wished. All at once, she did find herself crying. It was the first time she had cried over Long Wolf in months. It was also the first time she had cried over him with Samuel.

Samuel vacated the couch. He offered Jackie Lynn a hand and gently pulled her to her feet. He pulled her into his arms. "That's okay, Jackie Lynn, cry all you need. I'm here. I know it hurts." Samuel wished he could take away her pain, but he could not. He was glad he had come over.

Jackie Lynn allowed herself to freely cry for several moments. She slowly reined in her haywire emotions. *It feels nice to be held and comforted by a man*, she allowed herself to accept. Long Wolf had always had a special knack for calming her and making her feel better by holding her. She had not realized how much she missed that until now. "I'm sorry, Samuel…." she began to apologize, pulling back from him.

"No…no," he interrupted her. He led her to the couch, and the two of them sat down side by side. "Do not apologize to me, Jackie Lynn. I did not come over here expecting you to hold back your emotions. I came to comfort you. You needed a good cry. I'm glad I could be here for you."

"I appreciate it, Samuel. More than you know," Jackie Lynn said. She was looking into his caring eyes. *He such a nice man.* She felt better. It occurred to her all at once, *He's all alone on Christmas Eve too.* "Samuel, where are you celebrating Christmas?" she asked.

"I'll go to my sister's place tomorrow for dinner," he answered. He sounded a little despondent himself.

"So you don't have dinner plans tonight?"

"Tonight? No," he replied.

"How would you like to come to dinner with me?" She was amazed to hear herself ask. *He's been so sweet, and he still misses his wife. He shouldn't be alone on Christmas Eve.* "Flora is hosting Christmas this year."

"Oh, I don't want to intrude…" he started to object.

"You would *not* be intruding. We would be happy to have you. So how about it?"

"Well, when you put it like that…" he said with a chuckle, "How can I refuse?"

"You can't," Jackie Lynn prodded. "Why don't you come back by about 6:00? You can drive us to Flora's."

"Okay. Thanks, Jackie Lynn," he said with a smile.

"Thank *you*, Samuel," she said in sincere gratitude. She was glad to see his blue eyes dancing with happiness. He had helped to lift her burden a bit. She was glad to be helping him as well.

* * * *

Katie Rose was getting ready to go to Flora's for Christmas Eve dinner. She had showered, dressed – in a Christmas sweater and dress slacks – put on makeup, and was fixing her hair. BJ came into the bathroom. He was wearing the gifts Katie Rose had bought him for Christmas: a beige men's sweater, with a black diamond pattern running throughout, khaki pants, tan dress socks, and light brown, casual, leather, Rockport shoes.

"You look nice," she told him with an approving smile.

"So do you," he said as he came up behind her and kissed the side of her neck. "Except…something seems to be missing…"

"Oh, and what is that?" Katie Rose asked with curiosity. She turned sideways on her vanity chair to face BJ. Katie Rose still had not talked to BJ about Garrison. She did not intend to until after Christmas anyway.

"This," he answered. BJ brought his hands from behind his back and held out a small box to her.

"What is this?" she questioned. BJ had given her a bottle of perfume and a nice card for her Christmas gift.

"Why don't you open it and find out," he urged. BJ was anxious to see Katie Rose's expression.

She pulled the red Christmas ribbon loose. She tore into the paper with excitement. She lifted the top off the box and saw what looked like a ring box. *What is this? He's already proposed. It can't be a ring. Unless it's for the other hand.* Katie Rose pulled forth the ring box and snapped open the lid. Two, small, sparkling diamonds met her eyes.

"BJ!" she exclaimed, as she carefully released the earrings from their holder. "These…these are beautiful. But…you…you can't afford something like this."

"You are my fiancé. I wanted to do something extra special this Christmas to celebrate that. Don't worry about what I can afford. There is plenty of overtime pay to be made. So I'll find a way to pay for the earrings. Put them on. I want to see how they look."

Katie Rose placed the earrings in her ears. As she looked at herself in the bathroom mirror, she saw tears standing in her eyes. *He loves me so much. He deserves better than what he is getting. No more Garrison. I'll find a way to make him disappear from my mind. I can't hurt BJ.*

"I love you, Katie Rose. Merry Christmas," he said, and bent to give her a kiss.

"I love you too," she said, and met his lips for an eager, thank you kiss.

* * * *

Mason's plane arrived ahead of schedule the next morning. Callie was waiting for him when he came through the gate. She tossed herself into his arms, and the two stood kissing for several moments. They were oblivious to all the hundreds of others who were walking past them in the airport.

"Merry Christmas, Callie," Mason said with an enormous smile when they eventually came up for air. It was early in the morning, but Callie still looked extraordinary. She had pulled her hair back in a ponytail but left a few stray curls along her face. She had taken the time to put on makeup for him. The flesh her low-cut, V-neck sweater revealed teased Mason a bit.

"Merry Christmas, Mason," she said back. His hair was uncombed and he badly needed a shave. But Mason still looked incredible to Callie. She was glad to have him home.

He dropped his arm around her waist. Callie placed hers on top of his, slipping her hand into the back pocket of his jeans. "Let's go home. I don't want to waste a second of this day," Callie proposed in a husky voice.

"Me either," Mason agreed.

Callie's eyes glowed with love as they briskly raced off.

Chapter 18

Suggestions & Suspicion

It was January. Jackie Lynn was having dinner with Flora and Mary Julia. They had gone to a nearby Mexican restaurant – Border Patrol. The smell of hot, steaming fajitas at a nearby table made all of their mouths water. They snacked on chips and salsa and drank their soft drinks while they waited for their dinner orders to arrive. The restaurant was fairly crowded. They served good food.

Festive Mexican music could be heard throughout the restaurant. Colorful Mexican paintings decorated the walls. Several televisions were positioned up high all around the restaurant. They all were tuned to some sport's channel. The sound on them had been muted. None of the ladies were paying any attention to them anyway.

This was the second night Jackie Lynn had been out to dinner this week. She went to dinner with Samuel a few nights ago. Once again, she enjoyed herself. Samuel asked her if she would like to see a movie with him the following weekend. Jackie Lynn was ambivalent, so she declined Samuel's offer. Going to the movies together seemed more like a date than going out to dinner did. Plus, it would mean Jackie Lynn would have been seeing Samuel twice in the same week. The last thing she wanted to do was lead Samuel on. He was lonely, and truth be told, so was she. However, she still could not imagine herself ever loving any other man but Long Wolf.

As if her friends could read her mind, Flora asked Jackie Lynn, "How did your dinner with Samuel go the other night?" She dipped a chip in the mild sauce and stuck it in her mouth.

"It went well," Jackie Lynn told her friends with a smile. "I like Samuel. He was always such a wonderful friend to Long Wolf, and he's a good friend to me as well."

"Is that all he is...a friend?" Mary Julia dared to inquire. She also placed a chip – hers with hot sauce – into her mouth. She immediately took a drink of soda.

"Yes. Samuel is only a friend," Jackie Lynn assured both of her friends. "It's much too soon for our relationship to be anything but friendship." Jackie Lynn mixed the two sauces and also indulged in some chips. That was the only thing she did not like about eating at a Mexican restaurant. She always ended up overeating, because the chips and salsa were so addictive.

"But...if it weren't so soon...as you put it? What might your relationship with Samuel be?" Flora probed.

"I don't know. I can't even think that way, Flora. I can't imagine another man being in my life. My heart was given entirely to Long Wolf, and it still belongs to him," Jackie Lynn maintained with loyalty. She had a somber expression on her face.

"Jackie Lynn," Flora spoke her name with compassion. She reached to pat her friend's hand. "I understand. I was shattered when I lost Kenny, and I still love him. I always will. But life goes on. And you know what? Kenny and Long Wolf would want it to go on. You don't honestly believe Long Wolf would want you to be alone, pining for him, the rest of your life, do you?"

"Flora's right, Jackie Lynn," Mary Julia joined in. "Long Wolf loved you a great deal. He would want you to be as happy as possible. Samuel is a good man. He might be able to help fill some of the gap Long Wolf's death has left in your life."

Jackie Lynn challenged her friends, "Neither of you are dating. Why are you encouraging me to do so?" She chomped down on another beckoning chip.

"I would date again if the opportunity arose," Flora alleged, dipping another chip in the salsa as well. "I don't know what man would want me now that I've gotten so much heavier, and it's hard to begin dating a stranger anyway. But I've had amazing luck with two men in my life, which I loved and lost. Never mind the horrible experience I had with Jacob. But you know Samuel, Jackie Lynn. Long Wolf thought highly of him. You should not deny yourself the chance to get to know him better – the chance to bring happiness back into your life. You are doing disservice to Long Wolf's memory if you do."

"I agree," Mary Julia chimed in once more. She pushed the hot sauce to the side, as she waited on a refill for her drink. "And for the record, I would also date again if the opportunity arose. My divorce from Jonathan, after being married for so long, was traumatizing, to say the least. And for a while, I did not think I ever wanted another man in my life. But I do miss the companionship of a man. Not that I don't enjoy hanging out with the two of you. It has been wonderful we could be there for one another, as we have."

"Amen!" Flora agreed. She raised her plastic Coca-Cola glass in the air.

"I'll second that," Jackie Lynn agreed with a grateful smile, raising her own glass. Mary Julia followed suit with her glass full of ice. The three ladies clicked them together in a toast. "I truly don't know if I could have overcome my grief over Long Wolf's death if it hadn't been for the two of you."

"Why don't you take our sage advice then?" Flora encouraged. She pointed a chip toward Jackie Lynn and shook it. She had not dipped it in the sauce yet. "Don't close yourself off, Jackie Lynn. Let happen what may with Samuel. You may find you are glad you did."

"I promise I'll give it some thought. How would that be?" Jackie Lynn asked both her friends with a warm smile. She drank some more of her soda.

"It's a terrific start!" Flora stated with enthusiasm.

Their server came to the table with their dinner orders. Once he had unloaded the hot plates from his arms, he scurried away with Mary Julia and Jackie Lynn's glasses to get them a refill. Jackie Lynn was still thinking about what her friends had said. *I don't know if I'm ready to date again,* she was still debating. *But I can still be a friend to Samuel. Dinner every now and then certainly cannot hurt.*

* * * *

Jackie Lynn had only been home a little over an hour. She had already changed into her pajamas, and she was sitting on the couch, with her legs folded under her, reading a book. The phone rang ripping her out of her solitude. Jackie Lynn glanced at the clock on the mantle. *It's after ten. Wonder who is calling this late?* she mused.

Jackie Lynn picked up the telephone on the third ring. "Hello," she said.

"Hi. I'm not calling too late, am I?" It was Samuel's voice.

"No," Jackie Lynn assured him. "I went to dinner with Flora and Mary Julia tonight, so I haven't been home that long. I was just winding down by reading a good book."

"Oh, really. I enjoy reading too." Samuel shared. *Something else we have in common.* "What book are you reading?"

"I doubt you've heard of it. It's a women's fiction novel by a local author. It's called Bluegrass. It's about the trials and tribulations of a young actress."

"Sounds interesting," he commented. "I lean more to murder mysteries."

"Oh, I enjoy those too," Jackie Lynn shared.

Samuel changed the subject then, asking, "So how did dinner with the ladies go?"

"Fine," Jackie Lynn replied. *They were trying to match make and set me up with you.*

"Well, I was thinking about you and thought I would give you a call. I didn't mean to interrupt your quiet time."

"No, you didn't. Really," Jackie Lynn asserted, even though he had somewhat disturbed her.

"I wanted to tell you again that I enjoyed being with you the other night, Jackie Lynn," Samuel confessed. "I also wanted to try and twist your arm again. Have you given any more thought to going to see a movie with me this weekend?"

Quite a bit! Especially after the talk with the girls tonight. "Actually, I have," Jackie Lynn admitted.

"And...?"

"And...it sounds like fun. Yes, I will go to the movies with you this weekend, Samuel," Jackie Lynn said with a chuckle. *He is easy to talk to, and I do feel comfortable around him. What could sharing a movie hurt?*

"Wonderful!" Samuel almost cheered.

Jackie Lynn was glad to hear the happiness in his voice. *I'm doing the right thing. This isn't some big romance. Just two friends of the opposite sex going out together.*

"How about we go to dinner first? I'll bring the paper with me. And we'll decide what movie we want to see while we eat. How would that be?"

"That sounds great!" Jackie Lynn agreed with enthusiasm.

"Good!" Samuel rejoiced again. "Well, I'm not going to keep you. I'll let you get back to your book and settling down for the night. I'll plan on picking you up at 6:00 p.m. on Saturday."

"I'll see you then," Jackie Lynn concurred.

"Bye," Samuel said. "Have a good night."

"You have a good night too," Jackie Lynn returned his well-wishes.

I will. You won't regret going out with me, Jackie Lynn. I'll take things slow. I won't push anything. But I enjoy spending time with you, and I'd like to see our relationship grow in time.

As Jackie Lynn hung up the phone, she realized she was smiling. *Maybe talking to Samuel, and spending time with him,* is *good for me. After all, the girls have never led me astray. Long Wolf, I'll always love you, but Flora and Mary Julia are right. You would not want me to be lonely.*

Jackie Lynn picked her book up and began reading where she had left off. She felt content and at peace – a good feeling after so many months of painful turmoil.

* * * *

It had been over a month since Katie Rose had talked to Garrison. Still, she could not totally shake him from her mind. She hated making love with BJ anymore.

If Katie Rose did not fantasize about being with Garrison, she could not have an orgasm. *Yet, I'm betraying BJ when I allow Garrison to enter my thoughts in the bedroom.* This was exasperating for her. Katie Rose could not believe this nonsense was occurring, and she did not have a clue what to do about it. *I thought everything would be better by now. Why does it seem as if it's only getting worse?*

BJ had observed changes in Katie Rose. She was less talkative and more contemplative. He was also aware of a difference in Katie Rose when they made love. Sometimes their lovemaking was very intense, and BJ could tell Katie Rose was almost delirious with pleasure. Other times, he feared she might only be going through the motions with him and faking her enjoyment.

BJ was distraught. He wanted every one of their sexual experiences to be extraordinary, for both of them. However, when he questioned Katie Rose, she assured him everything was 'great'.

BJ wondered if their wedding was what had Katie Rose so uptight. It was only three months away now. *Is she having second thoughts about marrying me?* BJ did not want to ask this question. *What if Katie Rose says yes? What do I do?*

Regardless of his fears, BJ made up his mind he needed to talk to her. BJ wished for them to have the happiest of marriages. Therefore, he wanted to make sure all was well before their wedding day arrived.

He and Katie Rose were relaxing on the couch after dinner one evening. Her mind seemed to be miles away. *I need to find out exactly what is going on in that head of hers.* "Katie Rose," BJ called in a soft voice. Since she was so deep in thought, he did not wish to startle her.

"What?" she asked. Katie Rose could not help but notice the solemn expression on his face.

"A penny for your thoughts," BJ said and reached to gently caress one of her shoulders.

You wouldn't want to even pay a penny for what I was thinking, Katie Rose concluded. She had been thinking about Garrison again. He was at Greathouse again today. They had not spoken, but he had given Katie Rose a hard stare. Katie Rose attempted not to make eye contact, but she was not able to help herself. She dashed in the opposite direction and took refuge in her office, but she thought about Garrison all day, as she had been tonight.

"I don't know what I was thinking." Katie Rose decided to be deceptive. *Garrison is out of our lives. There is no sense talking about him with BJ. I need to put him out of my mind.*

"You've seemed uptight about something for some time now," BJ stated. "I've asked you what was bothering you, and you always say 'nothing'. But something is on your mind a lot. I need for you to tell me what it is. It's important we share things, Katie Rose. You can tell me anything."

"I know," she said and gave him an obliging smile. Katie Rose also reached and began rubbing BJ's hand. "I don't have anything I need to talk to you about. Everything is fine."

"How about the wedding? Is everything fine with that too?" he gathered the courage to question.

"The wedding?" Katie Rose asked and shrugged her shoulders. "Mom, Flora and Mary Julia are all helping out with that. Everything is coming together great. Why do you ask?"

"Well…I don't mean the wedding exactly. What I'm actually asking is…you aren't having doubts about marrying me, are you?"

"What?!" Katie Rose declared in astonishment. "Why would you even think that, BJ?"

"I don't know. Your mind is always wandering lately. I thought maybe you were worrying about what you are about to get yourself into. If you are having doubts, I need to know," BJ insisted.

"No," Katie Rose stressed. "I am *not* having doubts about marrying you, BJ. That isn't what all this is about."

"What is the 'all this' you mentioned?" he dared to continue to scrutinize.

Why did I put it like that? Katie Rose reprimanded herself. "I don't know," she hedged. "I guess 'all this' is…a little bit of everything. You're right; I do have a lot on my mind. But everything is fine with us. In fact, I look forward to marrying you, BJ. Then I'll truly be all yours, and nothing can come between us."

"What could come between us?"

Nothing. Because I won't let it. "Nothing!" she spoke out loud as well. Katie Rose was trying to convince herself as much as she was trying to persuade BJ.

"Okay. I only have one more question. Is everything okay between us sexually? Are you always satisfied?"

"Geez, BJ. What is with you tonight?" Katie Rose was getting annoyed. She did not like these pointed questions. She was not being honest with BJ, and she did not intend to be. Katie Rose did not plan to tell him about her thoughts of Garrison – especially not in reference to their sex life.

"Katie Rose, it's important that we be able to talk about *everything* freely. I want us to have a great marriage."

"Me too. And we will," she pledged. She drew in and gave him a prolonged kiss. Garrison's image popped into Katie Rose's mind. *Damn!* she thought. She jerked back from BJ.

"What? Why'd you pull away like that?" BJ interrogated.

"Because you wanted to talk, and I knew what kissing you like that would lead to. I was only trying to give you taste of the passion I have for you," Katie Rose pretended. *I hate these lies!*

"Sometimes you are filled to the brim with passion. Other times, you only seem to be going through the motions. Why?"

Because in my head I'm with a different man some of the time. Stop it! Stop thinking this way! However, her reflection was true. "I don't know. Sometimes I'm more tired than others," she proposed. "Maybe it's hormones. I'm not sure. But there *isn't* a problem with our sex life. You're a little paranoid tonight, hon." *There is a problem. But it will get better. It will* all *get better once I get Garrison out of my head. It has to happen. I only wish I knew how.*

"Maybe I *am* being paranoid," BJ agreed. "But I had to make sure. I love you, Katie Rose. I want us to be happy. And things have been…I don't know…different between us these past few months. Not different bad. Just different. I wanted to make sure everything is okay."

"Everything is…read my lips…*o-k-a-y!*" she promised him. "Believe me."

"Alright," he conceded. "But you'll tell me if anything is wrong. Right?"

"Right," she consented. *As long as it is something you need to be concerned about. Garrison is nothing for you to worry about. Because he isn't in my life anymore. I'll find a way to erase him from my mind. I will!* Katie Rose was determined.

* * * *

Mason was home, at long last. He and Callie were inseparable. They could not get enough of one another. They made love over and over. They talked incessantly. They kissed, cuddled, or touched. It seemed they barely took time to eat. Each of them understood time was of the essence. They did not want to waste even a second.

Mason was supposed to be home for only two weeks. Then he would be on the road again for several weeks. Savage Pride was scheduled to make more appearances on a variety of television shows and to play many more concerts.

His life was hectic, but it was crucial for him and Savage Pride to get as much exposure to the public as possible. The band's first single was still hanging in the top ten on the charts, and they had released a second song, which had debuted at number nineteen. The more Savage Pride promoted their music, the more familiar, and popular, their music was becoming. Mason's dream was coming true. He was becoming a recording star. People were falling in love with Savage Pride's music, and Mason was proud to have written many of the band's songs.

Callie had mixed emotions about Mason's newfound success. Since Mason was so happy, she was happy for him. However, she did not like the fact they had to be separated so much. Callie had a pervasive fear that Mason's musical career would eventually come between them.

She and Mason were snuggling on the couch Sunday evening. Callie shared with Mason that she dreaded going to work the next day. "I don't want to be separated from you," she said and gave him a prolonged, persistent kiss. "Just having the evenings together is not enough time."

"I agree," Mason told her with a conniving grin.

"So what do I do? Call in sick? Sneak you into work with me? We'd have to find an office...or some other place...with a door that locked," Callie teased.

"Uh-huh," Mason agreed. He was feeling very contented. Of course, he and Callie had made love many times that weekend. "I might have another solution."

"What?" Callie asked with curiosity. "I haven't been at this job long enough to have any vacation time. Do you want me to call in sick? I probably won't get paid...but..."

"Who cares," Mason proclaimed with a silly, almost goofy smile. "Callie, my musical career is taking off. It isn't only a pipe dream anymore. Why don't we take a chance? What is the worse thing that would happen if you quit your job?"

"Quit my job?" she repeated. She was studying him with intensity. *Is Mason serious?* "Don't tease me like that, Mason."

165

"I'm not teasing," he assured Callie. "Money is already coming in well from the sales of Savage Pride's CDs. We aren't millionaires yet. Far from it. But if we watched expenses, we would be alright living off of what is coming in from my musical career. Would you hate it if you had to quit your job?"

"Of course not. But what are you wanting me to do instead?"

"I want you to come on the road with me, Callie."

"Are you serious?" she grilled, her eyes full of excitement.

"Yes. It's not all glory though. You'd be on a bus with a bunch of rowdy, smelly guys. We'd have to sneak away for our private time. But at least we'd get to see each other each day. Being separated for weeks on end is killing me," he confessed.

"Me too," she agreed, nodding her head up and down. "I only have one question."

"What's that?" he asked.

"When do you want me to quit?"

"How about you go in tomorrow and give them your two week notice. That way you aren't burning any bridges. And you can leave with me when the tour starts in two weeks."

"That sounds great!" Callie screeched, throwing her arms around Mason's neck.

"You may not think so after a week or so on the road."

"I've lived in much worse ways," Callie uttered. Bad memories of when she had run away from home all those years ago came back to her. She could survive 'bus' life. She could survive anywhere as long as Mason was by her side. "I'll give my notice tomorrow. I can't wait to be by your side each day again!" Callie declared with newfound enthusiasm.

"I love you, baby," Mason said and smothered her lips with his.

"I love you too, Mason," she professed, wrapping her arms around his shoulders and her legs around his lower half.

"What again?" Mason inquired with a devilish spark to his eyes.

"We're going to spend a lot of time sneaking away to private spots on the bus," Callie maintained, giving him a greedy smile. "For now, let's make up for lost time."

"You don't have to ask me twice," Mason told her and began to kiss her and caress her body.

Chapter 19

Forbidden Fruit

It was the first week of February. The air was brutally cold – in the teens, with a subzero wind chill. Katie Rose was given the opportunity to escape this harsh environment for a few days. She would be flying to Anaheim, California. She was not going there to visit Disneyland. She was going there to meet with another prospect for Greathouse Construction. She was elated about this opportunity, because Greathouse had never built anything so far from home before. Her father had always stuck with the bordering states.

There was one major problem. The prospect had heard about them through the Gates Tower's project. They were looking to have a similar building erected in Anaheim. If Greathouse was contracted to construct this building, there was a good possibility that Parker Architecture would be as well. So Garrison was prone to be in California. Katie Rose would see him, and probably even have to interact with him, since she was not taking any other members of the Greathouse staff with her. She was more than a little uneasy about this fact.

Katie Rose still had not been able to erase Garrison from her mind. They had not talked to one another in over two months, and she saw less and less of him at Greathouse. But she still thought of him on occasion, especially at the worse time – when she and BJ were making love. She had finally given up and allowed herself the pleasure of fantasizing about Garrison while being intimate with BJ. *BJ doesn't know what I'm thinking about. As long as he never finds out, everything will be fine.*

Katie Rose's wedding was only a little over two months away. All of the preparations had been made. They had hired the caterer and DJ, rented a hall, passed their marriage preparation classes, and been given the green light – as well as a scheduled date at the church – by Katie Rose's parish priest. Katie Rose and her mother had picked out a beautiful wedding gown. Katie Rose had gone with BJ to pick out and reserve his tux. Katie Rose had asked Callie to be her Maid of Honor. BJ had asked his boss, Mitch, to be his Best Man. This would be their only wedding party, since BJ did not have a lot of other male friends. Mason was supposed to stand in for their father and give Katie Rose away.

Katie Rose had no intention of canceling the wedding, even if she did dream of Garrison on many occasions. Everything would be perfect between BJ and her once they got married. Her attraction and kiss with Garrison had only been a passing mistake.

* * * *

BJ took Katie Rose to the airport. She flew out on a Sunday morning.

"I'll miss you," he told her. He was holding both her gloved hands and gazing into her eyes.

"Me too," Katie Rose agreed. They were standing on the curb, shivering, outside the doors to the airport. She had already checked her one suitcase with the curbside baggage handler. She also had one, small, carry-on bag, slung over one shoulder. Her purse was over the other. She was eager to be on her way. They both needed to get in out of the frigid air.

Katie Rose bent forward to give BJ a departing kiss. He gave her a peck on the lips. He released her hands and pulled her to him for a devoted embrace. "You're going to call me each night, right?" he questioned, pulling back from her so he could look into her enthralling green eyes.

"Of course," she agreed with a confirming smile.

BJ pulled her in for a couple more hurried kisses. He grudgingly released her. "Bye. I'll see you soon."

"Bye," she said and turned and started away. She grabbed the chilled handle and pulled open the heavy glass door. Before she went through the second one, she turned and watched BJ climbing into his car. It had been parked beside them, running, with the flashers on. *It's nice to be missed by someone*, she thought, feeling warm and fuzzy, despite the arctic weather. She pulled open the other glass door and stepped into the airport.

* * * *

It did not take Katie Rose long to run into Garrison. They were on the same flight to California. She saw him first. She had already been seated in her aisle seat. He was placing his large carry-on in one of the overhead bins a few rows up from her. He had taken off his winter jacket and slung it into his seat. Garrison was wearing a gray T-shirt. Katie Rose could see his chest and arm muscles ripple as he reached into the air to secure his luggage. She also noticed the curve of his butt cheeks in his jeans. She hated the familiar yearnings seeing Garrison again arose in her. She pulled one of the airplane magazines out of the slot in front of her and attempted to focus on reading it instead.

* * * *

Garrison first saw Kate in Chicago at Midway Airport. She had already taken a seat at the gate and appeared to be reading a book. She had not curled her long hair. In the work environment, it normally had some wave to it, or Katie Rose had it pulled back in some manor. Today, her shimmering, straight, ebony hair lay unruffled down her back and along the sides of her face. *It looks attractive this way as well. I'd love to run my fingers through it, or feather it over my bare chest. Cool it, Garrison!*

Katie Rose had on an aqua sweater, which conformed well to her bust line. She also was wearing blue jeans and sneakers. She looked very relaxed. They had a half hour layover until their connecting flight to Los Angeles arrived.

Garrison was trying to keep from staring. *We'll probably be on the same shuttle from LAX Airport to the hotel. I knew I would be seeing* her *this trip, but I didn't know it would be so soon. Why does the sight of her always make it hard for me to breath normally?* Each time he had seen Kate at Greathouse, over the past two months, had been torture.

He wanted to chase after her – to convince her he was the man for her – but then her cruel words would come back to him. Garrison refused to give in to his desire. He would not prove to Kate that he was only a playboy –

someone who wanted to break off her engagement. *If Kate is foolish enough to marry into a passionless marriage, then so be it.*

Garrison turned and headed toward one of the airport stores. *I'll find something to read as well. I don't want Kate to catch me staring at her. Maybe I can stick my head in some book on the shuttle from the airport. Then we won't have to talk.* He scampered off to the store.

* * * *

Their prospect, McMillan Brothers, had arranged to have a gentleman waiting for them at the gate at LAX Airport. He was holding a sign which read, *Greathouse Construction & Parker Architecture.* Katie Rose felt her stomach tumble. *Garrison and I are going to be riding in the same car to the hotel.* She turned her head and saw he was only several paces behind her.

"Hello, I'm Katherine Rose Greathouse," she introduced herself to the man with the sign.

"Hello, ma'am," the gentleman replied and shook her hand. He was wearing a black hat, suit and shoes. He was clearly a limo driver.

Katie Rose looked down at her feet as Garrison approached them. "I'm Garrison Parker from Parker Architecture," he announced himself. Katie Rose's spine tingled as she heard his baritone voice resonate. *I've missed hearing his voice,* she recognized.

"Nice to meet you, sir," the driver replied. "We'll go and retrieve your luggage. Then I'll lead you to my car. Welcome to Los Angeles. I hope you'll enjoy your stay in Anaheim."

"Thanks," Katie Rose and Garrison said, almost in unison. As the three of them walked off, Katie Rose could not help but notice Garrison's memorable, fantastic smell. *I've missed his cologne,* she accepted with guilt. She moved away a bit, placing the limo driver between them.

Garrison had also caught a whiff of Katie Rose's scent. *How am I going to be able to stand riding in the car with her? She smells delicious.* His mouth was almost salivating. He was glad when Kate moved a few paces away. He moved a few paces to the other side of the limo driver. The three were walking at a wide berth. Other visitors dashed around them on both sides, as they raced through the airport.

When they came to the first escalator, Katie Rose was relieved the limo driver was a gentleman and let her get on first. There was no room for them to stand three wide on the escalators. When they arrived at baggage retrieval, the limo driver retrieved a cart. As Katie Rose and Garrison identified and pulled their suitcases off the conveyor belt, the limo driver took them and placed them on his cart. The three fell into horizontal file again and walked to the limo.

The man opened the door for them and ushered them inside the dimly lit, air-conditioned car. The windows were darkly tinted for privacy's sake. Katie Rose sat on one side, facing the front of the car, and Garrison sat on the other side, facing the rear of the car. The limo driver shut the door and went around the back of the car to load their suitcases into the trunk. Katie Rose found it strange to be in air conditioning, since it was so frigid back home. Here, in California, the sun was shining brilliantly. She guessed the temperature to be in the upper seventies. She rolled up the sleeves to her sweater. She had taken her heavy coat off in the airport. Her gloves had been stashed in the pockets of this coat. She tossed her coat on the seat beside her, with her carry-on bag and purse.

She could sense Garrison was looking at her. As she looked up and their eyes met, her suspicions were confirmed. "Hello, Kate," he spoke first. Once again, her spine tingled from the echo of his deep voice, and *his* cologne infiltrated her thoughts.

"Hi, Garrison," she politely replied. His handsome eyes, fixated on hers, caused her heartbeat to speed up. *This is ridiculous! You can ride in this car with this man. He's no one to you!*

Katie Rose gathered her purse from the seat beside her. She reached into the first compartment and pulled forth a small novel. *Read! Read and ignore him!*

Garrison was still studying her. *She's dismissing me*, he thought with some irritation, as he watched her open her book. *That's fine. We don't need to make small talk. We are here to work. I can handle a work-only relationship. I'm not some teenage. I can ignore the fact she is lovely and smells so extraordinary.*

Garrison unzipped the top compartment to his carry-on case. He pulled forth the book he had bought in the airport. *Two can play at this game*, he decided as he opened the book and stuck it in front of his face.

It took forty-five minutes to get from the Los Angeles airport to the Holiday Inn Anaheim Resort because of the heavy traffic flow on the freeways. Even though both Katie Rose and Garrison had turned many pages in their respective books, neither of them had absorbed much of what they had read. They were too engrossed in ignoring each another and disregarding forbidden pleasures.

* * * *

When they arrived at the Holiday Inn, the limo driver brought their luggage into the lobby and sat it inside the door. Both Katie Rose and Garrison gave the gentleman a tip. Katie Rose picked up her suitcase and Garrison retrieved his, and they proceeded to the counter to check in. There were two clerks available, so one took Katie Rose and the other took Garrison.

I can get my key and go to my room. I won't have to see Garrison again until tomorrow morning when we meet with the prospect, Katie Rose was thinking with some relief. However, when she heard the other clerk say to Garrison, "You're in room 509, sir", she felt sick to her stomach. *I'm in 511. That's right next door. How can our rooms be that close?*

Katie Rose picked up her luggage and started to walk toward the elevators. *I need to go to my room and be alone for awhile. This will all work out fine. Being with Garrison again is stressing me out, that's all.*

Garrison piddled around in the lobby for a few more minutes. He checked out the brochures on the table – even though they were on Disneyland and he would not be going there. He had also heard Kate's room number, so he knew their rooms were adjoining. He wanted to give her a second to catch an elevator, so they did not have to ride up together and walk down the hall to rooms that were *much too close.*

It's okay. It won't matter. Even though we're side by side, we'll probably never see each other – except for going to the meetings, and we'll see each other then anyway. It will all be okay, he assured himself. He picked up his suitcase and headed off to the elevators.

* * * *

The first thing Katie Rose did when she got to her room was call BJ and let him know she had gotten there okay. They did not talk long, since Katie Rose wanted to go and get something to eat. She had eaten brunch at 10:30 a.m., before her flight to Chicago Midway. Even though in California it was only 3:30 p.m., Katie Rose's body clock was still on its 'back home' time, which made it 6:30 p.m. A few bags of peanuts, cheese crackers, graham crackers and soft drinks were all she had consumed since 10:30. So Katie Rose was famished. When she hung up from talking with BJ, she vacated her room and went to the restaurant downstairs.

Garrison was already sitting at a table drinking a soft drink when the hostess showed Katie Rose to her table. Naturally, it was right across from Garrison. *Why can't I get away from him?*

Garrison watched as Katie Rose picked up her menu and hid behind it. *Are we constantly going to be in one another's face*, he was thinking in frustration. He had already ordered his dinner, so his menu had been taken. He looked away toward the window when the waitress came back to take Katie Rose's order and her menu.

Both Garrison and Katie Rose tried to disregard one another. On occasion, Garrison would catch a glimpse of Katie Rose glancing at him and vice versa. He wolfed down his food and left without a word. Katie Rose was thankful when he at last got up from the table. She watched him vacate the restaurant with relief. *Now I can finish what's left of my meal in peace*, she mused. She relaxed for the first time since setting eyes on Garrison that day.

* * * *

It was almost 7:30 p.m. when Katie Rose left the restaurant. She decided to go and take a look at the whirlpool. She was debating whether or not she wanted to go to her room, change into her bathing suit and spend a little time in the steamy swirling water. The warm, gentle massage of the hot tub would sooth her taut nerves. She could use something extra to help her settle down tonight. Garrison had her severely stressed out.

On the way to the pool area, she passed the fitness center. And there *he* was again. Garrison had taken his shirt off. He was all alone in the workout room, using some machine where you bent your arms at the elbows and closed and opened some weights across your chest. Katie Rose could not help observing the rippling muscles in his arms and chest. It caused things to ripple within her body. *Forget the whirlpool! I need a shower – a cold one!* she thought in frustration. She twirled and darted toward the elevators.

Garrison slammed the weights together in aggravation one last time. He had seen Katie Rose looking at him and rushing away. *What is going on today? We can't seem to get away from one another. This trip is going to be pure hell!* He walked over and picked up a towel from a nearby table and wiped the sweat from his brow. *I'm going back to my room, take a shower, and settle in for the night. I need to put* her *out of my mind!* He pitched the towel in the dirty laundry container, snatched up his discarded shirt, slipped it back on, and vacated the room in a huff.

* * * *

Katie Rose was in the bathroom, splashing her face with cold water, when she heard the door to the room beside her slam. *Is that Garrison?* A few seconds later, she heard water running in the bathroom beside her. *It is him. He's getting ready to take a shower.* Katie Rose had already stripped off her sweater and jeans. It was much too warm for sweaters and long pants in California. Not to mention the fact Garrison raised her temperature a few degrees every time she saw him. She was standing there in her bra and panties. She was glad she had brought short-sleeved blouses and T-shirts to wear for the rest of her stay.

Katie Rose discarded her underwear, turned on the shower, and stepped inside. She did not wait for the water to heat up. She wanted it to be lukewarm. *He's right beside me, naked.* Katie Rose reached to turn the water a bit cooler. The cold water was not helping her much. She was still envisioning Garrison's soapy wet body – *so close.* She turned her face up to the water and practically drowned herself, trying to expel these uninvited visions. Nothing was working.

When Garrison turned off his shower, he could hear water running on the other side of the wall from him. *Kate is taking a shower at the same time as me. Figures. We've done everything else in unison today.* He jerked a towel from the rack, picked up his comb, razor, shaving cream and aftershave from beside the sink, and stomped out of the bathroom. He could not stand to stay in the bathroom and listen to Kate showering. Each time he heard the water splash against the wall, he pictured being in that shower with her. It was driving him insane. There was a sink just outside the bathroom, so he could dry off, shave, comb his hair, and splash some aftershave on in the other room. And so he did. He also slid some boxer shorts over his arousal.

Garrison plopped down on the bed, switched on the television, and turned up the volume. He was attempting to drown out any sounds from the room beside him. *God, she'll be sleeping on the other side of the wall from me. I've got to somehow put* her *out of my mind.* He tried to focus on some dumb television show.

When Katie Rose stepped out of the shower, she found herself straining to hear more sounds of Garrison. The only sound she could make out now was his television. She dried herself off and rubbed some lotion on her legs. She had shaved her armpits and legs while she was in the shower. She stepped out of the bathroom, put on deodorant and combed her hair. She opened up her suitcase, pulled forth a black negligee and slipped it on. It was then she beheld *the door.*

That door connects to Garrison's room, she took a second to conclude. Her heart was all the sudden racing. As if the door was a magnet and she was steel, Katie Rose was drawn to it. She walked over and fingered the lock. Her mind told her not to do it, but she switched the lock open. She was staring at another closed door. She reached out and grabbed the knob. *Shut your door and lock it!* her conscience was telling her. But her mind and body were saying, *Get him to open that door!*

Garrison had gone to get a glass of water. He heard a clicking noise and thought he saw his connecting door to Kate's room move. *I must be imaging that.* However, he walked over to the door. He softly turned his lock and opened the door. He was stunned when he found Kate standing in the doorway. Katie Rose was equally astonished to be face-to-face with Garrison.

They stood in silence staring at one another for several bewildering moments. *What is she doing there? She's absolutely beautiful. I can see the whole imprint of her gorgeous body in that short, shiny nightgown. I can't stand this!*

Katie Rose's senses were reeling too. She was studying Garrison's lingering, yearning eyes and staring with her own eyes at his wet hair, bare chest, and the swelling in his boxer shorts. *I want him so bad!* She could not deny this thought, because it was true. Her desire for Garrison was earthshaking and unparalleled.

"Garrison...I...I...can't take this any longer," Katie Rose managed to utter.

Me either, he thought but did not say. Instead, he reached and pulled her into his arms. Their lips met in urgency, and they stumbled backwards into his room, kissing and caressing. "God, you smell extraordinary!" Garrison exclaimed in a rasping voice, planting hot kisses along her neck and shoulder blade.

Katie Rose had bathed with some shower gel she had brought from home. Since it had a fruit aroma, she smelled almost good enough to eat. "You do too," she said in a heated gasp. Garrison had a clean, fresh scent. It was a mixture of deodorant soap, shampoo and aftershave lotion. Katie Rose wanted to lose herself in this smell.

They staggered over to the bed and tumbled together atop the mattress. Garrison reached to grab the remote and silenced the loud television. He did not want any disturbances. He was still having trouble believing this was coming to pass. *How many nights have I dreamt of this very thing?*

Katie Rose was thinking the same thing. *It feels incredible to* actually *be in his arms.*

Garrison slipped the straps from her negligee off her shoulders. He began to kiss the top of her chest and between her breasts. When his large fingers began to tease her erect nipples through the silk fabric of her nightgown, Katie Rose could not catch her breath for a moment. His lips and hands felt stupendous touching and teasing her body.

Katie Rose reached to erotically touch Garrison as well. She stroked his hardness through his satin boxers. He closed his eyes, tossed back his head and exclaimed, "Oh…Kate!" *Her fingers feel glorious!*

Katie Rose grasped the side of his boxers and began to tug them downward. "No…Kate…wait!" she was taken aback to hear Garrison exclaim. *Why?* she wondered.

Garrison saw the befuddlement on her face. *She's used to things moving very fast with BJ. I'll show her how making love should really be – slow and mind-blowing. You're in for a treat, my lovely Kate.* "We are going to take our time. I want to savor being with you as long as possible," he confessed.

Garrison took both her hands into his. He tenderly pulled her arms upward and placed her hands on his shoulders. "Let me pleasure you for a while. You can touch and pleasure me later. Just lay back, relax and enjoy."

Before Katie Rose could protest, Garrison began to kiss her lips again. She wanted to touch him in the worst way and was perplexed about being a recipient, and not a participant, in what was taking place. But Garrison was taking her to new heights of passion. So Katie Rose did as he asked. She laid back, relaxed and relished each moment. She was lost in dizzying bliss.

Chapter 20

Compromising Positions

Katie Rose awoke at 5:00 a.m. She rolled over and looked into the peaceful, slumbering face of Garrison. *Oh, God! What have I done!* It had *not* been all fantasy and dreams this time. She had truly had sex with Garrison – mind-altering sex. Just the thought of it had her body quivering in delight again.

She reached to caress the sides of his handsome face. He stirred at her touch and opened his eyes. As soon as he focused, Katie Rose could see a smile spread across his face. *My lovely Kate is still here.*

Garrison rose up a little to take a glimpse at the bedside clock. He smiled even wider when he saw the time. "It's still early. Our first meeting isn't until ten. Did you wake me for any specific reason?"

"I…" *I didn't mean to wake him up, did I?*

Garrison did not wait for her response. He closed the distance between them and began kissing her sweet lips. He also ran his hand down her back and along her buttocks awakening all of the nerves throughout her body.

"Garrison, what are you doing?" she asked in a frenzied gasp.

"What do you think I'm doing?" he asked in a throaty voice.

"Again? After…the…the other time?"

He was pleased by the amazement he heard in Kate's voice. *BJ must be good for only one round. You've been so deprived, Kate. But no more. I'll show you how you deserve to be treated.*

"Oh, yes…again. And again and again and again. We're only getting started," Garrison declared with zeal. His mouth left her lips and began to trail downwards, starting with her breasts.

As if Katie Rose was on a rollercoaster that had just plunged over the first gigantic hill, she was senseless in exhilaration and breathless all at the same time. There was no thought of stopping Garrison. She wanted what he was doing to go on and on and on.

* * * *

A bump in the road woke Callie. The bus was roaring down the expressway. It was still early, but the sun was rising. They were on their way to another city for another concert the next evening. She had survived her first week of being on the road with the guys.

The tour bus was much larger than Callie had imagined it. It was a home on wheels. There was an upper and a lower level. The upper level had an entertainment area, complete with a nineteen inch television, VCR, DVD player, a small bar, and two sofas. Each sofa had foldout tables on each end. There were three-inch deep coasters made into the table to securely hold drink glasses as the bus bounced along down the asphalt.

The upper level also held a bathroom with toilet and shower. There were four bunks. Two hung on one side of the hallway and two on the other. A sliding curtain hung in front of each set of bunks. There was a compact kitchen, with a small stove, refrigerator, microwave, toaster, sink, cabinets to store dishes and glasses, and drawers for silverware and the like. In the center of this kitchen area was a tiny table with four chairs.

The lower level was a giant lounge area. There was a full-size sofa with tables and coasters. There were also two love seats. This area also sported a safe, a small bar, and a twenty-eight inch television with a VCR, DVD Player, Playstation and surround sound system. Two large bedrooms were also in the lower level – one at each end of the bus. These bedrooms had couches that folded out into beds. One of these bedrooms had its own private toilet and shower off from it. The lighting throughout the bus was fiber optic.

The bus slept up to ten people. There were ten on board – the driver, four members from Seventh Sign, three other members from Savage Pride, and Mason and herself. The worse part of bus life was trying to find private time. With so many other men dallying around, it was next to impossible.

At least most of the guys were respectful of Callie's presence. There were only two that had made lewd comments to her behind Mason's back. These were both members of Seventh Sign. One of them, Mick, had even cornered her coming out of the shower one evening. Of course, he had been drunk and stoned. Callie had pulled her robe tightly closed with one hand and with the other pushed his strung-out, cackling form out of the way. She did not tell Mason about this incident. Callie did not want to stir up any trouble. Fawn was not happy about her being along. Callie did not want to give her any ammo to have her tossed off the bus. *Fawn will never be 'hanging out' with Mason all alone again!* She was determined.

It was difficult for Callie to get used to the smell of marijuana and liquor again. It brought back terrible memories of her days as an addict when she was a teenager. Even though Mason was not into either the drinking or drug scene, most of the other guys were. Callie would come upon them drinking and smoking weed in the downstairs lounge and in the upstairs entertainment area. A few of the guys also offered her a hit or a shot. She turned them down, but it was hard to be around this type of crowd again.

She and Mason had only made love once during the week, and this interlude was not under the most comfortable of conditions. Most of the beds were either small double-decker bunks or a couch in the downstairs lounge. They all took turns using the two larger bedrooms. Callie relished the one night she and Mason steeled away to one of these rooms. They even had a door with a lock. However, they still tried to keep the noise of their lovemaking to a minimum. Callie had not been able to relax and enjoy being with Mason as she did when they were alone at home.

Regardless of any discomfort being on the bus brought Callie, she was still happy to be with Mason. She would put up with anything in order to be near him once more each day. *Only five more weeks*, she was thinking. A wild idea suddenly struck her. She could hear the other two guys in the bunks across the hall, snoring. *They are still sleeping*, she concluded, bent on mischief.

Callie quietly climbed out of her bunk. She ascended the small ladder to the top bunk, where Mason was sound asleep. She carefully climbed on top of his body. He jumped and opened his eyes.

"Shh," Callie said and put her finger to her lips. "The curtains to our bunks and the bunks across the way are still closed. The guys in the other bunks across from us are still snoring. We have a few minutes of private time," she whispered.

"Oh, yeah," Mason said in a quiet, groggy voice. A smile was forming on his face.

"Oh, yeah!" Callie said with enthusiasm and started kissing him. *We have to take advantage of private time whenever we can.*

Mason rolled sideways, so they would have more room. He began returning Callie's kisses with unveiled appetite. *God, I love this woman!* he was thinking. He was extremely glad he had brought Callie along with him on the road, even though it was hard on her. It was worth it for them to be together. *I'll find a way to make it up to Callie when we get home.* Right now, he lost himself in crazed need.

* * * *

The wakeup call came at 7:30 a.m., just as Garrison had requested. He reached over Kate's back to pick up the receiver and silence the phone. When Katie Rose felt Garrison's cozy body touching her back side, she could not believe she felt aroused again. *I must be losing my mind. I need to get away!* She began to scoot her body sideways to slip out of bed, but Garrison wrapped his arms around her and restrained her.

"Where do you think you are going, little beauty?" he asked.

"Garrison, we need to get up. We both need to shower. And we need to get ready for the negotiation meetings..." she began to ramble.

Garrison could hear the panic in Kate's voice. He could also feel the tension in her body. *I need to calm her. I want her to start this day happy...not stressed.* "You're absolutely right," he agreed, and released her.

Katie Rose sat up on the side of the bed. Garrison rolled some more, placed his arms loosely around her waist, and planted a few kisses along her bare back before she could get up. "We'll take a shower and make ourselves presentable. Then we can go down to the restaurant and enjoy a relaxing breakfast together."

"O...okay," Katie Rose agreed, springing to her feet. The touch of his hot, wet lips on her back was causing her body to want to lie back down. *Not again!*

She was astounded when Garrison arose beside her, took her hand, and started forward saying, "Let's go and take that shower, shall we?"

"Um…I…I'm going to my room…and you'll…take yours here."

"Now, why should we do that? The tub is far big enough for two people."

"You…you…want to shower…together?"

"Yeah. Come on. I'll make sure you are nice and clean," he said in a husky voice. He stopped and softly ran his hands over both her breasts. "I promise I won't miss a spot."

Say no. Go to your room! Katie Rose's mind was screaming. But her desires got the better of her again, and she allowed herself to be whisked into Garrison's bathroom.

* * * *

It was Monday evening. Jackie Lynn's phone rang as Flora and Mary Julia were preparing to leave. They had come to her house that evening for dinner. The ladies were still taking turns hosting dinner at one another's houses at least one night during each week.

Jackie Lynn answered the phone and discovered it was Samuel. "I am visiting with Mary Julia and Flora," Jackie Lynn told him.

"Oh, that's right. I forgot tonight was your night to do dinner with them. The old memory isn't as sharp as it once was."

"Yes, you are getting *so* old," Jackie Lynn teased him with a chuckle.

Mary Julia and Flora beheld their friend sharing a lighthearted conversation. They guessed it was Samuel. He called almost every night now. Mary Julia and Flora gave one another a smile.

Jackie Lynn was enjoying Samuel's company. They went to dinner at least once a week and had been out to see movies together. They had even gone dancing a few times. Mary Julia and Flora were happy to see Jackie Lynn going out with a man, and Samuel seemed to be a good man. He was not pushing Jackie Lynn to do anything. He was only providing much needed companionship.

"Well…I'll let you go, so you can enjoy visiting with your friends," Samuel offered.

"I'll call you back in a little while," Jackie Lynn told him.

"Okay," he agreed. "Bye. Talk to you in a while."

When Jackie Lynn put the receiver down, she turned and saw her friends were examining her and grinning. "What's up?" she questioned.

"Nothing," Flora answered. "We are enjoying seeing you happy. Samuel seems to make you happy."

"As the two of you do. Being with, and talking to, *friends* always does make me happy," she told Flora. Jackie Lynn was still determined there was nothing more to her relationship with Samuel than friendship. Even though the few times he had held her, at Christmas when she had cried over Long Wolf and the few times they had danced, had felt really nice.

"We're glad you have a male *friend* in your life," Mary Julia added with a conniving sparkle to her eyes.

"Uh huh," Jackie Lynn dismissed her inference. "Why don't you girls come help me finish off some pie for dessert," she suggested and started toward the kitchen.

Mary Julia and Flora fell into step behind her. Jackie Lynn was putting them off about Samuel, and they decided to let the subject drop. The only thing that mattered to either of them was that their friend was happy, and Jackie Lynn seemed to be finding happiness once again.

* * * *

The negotiation meetings were held in the hotel's large conference room. Garrison put in his two cents about how impressed he had been with Greathouse Construction and how he looked forward to working with them again on the Anaheim project. Katie Rose also praised Garrison and Parker Architecture's skills. She assured the prospect, McMillan Brothers, they would be hard-pressed to find a better architecture firm for the project.

Katie Rose showed an impressive, lengthy Powerpoint presentation detailing who Greathouse Construction was, how they conducted business, and why McMillan Brothers should choose them to construct their building. It also featured the Gates Tower building, showing slides from start to finish.

Katie Rose committed to moving several of her staff to Anaheim for the duration of the project. She also assured Gerald McMillan they would hire the finest of construction crews to work on the project. Greathouse's Anaheim staff would keep in touch with her at Greathouse headquarters primarily by weekly teleconferences. But she also pledged to make several more trips to California for onsite inspections throughout the project.

The McMillan's and their decision makers seemed to be impressed with Katie Rose and Greathouse Construction and also with Garrison and Parker Architecture. Everyone left the first day's meeting feeling very good about the way things had progressed. They would meet with the financial backers and McMillan the next day.

They concluded the day's business about 5:30 p.m. Since Katie Rose's body clock was still on home time – where it was 8:30 p.m. – she was very hungry. She had also eaten little for breakfast and only half a sandwich for lunch. She had not had much appetite. She had been nervous about the important business presentation she was making, and every time she looked at Garrison, she also could not help thinking about what had come to pass with him. Eating was the last thing on Katie Rose's mind.

Garrison walked out of the conference room at Kate's side. He had picked up Kate's laptop, and was carrying it for her. The projector she had used belonged to the hotel, so they left it in the conference room. They were the last ones out. Everyone from McMillan had already left. "You did great, Kate!" he congratulated her. "Greathouse is going to go far with you at the helm."

"Thanks," she said and gave him a broad, glowing smile. "You did very well too. But your skills have impressed me from day one."

"We are both doing what we love and what comes naturally to us," he said with a delighted grin. "So… we are free for the rest of the night. What do you want to do?"

"Eat," she said without hesitation. She was heading in the direction of the restaurant.

"Yeah. You did not eat much for breakfast or lunch. Were you anxious about the meetings? Or were you anxious about *us*?" Kate had not said more than two words at breakfast. And the words she had spoken had been about business – not about the passion they had shared in his bed or in his shower that morning.

Katie Rose did not like the way Garrison referred to the two of them as *us*. She did not want to think of them as a couple. They had shared an astonishing night of sex. It had exceeded all of her expectations. But this sexual encounter did not automatically make them a couple. She glanced down at her engagement ring and felt an enormous wave of guilt. *I still have BJ waiting for me at home.*

Garrison saw Kate had looked at her ring. *She's feeling guilty. But she shouldn't. She doesn't belong with BJ. She belongs with me.*

"Kate, are you okay?" he asked, reaching to touch the side of her face.

His simple caress caused Katie Rose to feel tingles from her head to her toes. She was amazed by her physical reaction to Garrison's touch. "Garrison, please don't do that," she said in an almost pleading voice. They had come to a stop.

"Okay. I'd much rather do *this* anyway," he said and brought his lips to hers.

Pull away! she told herself. Instead, she parted her lips to allow Garrison to tease her with his tongue and to allow herself to tease him back. Their mouths remained joined for several more, long moments, and as usual, Katie Rose was breathless when their kissing ceased. *This has got to stop!* Yet her mind was already replaying scenes from the night before and it made her ache for more.

"Let's go get something to eat. Then we'll see what kind of arrangements we can make for going and doing some sightseeing." It was not what Garrison wished to suggest. He wanted to steal Kate away to his room and have his way with her. *I don't want her to think it's all physical between the two of us. I want more with Kate.*

Katie Rose was baffled by Garrison's odd suggestions. She had expected him to try and take her back to one of their rooms. Especially after the sweltering kiss they shared. He was throwing her off balance by switching gears. Garrison gently took Kate by the arm and began leading her toward the restaurant again.

I should go to dinner alone. I need to be away from Garrison. What we have done...are doing...is wrong! Even though Katie Rose's conscience was bothering her, she still could not make her mouth utter the words to ask Garrison to leave her alone. She walked off to share dinner with him. She tried to convince herself they would only share another meal and then she would part from Garrison for good.

* * * *

Jackie Lynn called Samuel back after her friends had gone home that evening.

"Have you heard from Katie Rose?" he asked her.

"No. I take it you didn't either."

"No. I'm sure she was busy all day. I'm so proud of her taking on this project. I'm sure Long Wolf has to be smiling his favor down on her. She's a real go-getter, Jackie Lynn. She is going to take Greathouse far."

"It's what she has always wanted. I know she wishes her father could be alive to see it."

"I'm sure she does," Samuel agreed. "I'm counting the days until Katie Rose takes the reins from me. If this trip goes well, it may give her the confidence she needs."

"It may, but she needs you there, Samuel. Don't be in a hurry to walk away," Jackie Lynn appealed.

"Jackie Lynn, I think very highly of Katie Rose. I would never leave her high and dry. Even when I step down as president, she can always call on me. I'll be glad to share my knowledge and help her out in any way. But the company is hers now. I'm a relic."

"A relic with much valuable knowledge and know-how. Katie Rose is wise enough to realize this fact, Samuel," Jackie Lynn argued. "You will still be president for quite a while longer."

"I hope not," Jackie Lynn was stunned to hear him admit.

"Why?" she questioned.

"Because I want to see Katie Rose take over and run things by herself. Long Wolf wanted things this way. I want to stand by his wishes. Besides, I've had my run. It's been fun, and I certainly wouldn't mind being a consultant to the company, but I'm ready to retire." *I'd like to spend more time with a certain special lady*, he did not share. Samuel was cautious not to get overly personal with Jackie Lynn. He did not wish to scare her away. They were enjoying one another's company a great deal and he did not want to do anything to jeopardize their harmony.

Jackie Lynn was touched Samuel wanted Katie Rose to succeed so greatly. It made her hold him that much higher in esteem. They went on leisurely talking for some time more.

* * * *

Dinner with Katie Rose was much like breakfast had been. She was much too quiet for Garrison's liking. He tried to convince her to take a taxi with him to a car rental place and go do some sightseeing, but Katie Rose said she was tired and wanted to go back to her room.

Alone! she was pondering. "I need to call BJ," she told Garrison with serious eyes.

I wish you'd call him and tell him you're in love with another man, Garrison was thinking. He kept his thoughts to himself. "I understand," he said.

They were both silent as they left the restaurant and took the elevator up to their rooms. At Kate's door, Garrison sat the laptop down beside her. He had a hard time walking off to his own door. He watched as she unlocked her door, picked up the laptop, disappeared inside the room, and locked the door behind her.

You should be coming to my room. I've got to let her call BJ. Kate is extremely loyal. BJ doesn't know about Kate and me. I'm sure she won't tell him over the phone. She'll pretend everything is okay. I'll give her some time.

When Kate walked into the room, she saw the message light on her phone was blinking. She picked up the receiver and pushed the button on the keypad to retrieve her message. Naturally, it was BJ. He asked how her day had gone and told her he was waiting on her call. He ended the message with, "I love you and miss you."

With a heavy heart, Katie Rose dialed BJ's apartment. He answered right after the first ring. "Hi," Katie Rose said.

"Hello," he said with merriment. "It's good to hear your voice. I thought about calling this morning at eleven, when I got a break at work. But that would have been eight there. I wasn't sure if you were up or not."

Oh, I was up alright. I was being kissed and caressed in the shower by Garrison, Katie Rose accepted in gut wrenching shame.

"Katie Rose, is everything okay?" BJ asked after a few moments of silence. "Did everything go alright in the meetings today?"

"Yeah. It all went fine. I'm just tired from all the stress," she lied. "It's only seven here, but it's still ten o'clock by my body clock."

"Yeah, I wish I was there to massage your shoulders or something," BJ said.

He's always so understanding. He's a wonderful man. What have I done?!

"You're sure everything has gone okay?" BJ inquired again after more moments of muteness on Katie Rose's end of the line.

"Yeah. It went really well. I have to convince the financial backers tomorrow. So that will be another stressful day. I'm going to turn in shortly."

"Okay. I'm not going to keep you. Why don't you go take a relaxing shower and settle in for the night? I just wanted to hear your voice. Good luck tomorrow. I love you," BJ said.

"I love you too," Katie Rose said. Tears came to her eyes and a sob caught in her throat. *I can't believe I have betrayed you like I have.*

"I'll talk to you tomorrow."

"Okay. Bye," she said in a quiet voice and hung up the phone before her emotions got the best of her. She bowed her head and allowed her disgrace to overcome her. Katie Rose began to wail.

Chapter 21

Moment of Truth

Garrison could hear Kate weeping. Their connecting doors were shut. Neither he nor Kate had shut them that morning. *The maid must have.*

Luckily, the lock on his side was not turned. He opened this door, too softly to be heard, and tried the knob on Kate's door. Her door was unlocked as well. He made his way into her room uninvited. Garrison walked over to her bed, sat down beside her, and gathered her shuddering body into his robust, sturdy arms.

"Garrison, wha...what are...you...do...doing here?" Katie Rose asked in a garbled voice.

"Shh, Kate, it's okay," Garrison said. His tone was soothing, and he was stroking her back.

"N...no!" Katie Rose protested, fighting to free herself from his arms. "It isn't...okay. Let me go!"

Garrison held her tightly, and he was much stronger than her. Katie Rose was weakened even more by being such an emotional wreck. "Stop fighting me, Kate. I only want to be here to comfort you. I know you are hurting. I'm not going to leave."

"I don't want you here," she proclaimed through her tears, beating on his shoulders with her fists. Garrison was so muscular her assault was harming Katie Rose's hands worse than it was hurting him.

"Cry. Scream at me. Hit me. Do whatever you need to," Garrison challenged. "I'm not going anywhere." *I love you*, the thought registered, and it was true. However, Garrison was not about to say these words to Kate.

189

She is confused and hurting enough over BJ. I won't confuse and hurt her more.

Katie Rose struggled for a few moments longer. Then she stilled her body and allowed Garrison to console her while she continued to cry. Her tears eventually subsided. She pulled back and looked into Garrison troubled eyes. "You can let me go now," she told him.

He loosened his hold, and Katie Rose was swift to separate from him. She leapt to her feet and walked over to the connecting door. Pointing to the open doorway, she said in a decisive voice, "I'd like for you to leave."

"No. That's not what you'd *like* for me to do," Garrison argued. "That is only what you believe I should do."

"Whatever," Katie Rose said in exasperation. "Either way, I want you to get out of my room."

Garrison stood and began walking toward Kate. As he drew closer, she backed up a few more steps. "Why are you backing away from me, Kate?"

"I don't want you to touch me," she answered, crossing her hands and holding them at her waist.

"Why? What will happen if I touch you?" he was taunting her. He had a half smile on his face. He took a few more steps closer.

"Garrison, stop," Katie Rose pleaded. Her eyes looked desperate.

"Did you know you are trembling?" he asked as he sprang forward and grabbed her.

"You're hurting me," she whined, as Garrison pulled her against his body again. Her hands were still crossed and they were being mashed against him. This did hurt, but Katie Rose was referring to more than the physical pain.

"I don't want to hurt you." *I love you*, his mind betrayed again. He gave her the lightest of kisses on her lips. Her body shivered all the more.

"Garrison, I can't keep doing this. It isn't right. I'm engaged. I can't break BJ's heart. I never should have betrayed him," she chattered. Tears of shame and frustration were starting again.

Garrison began to slowly lead her back toward the bed. The closer they got, the more distraught she became. By the time Garrison lowered them both to a sitting position again, Katie Rose was sobbing once more.

"Kate, listen to me," Garrison said as he planted small kisses along her forehead and wet, salty cheeks and lips. "This is tearing you apart. You're a wonderful, beautiful, caring woman, and you can't stand the thought of breaking a friend's heart. But that's all BJ is…a friend. You've got to accept that." *I know I'm the man you truly love. I have to somehow make you recognize this fact.* "Let me hold you, little beauty. We won't make love. I just want to hold you. Please let me stay and do that."

I should say no. I should put my foot down and make him go back to his room. Even if we don't have sex – did he say 'make love'? It's having sex, not making love – regardless, it's not right for him to be here. Why does part of me want him to stay so badly? Is it because my emotions are so haywire? "Garrison, I can't think right now," Katie Rose proclaimed, rubbing her head. She was getting an awful headache.

"That's okay. You don't have to think. Let's get undressed and I'll hold you in my arms until we both go to sleep." They were both still dressed in business attire. Garrison had taken off his tie, suit jacket and shoes and left them in his room, but he still had on a long-sleeved dress shirt and belted dress slacks. Kate had discarded her blazer and high heels, but she still had on a blouse, skirt and pantyhose.

"So we are going to get naked, but just go to sleep. Yeah, I see that happening," Katie Rose said with irate sarcasm.

"It won't be easy. You are lovely with your clothes on, much less without. But I can abstain from making love to you, Kate. I'll just hold you tonight, regardless of what my body might like to do." *I love you enough I can do this for you, Kate.*

"Stop saying that!" she screamed and held her hands to her ears.

"Saying what? he questioned. It was almost as if she had heard his thoughts.

"Making love," she clarified. "*We* didn't *make love*. We had sex last night, Garrison. It was *not* making love. You only make love with someone you are *in love* with. And we *aren't* in love," she argued, her eyes bloodshot with anger.

Speak for yourself, and I don't even believe that. *You* are *in love, Kate. But not with BJ.* "What makes you so sure we aren't *in love*?" Garrison dared to ask.

"I can't be in love with you. I'm engaged to another man. This is all so nuts!" She declared, raking her hands through the sides of her hair and holding on to the back of her head.

"You are engaged to a best friend. You love him, but you aren't *in love* with him. You're *in love* with me - and you know what, I'm in love with you too." He had not intended to broach this subject. Garrison's only wish had been to calm Kate, but she had led them into this forbidden territory.

"Don't say that, please," she begged, placing her hands over her face and shaking her head. *It can't be true!*

With tenderness, Garrison pulled her hands away from her face and kissed Kate. As usual, she could not keep her lips from responding. She also could not stop her body from reacting. There was a ravenous craving deep inside her for him. She had never felt this insatiable yearning for BJ. *Oh, God! It is true!* "What have I let happen?" she spoke out loud.

"You know it's true, don't you?" Garrison inquired with a budding smile. He kissed her again, before he gave her a chance to reply. "I love you, Kate. And you love me. I'm the man you are meant to be with. Not BJ."

But I'm engaged to be married in two months to BJ. I was so sure. Mom even loves him. How could I have fallen in love with another man? Is this all real?

"Look, I know you are confused," Garrison told her, stroking the sides of her face. "I'll help you figure it out. Don't shut me out, Kate. I couldn't stand that. And neither could you," he swore, kissing her lips again.

I don't think I could, Katie Rose accepted. *What in the world am I going to do?!* For the first time that evening, she wrapped her arms around Garrison's neck and began to insistently return his kisses. "I don't want to think for a while, Garrison," she told him in a winded huff. "Take me away. Like you did last night," she implored him.

"I'll do whatever the lady wants," he told her with fanatical zest, unbuttoning her blouse while he still enveloped her mouth with his sizzling, sensuous lips.

Chapter 22

Beauty

The negotiation meetings with McMillan Brothers' financial backers on Tuesday went well. They seemed awed by Greathouse Construction's impressive personal and business history, and they were also impressed with Katie Rose. Katie Rose gave them a list of former clients they could call for testimonial to their happiness with Greathouse Construction.

Even though they did not personally know Garrison Parker, they had heard of Parker Architecture. In fact, this company had done more work in the West than where their headquarters currently resided. They had originally been based closer to California. Parker Architecture had an impressive record as well. Overall, these ladies and gentlemen were satisfyingly wooed by both Katie Rose and Garrison.

Everyone left the meeting with a good feeling. Gerald McMillan told Katie Rose and Garrison he would be in touch within the next few days with an answer. Secretly, he whispered in Katie Rose's ear that both Greathouse Construction and Parker Architecture were a shoe in for the work.

Katie Rose was on cloud nine as she and Garrison left the meeting. It was 6:00 p.m. They would spend one more night in California. Their flight home left tomorrow morning at 10:00 a.m. With the time change, they would get home around 8:00 p.m.

Needless to say, Katie Rose was in no hurry to get home. She would have to talk to BJ when she got home, but every time she thought about this conversation, she thought her heart would break. The thought of hurting him was killing her. But as she looked over at Garrison, as they walked down the hotel corridors, he smiled, and her heart fluttered. Katie Rose understood this

193

talk with BJ was inevitable. She could not deceive herself any longer. She was in love with Garrison, head over heels. They had spent last night and this morning wrapped in one another arms making love. It only confirmed her feelings further.

"Let's go get some dinner. Then maybe we can check out the pool or hot tub. You did bring a bathing suit, didn't you?" Garrison asked.

"Actually, I did," Katie Rose told him. "For some reason I've spent more time in my room than anywhere else," she said with a knowing snicker.

Garrison looked over into her glowing eyes and his heart leapt in joy. Kate had yet to say the words to him, 'I love you', but he could feel it in her actions and see it shining in her stunning eyes. "Or…we can always stay in the room if that's what you'd rather do. I could be persuaded."

"Yes, I'm sure it would take a lot of effort on my part," Katie Rose teased.

Garrison was enjoying seeing her, at last, so relaxed. Her carefree smile warmed his heart. He stopped walking, put the laptop down, and pulled her into an embrace. "I love you, lovely Kate," he professed with earnestness. Devotion gleamed in his eyes.

I love you too, Garrison, she screamed inside. However, Katie Rose would not allow herself to say these sacred words to him. *I can't tell him I love him until I've set things right with BJ,* she made up her mind. Instead, she said, "Just kiss me, Garrison." *I'll show you through my passion for you that I love you.*

"I thought you'd never ask," Garrison said and covered her mouth with his. His kisses were persistent and sweet all at the same time. *She's still frightened to tell me she loves me. That's okay, Kate. I can wait. You'll say these words to me all too soon.* For now, Garrison was thrilled Kate was not still trying to turn him away. Progress was slowly being made.

* * * *

Savage Pride took the stage at the House of Blues in Myrtle Beach, South Carolina. As they launched into their first song, the crowd went wild. It was Savage Pride's signature song – Love of My Life – their first recorded, hit single. Their second single – Complexity – had shot to the number one this week. Their first CD was selling like wildfire all over the country.

Callie was standing along the front of the stage. Everyone stood at the House of Blues. There were small tables for drinks all around, but there were no chairs. It was designed for frenzied fans to be able to jump, cheer and dance as the concert progressed.

Callie was being pushed closer and closer to the stage by hysterical females, who wanted to reach up with the hope of touching Mason or his bass guitarist, Mark. Not only were Mason and Mark the two lead vocalists for Savage Pride, they were also the two heartthrobs. Their drummer, Dave, and their keyboardist, Robert, also managed to draw in their fair share of girls after the show.

Mason had been letting his hair grow, since leaving Greathouse. It was several inches past his collar. Tonight, he had on a light, black, sport's jacket. Underneath was a white T-shirt with an Indian figure on it. Around his neck, he had a string necklace with a small arrowhead daggling from it. He was wearing long, grey, cargo pants and black shoes. His vivid red, electric guitar glistened as the dazzling lights from the stage hit it.

Mark's blond, wavy hair was even longer than Mason's. He was wearing a flamboyant, red and gold, long-sleeved shirt, which was left mostly unbuttoned down the front to showcase his bare, hairy chest. He had a sparkly black scarf around his neck, which he would toss to one of the girls in the audience in good time. He was wearing stone-washed jeans, with a gigantic, flashy belt buckle, and sneakers. Mark's bass guitar was sparkling, neon yellow. As he gyrated around the stage, it appeared to leave trails of yellow light all around him.

Callie enjoyed watching Mark work the audience. Mason was more talented on the musical, songwriting side, but Mark knew how to capture and hold the women's attention. He was a real asset to the band for this reason. He also knew his way around the bass guitar and had an outstanding voice.

Callie watched Savage Pride playing and the women's hysterical reactions. It was pretty much the same at each venue. All the shows were starting to run together, and this was only her second week on the road with Savage Pride. She still had three more weeks to go. Truthfully, she would be glad when this tour was over. She fully supported Mason, but she longed to be alone with him again in their apartment. For now, she attempted to focus on the show before her.

* * * *

After dinner, Katie Rose and Garrison did decide to check out the pool and hot tub. When Garrison came back into Kate's room, he was disgruntled to find her in a lackluster, navy, one-piece bathing suit. He was wearing a pair of Polo Ralph Lauren, Jamaican, floral, micro fiber trunks.

"Is that the only suit you brought?" he asked Kate. He was scrutinizing her with disapproving eyes.

"Yeah. Why?" Katie Rose asked with confusion.

"Why would a breathtaking beauty like you be wearing such a…a plain…do-nothing bathing suit like that?"

"Thanks," Katie Rose replied in disdain. His derogatory comments hurt.

"I'm not trying to be mean, Kate," he said, seeing the distress in her eyes. "It's just…I don't think you have a clue how pretty you are. You aren't ashamed of your body, are you?"

"No," she answered, sounding unsure. *At least I don't think so.* She had not given much thought to the way her body looked. Katie Rose thought she was cute, but she had never looked at herself as some beauty. Growing up, Callie had been the beauty. Katie Rose had been a slow developer. She still looked like a little girl when Callie was all women.

"Okay. We need to make a visit to the gift shop in the lobby," Garrison told her.

"For what?"

"For a new swimsuit for you. I saw some bikinis in there. You are in bad need of one."

"No, Garrison. I'm fine in what I have on," Katie Rose began to argue.

"Yes, if you are ashamed of your body. But you said you aren't, right? Okay, well, prove it to me."

"I'm not ashamed, but I'm modest," Katie Rose argued.

"Hey, you know what they say. If you've got it, flaunt it. And lovely Kate, you've definitely got it," he said with assurance. He walked over and kissed her in the bend of her neck. "Come on. Do it for me. What else have I asked of you?"

'If you've got it flaunt It' used to be Callie's slogan. And she definitely had it – from the time she was thirteen years old – enormous

breasts and a woman's body. "You've asked more than you know from me," Katie Rose mumbled under her breath, with honesty and a bittersweet smile. Their attraction, their affair and their love had all been silently asked of her by Garrison. She had not been able to say no to any of it, and she was having a difficult time saying no to his current request. *What could it hurt to wear a bikini? I don't think I'm God's gift, like Garrison does, but my body looks okay.*

"Come on. Slide some jeans over your bathing suit. I'll throw on a T-shirt, and we'll go check out what they have in the store," he continued to prod.

"Okay," Katie Rose surrendered. She wanted to make him happy. *Lord knows, he does enough to pleasure me.*

Katie Rose went to retrieve some jeans from a drawer. She slipped some sandals on her feet. Garrison disappeared back into his room to grab a T-shirt and some shoes. He could not wait to see Katie Rose dressed in a sexy bikini. *She hasn't had a reason until now to dress sexy. She already overshadowed BJ so much. He never requested she dress in something more sexy because he isn't any competition for other men. He certainly did not want to make them look any harder than they already were. I don't care who else looks, because Kate is* mine.

Garrison was whistling a cheery tune as he rejoined Kate in her room. They left to go on their small shopping excursion. Katie Rose once again could not believe how powerless she seemed to be to deny Garrison anything.

* * * *

Samuel and Jackie Lynn got off the phone about 10:30 p.m. They had been talking for nearly an hour. It seemed their conversations got longer and longer each evening. She had agreed to go to dinner with him tomorrow night.

Jackie Lynn was concerned to learn he still had not heard from Katie Rose. This was not like her. Normally, Katie Rose always called to report in with Samuel. Jackie Lynn called BJ earlier that evening to find out if he had heard from her daughter. He assured Jackie Lynn all was fine with Katie Rose, and the first day's meetings had gone fine. She wondered if the second day's had as well.

Oh, well, Katie Rose flies home tomorrow. BJ said she sounded really tired last night. So maybe today's meetings were exhausting as well. I'll catch up with her when she gets back in town and so will Samuel.

Jackie Lynn turned off the light in the living room. She headed to the bathroom to get ready for bed.

* * * *

BJ called Katie Rose's room a little after 10:30 p.m. He could not believe he had not heard from her. *It's only 7:30 there. She could be wining and dining prospects*, he reassured himself to calm his worries.

He left a message on her phone and told her to call him no matter how late it might be when she got in. He ended the message by saying, "I love you. It will be great to see you tomorrow night when you get home."

* * * *

Garrison helped Kate pick out her new bathing suit. He picked out one that was too skimpy. She rejected that one, and so they settled on a bikini that was more modestly cut. It covered all of her breasts and rear end. The top did push a little flesh out into view though.

They did not go back up to their rooms to change. There was a bathroom in the hallway right beside the gift shop. Garrison waited in the hall for Kate to re-appear. She came back out about ten minutes later, carrying her other bathing suit.

Garrison took the other bathing suit out of her hands. She had been holding it in the naked spot between her breasts and waist. "That's better," he said with a smile. "Now, give me a 360°," he directed, holding up his hand and swirling his finger.

"Garrison, we are in the hallway," Katie Rose said, her cheeks coloring.

"So?" he questioned. "I don't care if other people see you, and you shouldn't either. You should be proud," he lectured. He spun his finger around again.

Katie Rose shook her head, held her arms out at her sides and began to spin around. She even playfully shook her behind when she saw no one was coming down the hall.

"Beautiful! Absolutely beautiful!" Garrison praised. He raised his fingers to his mouth and whistled.

Katie Rose giggled in embarrassment, like a teenager, and slapped at his hand. "Stop, Garrison," she chastised. But she was enjoying the way his eyes were admiring her. It did make her feel very pretty and appreciated. She was dumbfounded. BJ had told her she was pretty on many occasions, but it had never mattered like Garrison's comments. *But then again, I'm not in love with BJ*, she truthfully recognized.

The smile left her face and she felt sad for a few moments. Garrison observed the change in her right away and wondered what was wrong. "Is something the matter, Kate?" he asked with concern.

"It's...I'm not used to all this...that's all," she said.

Well, you should be. You should be treated like the beautiful princess you are. "Well, you are going to have to get used to it," Garrison said with an enormous smile. He dropped to his knees and planted a kiss in the middle of her flat stomach.

His silliness took Katie Rose totally by surprise. She was cackling out loud before she could stop herself. "You are nuts!" she proclaimed.

There was a couple coming down the hall toward them. "Don't mind us," Garrison said to these strangers as they drew closer. He stood back up. "We're two people madly in love."

The other couple smiled at them and walked past. Garrison put his arm around Kate's shoulder. "Let's go check out that hot tub, Miss Hottie," he said and started to whisk her toward the pool.

* * * *

It was 8:45 p.m. when Garrison and Katie Rose came back to their rooms. They spent over an hour playing in the pool and relaxing in the hot tub. Even though there were many other people in the pool and the hot tub was full, they were so focused on one another it seemed they were alone.

Garrison followed Kate into her room. They both tossed off their wet bathing suits in her bathroom. "We should shower off the chlorine, don't you think?" Garrison suggested with an unchaste grin. He was also leering at Kate's enticing, naked body.

"I know you're concerned about the chlorine," Katie Rose said with a naughty laugh. She dropped to her knees and kissed his growing erection. "It's still warm from the hot tub," she teased.

"It's getting hot...very hot," he said in a gasp.

Katie Rose stood and tossed her arms around his neck. "Something tells me we are going to do more in this shower than wash off chlorine."

"Oh, yes. Much, much more," Garrison promised, joining his lips with her delectable mouth.

* * * *

After making love in a long, steamy shower, both Katie Rose and Garrison were extremely relaxed. They strolled out of the bathroom arm in arm. "Your place or mine?" he asked with a silly, drunken grin. He was inebriated by love.

Katie Rose started to reply, 'hers', when she saw the message light flashing on her phone. Garrison saw the solemn expression that had appeared on her face and felt her body tense. He followed where her eyes were looking.

"BJ?" he asked, even though this was likely who it was.

"Yes," Katie Rose answered with a heavy heart. "I should call him. It's late at home. After midnight. He's bound to be worried. It's not right to do him that way."

"I know," Garrison agreed. "Do you want me to give you some privacy?"

"Please," she requested.

"Will you come to my room after? Or do you want me to come back here?"

"I'll come to you," she told him.

"Okay. But I'll hold you to that. No guilt trips, okay?"

"Alright," she consented.

Garrison walked through the connecting doors back into his room. He even pushed his door closed – although he left it open a crack. He went over and sat on the side of his bed. He was missing Kate already. He had been envisioning the two of them snuggling for a while and falling contentedly asleep in one another's arms. Now, he would have to deal with her turmoil over BJ again. Garrison would be glad when she eventually got to talk to BJ and tell him the truth. Then Garrison and Kate could be together always, as they belonged.

Katie Rose sat on the side of her bed. She picked up the phone receiver and in dismay, dialed BJ's number. He answered before it could ring a second time. *I bet he's been waiting on my call.*

He confirmed her suspicions. "I've been waiting up for your call. I'm watching the *Late Late Show*. How did everything go today?"

"Great!" she answered, trying to sound enthusiastic. She only wanted to set BJ's mind at ease and go and be with Garrison. Her conscience twisted in pain at these thoughts, but they were true. She was done with pretending they were not. "Look, BJ, it *is* late. I'm not going to stay on the phone. You need to get to bed. I'm flying home tomorrow. I'll see you then and we can talk about everything. Okay?"

She seems to be in a hurry to get off the phone. She sounded odd last night, and she is acting strange again. "Katie Rose, are you sure everything is okay?"

"Positive!" she declared, trying to convince him and herself as well. "We'll talk tomorrow, okay?" *I dread this talk.*

"Okay," he conceded with reluctance. "I love you."

"M...me too," she replied. *What's wrong with me? Why didn't I say it back? I do love BJ. Even if it isn't the way I thought I loved him.*

"I'll see you soon. Call me when your plane leaves Chicago, so I know what time to pick you up when your plane lands at home."

"Alright," she agreed. "Bye."

Katie Rose was relieved when she heard BJ say 'bye' and she was able to hang up the phone. She looked down at her ring finger, at the empty place where the engagement ring had been. She had taken it off last night right after she and Garrison made love – after she realized her love for him. She picked it up from the nightstand this morning and placed it in a small zipped compartment in her purse. *I need to remember to put the ring back on when I get on the plane in Chicago. It's a lie, but I need to talk to BJ before he sees I'm no longer wearing his ring. Oh, I wish I didn't have to go home tomorrow*, she lamented.

Katie Rose got up from the side of the bed and walked over to the connecting door. She pushed Garrison's door open and saw him sitting on the side of the bed waiting for her.

"You okay?" he asked with apprehension.

"I will be," she told him as she sat down on the bed beside him. She kissed his lips and said, "Hold me, Garrison." *Your love will make it all okay.*

He took her in his arms. He was pleased she had come to him, and he was thrilled to hear her ask him to hold her. *You're mine now, Kate,* he conceived with enchantment.

Chapter 23

The Reservation

Katie Rose woke about five in the morning. She could not go back to sleep. She watched Garrison doze and thought about going home later than day. When she contemplated the talk she was going to have with BJ, her stomach turned. She got up, walked over to the window, pulled back the curtain a bit, and stared out at the city lights glowing in the darkness.

Garrison must have sensed she was no longer in bed with him. He awoke with a start. He could see the silhouette of Kate standing by the window. He gave himself a few more seconds to fully awaken, thinking perhaps he was only dreaming. When he was certain Kate was not in bed with him, he crawled out of bed and padded over to her.

Kate jumped as he encircled her waist with his arms. She had not heard him come up behind her. She had been deeply in thought. "What's wrong, Kate? Are you having trouble sleeping?"

"Yes," she said, and nodded.

"What's troubling that pretty head of yours?" Garrison questioned.

"Going home today. Talking with BJ," Katie Rose replied in a detached tone.

"Would you like to put off that talk for another day?" she was surprised to hear him ask.

"I'd like to put it off indefinitely," Katie Rose confessed. "I'd like to rewind time. Back to when BJ and I were only friends and nothing more. I've screwed up really bad, Garrison," she bemoaned.

"Well, you *can't* put your talk with BJ off forever, but I could give you another day," he said.

"What are you talking about?" Katie Rose probed, turning in his arms.

"Last night when we were relaxing in the hot tub, you mentioned visiting your father's grave at the Reservation. I told you my dad was buried there as well. I said I'd like to go visit my dad's gravesite too. Why don't we do that? The Reservation is sort of on the way."

"And what are we going to do? Skydive out of the jet? I don't think they make a stop there, Garrison," Katie Rose pointed out.

"We can always change our tickets and fly to whatever airport is closest to the Reservation. We can rent a car, go visit the Reservation, and drive back to the airport for our flight home. What do you say?"

"I say…it's very tempting. But…I need to get back. What about Greathouse? I haven't even checked in with Samuel. He's probably wondering what in the world is going on. You kept most of my free time tied up…."

"Gladly so," Garrison said. Katie Rose could see the smile come upon his face. "So you call and check in with Samuel. Tell him everything went wonderfully. Explain to him you need a day of R&R to recoup, and you are going to visit your father's gravesite. He'll understand. You have excellent people working with you at Greathouse, Kate. The company will not fold because you take a day for yourself. Trust me."

"And I suppose Parker Architecture will not fold if you are gone an extra day either."

"No, it won't," Garrison assured her. "Let's do it, Kate. I don't want our alone time together to end yet. Say yes."

She did *not* want to go home, and she did *not* want to end their magical one-on-one time either. Plus, maybe going to the Reservation, to her father's gravesite, would help her to gather needed strength and wisdom. "As usual, I can't seem to say no to you," Katie Rose said. She was smiling as well.

"You won't regret it, Kate," Garrison promised. "Now come back to bed with me a while. I'll help you de-stress."

"I bet you will," she said with a knowing snicker. Katie Rose allowed herself to be led away with Garrison. She was relieved to be given another day's reprieve from her heart wrenching revelation to BJ.

* * * *

204

Callie had gotten up from her bunk and gone to the bathroom. When she opened the bathroom door to come out, she almost ran into Mick – the drummer for Seventh Sign. He was standing in the hallway, staring at the door. The stench of marijuana and alcohol nearly knocked Callie out. *He's been drinking and getting high all night again*, Callie concluded with pity. *He's an addict. Just like I used to be.*

"What are you doing up so early, baby doll?" Mick asked in a slurred voice.

"Well, since I came from the bathroom, that should give you a clue," Callie answered in a gruff voice. She only wanted to go back to her bunk – the one right below Mason's. Mick's large, tattooed body was blocking her way. He had tattoos of green snakes all up and down his arms. Mick's long brown hair was dirty and unruly looking. He had on the same mesh shirt and torn jeans from the concert last night. He smelled of perspiration. "Were you waiting to take a shower?" Callie asked. *You sure need one!*

"Why? Would you like to climb in the shower with me, baby doll?" he insinuated, leering at her. "Is that why you are slinking around in that see-through nightie? Looking for some action from a real man?"

"I have a real man!" Callie spat in disgust, giving Mick a shove.

"Yeah. I've heard some of the noise you and Mason make in those bunk beds. You only whimper with Mason. I bet I could make you scream."

"Scream to get away from you maybe."

"Why don't you come in the shower with me and we'll find out," he suggested. He clasped her arm as she tried to push past him.

"Let go of me, you ape!" Callie demanded, raising her voice.

Mason heard her voice. It awoke him from his sleep.

"Ape, huh. You want it monkey style," Mick continued to taunt. He pulled Callie's alluring, extraordinary smelling body up close to his.

She raised her foot and brought the heel of it crashing down on top of his toes. "Ouch! Son of a bitch!" Mick screamed and released her. "Goddamn, little whore! I think you broke my toes."

Mason was coming toward them. "What's going on?" he asked, seeing Mick hopping up and down.

"Neanderthal here thought he would get cutesy with me. So I taught him some manners," Callie explained.

"Bitch! She's a bitch!" Mick was shouting and pointing toward Callie. He stumbled into the bathroom and shut the door.

Mark and Dave – the two other members of Savage Pride, who had been in the bunks across from Callie and Mason – were coming down the hall. "What's all the shouting about?" Mark asked.

"Mick was being a jerk. And Callie set him straight," Mason told them. He put his arm around Callie. "Are you okay?" he asked, as he started to lead her down the hall toward their bunks.

"I'm fine," Callie assured him. "I should have put my robe on for one thing. I didn't think anyone was up. He was drunk and stoned."

"Next time, why don't you wake me up and I'll walk you to the bathroom," Mason suggested.

"I don't need a babysitter, Mason," Callie argued.

"Obviously. Mick may have to have his foot put in a cast. But I don't want the guys harassing you, and they won't do it if I'm by your side."

"Are we going back to bed," Callie asked.

"Well, it looks like Mark and Dave are up, so we would have our bunks all to ourselves for a while," Mason said with a suggestive snigger.

"First, I'm propositioned by a smelly monkey, and now by a handsome prince. Something must be in the air," she teased, trying to make light of her escapade with Mick. However, it had bothered her. She learned to fight when she lived on the street all those years ago, but Callie did not like being put in this position again.

"It's always in the air where I'm concerned," Mason told her, as he pulled back the curtain to their bunks.

And all of the rest of the guys too, she could not help but consider in turmoil. Callie lay down in her bunk and waited for Mason to join her. *Maybe Mason's right. Let's make the best of things.*

* * * *

Garrison made all the arrangements for Kate and him to fly to the Reservation. They arrived at the Reservation at 4:30 p.m. Their plane left the Los Angeles airport at 9:00 a.m. It was a five hour flight with a half hour drive from the airport. They gained two hours with the switch between California's Pacific Time Zone and the Central Time Zone they were now on.

Katie Rose called and left BJ a message at the apartment, while he was at work. She simply told him she was going to visit the Reservation and would be home a day later than planned.

She also called Samuel. She shared the good news about the meetings with McMillan Brothers and their financial backers. Katie Rose also informed him she would be gone another day. "I'm going to visit my father's gravesite at the Reservation," she explained. Samuel was taken aback by this news, but he wished Katie Rose well and assured her all would be okay at Greathouse while she was away.

Katie Rose and Garrison planned to visit their fathers' gravesites together, spend the night at the Reservation, and fly back home the next day. Chief Ironhorse welcomed them to the Reservation. "Welcome, Emerald Sea, it is good to see you again, and not for such a sad occasion as before. Soars Like an Eagle, the same is true for you. The last time I saw you was a few years ago when your father died. I'm pleased you have returned."

"I am as well," Garrison told him. He had always loved the Reservation, but the fighting between his parents, his father's dismissal, and his burial here had given the Reservation a bitter cast in his mind. Now, coming here again with Kate, sharing their Indian heritage, was a whole new beginning for him. He looked around him at the lush green forests, the mountains, and the streams, and he sighed peacefully. It almost felt like coming home to him.

Katie Rose was also feeling much more at peace about being back at the Reservation. The sad memories from her last visit were not so pervasive anymore. She was looking forward to visiting her father's resting place.

When they told Chief Ironhorse the reason for their visit, he said without a smile, "It is white man's ways to go and visit gravesites. Your fathers' earthly vessels are here, buried in our soil, but their spirits are with you wherever you are."

Katie Rose could certainly believe this statement. She had felt her father's spirit many times since he had died. She wondered what he was thinking of her after all her transgressions with Garrison these past few days. Part of her reason for being here today was to get even closer to that spirit and seek some guidance from it.

"So can we go to the gravesites, or not?" Garrison asked. He thought maybe the chief was prohibiting them from doing this.

"Of course. You can travel this Reservation freely and visit any part of it you like. If it makes you feel closer to the spirit to visit where your fathers' bodies are laid, feel free to do so. We are happy to have you here."

Katie Rose found the chief to be a strange man. He could be cold and harsh one minute, and warm and inviting the next. She guessed it was his way. His traditions had been trampled and disregarded by most of the world, so she could understand why it was so important to him to see them upheld at the Reservation.

"Thank you, Chief Ironhorse," she told him. Despite the fact it was taboo, she gave him a brief hug.

She and Garrison started away to go and hike the trails and visit both of their fathers' graves. Fortunately, both graves were fairly easy to find. Katie Rose looked for the old willow and Garrison's father was buried beside a small pond. They both took some silent time at the graves to reflect and to silently talk to their fathers' spirits.

Garrison said to his father's spirit, 'Dad, I've been brought back home by the beautiful Emerald Sea. I was here with you when she was named to our tribe. I wanted to stay at the Reservation always then, but maybe I wasn't meant to. All things happen for a reason. I'm an architect now, and Emerald Sea runs a construction company. We make the perfect match in business, in our Indian heritage, and in so many other ways. I love her, dad. Show me the right path to take to help her through the difficult time she is about to encounter. She is a very caring woman, and it is going to hurt her a great deal to do what she must. Give me strength and wisdom to help her as best I can.'

Katie Rose also carried on a silent conversation with her dad's spirit. 'It's me, daddy. As if you didn't know. I talk to you a lot in my head and have ever since you died. But I feel really close to you here, under this willow tree, where you and my grandmother are buried. I hope you aren't ashamed of me. What I've done these past few days hasn't been right. Or maybe it's more like what I've done the past few years, with BJ, that hasn't been right. I need to tell him the truth. I wish you were here, daddy. You always gave me such strength.' A warm wind whipped through Katie Rose's hair. It gave her a chill, because it felt as if someone had gently ran their fingers through her hair. Her dad used to do things like that to soothe her. 'I love you so much, daddy. I'll make you proud again. I'll do what's right. I'll tell BJ the truth.'

Garrison dropped to his knees beside Kate and pulled her into a loving embrace. It was not until Katie Rose felt his arms around her that she realized she was crying. "It's okay, Kate," he reassured her. "It's all going to be okay."

"I know," she told him, smiling through her tears. She felt it in her heart. It was like her father's great arms were holding her as well. His spirit was strong here. Katie Rose was happy Garrison had talked her into coming.

* * * *

Samuel picked Jackie Lynn up for dinner about 6:00 p.m. Since they were doing casual dining, he was dressed in a long-sleeved polo shirt and navy slacks. The shirt had effervescent, vertical, orange strips. Samuel loved to wear the brightest of colors, even in the dead of winter.

Jackie Lynn, in contrast, was dressed in black slacks and a pale pink, V-necked sweater. She had on pink lipstick and nail polish to match her top. Her wavy locks did not have a hair out of place. She always looked so spectacular.

They went to a Chinese restaurant called Mei's. The food was fantastic, but the portions were more than they could eat. They ended up splitting one dinner. The walls of the restaurant were decorated with pictures from China. There was a small bonsai tree on each table. The lighting looked like huge covered balls hanging from the ceiling. There were instrumental Chinese melodies playing quietly from small speakers positioned by the ceiling. The smell of curry and soy sauce made their stomachs growl, as they waited for their dinner to arrive. Their waitress, a small Chinese woman with an infectious smile, and broken English, brought them drinks and took their dinner order. Samuel was drinking a 7-Up and Jackie Lynn was drinking iced tea. The restaurant was not packed, but there were several other people eating here.

"I talked to Katie Rose today," Samuel told Jackie Lynn.

"She's due home tonight. Why'd she call you now? Just finally got a chance?" she questioned as she took a drink of her tea.

"Actually, she isn't coming home quite yet," Samuel shared, playing with his straw. He did not want to worry Jackie Lynn, but he was concerned about Katie Rose. He wondered why she suddenly decided to visit her father's grave after ten months.

"More business meetings in California?"

"No…actually she took today for herself. She was going to stop by the Reservation …and visit her dad's grave."

"The Reservation?" Jackie Lynn repeated. She sounded concerned. Her somber eyes relayed this concern as well. "Did something upset her in California? BJ said the business meetings went extremely well."

"That's exactly what Katie Rose told me. She sounded really excited about the McMillan project. Maybe Katie Rose wants to visit her father's grave and talk with him about it, because it's something new – different than Abraham would have taken on. I don't know for sure. I thought it was strange."

"I think it is a *lot* strange," Jackie Lynn confessed. She looked distressed.

"Jackie Lynn, I didn't mean to worry you," Samuel said. Her placed his hand on top of hers and gave it a tender squeeze. "I'm sure Katie Rose is fine. I'll just be glad when she is back. Maybe you can get to the bottom of what this trip was about for her."

"You bet I will," she assured him. Jackie Lynn sensed all was not right in her daughter's life. Katie Rose had always been 'daddy's girl'. If something was troubling her, she looked to Long Wolf to help 'fix it'. *I'll have to find out what's wrong. I'll step into Long Wolf's shoes and help Katie Rose with whatever is bothering her.*

"Hey, don't worry. I'm sure it's nothing," Samuel tried to reassure her, patting her hand.

Their waitress brought their dinner to the table, and they set about dividing up the Chicken-Ala-King and rice.

Chapter 24

Strike Three

Seventh Sign and Savage Pride's next concert was in Nashville, Tennessee, at the Gaylord Entertainment Center. Fawn came aboard the bus when it arrived in Nashville. She had clipped her hair even shorter and had it colored almost orange. Mason told her it looked nice.

Nice, if you like carrots, Callie was meanly thinking. She observed Fawn had on makeup, and she caught a whiff of her perfume as she passed by. She hated when Fawn showed up. Fawn always made a point to talk to Mason. She did not talk to every one of the other guys, so Callie did not see why she had to single Mason out. She thought it was because Fawn missed their alone time. *That's too bad, Fawn. Mason is mine. You don't need alone time with him.*

Fawn asked Mason if he could step outside so she could have a talk with him. Callie started to follow them out. "Callie, this is between Mason and me. Can you please wait in here and give us some privacy?" Fawn requested.

"What is so private I can't hear it too?" Callie challenged. She had an annoyed smirk on her face.

"It's business," Fawn clarified in a curt manor. She kept walking toward the bus doors with Mason in tow.

"Well, *Fawn*, Mason's business *is* my business," Callie informed her, sounding snappish. She continued to follow.

Mason stopped and turned toward her. "Callie," he addressed. "I'll only be gone a minute. Wait here for me, and I'll fill you in when I get back." His eyes looked aggravated.

Callie detested Mason was taking Fawn's side. She saw no reason she needed to be excluded from any talks. She considered sharing her opinion with Mason, but she thought better of it. *I'll wait and see what Fawn wanted when Mason comes back*, she surrendered.

She plopped down in one of the high backed bus seats in the front of the bus to wait for Mason's return. "I'll be back in a second," he said with a reassuring smile. He could tell by Callie's rigid facial expression and body language that she was unhappy about being excluded. *Wonder why Fawn is excluding Callie?* The sooner they left the bus, the sooner he would find out, so Mason grabbed a jacket and followed Fawn out of the bus.

Mick was standing outside waiting for them. He was somewhat hopping from foot to foot. It looked as if he was trying to ward off the cold, but it was mostly because his foot was hurting. Callie had sprained his three middle toes.

It was February thirteenth. Tomorrow was Valentine's Day. The sun was shining, but it was still a cold day – twenty-five degrees. Fawn was wearing a long, brown, leather coat, but the brisk winter wind was still chilling her. The guys were both in short winter jackets and jeans.

"Do you guys want to sit in my car?" Fawn offered.

"Sure," Mick said and started walking toward the neon blue sport's car. "Why don't you make it a talk while driving? I'd love to take a spin in your car. I'll even drive if you'd like."

"I bet you would, but I'm fine with driving my own car," Fawn said.

She pressed the button on her keyless remote to unlock the doors. The horn beeped, the headlights flashed, and the two door locks clicked open. Mick opened the passenger door. He stepped back and waited for Mason to slide into the small back seat. He hopped in the front and closed the door. Fawn settled into the driver's seat, starting the car and the heater.

"The engine sounds sweet!" Mick commented on the rhythmic sound it was making.

"Uh-huh," Fawn agreed with pride. She popped the clutch and started away. "I didn't bring you both out to talk about my car." Fawn shifted gears and roared on down the highway. She did not get far before she had to stop for a red light. They were driving around in the city.

"What did you bring us out for?" Mason inquired.

"I wanted to talk about the incident that took place between Mick and Callie yesterday morning," she shared with Mason, glancing at him in the rearview mirror as she started down the road again.

"Oh, okay," he agreed, nodding his head. He volunteered with a sneer. "Someone was being a jerk, because they were drunk and stoned, and Callie set that someone in his place."

"You're full of shit, Mr. Goody Two Shoes – too good to drink or smoke weed. I was only being friendly, when that little bitch attacked me!"

"Watch your mouth, Mick!" Mason warned, yanking on his seat.

Fawn gave the steering wheel a hard jerk to the right and pulled the car to a skidding stop on the side of the road. "I'm not going to have the two of you fighting while I'm driving!" she told them with authority. "We all need to have a civil conversation here."

"I don't think Mick knows how to be civil. But I'll sure teach him if he doesn't watch his step."

"Are you threatening me?!" Mick asked, turning in his seat and glaring at Mason.

"No, that isn't a threat, Mick. It's a promise," Mason spat, returning his fiery stare.

"Guys, that enough!" Fawn declared, playing referee.

"Yeah, it is enough, Fawn," Mick agreed. "I don't know who this upstart thinks he is, but he can't come on Seventh Sign's bus and start ordering us around. It's obvious he thinks he owns the joint, what with bringing his girlfriend along. What if we all decided to bring someone along?"

"You guys bring complete strangers on the bus on a regular basis, in each city," Mason squabbled.

"Yeah, but we have fun with them and send them on their way. They don't travel with us. You don't get to listen to us fooling around with them over and over as the bus bounces down the road. That little honey is a damn nympho. No wonder you wanted her along."

Mason reached up in the front seat and grabbed Mick by the sides of his jacket. "I told you to watch your mouth," he repeated, giving Mick a hard shake.

Fawn slapped at Mason's hands. "Mason, knock it off!" she screamed through gritted teeth. He begrudgingly released Mick and sat back in his seat.

"That's it, Fawn! You need to arrange to have Mason and his band removed from our bus. Seventh Sign no longer wants them as our opening act."

"Fine by me!" Mason proclaimed, fighting not to send a fist sailing into the side of Mick's unguarded face.

"Mick, you need to simmer down," Fawn told him.

"Me simmer down. That little..." he caught a glimpse of Mason's fuming face and decided not to curse Callie anymore. Mick did not wish to fight Mason. Mason was a good sized man, and while Mick looked tough, with all of his snake tattoos, he was a coward. "Mason's girlfriend damn near broke my toes. We are going to have to use Savage Pride's drummer tonight, because my toes are too swollen to work the foot pedals on the drums. I have reason to be upset."

"And Callie had a reason for mashing your toes." Mason continued to defend her honor.

"Okay, I've heard enough," Fawn said. "Mick, I'm going to take you back to the bus. Mason, you and I need to talk some more."

"Alright," he agreed. He wanted to get Mick out of the car, before he lost his cool and strangled him. He could not believe he was making an issue out of the incident with Callie. If anyone was wrong, it was Mick.

Fawn turned the car around and drove back to the bus. Since she had not gone far, it did not take her long to get back. Mick hopped out of the car and stormed back toward the bus. Mason climbed out of the back seat and sat in the front. Fawn sent the car zooming away again as soon as he closed the door.

"Where are we going? I don't like leaving Callie alone with that jerk," Mason told Fawn, looking over his shoulder at the receding bus.

"Callie will be fine, Mason. It's obvious she can take care of herself. But we *do* have a problem."

"No, we don't. I'll stay by Callie's side from now on, so she won't have any more run-ins with the guys. Drugs, alcohol, and pretty women in negligees do not mix."

"No, they do *not*," Fawn agreed, glancing at Mason, and then focusing on the road again. "That's why Callie should not be on the bus with you. I had my reservations about you bringing her along. Now, I'm convinced my worries were valid. I think we should send Callie home, Mason. We can fly her home from Nashville."

"Fawn, that is ridiculous!" Mason disagreed. "You can't let Mick get away with being a jerk."

"It doesn't matter whether Mick is a jerk or not. What matters is Seventh Sign is doing a concert tour, and they need their drummer, and now he can't play for a few shows. Your drummer can fill in, but what if it had been Christof, their lead singer. Are we going to put you in as lead singer of Seventh Sign? Savage Pride's fans love you, Mason, but Seventh Sign's fans would not appreciate the substitution. Music and concerts come first, Mason. This isn't a vacation you and Callie are on. This is business. I have to look out for the bands' welfare first – both Seventh Sign and Savage Pride."

"Okay, look, I understand where you are coming from," Mason relinquished. "But there won't be any more trouble. Okay? This is our second week on the road, and this is the first incident. I'll make sure there aren't any more. You've got my word, Fawn. Besides, tomorrow is Valentine's Day. You can't separate two people who are madly in love on Valentine's Day."

Fawn glanced at Mason again. She could tell by his pained facial expression and the pleading sound of his voice how important Callie staying with him was. She was leery to say yes to him, because she did not want any more trouble. *Should I give them another chance?*

"Come on, Fawn. It will be okay. You'll see," Mason guaranteed her.

"It better be, Mason," she warned, squeezing the top of the steering wheel with both hands. "I'll have to talk to Seventh Sign. If Mick convinces them all Callie has to go, there may not be anything I can do. It is their tour bus; you are just along for the ride. We can't start getting the word out that you piss off big name bands."

"I know," Mason conceded. However, it would not be long until Savage Pride was out on concert tours alone. "Give me another chance, Fawn. That's all I'm asking."

"Alright," she agreed with hesitation. "If I can smooth things over with Seventh Sign, I'll let Callie stay on board, but we are going to have to revisit this issue with future tours."

"Fair enough," Mason agreed with a grateful smile. "Thanks, Fawn."

Don't thank me yet, Mason. I'm may have to put an end to Callie traveling with you. Fawn pulled the car into a parking lot and turned around, heading back toward the bus. Mason wanted to get back to Callie, and their talk was finished – *for now.*

* * * *

Callie had pulled up one of the window shades and was watching for Mason to return. She saw them come back the first time, and Mick jump out of the car. She also watched Fawn take off again with *only* Mason. *Where's she going with him? Was this a trick to get Mason all alone?* she wondered, enraged.

Mick came stomping aboard the bus. He glowered at Callie and said with a triumphant smile, "You're going down, you little witch!" He raced off toward the lounge on the lower level.

He's probably going to get drunk or stoned again, Callie ascertained. She remained sitting by the window, waiting for Mason to return, and anxiously counting the minutes. Fawn pulled back up about ten minutes later. Callie grew even more infuriated when she witnessed Mason coming around the car and giving her a hug. *What's going on between those two? What did Mick mean about me going down?*

Fawn and Mason came onto the bus. Fawn passed by Callie with nary a glance or a word. Mason came over and sat in the seat beside her. "What was that all about?" Callie asked. She was giving him an intense stare.

She looks angry, Mason noted. "Did Mick say anything to you?" he inquired.

"Yeah. He said I was 'going down'. What's that supposed to mean?" Callie asked. "What's Fawn up to?"

"Fawn isn't 'up to' anything," Mason replied. "Mick is trying to stir up trouble. He's demanding Fawn have you removed from the bus because you sprained his toes."

"Oh, that's convenient for Fawn, isn't it?" Callie accused with ire.

216

"What do you mean? This has nothing to do with Fawn. It's Mick," Mason retorted.

The fact he was defending Fawn made Callie even angrier. "What's going on between you and Fawn, Mason? Why'd she take off with you like that? Where'd she take you?"

"We took a ride so we could talk about this incident with Mick. Fawn is going to talk to Seventh Sign and get them to allow you to stay. You should be grateful to her - not badmouthing her," he told her.

"Yeah, right!" Callie said with heavy sarcasm and rolled her eyes. "Fawn has wanted me off this bus from the start. She's probably ecstatic that this thing with Mick has come up. She wants you all to herself, Mason."

"Callie, that is ridiculous!" he argued, raising his voice a notch to match hers. "She's down in the lounge right now talking to Seventh Sign to smooth things over. If you get to stay, you have her to thank. For the hundredth time, you have no reason to be jealous of Fawn, Callie. You need to stop all this foolishness. It's getting old."

"If I have no reason to be jealous, why did you hug Fawn when you got out of her car, and why are you defending her?"

"I hugged Fawn because I was grateful to her for sticking her neck out to help us. It's business first for her, Callie. She could order you off the bus today for the sake of business, but she is smoothing things over for us, so we can be together for Valentine's Day."

Yeah, and because she wants to get in your good graces, so she can seduce you at some point, Callie pondered, but did not say.

Mason could tell Callie was seething. He despised she was so jealous of Fawn. He did not understand why Callie did not trust in their love enough to realize he would never betray her. Not with Fawn. Not with *anyone*.

I'm not going to make things any better by arguing with Mason, Callie concluded. She had become aware of his silence and the fact he would not look at her. *I need to keep on doing what I've been doing. Make Mason happy and keep a close eye on Fawn. She won't win. I won't let her.* "Alright, Mason, I'll give Fawn the benefit of the doubt," Callie agreed. But she was never going to forget that Fawn would always be the enemy. "But I'm not leaving this bus. No matter what *she* says."

You may not have a choice. Mason believed Fawn would be able to work things out with Seventh Sign this time, but he needed to make sure nothing else came up. *If Seventh Sign puts their foot down and orders Callie to leave the bus, there is little I can do about it.*

"Take it easy on Fawn, Callie. She's done extraordinary things for Savage Pride so far. It won't be long 'til we are on our own. Then I'll have some say in whether you come along on the bus with us or not. Right now, we are at other people's mercy. We've got to work with Fawn, okay?"

"Yeah," Callie conceded with dislike. "I'll do whatever it takes for us to stay together. That's what's most important to me, Mason. More important than anything."

"Good. Me too," he said with a grin. He bent to give Callie a small kiss on the lips. "It will all work out, baby," he tried to reassure her.

Yes, it will. Fawn will not get the upper hand. I will not let her, Callie was determined.

Chapter 25

Wedding Ritual

Darkness settled in at the Reservation. Both Garrison and Katie Rose had relished their day there. They spent the remainder of the daylight hours, after visiting their fathers' graves, walking trails through the woods, and along the mountains, and enjoying the beauty and serenity of the land. Garrison had gathered food and drink from some of the Indian women before he and Kate set out. They stopped by a quiet stream and shared lunch – dried venison, wild rice, berries and cornmeal – and had herbal tea to drink.

Katie Rose was amazed Garrison would eat this strange food. She was used to BJ, who was extremely picky about food. He was a traditional 'steak and potatoes' man. She felt even closer to Garrison after spending the day sharing their Indian heritage. In fact, her heart was filled to the brim with love for him now. She decided to put BJ out of her mind. She would worry about him when she got home the next day.

A massive, rolling bonfire had been built at Big Rock. Katie Rose and Garrison settled in with the tribe around this luminous spectacle. The orange, red and yellow, tall, leaping flames looked exquisite against the backdrop darkness of night.

A few of the younger Indian girls, gurgling with laughter, tried to entice Katie Rose and Garrison into joining in a *rather erotic* circling dance around the fire. With a sinister grin, Garrison tried to prod Kate into joining in the dance too. She stubbornly refused.

The girls were dancing to arouse the attention of a male they were interested in. Before the dancing was finished, the male companion of each young girl's choice had eagerly accompanied her. They danced then, going around and around the fire several times, in intimate embraces, before the couples each took turns leaving the crowd.

"Come on, Emerald Sea, let's dance," Garrison coaxed again. They had been calling one another by their Indian names all day. It only seemed fitting with where they were.

"No!" she protested again. But she had a glorious smile on her face.

"Why not? This dance is clearly for lovers, and we are lovers..."

"Shh...Soars Like an Eagle," she cautioned. She did not wish to be overheard. If you chose one another as 'lovers' at the Reservation, you were choosing one another as life partners. She already had a fiancé. *And it isn't Garrison*, she thought, in despair, for the first time that day. *Put* him *out of your mind!* she commanded, squelching thoughts of BJ once more.

"What can a dance hurt, Emerald Sea?" Garrison continued to pursue, rising and offering a hand.

"Sit back down!" she ordered. However, an Indian girl appeared on the other side of her, offering her a hand and urging her to join in the dance.

What could *it hurt?* Katie Rose could not help wondering. She enjoyed being at the Reservation and sharing Indian customs a great deal. She did not want it to end yet. She rose to her feet. "One dance," she told Garrison with an idiotic smirk across her face. With the rapid pounding of the drums, it was hard to sit still anyway.

She took Garrison's hand and he helped her up. He gently urged her into the dancing circle of people. He came in behind her, placing his hands on each side of her waist, as they bounced back and forth and began to circle the fire. He had her pulled against his body, and after only a few rounds, Katie Rose could feel him growing aroused. He carefully turned her in his arms, and she could see the passion burning in his eyes. Her eyes mirrored his. He pulled her into an embrace, and the two of them shared a slow dance around the roaring flames, even though the beat was still brisk. Katie Rose was growing very warm, and this warmth was not merely because of the heat from the fire.

"I need to sit down," she told Garrison.

"I think we need to *lie* down," he unchastely suggested.

"We have no place to lie down here," she whispered. She was remorseful, because her body was reeling to find a private spot to *lie down* with Garrison.

He led her away from the fire. They started along a torch lined path, toward the teepees and cabins. Garrison stopped a short distance along the path and pulled her to a stop. He collected her in his arms and they shared a scorching, persevering kiss.

"Ga...Soars Like an Eagle...you need to stop!" Katie Rose said in alarm, a few moments later, when she was able to pull back a little. She was relieved to see there was no one coming along the trail. She did not wish to be caught in a passionate embrace. Their people might misunderstand. *Although, actually, they would be right. She was unquestionably in love with this man. But the tribe would expect something that could not occur – an Indian wedding ceremony.*

"Why do I need to stop, Emerald Sea?" he questioned.

"Maybe you haven't been here enough to know the rules. But you cannot...*we*...can *not* physically express our love here. It means marriage to the Indian community."

"And would that be such a terrible thing?" he inquired.

"Have you lost your mind?" she replied with a question. *What was he doing... proposing?*

"I've definitely lost my mind," he answered. "I'm totally insane! Insane in love with you!" he proclaimed with zest and a fanatical cackle, trying to sneak another kiss.

Katie Rose pushed away from him. But she was giggling as she said, "O..kay, mad half-Indian man. Regardless...you need to behave *here*." She was glad she had pulled away, because there were tribe members – two men and two women – coming toward them along the path. Katie Rose fought to separate herself from Garrison's arms. He released her at the last minute.

The Indian men and women were staring at Katie Rose and Garrison as they walked past. Katie Rose nodded at them and gave them a deceptive smile. Once they were a little ways along the path from them, and Garrison did not think they could see any longer, he reached and grabbed Kate again. "Can I steal another kiss?"

"No!" Katie Rose objected. "We need to go to our *separate* sleeping quarters for the night."

Katie Rose shook free from his loose grip and started along the path again. Garrison scurried to follow and slid his arms around her waist. Katie

Rose could feel his hot breath on her ear as he whispered, "Let's find some private spot, and spend the night together."

"There are no private spots here, Soars Like an Eagle. You need to behave!" she swatted his hands, trying in vain to get him to release her.

"Can't we at least try and find a private spot? Please," he pressed.

His steamy air, blowing on her ear and neck, was turning Katie Rose's legs to jelly and weakening her resolve to say no to the man. Her physical need for him was voracious. She did not want to spend the night in separate places. They had come close to making love by the stream earlier that day, but Katie Rose had stopped Garrison, for fear of someone coming upon them. She was having a fierce time saying no a second time.

"Where do you suggest we go? We can't stay outside. The nights are a little chilly for that. This isn't California." she said, entertaining the notion of sneaking away for the first time.

"I wasn't suggesting we sleep outside on the cold ground, with nothing for cover. Let's go to the cabins. We'll let them direct us to our places for the night – separately. Then I'll come to you. I'll sneak out before morning. No one will be any the wiser."

This time of year, most of the tribe slept in the cabins on the hill, because it got too cold to sleep in the teepees at night. They heated the cabins with fireplaces.

"Alright," Katie Rose found herself agreeing against her better judgment. But we have to be careful," she warned.

"We will be," Garrison promised. They scampered along the trail to the cabins.

* * * *

Katie Rose was in her bedroom in one of the cabins. The bedroom was rather plain. It consisted of an immense log frame bed with a thick feather mattress, pillows and comforter. A solid wood side-table, with large round legs, sat by the bed. Unlike the teepees, which were lit by lantern light, the cabin had electricity. A lamp made out of deer antlers, with a rawhide lamp shade, sat on the side-table. Aptly, there was a painting of a dream catcher on the shade. The wood floor was covered beside the bed with a hand-weaved rug. It was ivory and brick red with a diamond pattern running throughout. Katie Rose found it pleasant that the whole room smelled of wood.

She had been in this bedroom about twenty minutes. Garrison had been taken to an entirely different cabin. *Maybe he has changed his mind, and he isn't coming*, she concluded. She walked over to the bed and had a seat on the mattress. She turned off the antler lamp on the side-table. *I need to get some sleep anyway. Our flight leaves at ten tomorrow, and it will be a long, stressful day. I dread seeing BJ.*

She had just lain down in the bed when she heard a soft knock on her window. She sat up and saw Garrison standing there. She stood and crept over to the window, quietly sliding it open.

"Is there a beautiful squaw in here waiting for her handsome warrior?" Garrison asked, giving her a brief kiss.

"Shh…Garrison," Katie Rose cautioned. She stepped back so he could crawl in through the window.

"Who?" he asked in a soft voice, as he crawled inside.

"What do you mean *who*?" Katie Rose questioned in puzzlement.

"I'm not Garrison here."

"Oh, sorry, Soars Like an Eagle. Whoever you are, we need to be very quiet," Katie Rose advised.

Garrison turned and softly closed the window. "I'll do my best not to make you scream," he murmured, pulling her into his arms. He began to kiss her in reckless abandonment, slowly walking her backwards toward the bed. They tumbled upon the mattress. The feel of feathers upon his body felt odd to Garrison. Katie Rose, on the other hand, was oblivious to anything other than being with Garrison.

He grabbed hold of the buffalo skin nightdress she had been given to sleep in. He began to hoist it up, intent on pulling it from her body. All at once, the door to the bedroom was shoved open. A blinding lantern light illuminated the room, as well as Garrison and Katie Rose's shocked faces. Chief Ironhorse was holding the lantern.

"Soars Like an Eagle, Emerald Sea, what is going on?" the chief demanded to know in a strong voice.

"Chief Ironhorse," Garrison addressed him. "What are you doing here?" He released Kate and leaped to his feet. Katie Rose slid to a sitting position on the bed. She was looking back and forth between the imposing chief and Garrison. *What is going to happen?*

"Soars Like an Eagle, this is my cabin, and this is *not* white man's land. We have our own rules on the Reservation. You cannot sneak into a squaw's window at night. It is to shame the gods to do so. You will not displease the gods," he explained. His face was set in granite and it was clear he was angry.

"I'm sorry," Garrison apologized, although he was not contrite. He only wanted Chief Ironhorse to leave and give him and Kate the privacy they deserved.

"No. You are a man in love, and Emerald Sea loves you as well."

"Yes, that is true. I do love her," Garrison agreed. *Maybe he does understand. Maybe he'll leave us alone.*

"Is this true of you as well, Emerald Sea? Do you love this man?" the chief grilled her.

Katie Rose looked into his stern probing eyes. *I can't lie to him.* "Yes, it is," she said with certainty.

Garrison's heart leapt upon hearing her precious words. It was the first time she had admitted it. He wanted to take her back into his arms all the more. "Can you please leave us alone now?" Garrison had the gall to ask Chief Ironhorse.

"No. You cannot continue what you were doing. You can be together as such tomorrow night and every night thereafter," he told them.

No, we can't, because we'll be home tomorrow. Maybe tomorrow night, after I tell BJ, but probably not, Katie Rose was thinking with unhappiness and apprehension.

The chief's next words shook Katie Rose to the core. "Tomorrow, I will arrange for the Road Chief to perform an Indian wedding ceremony. Then the two of you will be bonded for life. You will not need to sneak around to be together anymore."

"A...you are going to arrange what?" Garrison asked. He was shocked by the chief's declaration.

"At the Reservation, if you take a squaw to your sleeping quarters, you are telling the tribe you have chosen her as your life's partner. You have done such tonight, Soars Like an Eagle, by sneaking into Emerald Sea's room. It is custom to have the wedding ceremony the next day. I will arrange it."

Katie Rose's mouth dropped open, and she was struck dumb. This *was* the custom. She had learned this fact from her father long ago. If fact, even her mother told her this was the way things were. Jackie Lynn had shared that she and Long Wolf had come to the Reservation before they were married, and they were very cautious about displaying their love for one another. Katie Rose could not believe she had put herself in this position. *What was I thinking trying to be with Garrison in this manor, in the chief's own house? Well, obviously I was* not *thinking. That's the problem. What are we going to do?*

"Chief Ironhorse, I did not mean to anger the gods," Garrison explained, catching a glimpse of Kate's mortified face. "I will leave and go back to my cabin. We'll pretend this incident never occurred. I am sorry. Is there some way to apologize to the gods?"

"Not apologize to the gods. You will please them tomorrow when you and Emerald Sea become one," he maintained with obstinacy.

"We have to go home tomorrow," Garrison disputed.

"You can leave after the wedding ceremony," Chief Ironhorse upheld.

"Our flight leaves at ten. We'll have to leave by nine-thirty at the latest. How early can you plan this wedding ceremony and how long will it take?" Garrison was challenging him.

"We will plan to have the ceremony at seven. That will give us over two hours. That is far long enough. Emerald Sea, I will send some of the women to bring you clothes to wear and help you prepare. Likewise, Soars Like an Eagle, some of the tribesmen will help you get ready. You should come with me, so you and Emerald Sea can get some sleep."

"Is this ceremony legal?" Garrison questioned. Katie Rose was still a dumb mute. She could not comprehend what to say.

"Not by white man's laws. You can go to a Justice of the Peace when you leave here. But in the eyes of the Reservation and the gods, you will have entered into a lifelong bond with Emerald Sea. There is no breaking this bond."

"And what if we refuse to go through with this ceremony?" Garrison defied.

"If you refuse, I will ask you leave right away. Do not ever return. You will have angered the gods. You will no longer be welcomed at this Reservation. The tribe will no longer know you," Chief Ironhorse dictated.

"My God," Katie Rose finally uttered. She looked horrified.

"You can pray to your God or any of our gods. It will do you no good," the chief reprimanded her. "The only way to set things right is by going through the ceremony tomorrow. The choice is yours. What will it be?"

"Can we have a second to talk?" Garrison asked.

"Of course," the chief agreed. "But not in this bedroom. Step out into the main room of the cabin. I will make sure you are not disturbed."

"Kate," Garrison addressed her as such, for the first time that day. He offered her a hand and helped her to her feet. She was trembling. "It will be okay," he tried to assure her. But he was not sure. Her Indian heritage meant a lot to her. He was proud of his as well. He did not wish to walk away from it.

Chief Ironhorse addressed his wife, son and daughter-in-law, who were sitting upon the wood floor on a bearskin rug by the fire. They arose and headed out of the room. "Come sit in front of the fire. The god of fire may be able to shed some light and help you to make a wise decision. I will wait outside. Come and get me when you are finished talking, Soars Like an Eagle. I will either walk you back to your cabin, or escort both you and Emerald Sea off the Reservation. The choice is both of yours to make."

Garrison and Katie Rose took a seat on the bearskin rug in front of the fireplace, where Chief Ironhorse's family had been a moment before. It was warm here, but Katie Rose felt cold. She was confused and worried. *What are we going to do?* she thought once again, looking around her in panic.

The cabin was pretty plain. There was the bearskin rug she and Garrison sat upon, and there were a few other hand-woven rugs covering other parts of the wooden floor. There was a buffalo skull hung on the stone over the fireplace. The mantle held a few items of hand crafted pottery.

A cedar futon couch sat behind them. An oval, brick red and ivory table, with the picture of a buffalo atop it, resided in front of the couch. There were two, wood end-tables, with antler lamps upon them and two log chairs with feather cushioning. A rocking chair made out of logs was sitting off to the side of the fireplace.

The cabin did not have a kitchen, because the cooking was done in the fireplace. There was a log dining table and several log chairs. Other than that, there was one bathroom, and four separate bedrooms – one of which she had been given as the family's guest for the night. *I should have respected their home.*

Garrison disturbed her deep musings. "Kate, we need to talk about the chief's dictate. He's waiting for our answer."

She looked over at him. The firelight was dancing on his face. He looked so very good-looking. She wanted to get up and leave this place with Garrison and never return. *And that's exactly what I'll have to do – never return – if I don't go through with this wedding ceremony.* "What can we do? Chief Ironhorse is extremely strict about the rules of the Reservation. We should not have tried to break them," she said with remorse, looking into the fire again, as if she expected the fire god to really give her some magical answer.

"Okay. But we did. Now, we need to make things right. We should go through with the ceremony tomorrow morning."

Katie Rose looked back over at him in shock. "Do you realize what you are saying, Garrison? How can I marry you when I haven't broken my engagement to BJ? And it's all so nuts anyway. A few days ago, we weren't even speaking to one another. Now we are planning to marry. How does that make sense? We *both* need psychiatric help."

"Kate, it will be no big deal," Garrison assured her. "You heard what the chief said. It isn't a legal ceremony, so we won't actually be married. Not when we leave here anyway. I agree it's a little soon for us to be talking marriage in the *legal* sense. But spiritually, which is basically what all of your Indian ceremonies are based on, I'm all yours already. Bond me to you for life. I sure would not mind."

Katie Rose's heart was touched by Garrison's last words. *He's madly in love with me, and I'm out of my mind with love for him. That's more than I have with BJ, and I have planned to marry him in a legal sense.*

"So I guess I'm basically proposing," Garrison said with a striking grin. He took Kate's hand in his. "So what will it be, Emerald Sea? Will you be my squaw for life?"

"Garrison, this isn't a joke," she argued with trepidation.

"I'm not joking," he assured her.

Katie Rose scrutinized his eyes and saw he was serious. He was genuinely asking her to go through with the ceremony – to be bonded with him in front of their tribe for life.

"I have a hard time saying no to you," she confessed, moved he loved her so much.

"Then don't. I'll go tell the chief it's a go. We'll stand before the Road Chief and the rest of the tribe tomorrow morning, and we'll agree to become lifelong Indian partners. Does that sound so terrible?"

Katie Rose's heart was beating very rapidly. She reached and touched the side of Garrison's handsome face. *Can I do this? What other option do I have? I don't want to walk away from my Indian heritage.* "Alright," she agreed.

Garrison scooped her into his arms and squeezed her to him. "It will be okay, Emerald Sea. I love you very much."

"I love you too, Soars Like an Eagle," she professed for the first time. The chief had asked her if this was how she felt, and she had acquiesced, but this was the first time she had actually spoken the words to Garrison. He was overjoyed to hear them. He showered her face and lips with elated kisses.

"Garrison, stop!" Katie Rose protested, pushing back from him. "That's what got us in this mess in the first place. You need to go and talk to the chief."

Being railroaded by the chief into an Indian wedding ceremony is worth it to hear you say you love me! Garrison was thinking in delight.

He released Kate and sprang to his feet. "I'll see you tomorrow morning, beautiful squaw. Happy dreams!"

Katie Rose watched Garrison leave. *He's so happy! He really does love me, and I love him. That's all we'll be doing tomorrow – showing our love for one another – and it won't be a lie, because it's how we really feel. As Garrison says, it will all be alright.* Katie Rose suddenly felt much better about the whole thing.

Chief Ironhorse came back in a few minutes later. "Go back to bed, Emerald Sea. I will walk Soars Like an Eagle back to his cabin. You will be awakened in the morning for the ceremony. You are doing the right thing, young one. The gods have spoken and chosen the two of you to become life partners. It will be our tribe's pleasure to see the favor of the gods rain down upon the both of you. Go now and get some sleep."

Katie Rose went back into her bedroom, closed the door, and walked back over to the bed. She lay down and closed her eyes. *Go to sleep*, she told herself. *Everything will be okay again after the ceremony tomorrow.*

* * * *

Katie Rose was awakened around dawn by Chief Ironhorse's wife and daughter-in-law. The wedding dress they brought her was buffalo skin, woven with symbolic colors: White – East, Blue – South, Yellow (Orange) – West, Black – North. Katie Rose's long, straight hair was combed to bring out its natural sheen. A buffalo skin diadem was placed around Katie Rose's head. The headband, the entire back of the dress, and the sleeves bore the same symbolic mix of colors woven into the front of the dress. Flying Swede fringe ornamented the arms and bottom of her dress. Red beads held the plentiful silver cones and horsehair decorations in place. She was given knee-high moccasins to wear on her feet. Her attire was topped off by adorning Katie Rose with turquoise and silver jewelry – earrings, necklace and bracelets. Chief Ironhorse's wife explained jewelry was seen as a shield against the evils of hunger, poverty and bad luck.

Some of the tribesmen brought Garrison his attire. He was given a hip-length, white native shirt, and black pants and shoes. On his head was worn a turquoise and silver headband, and he had wide bracelets to match for both wrists. He was also given a Concho belt – oval sterling silver pieces, inlaid with handmade turquoise stones. Obviously, like traditional, non-Indian wedding ceremonies, the focus was to be on the bride.

Garrison and Katie Rose were asked to wash their hands in a special basin – a symbol of purification and cleansing. They were told this ceremonial washing of hands was to wash away past evils and memories of past loves. Katie Rose could not help but momentarily think of BJ in sorrow – *He's a past love, and he doesn't even know it. Am I doing the right thing?* she could not help but wonder. However, she realized, *it's what I* must *do.*

Within a half hour, they were both led to Big Rock. The Road Chief and Chief Ironhorse were waiting for them. Both were wrapped in Buffalo Robes with symbols of Great Spirit upon them. "The Road Chief will perform this sacred ceremony," Chief Ironhorse told them. "His role is to lead the two of you and all of the rest of the tribe down the path of life. Since he will be speaking our native language, I will translate for the two of you."

The music started up then – tense, pulsating and forceful drums, rattles, flutes, and whistles. It reminded Katie Rose of the music played at the courtship ritual the night before. As Garrison and Katie Rose were brought to stand before the Road Chief, Garrison smiled at her. He also took her hands into his to reassure her they were doing the right thing. "You look extraordinary, Emerald Sea," he spoke.

"You look quite dashing yourself, Soars Like an Eagle" she said and returned his smile. She was stunned by how relaxed she felt, now that she was back in Garrison' presence. *This all seems right*, she was astounded to find herself concluding.

The loud, boisterous music was silenced for a moment by a gesture from the Road Chief. The Road Chief asked that the love flute be played for the couple. "Legend has it this flute, carved out of cedar, holds the power of attraction. It is used to enhance courtship," Chief Ironhorse explained. The Road Chief gestured and one of the women began to play it. Its calm, yet pleasing, tune gave Katie Rose an even more peaceful feeling.

As the flute sang in the morning twilight, some of the other women brought over decorative, woven, willow baskets. These baskets held cornmeal – a symbol of fertility. The Road Chief turned Garrison and Katie Rose toward the East – the sacred direction where no harm shall pass. They were prompted to open their ceremonial basket. Katie Rose's cornmeal was yellow, which symbolized female. Garrison's cornmeal was white, which, of course, symbolized male. Katie Rose and Garrison were instructed to combine the two corn meals in another basket. They were each given a pestle and told to make corn mush out of them. They bent over the basket and did as asked.

"With this combining of the two corn meals, male and female are made into one," Chief Ironhorse told them as the Road Chief announced these same words to the rest of the tribe.

The drums began to pound, rattles to shake, and whistles to blow, celebrating the joy of this union. Katie Rose and Garrison were lead to the fire, which had been burning the whole time. It was different that the usual bonfires. There were three separate fires – one giant one in the middle and two smaller ones, to the left and to the right of the big fire. All three fires were encircled by a single, narrow, stone border.

"The fire is one of the ways to communicate with mother earth," the Road Chief explained, through Chief Ironhorse. "We will now proceed with the Fire Ceremony. Symbolic of the separate lives of the couple and the union of one. Braves, bring forth the seven types of wood. We will ask the gods to bless the wood and fire circle by prayer and song."

As the tribesmen brought the seven woods and laid them on the main fire, the tribe's spiritual leader stepped forward. He began to pray animatedly in the tribe's foreign tongue. Then a group of tribesmen chanted a few joyous songs.

"The gods have blessed our fire circle," Chief Ironhorse told them as the Road Chief had deemed. "Now we will proceed with the Fire Ceremony. The large fire in the center represents the Great Spirit and the union of these two people – Soars Like an Eagle and Emerald Sea. The two smaller fires – one in North and one in South – represent this bride and groom. Come forth, members of our tribe, and sprinkle tobacco, sage, sweet grass and corn into the large fire to please the Great Spirit."

The drums pounded as the tribe lined up and marched in a rhythmic circle around the fire circle, sprinkling one or the other of the ingredients mentioned by the Road Chief into the large fire. Garrison squeezed Kate's hand and smiled at her again as they watched this ceremony proceed. As usual, she was savoring the ritualistic actions and the ceremony.

Once the last tribe member had tossed his offering into the big fire, the drums were silenced as the Road Chief addressed Garrison and Katie Rose. Chief Ironhorse interpreted, "Now, the bride and groom will offer a prayer to one another to seal their lifelong bond."

Katie Rose and Garrison had been given a copy of the prayer that morning. The words were beautiful. She could not recite this prayer and not mean it. She and Garrison – or Soars Like an Eagle – would be bound for life in her mind and heart once she uttered these sacred words.

"Are you ready?" Garrison asked her, looking into her eyes and giving her hand another tender squeeze.

"Yes," she agreed, gazing deeply into his eyes. *There is no turning back now. And I don't want to.* She began to speak the words. "Soars Like an Eagle, now you need fear no storm, for each of us will be shelter to the other. Now you will feel no cold, for each of us will bring warmth to the other. Now there will be no more loneliness, for each of us will be companion to the other. Now we are two bodies, but there is only one life before us. Now we pledge our love and fidelity to one another, to the gods, and to everyone present here. Now we will go to our dwelling place, to enter into the days of our togetherness. And may our days be good and long upon the earth."

As Garrison recited the same hallowed words to Kate – Emerald Sea, Katie Rose was so moved she began to cry. *This ceremony might not be legal, but I feel the binding of our souls.* She would never be able to walk away from Garrison now. She did not want to. She wanted to always be by his side. What she did not know was Garrison was feeling the same way.

"Now that you have spoken your vows to one another, go into the Fire Circle," the Road Chief and Chief Ironhorse spoke, interrupted the couple's silent litany. "Push the two small fires into the large stack."

Katie Rose went to the fire in the North and Garrison went to the fire in the South. They picked up something that looked similar to a rake, made out of all wood, and they pushed their small fires into the giant one. The drums, rattles, and whistles sounded wildly again, and the tribesmen and women all sang praise to the Great Spirit.

"Two lives are now merged into one," the Road Chief and Chief Ironhorse declared. The Road Chief raised his arms toward the sky, chanting and shaking a rattle of his own. A few moments later, when Katie Rose and Garrison were in front of him again, he said, "Let us consecrate this union." Chief Ironhorse repeated his words.

We couldn't do this in the privacy of his cabin, but he wants us to do this right in front of everyone, Garrison was thinking with humor and nervousness. *Surely consecrating the union must mean something different here.* He glanced at Kate and he saw her bewilderment. Once again, they were on the same wavelength.

Chief Ironhorse's wife brought forth a double-spouted, pottery, wedding vase. "One spout signifies the bride and the other the groom," the Road Chief and Chief Ironhorse explained. "The looped handle on the other side of the vase is symbolic of the unity of marriage. Drink the nectar from this vase together to consummate the marriage."

The chief handed the vase to Garrison. *Oh, okay. This I can handle*, he thought with a relieved chuckle. He bent down, so his and Kate's heads were even. He tipped the vase, and he and Kate drank from the two spouts in perfect unison.

"It is done! This couple is now one! The gods and the Great Spirit are smiling down on them! They are bonded for life. Nothing can break this bond," the Road Chief proclaimed in a loud voice. Chief Ironhorse repeated his words. There was a pleased smirk on his face.

The drums began to beat one last, uproarious time. As in a traditional wedding, Garrison pulled Kate into an embrace. "I want to kiss my bride," he told her.

"Good. Cause I want to kiss my groom," she said, laughing. The two joined lips and the drums, rattles, and whistles became even louder and more energetic. The music sounded almost explosive. Katie Rose was married to Garrison – if not legally, then in her heart and soul, where it mattered. There was no fighting this fact anymore, and she no longer wished to. She was euphoric.

Chapter 26

Valentine's Day

Garrison and Katie Rose got to the airport about 9:00 a.m., an hour before their flight. They left the Reservation right after the wedding ceremony. Garrison had removed the turquoise and silver headband and bracelets, but other than these items, he was still dressed in his wedding garments, including the silver turquoise Concho belt. Katie Rose's still donned the colorful buffalo skin diadem, dress and knee-high moccasins. Being dressed in this manor made her feel like she was Emerald Sea – the woman who had married Soars Like an Eagle. She did not want this fantasy to end any sooner than it had to.

As they walked to their gate, two teenage boys stared at her and Garrison as they walked past. "What's up with that? It's Valentine's Day...not Halloween," she heard one of them rudely state.

"Oh no!" she suddenly spoke. Her voice sounded alarmed and her face looked stricken.

"What's wrong?" Garrison asked, studying her intensely.

"Today is Valentine's Day. I hadn't even thought of it. I totally lost track of time with all we've been...doing...these past few days." She caught glimpses of bears and candy with hearts and Valentine cards in the airport stores now. She had been so fixated on Garrison she had not even noticed them until now.

"I hadn't thought of it either," Garrison admitted. "It's fitting though, isn't it? Getting married on Valentine's Day."

Getting married maybe. But breaking someone's heart, no. She was thinking of BJ. *God, what if he's got something special planned. Could I have had any worse timing?*

Kate must be thinking about BJ. She dreads telling him the truth anyway, but doing it on a day that's special for lovers will make it even worse. "Hey, it will all work out," Garrison assured her, putting his arm around her and pulling her close.

I sure hope so, Katie Rose was almost desperate. There was a sick feeling in the pit of her stomach all of the sudden. She walked through the airport at Garrison's side, trying to gain strength and perseverance from the touch of his brawny arm around her.

* * * *

Jackie Lynn returned from a grueling morning in court. She was senior partner at Grayson & Associates Law Practice, where she had worked for many, many years. She disappeared into her office, hoping to take refuge for a few moments.

A huge bouquet of dazzling red roses in a sparkling crystal vase caught her eye at once. The arrangement was sitting in the middle of her large oak desk. They had apparently been sat there by the receptionist, who must have signed for the flowers. Jackie Lynn's heart rose and then fell with a crash. Long Wolf had always sent her flowers on Valentine's Day. *For a second, I thought...* These flowers were not from him. *They must be from Samuel.*

She walked over to the desk and pulled the card out of the tiny envelope. The message was simple, yet sweet: 'Jackie Lynn, I hope these flowers brighten your day. You have brightened many of mine lately. Happy Valentine's Day, Samuel.'

She sat down at her desk and began to dial Samuel's number at Greathouse with reluctance. Dialing this number made her heart ache, since it was Long Wolf's old number. Samuel resided in Long Wolf's office. He was acting President of Greathouse Construction, so this was only right, but it was tremendously difficult for Jackie Lynn to call this particular number.

"Greathouse Construction, Samuel Lewis," he answered the phone on the second ring.

"Hi, Samuel," Jackie Lynn replied.

"Jackie Lynn, what a nice surprise! This is the first time you have called me at work," he commented on.

"Yeah...I know. It's the first time I've dialed Long Wolf's number since...well...you know."

Samuel apologized in a contrite voice, "Oh, I'm sorry. I hadn't thought about that. Does it bother you that I took his number? Katie Rose and I talked about this when she asked me to step in as president. She thought it was best I take her father's number and have all of my calls from my old number forwarded here."

"It's fine, Samuel," Jackie Lynn insisted. "It was just a little..."

"Unsettling. I'm sure," Samuel filled in the blanks. "Perhaps you should call me on my cell phone if you want to call me at work in the future."

"No. It's okay," she told him, as well as herself. "This is your number now. It has been for several months. That's as it should be."

"Well, it will be Katie Rose's soon. That is, if she ever comes home. She should be on her way now – If her flight hasn't been delayed or canceled. I don't know whether she is coming in later today or not. I'm anxious to talk with her."

"Yeah. Me too," Jackie Lynn agreed. "The reason I called...you might have guessed...was to thank you for the beautiful roses and the sweet card. They did brighten my day. Even if they did make me a little sad at first."

"Sad? Why?"

"Long Wolf always sent red roses on Valentine's Day. I'm sure most every husband does..."

"Oh, my gosh! I should have realized," Samuel chastised himself, slapping himself in the forehead. "My intention was not to make you sad..."

"I know that, Samuel, and I'm not sad now. I'm enjoying the beauty and smell of the flowers sitting in the middle of my desk," she said, sounding more upbeat. "It was nice of you to think of me."

I think of you quite often, Samuel pondered to himself. "Hey, it's almost lunchtime. Why don't we get together someplace for lunch? I could meet you somewhere. What do you say?"

"I could certainly use a break. I had an exhausting morning in court," Jackie Lynn shared.

"I'm at a stopping point. Where would you like to meet, or do you want me to come by and pick you up, and we'll leave the downtown area?"

"No, you don't need to do that. I don't want to pull you away from work for that long," Jackie Lynn was considerate.

"Hey, getting you away from downtown is the least I could do, after being such a clod. I shouldn't have sent the flowers…"

"No, Samuel. You sending the flowers was fine. I shouldn't be such a basket case about everything," Jackie Lynn argued.

"You are far from a basket case, Jackie Lynn. You are still grieving, and that is fine. I want you to feel free to share your feelings with me, okay?"

"Okay," she agreed.

"How about I pick you up out in front of your building in about ten minutes?" he suggested.

"Alright," she agreed with an easy laugh. She actually was looking forward to getting away from the downtown area awhile, and she enjoyed Samuel's company a lot. "I'll see you then."

They hung up, and Jackie Lynn looked with fondness at the roses Samuel had sent, instead of her initial sadness. *He's such a thoughtful man.* She was beginning to like talking to him and spending time with him more and more. He eased the loneliness of not having Long Wolf in her life. She got up to go and retrieve her coat and to head down to the lobby to wait for him. She was looking forward to lunch.

* * * *

The Fasten Seatbelt light had been turned off. Katie Rose got up to go to the bathroom. Garrison got up with her and was tagging along close behind her. "Do you have to go to the restroom too?" Katie Rose asked him. She could not figure why else he would be following her.

"Yes," he answered, although he had a sinister grin on his face.

Katie Rose stepped into the bathroom and closed the door. She emptied her bladder, washed her hands, and opened the door. When she did, Garrison was standing right there. He walked forward, pushing her back into the tiny, compact space. "Garrison, what are you doing?" Katie Rose asked with an uneasy chortle.

She watched him lock the door. "Having a little alone time with my *wife*," he briefly explained.

He warmed Katie Rose's heart each time he called her his *wife*, even if it was not exactly true. Yet, in their hearts it was, and that was where it counted. Before Katie Rose could respond to his words, he covered her mouth with his. Garrison's kisses were frenzied and famished. They instantly drew Katie Rose in and caused her body to stir in response.

"You know…" he murmured, turning her so her back was to the sink. They could barely move. Their two bodies took up all of the empty bathroom space. It was an extremely small area. Garrison did not care. His need to be with Kate – *my Emerald Sea* – was greater than any obstacle. "That drinking the nectar thing from the pitcher…this might be okay in the Indian community to consummate a marriage. But I have something a little different in mind."

"Garrison, we can't do *that* in here," Katie Rose protested, but there was a slight, conniving smile on her face. *Can we?* She was flabbergasted to learn that the thought aroused her. BJ had never been imaginative when it can to their sex life. It was pretty much the same thing each time.

"I think we can manage it," he said in a rasping voice, with confidence.

He reached to lift her dress and pull down her underwear. He lifted Katie Rose off her feet and sat her on the minuscule sink. He planted a few more sizzling kisses on her wanting lips and along her collarbone. Katie Rose returned his kisses with force, raking her fingers through the sides of his hair. Garrison's hair was the only thing she could reach, and she *oh so much* had to touch him. She was senseless in need. Her appetite for this phenomenal man was unappeasable.

"Happy Valentine's Day, lovely Emerald Sea! I love you beyond reason!" he proclaimed. Garrison dropped his pants and underwear.

"I love you too, Soars Like an Eagle," Katie Rose declared as she relaxed to allow him to take her on another impassioned journey to paradise. She had never been happier in her life. She never wanted to be parted from this man.

* * * *

Their plane landed at 1:00 p.m. It was a direct flight from the Reservation. It had not taken them long in the bathroom. Their want for one another had been much too overpowering. When they vacated the bathroom, there was a lady waiting in the passageway. She gave them a strange look when she saw first Garrison and then Katie Rose emerge. Katie Rose averted her eyes. She could feel her cheeks burning in embarrassment. She was not ashamed of what she had done, however. Being with Garrison, wherever they were, all seemed much too right for her to feel shame.

They had gone back to their seats and Garrison had napped for most of the remainder of the flight. Katie Rose, on the other hand, had been keyed up. She tried to concentrate on reading a book, but did not comprehend most of what she read. She wished she could turn the plane around and go back to the Reservation. Needless to say, she did not want to go home.

But now she was home. As she and Garrison walked through the airport, hand in hand, Katie Rose tried to savor what little time they had left together. They went to baggage retrieval and Garrison pulled Kate's suitcase off the luggage belt and carried both bags. They even shared a taxi from the airport.

When Katie Rose arrived at BJ's apartment, she was relieved when she did not see his car. She had feared he might take off work for a surprise homecoming for her, since it was Valentine's Day. Then again, she had not called him to tell him when her flight was coming in. She had not wanted him to know.

Garrison got out of the taxi and carried Katie Rose's suitcase to the door. He stood in the hallway and gave her one, final, yearning kiss. When they separated, Katie Rose had tears standing in their eyes. "We won't be apart for long," Garrison pledged. "Call me after you have talked to BJ."

"I will," she promised. She gave him another brief kiss. She unlocked the door, picked up her suitcase, and stepped inside.

"I love you, Emerald Sea," Garrison said, before she closed the door.

"I love you too, Soars Like an Eagle," she said with earnestness. A few tears escaped and rolled down her cheeks.

"Don't cry, little beauty. I'll see you again soon," Garrison reassured her, bending to gently kiss her tears away.

"Bye, Garrison," she said and pushed the door shut. Otherwise, she would end up pulling him inside. She did not want to separate from him.

When Katie Rose turned from the door and looked over on the coffee table, she began to cry even harder. There was a huge box of chocolates, shaped like a red heart, some long-stemmed red roses, and a card with her name on it. "Dammit! Why does it have to be Valentine's Day!" Katie Rose spoke out loud, even though there was no one to hear her. *This is hard enough, without all this!*

She plopped down on the couch, put her head in her hands and sobbed. She refused to open the card. It would be professions of love from BJ, and she could not take this torture. *I'll tell him tonight about Garrison, whether it is Valentine's Day or not. This deception has got to end.*

* * * *

The phone rang at BJ's apartment around 3:00 p.m. Katie Rose did not answer it. She figured it would be BJ, and she did not wish to talk to him until she could see him face to face. Actually, she did not want to talk to him at all, but she had no choice. It had to be done, and the sooner the better. *I should have been honest with BJ all along. Then maybe I wouldn't be in this predicament.*

Katie Rose heard the answering machine click on. She waited to see if BJ would leave a message. Instead, it was BJ's boss, Mitch. *Why is he calling here? Where is BJ? Isn't he at work?*

Katie Rose picked up the phone before Mitch could say much more than his name. "Hello," she answered. "This is Katie Rose."

"Katie Rose! Good! I'm glad you answered. I didn't want to have to leave this as a message on the answering machine."

"What? Where is BJ? Isn't he at work today?" she rambled all of her questions to Mitch.

"Yes, BJ is here...or rather he *was*. Katie Rose, there is no easy way to say this, so I'm just going to tell you. Here goes...BJ was hurt today in a freak accident. EMS took him to the hospital a few minutes ago. I knew you were coming home today, because he's been talking about you all day..."

"Never mind about me!" Katie Rose stopped him. "What kind of accident was BJ in?" *BJ obviously was hurt bad or EMS wouldn't have taken him to the hospital.*

"We had a truck hoisted in the air. The lift broke. BJ tried to jump out of the way…but…it caught his left leg. I won't lie to you, Katie Rose…it looked bad."

"What do you mean it looked bad? What hospital did they take him to?"

"University. I think BJ will be okay, but I'm not so sure about his leg. It was crushed. I'm closing up shop now and going over to the hospital. I knew you would want to know, so you could be there. I'm very sorry, Katie Rose. It was faulty equipment. I'll, of course, pay all of BJ's medical expenses."

My God! She was thinking. *Did he say BJ's leg was crushed?* "I'm leaving now, Mitch. I'll see you at the hospital."

All thought of telling BJ about Garrison was gone. She was only worried about BJ's welfare. Katie Rose might not be in love with BJ, but she did love him a great deal as a friend, and she could not stand the thought of something terrible happening to him. She hung up the phone, grabbed her coat, and raced from the apartment.

* * * *

Savage Pride was in Chicago at the United Center. The United Center was home to the Chicago Bull's and Blackhawk's and was one of the largest arenas in the United States. The shape of the arena was oval and it seated many thousands. Almost all of those many thousands of seats were filled with eager, noisy fans of both Savage Pride and Seventh Sign tonight.

The concert started at 8:00 p.m. Mason wished Callie a Happy Valentine's Day earlier in the day, but he had not done anything special. Callie had bought a card before they left for the tour. She gave Mason the syrupy love card, after they had made love that morning. She was not hurt by the fact that Mason did not have a card for her, because they had been traveling constantly. It was not like Mason could hop over to the corner store.

The first song Savage Pride played was Love of My Life. Normally, they launched into their second hit – Complexity – next. This time, the lights were brought down low, and a single spotlight was shown on Mason. He picked up his acoustic guitar, stepped to the microphone, took it out of its holder, and began walking up the part of the stage that stuck out farther into the audience. The girls on the floor by the stage went wild, screaming at the top of their lungs, sticking their arms out, waving and almost crushing Callie up against the front of the stage. *What is he doing?* she wondered. She noted he was looking directly at her and smiling. *He's coming toward me.*

When Mason got to the end of the stage, he dropped down on his knees in front of Callie. Other women were reaching around her, trying to touch him. Callie wanted to turn and slap them. *Chill!* she was thinking, but she knew the frenzy would not die down.

"Callie, the real love of my life, I have a present for you for Valentine's Day. I have written a special song for you," he told her, gazing into her eyes.

Callie's heart leapt with love and excitement. *It's been ages since he's written a song for me!* Suddenly, the pushing, screaming, annoying women all around her ceased to exist to Callie. She was fixated on Mason. She could not wait for the song to begin.

"This song is called '*Baby*'."

My nickname, Callie identified. *Sing, Mason, sing!* She looked as star struck as every other woman there. But what was shining in Callie's eyes was love and not merely infatuation.

Mason began to strum his guitar and sing, "Baby, you're my sunlight through my days. I love you. You have made my life complete. And ohhhh…we belong to..get..her. You're my ba..by."

After the slow refrain the rest of the lights came up as the band kicked in and the song became much more upbeat. The backup singers also began to croon. "Baby, baby, baby, baby…"

Mason unfastened the strap to his acoustic guitar and laid it on the stage beside him. The electric guitar, keyboard and drums were playing a souped-up musical accompaniment. Mason began the first verse. "Callie, young girl who teased and made me crazy. Made me oh so crazy. We parted and you went and grew into quite a fine, beautiful lady. What a fine, beautiful lady. Baby, thanks for coming back into my life. Back into my life…" He followed by singing the refrain with the band, and then flowed directly into verse two, "Callie, lovely lady. Light of my life. Splendid light of my life. We started as best friends and grew into lovers. Oh, what blazing lovers. Baby, I'm so thankful to have you in my life. In my life…" The band sang the refrain again and Mason started into the third and final verse,

"Callie, my special baby. Special baby. I asked you to become my wife. Become my wife…my better half. You said yes. Miraculously, you said yes. And now we will spend the rest of our lives together. Our lives together. Oh, how I love you, my Callie baby."

Callie was overwhelmed with emotion. There were tears standing in her eyes; she was tremendously touched. It meant so very much that Mason had written a song for her. He could not have given her a better Valentine's present. This special song beat any syrupy love card he might have purchased.

He and the band had just begun the final refrain when one of the girls from the audience managed to clamber onstage with Mason. She had on a T-shirt that said, 'Be Mine' in the middle of a giant red heart. She hoisted this shirt over her head. She had nothing on underneath. She was slinging her big breasts right in Mason's face. He could not help but have his attention diverted from Callie. Nor could he help but look. Mason stumbled over a few of the words in the refrain.

The security team immediately grabbed the girl and escorted her from the stage. Mason looked back at Callie in embarrassment and finished the refrain, "…You're my ba..by." He glanced over at where they were dragging the girl through the crowd. He bent and gave Callie a long kiss. "Sorry about that, baby," he whispered.

Callie was upset, but the excitement of having Mason write a song and serenade her replaced all that. Savage Pride launched into Complexity, and the concert continued. "You're the luckiest girl in the world," a woman on the right side of Callie screamed in her ear, as she danced back and forth, bumping into Callie.

"Yes, I am," she agreed with an overjoyed smile and went back to watching Mason perform.

* * * *

Callie greeted Mason backstage after Savage Pride had finished. "Thank you so much for my song," she screeched, throwing her arms around his neck and giving him an excited, feverish kiss.

"My pleasure," Mason said in delight, grinning. "I'm glad you liked it."

"I loved it!" she corrected. "And I love you!"

"I love you too, baby," he said and gave her another kiss.

They both heard a strange woman scream, "I love you too, Mason!" Charging toward them was the girl who had hopped on stage earlier. Fortunately, she had her T-shirt back on. Callie intended to see to it that it remained that way.

How'd she get back here? Both Mason and Callie were thinking.

Callie released Mason and stepped in front of him. She stepped forward a few paces and got a stronghold on the girl's shoulders as she dashed forward. Callie brought her to an abrupt halt. "You don't belong back here!" she growled, practically spitting in the girl's face.

"I want to see Mason," the girl said, looking over Callie's shoulder in desperation. "I love him."

"Yeah, well, how'd you love to love him with your eyes gouged out?!" Callie threatened. She raised her left hand and stuck her engagement ring in the girl's face. "This is my engagement ring from Mason. I'll scratch your damn eyes out with it, if you don't leave him alone."

"Callie!" Mason said, stepping forward and grabbing her shoulders. About then, with relief, he saw one of the security guards approaching this strange woman again.

"Come on, Miss. You're not allowed back here," the guard said, clutching her from behind.

"I want to talk to Mason."

"Well, you can't!" Callie shouted. *You already ruined my song.* "Get her out of here!" Callie ordered the security guard. "And make sure she is gone for good this time!"

The security guard nodded and began pulling the woman away. "Bye, Mason. I'll see you again," the girl said in a dreamy voice, still reaching out toward him as the security man dragged her away.

"Not if you value your eyes!" Callie further threatened, shaking her fist toward the girl.

Fawn stepped forward out of the shadows. She had on one of her signature berets – red tonight, appropriate for Valentine's Day. She also had on a bright red poncho, with a white, long-sleeved T-shirt underneath. She had on black slacks. Since Fawn was already slim, these almost made her look overly small. "What's going on?" she questioned.

"Just a fan a little out of control," Mason explained with a pitying grin.

"Sounds like it is more than a *fan* that is out of control," she said, giving Callie a concentrated stare.

"Everything is fine, Fawn," Mason assured her.

"It is now," Callie agreed, putting her fist down, as she saw the girl disappear from sight.

Fawn stepped over to Mason and Callie. "Mason, these are your fans. It's up to security to keep them in line. Callie cannot be threatening them," she warned.

"I'm right here, Fawn. Don't talk about me like I'm not in the room. If you have a problem with me, you tell me," Callie challenged. "What are you doing? Looking for another excuse to throw me off the bus?"

"I'm hoping you don't give me one," Fawn answered with a disapproving frown.

"She won't," Mason promised, pulling Callie to his body. "Simmer down," he whispered in her ear. He began to pull her toward the bus. Callie and Fawn were still glaring at each other as Mason led Callie away.

She's trying to come between us. I wonder if she purposely let that girl come backstage, Callie contemplated. She wanted to scratch out Fawn's eyes too.

"Why don't we go back to the bus, and I'll sing your song for you again. Just to you this time," Mason suggested.

This idea directed Callie's attention away. "That sounds great!" she said and smiled for the first time in several long moments.

Mason continued to walk her away. *I've got to keep Callie's jealous streak under control. She still has that cruel streak she had when she was a girl. I can't let things get out of hand. I don't want her thrown off the bus, and she may not give Fawn any choice. Especially if she gets in a fight with a fan – or God forbid, Fawn.*

Chapter 27

Guilt & Jealousy

It was Friday morning. Katie Rose had spent the night at University Hospital. She was napping in a recliner by BJ's bed. He was fast asleep, still was not aware of what had happened to him.

When she had gotten to the hospital yesterday afternoon, BJ was already in surgery. Several hours later, the surgeon came out and announced to Katie Rose and Mitch that he had removed BJ's left leg below the knee. The surgeon assured them that, with proper healing and rehabilitation, BJ should be able to be fitted with a prosthesis and walk, run, or do any of the things he always had done. Katie Rose was still horrified that BJ lost his leg. She burst into tears, and Mitch held her and comforted her for some time.

Once she got her wits back, Katie Rose left the hospital while BJ was still in the recovery room. She wanted to go home and change clothes. She did not want any extra reminders of her time away with Garrison. *Not now!* The first thing Mitch had commented on when he saw her was the fact she was dressed in an Indian wardrobe. But his question to her was what rattled Katie Rose. "Where is your engagement ring?"

Katie Rose had forgotten to put it back on. It was still in the zippered compartment in the back of her purse. She pulled it out at the hospital and slipped it on her finger. She told Mitch she had come from an Indian Reservation, which was true. Then she lied, telling him they had prohibited her from wearing her engagement ring there. Katie Rose hated telling so many lies. She thought it was all going to end, but now she was not sure of anything. The only thing she knew for certain was she intended to stay by BJ's side and help him recover. Her heart was breaking for him.

* * * *

Garrison waited and waited for a call to come from Kate. However, the night passed without one. He got little sleep. The fact he had not heard from her made him nuts. When he got into his office that morning, the first thing he did was call Greathouse Construction. He was dying to know if Kate had talked to BJ yet.

Carla answered the phone, "Greathouse Construction. Ms. Greathouse's office. Carla speaking."

"Carla, how's my favorite secretary this morning?" Garrison spoke, sounding much more upbeat than he was. "This is Garrison Parker. May I speak to Ms. Greathouse please?"

"She isn't in today, Mr. Parker," Carla replied.

"She isn't. Is she out on business? Ill?" he probed.

"No. Her fiancé was involved in a serious accident yesterday. She is at the hospital with him."

"An accident?!" Garrison asked in alarm. "What kind of accident?"

"I'm not sure what happened. All I know is a car fell on him where he works. He had to have his leg amputated."

"My God!" Garrison gasped. *No wonder I haven't heard from Kate.*

"Yeah. I know. It's horrible," Carla said, sounding flustered. "If you need to speak to someone about Greathouse business, I could put you through to Samuel Lewis."

"No, Carla. That's okay," Garrison said in a monotone. He was still reeling from shock. "What hospital is Ms. Greathouse's fiancé at?"

"University," she informed him.

"Okay. Thanks, Carla. I appreciate the information. Have a nice day."

"You too, Mr. Parker," she replied.

They ended their call then. *What should I do?* Garrison was wondering. He wanted to rush off to the hospital to comfort Kate. But he could not. He also did not think it wise to call her. *BJ and I are not exactly friends. I can't call his room and give him my condolences. Kate must be going crazy. She can't tell BJ about us now. I'm sure she'll stand by his side and help him recover. That's the sort of kindhearted lady she is. BJ is a good friend, if nothing else.*

Garrison felt helpless. *I'll just have to wait for Kate's call. No matter how hard it is to sit back and do nothing.* He went back to concentrating on work, although it was next to impossible to do so.

* * * *

BJ was shocked to the core when the doctor relayed the news that part of his leg had been amputated. Katie Rose was right by his side, holding his hand, and struggling to remain strong and not to cry. She held BJ and assured him that all would be okay. She even gave him encouragement when the doctor talked of fitting him with a prosthesis as soon as possible.

Katie Rose was amazed when they sent BJ home after only two days. He was supposed to go to a rehab center each day and work out several hours. The doctor said his leg should be healed enough in two weeks to fit him with a permanent prosthesis.

BJ was exceedingly depressed. The doctor explained to Katie Rose that this depression was normal. "He will likely go through a bereavement period. Almost as if he had lost someone close to him. He also might have phantom pains, as if the leg is still there. With your support, he should come through all this fine. It will take time. It will also take a lot of work, if he intends to lead a normal life again."

Katie Rose hired a nurse to look out for BJ's needs, so she could go back to work. Samuel assured her she could take off longer if need be, but Katie Rose needed to get back. Truthfully, she wanted to get away from BJ's misery for a while.

"I'll see you this evening, BJ," Katie Rose told him and gave him a peck on the lips. BJ was sitting in a wheelchair at the breakfast table. He had to be at rehab at 8:30 a.m. "Nurse Abbott is here if you need anything. And she is going to drive you to the rehab center. I'll be checking on you."

"Okay," he grumbled. "I'm sure you are glad to be getting away from the cripple."

"Don't say that, BJ!" Katie Rose reprimanded him with an annoyed, puckered brow. "You are not a cripple. You'll be up and walking and doing everything you did before in no time."

"I hope so," he said. He was staring off into space. "I want to walk you out of the church after we get married. I don't want to be sitting there in some wheelchair and have you push me out of church."

Katie Rose took his chin in her hand and made him look her in the eyes. "You *are* going to be standing in the front of the church waiting for me, and you *are* going to walk me out of church after we are married, BJ," she told him with conviction. *What am I saying? It doesn't matter whether I'm going to marry him or not. What matters is giving BJ the incentive to walk again.*

"I love you, Katie Rose," he told her. He sounded a little choked up.

Katie Rose's heart twisted with pain. She hated seeing BJ hurting so much. She was determined to do whatever it took to take away that agony. "I love you too, BJ. You'll be standing and walking again soon. You'll see," she assured him. *I do love him. He's one of my best friends. How am I going to deal with no longer having him in my life?* Her heart was very heavy. "I have to go," she said, and gave him a kiss on his cheek and forehead.

She scurried toward the door. Work would be a welcome relief. She loathed perpetrating these lies, but it was essential she continued to do so. BJ's recovery was her primary goal.

* * * *

Katie Rose had not been in her office a half hour when her intercom sounded. "Ms. Greathouse, Garrison Parker is here to see you." Katie Rose felt her heart soar and at the same instant an awful beleaguering guilt. "Ms. Greathouse, can I send Mr. Parker in?" Carla asked, bewildered by her boss's silence.

"Oh…yes…Carla. Of course," Katie Rose stammered.

A few moments later, Garrison walked through her door. He closed the door behind him, hung up his long winter coat, and approached her desk. Katie Rose had to fight to keep from leaping to her feet and throwing her arms around him. As usual, his robust body and handsome face caused her breath to catch in her throat.

"Kate, I am so sorry to hear about BJ," Garrison spoke. His eyes relayed sympathy. "How's he doing?"

"How…how did you know…?" she inquired, looking dazed.

"I called Friday looking for you, and Carla told me…"

"I'm sorry I didn't call, Garrison. The time was never right…" Her eyes were remorseful.

"Kate, I understand," he told her coming around her desk. "Please stand up. I want to hold you. I'm sure you could use some big, strong arms around you about now."

Katie Rose did as he asked. She longed to be held by him. When he slid his arms around her, she felt like she had died and gone to heaven. She burrowed her head into his shoulder, inhaled his scent, and lost herself in his safe and secure arms.

"Thank you," she murmured when she pulled back from him several moments later. She had a pained expression on her face. "I did need that."

"What happened, Kate? Carla told me a car fell on BJ."

"He was at work, and they were working on a truck. The lift broke. Thank God, BJ managed to jump partly out of the way, or he would have been killed. They had to amputate his left leg below the knee."

"My God!" Garrison professed with pity. "How's he doing?"

Garrison's concern for BJ moved Katie Rose's heart. "As well as can be expected. He's depressed. He needs me to help him through this terrible time. Our wedding gives him incentive to get out of his wheelchair and to walk again. I won't take that away from him. I can't!"

"And I won't ask you to," Katie Rose was relieved to hear Garrison say. "Tell him what he needs to hear right now. But you can't actually marry him, Kate. I'm the man you love, and you love me. That's all that matters."

"I do love you, Garrison," Katie Rose professed, reaching to stroke the side of his cleanly shaven face. She found herself fighting tears. She wanted to be with him a great deal, but she could not. Not until BJ had fully recovered.

"We'll find a way to work it all out, Kate," he promised her, gazing with adoration into her eyes. He cherished hearing Kate say she loved him. Garrison wanted to hear it over and over again. "Why don't we start by having lunch together today?"

"Where?"

"My house. It's not far from downtown."

She was surprised to hear he had a house. "You have a house?" she questioned.

"Yes. About ten to fifteen minutes away from the city. It's a small, brick, startup house, but it's a beginning. It's only has two bedrooms, and a carport instead of a garage. Right now, the spare bedroom is my computer room, but it could always be converted into a nursery…"

"Whoa, Garrison…let's not get ahead of ourselves," Katie Rose cautioned.

"Well…if planning to have a child with the woman I love is getting ahead of myself… I'm game to get ahead of myself. We could make beautiful children, Kate. I'm game to practice for a while though. How about we start with lunch today?"

Katie Rose knew what he was inferring. She wanted to suggest they make it breakfast, and they leave right now. Instead, she said, "I don't know, Garrison…"

"What's to know? We need to take advantage of whatever time we can find to be together. I can survive not having you all the time if we steal away when we can. I can't survive not having private time with you at all. You won't be fair to yourself either, Kate. Being BJ's nurse is a wonderful, selfless thing, but don't punish yourself. Say we'll meet for lunch."

"What time?" she found herself asking. His lips dangling within inches of hers were making her dizzy with desire. *I can survive the lies if I'm still able to spend intimate time with Garrison. I'll go crazy if I don't.*

"Is eleven o'clock too early?"

"Eleven will seem like an eternity," Katie Rose uttered the truth, sounding breathy. "But that's fine."

"I'll pick you up at eleven out front," Garrison told her. "I can't wait until then."

"Me either," she agreed.

He kissed her – a fiery sample of what was to come later. Katie Rose melted in his arms and returned his kisses with decadence. She could not wait until eleven o'clock rolled around. She needed their time together.

* * * *

Katie Rose was lying wrapped up in Garrison's arms when she heard her cell phone ring. It was in her purse in the living room. "Crap!" she cursed.

"Let it ring," he advised her, kissing the back of her neck. "They can leave you a message."

"They can, but what if it is something to do with BJ?" she said with unease.

She untangled herself from Garrison's arms and dashed from the bedroom. She answered the phone on the last ring before it rolled to the answering service. "Hello," she gasped.

"Katie Rose?" It was her mother's voice.

"Hi, mom," she said. Katie Rose glanced over her shoulder and saw Garrison was standing in the entranceway to the living room. He was still completely naked. He had followed her from the bedroom.

"Sweetie, you sound a little out of breath. Is everything okay?" Jackie Lynn questioned.

"Yeah, it's fine," she replied. "I was worried it was someone calling about BJ. That's all."

"Sorry. I didn't mean to scare you. Carla said you had left for lunch. I was calling to see how BJ was doing."

"He's doing okay. He should be in therapy right now. The nurse was taking him. He wants to be able to stand at the front of church and watch me walk down the aisle to him, and he wanted to be able to walk me out of the church after our wedding. The doctor says if he works really hard, he should be able to do it. I'm willing to give him an incentive. I want him well."

"Of course you do. We all do," Jackie Lynn told her.

Katie Rose could hear how much her mom cared about BJ. *It's going to break her heart too when I have to break things off with him.* "Listen, mom, I hate to cut you short, but I need to get a bite to eat, and get back to work. I wasn't there at all last week, so I have some catch up to do."

"That's fine, sweetie. Keep me up to date on BJ, and let me know if I can do anything. I'm here for you guys. I love you both."

"I know, mom," Katie Rose said, feeling another little tweak of pain in her gut from her mother's last words. "*We* love you too," she answered, feeling even more misery.

They hung up, and Katie Rose turned to face Garrison. She began to ramble, "We need to get dressed. We need to be getting back." She darted past him. She was headed to the den. Her suit was lying over the back of his desk chair. Her blouse, stockings and bra were scattered on the floor, from the den to the bedroom, along with Garrison's shirt, pants and underwear. They had been in an insistent hurry.

Garrison followed Kate into the den. He could tell she was troubled. "Your mom was calling about BJ, wasn't she?"

"Yes," she brusquely answered. She vacated the room with her suit draped over her arm. She bent to pick up her blouse, bra and stockings as she moved into the bedroom. She was headed toward the bathroom off the bedroom. "I'm going to go in the bathroom and freshen up."

"Why don't you let me help you with that?" Garrison offered with a devilish smile.

"Garrison, we don't have time. I'll already be gone for over an hour. I need to get back to Greathouse. I wasn't lying when I told my mom I had some catching up to do."

"I know," he conceded a little sadly. "You're feeling guilty about us, aren't you?"

"A little," she confessed. "I hate all the people this is going to hurt. Mom loves BJ too. He's already part of the family to her."

"But I bet your mom loves you most of all. Am I right?"

"Yes. What's your point?" she asked. She was edging closer and closer to the bathroom. She did not have time for a longwinded conversation with Garrison.

"I'll bet your happiness will be what is most important to her. And I can bring you that. She'll see that in time. I intend to show her. I intend to show everyone. Most especially..." he walked over to her and pulled her into his arms. "you. Your happiness is extremely important to me, Kate."

"If that's so, you need to let me go into the bathroom and freshen up," she said, fighting the impulse to kiss him. Garrison could not hold her without her wanting to kiss and touch him. The two naturally went hand in hand.

"Fair enough. I'll leave you alone...for now. I'll go freshen up in the other bathroom. We'll get dressed, and I'll get you back to work."

"Okay," she said. She squirmed out of his arms and bolted into the bathroom. She shut and locked the door. She did not want Garrison to sneak into the bathroom. She did not need the temptation or distraction. She wanted to freshen up, get dressed and get back to work. She needed some time alone to think. It was impossible for her to think clearly when she was with Garrison. Her love for him was so intense it scrambled her senses.

Garrison hustled to the other bathroom to clean up. *I'll take her back to work. But I won't allow her guilt to come between us. We love each other and we belong together. I feel for BJ, but he and everyone else will have to accept Kate and I belong together.*

* * * *

Callie and Mason were sitting in the upper level entertainment area, watching *The Late Show with David Letterman*. It was almost midnight. The bus was barreling along down the highway. Savage Pride's next concert was not until tomorrow night. They would spend most of the day tomorrow traveling to their next location. They were both dressed for bed. Mason had on boxer shorts and Callie had on a gown with a long robe over the top. *So I don't tempt any of the guys, like Mick.*

All of the members of Seventh Sign, and the drummer from Savage Pride, were having a mini-practice session in the lower lounge. Music and singing emanated from there, as well as an occasional whiff of marijuana, which Callie tried to ignore. The other two members of Savage Pride had already gone to their bunks for the night. These guys could sleep through anything.

At midnight, Mason turned off the television. "Are you ready to go to bed?" Callie asked him. She stretched to indicate she was tired. She hoped she was sleepy enough to doze through the band's music. She was more of a light sleeper.

"Yeah. But can we talk for a second first?"

"About what?" Callie asked. She did not like the serious expression on Mason's face. "There isn't more trouble with Fawn is there?"

"Fawn...no. That is, if you don't keep insulting her," Mason pointed out with a disapproving grimace.

"Insulting her? When did I do that?"

"You were practically in her face the other night when she warned you about threatening that groupie."

"She was talking about me like I wasn't in the room. Which is her wish. She'd like me to be several states away...at home."

"Callie, I don't understand why you don't like Fawn. Or...on the other hand...I do. You are jealous of her. But you have no need to be. I don't know how I can prove that to you. You are the only woman I am interested in. You don't need to threaten fans either."

"That kooky woman swung her tits in your face, Mason. I wasn't going to give her the chance to take off all her clothes the next time."

"And what if she had?" Mason questioned.

"Is that what you wished she had done?" Callie challenged.

"Why do you automatically assume that? Again, Callie, you are the only nude woman I want to see."

"Yeah, right," she said with mockery, shaking her head.

"Why do you doubt that? What have I done to prove otherwise? The other guys run off to strip clubs. Have I gone with them? No! And I didn't go even when you weren't here, so don't say it's only because you are watching me. This lack of trust really bothers me, Callie."

"It's not a lack of trust…not exactly. It's just…men are predisposed to want to fool around with lots of ladies…and it's in your face. I don't want it in your face, tempting you…that's all."

"I could be tempted by a picture in a magazine, or some beautiful chick on television or at the movies. What are you going to do, take away all the magazines, not let me watch television or see movies? Then there would be no temptations. You can't lock me away from the world, Callie."

"So you do admit you are tempted by other women," Callie tried to make her point.

"I notice other women's beauty. Does that mean I want to sleep with them all? No! I would not have asked you to marry me if I wasn't sure you were the *only* woman I wanted to be with. I don't intend to cheat, Callie. You need to get that through your hard head. You've been acting like a child these past few days. I don't like this."

"How have I been acting like a child…"

"Being rude to Fawn. Threatening fans. That is childish. It needs to stop. I want you with me, Callie. Don't give Fawn reason to have you removed from this bus. I'll be very disappointed if you do. You need to get a handle on this jealousy thing."

Callie did not like when Mason tried to tell her what she should do. She had never liked being told what she should do, not even by her parents. However, Callie did not want to be separated from Mason, so she would have to play by his – *and Fawn's* – rules.

"I'm sorry," she grumbled. Mason could tell she was not genuinely remorseful. She was angry. Callie was a stubborn, high-spirited woman. He loved her because of these qualities, but it could also make her difficult to get along with when she was on a different side of an issue.

"We'll work on it together. Okay?" he tried to appease her.

"Whatever," she quipped. She stood. "I'm going to bed. Are you coming?"

"Yeah," he said. He rose to his feet as well. "Don't be mad, Callie," Mason pleaded. He placed his arm around her waist. "I want you with me, that's all."

"That's all I want too," she told him. *And I'll do what I need to do to be able to stay by your side. But I'll still keep my eye on Fawn and all the other women vying for you. They won't pull you away from me.*

Chapter 28

Deception

It had been a month since Valentine's Day – the day of BJ's accident. BJ had been fitted with his prosthesis two weeks after the surgery. He was working extremely hard to be able to walk normally again. The plan of walking Katie Rose out of the church was his main incentive. The doctor had stressed to Katie Rose that motivation would perhaps be the most important factor in BJ's recovery. She still fully intended to provide this enticement for him.

However, BJ's other needs put Katie Rose under incredible stress. At first, Katie Rose put BJ off physically by using the excuse that he was still healing, and she feared she might hurt him. Now, she was trying to justify their lack of intimacy over the fact he must be 'tremendously tried' after all of the strenuous physical therapy he went through each and every day.

Katie Rose went to some of BJ's physical therapy sessions. She could not believe all they put him through. The PT laid BJ down. He rolled up a towel and placed it under BJ's damaged leg. "Now, BJ, I need for you to push down as hard as you can – twenty times," he instructed. BJ did as asked, even though it was obvious this was painful and extremely difficult for him.

Then the PT helped BJ to roll over onto his side, with the limb on top. "Push your leg backwards; then lift it straight up as high as you can." The therapist encouraged him to repeat this exercise twenty times for three sets. Katie Rose was getting tired just watching the workout.

Next, the PT had BJ lie on his stomach and lift his leg toward the ceiling twenty times for three sets. Katie Rose was relieved when the therapist announced that this would be the last exercise for the day. "The motion of pushing back with the limb is an integral part of walking with a prosthesis," BJ's PT explained to Katie Rose.

Once they fitted BJ with his prosthesis, they taught him how to put the leg on and take it off. They gave him a few days at home to try to walk with it. This effort made Katie Rose a nervous wreck.

"Can I help?" she asked as she beheld him struggling to take his first wobbly steps. She wanted to rush to his side and take his arm.

"No. I need to do this myself," he snapped, panting. He wiped the sweat from his brow and he persevered on. Katie Rose thought her heart would break, but she tried to sound very optimistic – telling him he could do it and he would soon be walking perfectly again.

It was terribly difficult for BJ to bear weight on the prosthesis. For one thing, his limb was still exceedingly tender and sensitive. He wore the leg for only a couple hours a day at first, and he used crutches when he walked for support, to keep from falling and to take off some of the pressure.

During the first week of rehab, after receiving his prosthesis, the therapist focused on teaching BJ how to walk correctly. He walked between bars for support. He was learning to push back when his heel struck and swing forward when needed – learning the feel of walking with a leg that was not his own. The therapist explained, "This will take a while to get used to. Walking over twenty years with two legs and all of a sudden walking with a new one is a major change that takes the brain time to get accustomed to."

However, BJ was impatient. "My wedding day is getting closer and closer, and I'm determined to be able to walk perfectly by that day." His PT was happy with BJ's doggedness. It was definitely paying off.

By the end of the first week, BJ was able to walk in a room a little bit with no assistance at all; not fast, and with very small steps. *It's terrific to walk again with no crutches,* he realized.

BJ also did a lot of walking on the treadmill after the first week. "The treadmill will help to equalize your strides so your gait would be more natural," the therapist explained.

"Am I supposed to be holding onto the bars like this?" BJ had a death grip on them.

"That's fine," his PT assured him. "Walking on the treadmill is helping your stride, and also your endurance."

They also needed to work on BJ's balance. "One of the most important things when it comes to walking with a prosthesis is good balance. To develop this, I'm going to have you stand on just your prosthesis for as long as you can stand it," his therapist told him. BJ was elated to find he was getting better standing on the prosthesis for longer periods of time. This practice also correlated with easier walking and more confidence.

Another exercise his PT did for balance was with Therabands. His therapist put a band around BJ's good ankle, and he would have to stand on the prosthesis. "Now move your foot back and forth as many times as you can," he instructed. While BJ did this exercise, he would stand next to a railing for some support when needed. This procedure was a challenging feat, but turned out to be very helpful.

"Agility while wearing the leg was another key to success," his PT disclosed, taking BJ into an open room to play with a basketball-sized rubber ball. "What we are going to do is rotate in circles. I'll throw the ball to you and you throw it back to me. This exercise will help with side-to-side movement. It will also take your mind off of your leg, so you can start moving around without thinking constantly." They also went forward and backward, doing the same thing with various sized balls.

The therapist also revealed, "Gaining strength in the limb is important for walking with a prosthesis, both for ease of movement and endurance." To help BJ with this step in the process, his PT worked with the Therabands again. These were stronger than the ones he used for balance. The therapist put the band around the prosthesis and walked behind BJ. He would pull back on the band, so when BJ walked forward he had to swing the leg extremely hard. They went from side to side and backwards in this manor as well.

"I can feel the burn," BJ confided to his therapist after a strenuous workout.

"Good. That means it's working," his PT said with a pleased smile.

The last thing BJ's therapist did was to videotape him walking, so he could see what he was doing right and more importantly, what he was doing wrong. BJ would walk back and forth for a while with the camera rolling, then go back and analyze it. He observed he was pausing on his prosthesis pretty long and his walking was still off. The video showed him what he needed to work harder on, and he intended to. *I'm determined to get to the point where there is no pause at all, and my stride is normal.*

* * * *

As BJ gained confidence in his walking skills, he longed to be with Katie Rose again, in the physical sense. She was finding it harder and harder to turn him away. Not because she desired him. Katie Rose was too consumed by love for Garrison to have any desire to be with BJ, but she found herself in an incredibly uncomfortable position. She was running out of excuses to turn BJ away. After all, they were supposed to marry in a little over a month.

It was almost eleven o'clock at night, and Katie Rose was already in bed. BJ came into the bedroom. He took off his glasses and laid them on the side table, and he removed his prosthesis. He laid it on the floor beside the bed. He slid himself under the sheet and cover and into the bed with Katie Rose.

She turned off the light on her bedside table. Katie Rose had bought a solid walnut bedroom set for BJ. This furniture replaced BJ's particle board, side table, Chest of Drawers and headboard. The bedroom now had two nightstands, a King-sized bed, with a headboard and a footboard, a dresser, and a Chest of Drawers. The room looked much more lived in.

Katie Rose rolled over on her side, facing away from BJ. "Goodnight," she said. "I love you." She did not feel bad or hypocritical, because she would always love BJ as a friend.

BJ rolled over beside Katie Rose and placed his arms around her. She cringed as he also began kissing her neck. "My leg is all healed. I've got more and more energy," he said in a husky voice. Katie Rose could feel his hot breath on her ear and the side of her face.

"I know," Katie Rose replied. "You've been working so hard, BJ. But you still must be exhausted. I can wait until our wedding night."

"Trust me, Katie Rose, I'm not *that* exhausted," BJ assured her. He began to finger one of her nipples through her flannel pajamas, and she could feel his erection through the cotton boxer shorts he had worn to bed.

Katie Rose no longer wore negligees. She wore long-sleeved cotton tops and full-length bottoms. She was trying everything in her power *not* to encourage BJ sexually. Garrison was fulfilling her sexual appetite. They were still sneaking away whenever they could each day. Garrison understood why she was still staying with BJ and why she had not told him about her love for him. But Katie Rose could not imagine Garrison would accept her having sex with BJ. *I need to find a way out of this predicament.*

Katie Rose slid out of BJ's arms, sat up, and turned the light back on. BJ blinked at the offending light. He said with a suggestive smile. "You want the lights on? That's fine by me."

He reached for her again, but Katie Rose stood. BJ rolled onto his back and slid himself to a sitting position. He was studying Katie Rose with a mixture of unhappiness and bemusement. He was careful to make sure his disfigured stump was still covered.

What am I going to say to him? Katie Rose was agonizing over.

"So do I gross you out?" BJ asked. "Is that why you don't want me to make love to you anymore?"

"No, BJ! Of course not!" Katie Rose tried to assure him.

"Then why?" he pressed her.

I'm in love with another man. I'm only still with you *because I want you to get better.* "I want you to get your rest, that's all. You don't want to have a setback, do you? I know how important walking me out of the church is to you. I want you to be confident you can do that. Going to therapy tired won't help anything. We'll be married soon. We can be together all we want then."

BJ was not buying this argument. "Maybe you shouldn't be marrying me," he said with dejection, looking at where the bottom half of his right leg should be.

"BJ, don't say that," Katie Rose pleaded. She sat back down on the bed and slid herself over beside him. "I want to marry you," she lied. "This has nothing to do with your leg. One of our vows will be to love each other no matter what, right?"

"But we aren't married yet. So I won't hold you to that vow," BJ said in disgust. "I was a whole man when I proposed. Now I'm this cripple who is trying to be normal again. I'll always have this hideous stump. There is no getting around that."

Katie Rose yanked back the covers and sheets. BJ flattened himself up straighter against the headboard. "What are you doing?!" he asked in alarm.

"Showing you that your leg does not bother me," Katie Rose assured him. She tenderly removed the sock that was covering it.

"Katie Rose, stop!" BJ demanded, starting to pull away from her.

"No. You stop!" she ordered. She lowered her head and began to smother the scarred end of his stump with kisses. "I love you, BJ. All of you. This…" she pointed to his flinching limp, before she kissed it again. "is a part of you now. So I love it too. I want you to focus on what's important and that is getting better. There is plenty of time for us to be together...after we are married. It's only a little over a month. Think of how long we waited to be together the first time. We can wait now. We'll have a lifetime together soon."

Her heart twisted as she uttered this terrible untruth. At some point before the actual wedding, she would still have to break BJ's heart. She hated being dishonest with him, but she did not want him to give up. Katie Rose wanted BJ to be fully functioning again, before she ruined his life.

"Okay…" he conceded, wanting her to stop kissing his repulsive limb. He was still sliding away from her. He was propped on the edge of the bed. BJ only wanted to put the sock back on his stump and hide it under the covers again. He still had a hard time looking at it, and Katie Rose kissing it was making his skin crawl.

Katie Rose sat back up and studied BJ. "Are you okay?" He had broken out in a sweat.

"Yeah," he said. "Let's just go to sleep. You're right. My main focus should be on getting fully well."

"Yes, it should," she agreed. "Do you want me to sleep on the couch until the wedding?"

"What…? No," he protested. He had reached to grab his sock and was sliding it back on. He also slipped his leg back under the sheet and cover. "It's bad enough not making love to you, but not being able to fall asleep with you in my arms will be more than I can stand."

Katie Rose ached deep within. *You'll all too soon* have *to sleep without me in your arms.* "Alright," she agreed with an anxious smile. She crawled off of the top of the covers. She turned the light out, and she slid under the sheet and cover again, rolling over on her side. BJ placed his arms back around her. "Goodnight, Katie Rose. I love you so much," he said. His voice sounded shaky, and Katie Rose felt him tremble a bit.

"I love you too," she replied, feeling tears of remorse burn her eyes. *If only we had stayed friends and not become lovers. I'll miss you BJ*, she could not help but acknowledge. She stifled her tears and tried to relax and fall asleep in his arms.

* * * *

Greathouse Construction was awarded the McMillan Project in California. Needless to say, Katie Rose and Garrison were thrilled. Katie Rose was working diligently to put together a business plan, hire staff, and plan for Greathouse's grand new future. Garrison was as busy. He had pages and pages and pages of plans to draw.

BJ had physical therapy that evening for a few hours, so Katie Rose rushed over to Garrison's house. They usually only had a harried lunch hour together, so Katie Rose was overjoyed to have more than an hour to be with Garrison. Garrison was tickled to have the extra time as well.

Even though Garrison was a bachelor, his house was far different than BJ's apartment had been when Katie Rose had first started going there. Garrison had a comfortable wrap around sofa in the living room. He had a large screen television across from the couch, with a nice surround sound system. All of his furniture was real wood, and it all matched. He liked oak. He had two side tables and a coffee table in the living room made out of this wood. He had a small oak table and chairs in the kitchen and an oak desk in the den. His stereo system in the den was housed in an oak cabinet. His headboard, footboard, dresser, Chest of Drawers and two nightstands in the bedroom were also of this same wood.

The living room, hallway, den, and bedroom walls were decorated with beautiful oil paintings. Katie Rose had commented on them her first visit to Garrison's house. He had shared with her that he had painted these pictures – painting with oil was what he liked to do in his spare time. Katie Rose was amazed by Garrison's talent. Garrison was an awesome architect, and now, she had discovered he was gifted at painting as well. She never ceased to be awed by this vibrant man.

Garrison took his time pleasuring his lovely Kate that evening. "Now that's the way it should be between us," he told her. He was holding Katie Rose in his arms. They were both exceedingly fulfilled. "Soon, it will be like this all the time. When we are together all the time. How much longer do you expect this charade with BJ to last? He's up and walking around. It's getting closer and closer to the wedding day. You don't intend to tell him at the church, do you?"

Garrison was growing impatient. He was tired of having to sneak around with Kate to share their love. He did not want to hide it any longer. Garrison wanted to shout it to the world from the rooftops. He wanted to spend the rest of his life with his lovely Kate.

"I don't know, Garrison. I can't bear to think about telling BJ the truth; it breaks my heart. I'm going to lose a best friend, and I'm going to hurt him badly. I'm afraid he'll give up if I tell him too soon, and then he'll never walk again. The wedding gives him added incentive, and he's getting stronger and stronger, and walking better and better each day. I can't pull the carpet out from under him. At least not yet. We at least came to an agreement about the physical thing last night, so you'll have to tough it out a little longer."

"The physical thing?" Garrison questioned.

Katie Rose felt his body tense. *Why did I bring that up?* She felt Garrison turning her in his arms. He obviously wanted to see her face. He had a few candles burning in the bedroom to set a romantic theme. "It's nothing," she assured him. "Since BJ's getting strong…well…he wanted…to be together as lovers again last night…"

"And?" Garrison looked concerned.

"And nothing," Katie Rose asserted. "I love you. You are the only man I want to be with in that way now."

"Well…you couldn't exactly tell BJ that. So what happened?"

"He thought it was because of his leg that I didn't want to be with him. I proved to him it wasn't. So he agreed to wait until our wedding night."

"You proved to him it wasn't? How exactly did you do that?"

Katie Rose hated the jealousy she saw burning in Garrison's eyes now. *Why did I even start this conversation? Because I'm used to talking to Garrison about everything, that's why.*

"It was nothing, Garrison. I kissed his bad leg. That was all," she attempted to downplay.

Garrison sat up in the bed. "Kate, this whole sham needs to end," he declared with authority. "You should be sleeping in my bed at night. Not in BJ's. And I don't like you kissing him – on his leg, or anywhere else."

"I know, Garrison," she agreed. "It feels so empty now. I don't like it any more than you do, but I can't stop. Not yet."

"Then you tell me when," he demanded to know. His eyes were serious. Katie Rose hated she had ended their peaceful bliss.

"Before the wedding. I don't know the exact date. Whenever BJ can walk perfectly again. It shouldn't be that much longer."

"I don't want you sleeping with him anymore, Kate," Garrison dictated. "That doesn't need to be part of the deal. BJ lost his leg…not his manhood. He may say he'll wait until the wedding night, but it's only natural he'll try to persuade you otherwise. Especially if you're in bed with him. Why don't you tell him you are moving back in with your mother until the wedding? Then you can slip out at night and come here."

The plan was very tempting. Katie Rose actually gave it serious thought for a few long moments. "I'll sleep on the couch…at BJ's. I don't think it will fly if I move back in with my mom. She would wonder what was going on as well…"

"Who cares? Tell her the truth. Your mother will understand. She is eventually going to find out anyway. Why shock her at the same time you are dealing with BJ's emotions. This is the perfect plan."

Katie Rose was sitting up in bed too. She was studying Garrison's face and thinking over all he had said. It was going to come as an enormous shock to everyone when she finally broke it off with BJ. *Should I start being honest with people, and preparing them one by one? What if mom demands I tell BJ, and the whole thing backfires and he gives up? I can't take that chance. I don't know how she is going to react.*

"Garrison, I can't do that yet. I don't know how my mom will react, and I don't want BJ to find out from someone other than me. I promise you I won't sleep with BJ anymore. That should set your mind at ease. I'm sorry I brought all this stuff up. I didn't mean to spoil our time together. I still have another hour. Can we please stop talking about BJ and focus on the two of us instead? Please."

Katie Rose kissed Garrison. Garrison pulled her into his arms and stroked her back, along her spine. "I love you so much I think I'll go crazy sometimes," he professed, giving her another heated kiss before she could respond.

"I know. I feel exactly the same way," she responded, gazing into his eyes in veneration. "It won't be that much longer, Garrison," she pledged. "For now, let's make the best of the time we have. Okay?"

"Okay," he agreed. Garrison detested that she would still be living with BJ. But he needed to let Kate have the final decision when it came to BJ. If he pushed her to do something too soon, and BJ's recovery withered and died, Garrison feared Kate would not forgive him or herself. He wanted their new life together to begin unmarred. The very fact Kate would have to break BJ's heart would be hard enough for her. But Garrison was confident his all-encompassing love could help her come through this turmoil.

* * * *

It was Saturday afternoon. Jackie Lynn was strolling along at the Street Rod Nationals with Samuel. It had been many years since she had been to a car show. Long Wolf had not enjoyed doing these things. She was taking pleasure in looking at all the vibrant colored, shiny cars, showcasing their gigantic glistening engines.

This show was being held at the massive convention center in the middle of downtown. There were several thousand cars, and there was also a separate wing that housed what they called Women's World. Women's World was hundreds of vendors selling products for women. Jackie Lynn was checking out the cars with Samuel, and Samuel intended to walk through Women's World with Jackie Lynn. They were enjoying a nice leisurely afternoon.

It was March. The day was partly cloudy with a temperature in the low seventies. Samuel was dressed in a short sleeved cotton shirt. The shirt had bright prints of different colored street rods running all through the material. He had on black slacks and comfortable black loafers. Jackie Lynn had on a red T-shirt with a black and white checkered line running across her bust line. She had an unbuttoned black and white checked blouse over the top of the shirt. She also donned black Capri pants and black Hush Puppy flats.

Samuel had been rather quiet all day. When he and Jackie Lynn sat down to have a bite of lunch in the food court, she decided to broach the subject of his reserved mood. "You've been awfully quiet today. Is everything okay, Samuel?" she asked, as she doctored up her grilled chicken sandwich. She tore open a packet of mayo and spread it on the bun. She also had waffle fries and a coke. They were sitting across from one another at the end of a picnic table. Everyone else at the table was a stranger, and these strangers were all lost in their own conversations.

"I have a lot on my mind," Samuel replied to Jackie Lynn's question. He took a bite of his own chicken sandwich. He had gotten the same meal as Jackie Lynn. You could also smell the brats, hotdogs, hamburgers, fried chicken and polish sausages cooking.

"Anything you'd like to talk to me about?" Jackie Lynn pried.

"Actually…yes. First off, Katie Rose asked me if I want to head up the project in California. If I did, I would have to move to California for a year…"

"A…year?" Jackie Lynn repeated, almost choking on her sandwich. She had not anticipated this statement. She was amazed by the strange, empty feeling this information evoked in her all at once. *I would miss him.*

"At least a year. That's if all goes well. I don't think I'm interested. She's looking for ways to keep me with the company. It is time I stepped down…"

"Oh, Samuel, Katie Rose is going to hate losing you."

"Would you miss me if I went off to California?" he asked her out of the blue.

It's like he was reading my mind. "Yes, I would," Jackie Lynn answered with honesty.

"Well, that's settled then. I'm not going to do it."

"Wait, Samuel," Jackie Lynn cautioned. "Don't make this decision based on me. That wouldn't be fair to you."

"How is staying in town to spend time with a women I greatly enjoy spending time with not being fair to me?" he asked her.

Jackie Lynn was unsettled by the admiring look in Samuel's eyes. She broke eye contact and munched on a few fries before saying anything else. She was suddenly feeling uncomfortable. She did not want Samuel making life decisions based on her. *We are still only friends.*

Samuel reached to cup Jackie Lynn's hand with his own. "Jackie Lynn, I didn't mean to worry you. I do enjoy spending time with you, and you enjoy spending time with me. There is nothing wrong with that."

"No there isn't," she agreed, looking him in the eye again. "But I can't promise you we will ever be anything more than friends. And I don't want you to put your life on hold hoping for something more."

"I haven't been doing that. Nor do I plan to. I understand you aren't ready to move forward to any other relationship between us, and I'm fine with that. I want you to take however much time you may need to grieve Long Wolf..."

"And what if I never stop grieving him?"

"You probably won't," Jackie Lynn was shocked to hear Samuel say. "You will always miss him in some capacity. But it's gotten more bearable, has it not? Unlike in the beginning. It will continue to hurt less and less. I only want to be able to spend time with you; that's all. That's my only request. I can't do that if I'm in California. I'm ready to retire, Jackie Lynn. And Katie Rose is more than ready to take over the reins. She has proved that by pulling in this McMillan project. I'm very proud of her, and I'm sure Long Wolf is as well."

"For sure," Jackie Lynn agreed, giving Samuel a forced smile. Samuel seemed to care a lot about her and her family as well. This fondness meant a great deal to her.

"There's something else that is bothering me as well," Samuel said, picking at his fries.

"What?" Jackie Lynn asked, taking a drink of her soft drink. She was intensely studying Samuel's worried eyes.

"I saw something yesterday with Katie Rose that greatly disturbed me," he began with hesitation. "I don't want to go around spreading tales...and maybe I should be talking directly to her...but..."

"What, Samuel? You brought it up. Tell me what you saw that has you so worried."

"I saw Katie Rose in a car around the side of Greathouse Construction. She was with Garrison Parker. The two of them...well...they were kissing."

"They were – did you say they were kissing?" Jackie Lynn already knew the answer. She was just asking the question out of shock. *I thought Katie Rose dealt with her attraction to Garrison.*

Samuel merely nodded. "She's a month away from marrying BJ. This kiss wasn't an innocent peck, Jackie Lynn," Samuel shared. "I felt you should know. The two of you have always been close. Maybe you can talk to Katie Rose and get to the bottom of what is going on. Katie Rose might resent it if I bring it up. This is totally out of character for her."

"Yes, it is," Jackie Lynn agreed. *How can she be pursuing her marriage to BJ if she still has feelings for Garrison? I've got to talk to Katie Rose.* "Thank you, Samuel," she said and gave his hand a grateful squeeze. "I'll get to the bottom of things with Katie Rose. I appreciate you confiding in me about what you saw." *I can't allow Katie Rose to enter into a marriage if she has feelings for another man.*

"I hated to upset you, but...I care a great deal about Katie Rose...and I'd hate to see her make a mistake. She needs to get her head together before she marries."

"I quite agree," Jackie Lynn nodded. "You've done the right thing, Samuel," she assured him. Jackie Lynn intended to have a long conversation with Katie Rose as soon as possible. She *would* get to the bottom of things, and she *would* make sure her daughter did what she needed to do in order to be happy. She would *not* allow Katie Rose to marry BJ out of guilt if she was in love with another man. Jackie Lynn was appreciative to Samuel for sharing what he had seen. She felt that much closer to him.

Chapter 29

Relapse

It was Saturday, near midnight. The concerts had just ended. Fawn approached Mason. She said she needed to talk with him. She wanted to discuss the next series of tours – Savage Pride striking out on their own. This conversation sounded like sweet music to Mason's ears. He was tired of traveling with other bands and past ready for Savage Pride to make a stand on their own.

"Can we go and find an all-night diner, like we used to?" Fawn suggested with a reminiscent smile. She had on a stretch T-shirt that emphasized her ample bust line. The shirt had an imprint of some artist's painting across it. She was also wearing a black beret and black Capri pants.

Mason was agreeable to joining Fawn for a late night snack and discussing upcoming business. Callie had already gone back to the bus. She had left after Savage Pride had finished their opening act. Unlike Mason, she did not like to stay for Seventh Sign's concerts any longer. She had seen enough of them over the past four weeks. She had actually seen enough of Savage Pride's as well, but she was always at the concert during their performance, to show her support to Mason.

Callie was glad the tour was almost over. She was weary of traveling and drained from being cramped up on a bus with a bunch of guys. She was also tired of dealing with Fawn and all the groupies that obsessed over Mason. She only wanted to go home where she could have privacy and Mason all to herself.

Mason briefly considered going back to the bus to tell Callie he was leaving with Fawn, but for the last few concerts, she had already been asleep when he had returned. She was tired of traveling and ready to go home, and so was he. *I'll let Callie sleep. She would want to come with us, and there is no sense in that. Fawn and I are just going to discuss business.*

"Let's go," Mason told Fawn with enthusiasm. He caught sight of Mark, Savage's Pride's other lead singer. "Hey, Mark," he called. "If Callie is awake, can you t ell her I went to grab a late snack with one of the guys."

Mark eyeballed Mason strangely, looking from him to Fawn. *Hardly one of the* guys. *Surely Mason isn't going to run off with Fawn when Callie is here with him.* All the guys still believed Mason and Fawn had been having an affair before Callie came on tour with him.

"Can you tell her that for me?" Mason asked, stumped by Mark's odd silence.

"I guess so," he answered. *I don't like lying for you. Callie seems like an awesome chick. I can't believe you would do her this way.*

"Okay. Callie may already be asleep. Don't wake her or anything. I'll be back in a little while."

Mason went off with Fawn, and Mark ambled toward the bus. Still deeply absorbed in thought over Mason's betrayal to Callie, he walked into the upstairs entertainment area. Mark was unprepared when he came upon Callie. She was sitting on the sofa staring at the television. The *Late Late Show* had just come on, but she was not really watching it.

"Oh, hi, Mark. Is the concert finally over?" she asked, yawning. Callie was fighting to stay awake. She was waiting up for Mason. She had not changed out of her clothes yet – a T-shirt and jeans.

"Um…yeah," Mark replied.

"I guess Mason will be here in a few then," Callie said both to Mark and to herself.

"N…no, not exactly," Mark told her.

"What's that supposed to mean?" Callie asked. She was studying the weird way Mark was acting. "What's up?"

"Mason left with Fawn," Mark revealed. He could not bring himself to lie to Callie. *It's disgusting that Mason is cheating on her.* Mark liked Callie a great deal. He thought Mason had gotten his head together since Callie had been traveling with him. *His* thing *with Fawn should be totally behind him.*

"What do you mean he left with Fawn?" Callie questioned, sitting up straighter. She was suddenly wide awake.

"I'll be honest with you, Callie. I thought everything was over between the two of them. But when Mason asked me to lie for him a second ago…"

"Lie for him?"

"Yeah. He asked me to tell you that he went to grab a late snack with one of the guys."

"He told you to tell me that?" Callie inquired with misgiving. *He's gone off with Fawn, and he's having Mark lie about where he is going?* "What did you mean when you said you thought it was all over between Fawn and Mason," Callie began to interrogate.

Mark sat down with dejection. They heard some of the other guys talking with loud excitement as they boarded the bus. They went directly to the lower lounge. They would smoke some weed and have a few drinks to unwind before they went to bed.

"Answer me, Mark," Callie pushed.

Mark fidgeted with his hands and would not make eye contact with Callie. He hated to hurt her. *But she should know the truth.* "All of the guys believe Mason and Fawn were having an affair before he brought you on board. Mason was always running off with her late at night. They even came from her hotel room right before one of the concerts. I thought he had put that all behind him when he brought you along for this tour. After all, the two of you are engaged. It's disgusting he would take up with Fawn again right under your nose."

"Did…did you say…they…they came from Fawn's hotel room one time?" Callie repeated in a shaky voice. *Is my worse fear coming true?* They used to spend a lot of time together, but Mason had sworn it was merely friendship. *But how can I truly know.*

Callie knew too well what men could be like. She had been a prostitute for awhile when she had been a drug addict living on the streets. Most of the men who went off with her were married men; men sworn to love only one woman. "Oh, my God!"

"I'm sorry, Callie," Mark apologized. "This has got to hurt. But better you know about it than Mason get away with doing it behind your back."

Mark got up from the couch. "I'm going to go downstairs with the rest of the guys and have a drink. Do you want to join us? It might take the edge off a little."

It would definitely take the edge off. I can't believe Mason is cheating on me with Fawn. Callie was crushed. She felt as if someone had put something heavy on her chest. She could hardly breathe and she hurt through and through. In a depressed fog, she got up and followed Mark downstairs. All of the guys were already settled on the sofa and love seats – Christof, James and Sam from Seventh Sign, and Savage Pride's drummer, Dave. Luckily, Mick was off somewhere else, probably chasing some groupie. Robert, Savage Pride's keyboardist, also was not there. Christof and the others were passing around a joint and all of them had drinks in their hand. Mark went over to the bar and Callie followed him.

"What would you like?" he asked. Mark had no idea Callie was an alcoholic. She and Mason never joined in the partying, but he did not know why.

"I'll take a shot of whiskey, straight up," she replied with hollow eyes and a troubled frown.

"You might want me to mix a little Seven-Up or some Coke with that. That will pack a punch," Mark warned.

"Trust me. I can handle it," Callie told him.

"Okay," Mark said. He felt sorry for her and could appreciate why she would want a strong shot of liquor. He poured her a shot glass full and placed the small tumbler in Callie's hand.

Callie looked at it for only a moment. Then she tilted back her head and poured the liquor down her throat. It burned as it went down. She remembered this burn. She also remembered how mind-numbing alcohol and weed could be. "Give me another shot," she asked Mark.

"Callie, are you sure?" he asked.

"Yes," she told him with authority, holding out the shot glass with eagerness. Mark filled it again, and Callie swung the glass to her mouth, tipped it, and swallowed.

She turned and went over to the sofa, taking a seat. "Can I have a hit?" she asked Christof, who was holding the joint.

"You're kidding, right?" he said with a chuckle. The other guys also laughed. Callie and Mason never partook in the drinking and drugs.

"Far from it," Callie said, reaching to jerk the marijuana cigarette from his hand. She never even took a second to think about what she was doing. She simply placed the joint in her mouth and deeply inhaled. Callie wanted to get totally wasted. She did not care where this foolishness led her. She could not deal with the pain she was feeling over Mason's betrayal, and with enough alcohol and drugs, she could escape. Never mind that she was an addict. All Callie cared about at present was getting beyond the pain, and drugs and alcohol were her ticket.

* * * *

Mason and Fawn were gone almost an hour and a half. They spent this time getting a bite to eat and discussing the details of Savage Pride's upcoming tour. Fawn told Mason he would be home for a month. Then he and Savage Pride would begin their first, solo, six week tour. They would even be given their own tour coach. Mason was overjoyed.

Even though it was one-thirty in the morning, Mason was extremely keyed up with excitement. He opened Fawn's driver's door, bent into her car, and gave Fawn a tight, grateful embrace. Then he allowed her to speed off down the road to her hotel.

Mason bounded aboard the bus. He hated to wake Callie, but he simply could not wait to share his wonderful news with her. He heard music, loud voices and laughter coming from the lower lounge. This scenario was not surprising to him. It went on after every concert. He also did not find it odd that he heard a woman's laugh. The guys were always bringing women back to the bus with them. They would kiss them goodbye and send them on their way, before the bus headed out, never seeing them again. So was the way with being on the road – at least for most of the guys other than him.

Mason went to the bunks where he and Callie were supposed to be sleeping for the night. When he pulled back the curtain, he was surprised to discover Callie was not in either bunk. *Tonight wasn't supposed to be our night for one of the big bedrooms downstairs, was it?* he wondered. *Where else could Callie be? I'll bet she is awake if she is in one of the big bedrooms. She has trouble sleeping through all the noise when the guys are partying. Maybe I won't have to wake her after all.*

Brimming with excitement, Mason went to the steps and bounced down them into the lower lounge. He came to a screeching halt at the bottom of the stairs when he saw Callie sitting on Mark's lap. She was running her fingers through his hair and kissing him. Mark had his hand on Callie's breast, and all of the other guys were cheering the two of them on.

At first, Mason thought he was mistaking another woman for Callie. *That can't be Callie*, his mind refused to accept. However, as he took a closer look, his eyes confirmed it. *It is her! But how! Why?!* "What the hell is going on?!" Mason's bellowed, ending the riotous uproar.

All at once, there was silence. All eyes were focused on his gaping figure. Mason had his hands balled into fists, and he was fast approaching Callie and Mark.

Mark tossed Callie sideways on the sofa, removing her from his lap. He scrambled to his feet and stood, prepared to shield himself from Mason's assault. Callie saw Mason approach and also staggered to her feet. "Well, did you finish your business with 'one of the guys'?" she asked in a slurred voice. "I had 'business' with one of them too," she spat with an evil cackle, as Mason closed the distance between them.

Callie looked unruly. Her hair was grossly tousled, her T-shirt twisted, and her eyes were a bright, irritated red. "My God, Callie, you're drunk..." Mason proclaimed, catching a strong whiff of alcohol.

"And stoned! Don't forget stoned," she said with an uncultivated chuckle, waving her index finger in his face. She smelled to high heavens of marijuana too, but so did the whole room. A dull, smoky residue still hung in the air. "What's it to you anyway? I figured you intended to spend the night with Fawn...oh...excuse me...that *guy* you went to get a bite to eat with. Isn't that what Mark was supposed to tell me? How many other times have you lied to me, Mason? How many other times have you and Fawn slept together. Huh? Why don't you answer me?!" Callie demanded. She tottered forward and smacked his shoulder with her open palms.

Mason glanced at Mark with malice. *What in the world did he tell Callie?* Mason was angry, confused and hurt. *How could Callie do what she's done? How much further would she have gone with Mark...or these other guys...if I hadn't come in?* The questions were racing through his mind.

Mason wanted to tear into Mark, and he wanted to tear into Callie. He also wanted to run and hide. He wanted all that had occurred to only be a bad dream. "I don't know what this jackass told you..." Mason began, glaring at Mark. "Fawn and I just went to discuss business. That's all. I thought you would be asleep, or I would have come and told you."

"Save it, Mason!" Callie squabbled. "Mark told me everything. He said you and Fawn have been having an affair for some time. He told me how the two of you used to sneak around before I came on the road with you. How you came from her hotel room before one of the concerts. How long has it been going on, Mason?! Stop lying to me! Tell me the truth! Damn you! I loved you and trusted you! I believed you were different! But you're like everyone else in my life! They all betrayed me! Now you have too! I don't need any of you!" Callie became hysterical. She began howling and beating on Mason's chest.

Damn you, Mark! You'll pay for the lies you've told Callie, Mason was thinking. His furious eyes and stone-set face fully conveyed these thoughts to Mark. Mason swept Callie off her feet and into his arms. He carried her flailing, crazed, wailing body up the stairs. He carried her all the way off the bus. He stood holding her and walking back and forth in the cool night air until she had kicked, screamed and cried herself into a state of unconsciousness.

Mason took Callie back inside. He marched her down to one of the big bedrooms. The guys sitting in the lounge saw him rush past. None of them said a word. Mason stomped inside one of the bedrooms. He slammed the door behind him and locked it. The other guys glanced at one another in stunned silence. Their party for the night had been brought to a somber end. Slowly, one by one, they began creeping off to their sleeping places for the night.

* * * *

Callie awoke from a restless sleep about eight o'clock the next morning. The bus was moving along again. She was surprised to learn the movement of the bus nauseated her. The coach had pulled out an hour ago. They would travel all day Sunday and Monday. Seventh Sign and Savage Pride would not perform again until Monday night.

As Callie sat up in bed, the room spun, and she realized she had a splitting headache. It was only then she began to recall the night before. *My God! I got loaded!* she was thinking with agony and repulsion, as she massaged the front of her skull with both hands.

Mason had felt her move, so he too slid to a sitting position in the bed. He had slept little the night before. His mind had been too troubled by what had transpired with Callie.

When Callie eventually gathered the strength to raise her head again, she looked over at Mason. His eyes were bloodshot, and he had bags under his eyes from lack of sleep. He almost looked as if he had gone on a drunken drug binge as well. *Not unless he did it with Fawn.* As this dreadful thought registered in Callie's mind, all of the reasons for her behavior last night also came to light. *I found out Mason has been unfaithful to me with Fawn.* All at once, the pain in her head was not as poignant as the pain in her heart.

"What are you doing here?" Callie snapped at Mason. Her voice was extremely groggy. "I thought you would have left to go be with your *lover*, since your fling with Fawn is all out in the open now."

Callie's hateful, untrue words cut at Mason like a knife. *She believes this crap!* It hurt him deeply that she had so little faith in him. *How could Callie believe Mark's lies? What have I ever done to give her reason to believe such nonsense?* "Let's get the facts straight," he said in an acidic voice. "I went with Fawn and we *talked*. When I came in last night, you were the one who was being unfaithful. You were deep-throat kissing another man, and he had his hands all over your body. And all because you believed some stupid lies Mark told you about Fawn and me. How could you, Callie? How can you not have more faith in me…in our love…than that? If we don't have trust, I'm not sure what we have…"

"Exactly!" she barked, and then lowered her voice several octaves. The loudness had rung in her head, causing it to throb. "You've been lying to me for some time, Mason. So how can I trust you?"

"What have I been lying about?" he demanded to know.

"About you and Fawn. You didn't tell me the two of you were still hanging out when you were on the road the last time. I found that out from the tabloids. Then you tried to have Mark lie for you last night. If it was all so innocent, why did you lie? And what were you doing in Fawn's hotel room before a concert that one time? What reason would you have to go there with her…other than to fuck her? You treat me like I'm some dumbass, Mason. I've been around. I know what happens between men and women – especially in hotel rooms."

"I *was* in Fawn's hotel room *once*," Mason confessed.

Callie looked shattered, shook her head as if to say 'I knew it', and looked away from him. Mason grabbed her chin and turned her head, so she was looking at him again. The spin made Callie want to hurl. "Stop, Mason," she demanded, slapping at his hands.

"No. I want you to look me in the eye and listen to what I am saying. I went to Fawn's hotel room to call you. Nothing else! She offered me her phone – *Only* her *phone*! – because I had no privacy on the bus to talk with you..."

"And while you were there...she tried...and probably succeeded in seducing you. You never should have gone to her room with her, Mason..."

"God, you have no faith in me at all," Mason said in repugnance, releasing Callie's head. He crawled out of bed and stood looking down at her with disappointed eyes. "I have *not* slept with Fawn. Not in her hotel room that time. Not at all. You may not believe that, but it's the truth. You are...or at least you were...the *only* women I was interested in sleeping with..."

"What do you mean...were?" Callie inquired in fear.

"I'm not sure," Mason acknowledged. "What you did last night...and what you have said this morning...I don't know how to deal with all this crap. I knew you were jealous of Fawn...of any other woman...but this is more than that. This is...you don't trust me at all..."

"Because you lie to me. Because everyone in my life has let me down at some point..."

"So I will too. Is that what you're saying?"

"I don't know," Callie whined with remorse. Tears were running down her cheeks. She did not want for Mason to go. She loved him and she did not want to lose him, but she did not know how to get beyond this feeling he had betrayed her...*or if not yet, then he will.* This revelation shook her.

"I need to be alone for a while to think. If you need to take comfort in drinking or doing drugs or in one of the other guys, I can't stop you," he said with misery. "You're the one who has betrayed our relationship, Callie. All I've done is love you from the bottom on my heart. If that isn't enough...then...I just don't know."

With that, he walked over to the door, unlocked it and walked out of the room. He shut the door behind him as he left. Callie stared at the closed door and began to sob. The shaking movement of her body made her very ill. She scampered off to the bathroom. She vomited until there was nothing left but dry heaves. She had never felt so terrible in her entire life. She had spent many a day ill over drugs and alcohol, but this, mixed with her heartbreak over Mason, was almost unbearable. Callie truly felt as if she was dying. With incredible effort, she made her way out of the bathroom, crawled back into bed, and curled up in a protective ball. She laid there shivering, whimpering, and trying to decipher what she should do next.

* * * *

Jackie Lynn called Katie Rose about ten o'clock Sunday morning. It had been difficult to wait until ten. Jackie Lynn had been awake since seven and had been biding her time to make this important call to her daughter. She would have called at 7:00 a.m., but she had not wished to wake Katie Rose or BJ, especially BJ. He needed all of his rest after all of the stress he was putting his body through each day.

Katie Rose answered the phone. "I didn't wake you or BJ, did I?" Jackie Lynn asked.

"No. Not hardly. BJ is at the hospital in physical therapy. He doesn't even rest on Sunday. He is determined to be able to walk perfectly by our wedding. And time is growing short."

"Yes, it is," Jackie Lynn said, sounding more than a little distracted. "Your wedding is exactly what I'm calling about," she got straight to the point.

"Is something wrong? I thought everything was all planned," Katie Rose said.

She sounds so nonchalant about the wedding. How can she be kissing Garrison in a car one minute and planning her wedding to BJ like nothing is amiss the next. Katie Rose was not raised this way – to be deceptive. I have to get to the bottom of all this, Jackie Lynn mused.

"Mom, what's up?" Katie Rose inquired, worried by her mom's sudden stillness.

"That's what I need to know from you," Jackie Lynn dived right in.

"Me? How so?"

"Well…there is no easy way to say this…so I'll just come right out and say it. Samuel saw you kissing Garrison Parker in a car Friday afternoon. How is it you are about to marry one man in less than a month, but yet you are kissing another? I thought all this business with Garrison Parker had been worked out. What's going on?"

Katie Rose was awestruck. *Samuel saw us kissing!* She felt embarrassed, guilty and relieved all at the same time. *I need to tell mom the truth.*

"Katie Rose," Jackie Lynn called. "I need to know what is going on."

"I know," she articulated at last. "You deserve an explanation." *How do I even begin to explain?* "There is no easy way to say this either…I'm…I'm in love with Garrison Parker, mom. I'm not in love with BJ." *There, I've said it. It's all out in the open now.*

Jackie Lynn was stunned by Katie Rose's declaration. "Then…what are you doing? Why are you still planning to marry him? What you are doing makes no sense, Katie Rose…"

"I know, mom. Believe me, I know," Katie Rose assured her. "I have hated all this dishonesty. I don't like being deceitful to BJ, you, or anyone. BJ was supposed to have been told the truth, and so were you and everyone else. But his accident changed all that…"

"Katie Rose, you can *not* marry BJ because you feel sorry for him," Jackie Lynn pointed out.

"I know, mom. And I don't intend to. I'm only giving him hope. Hope he needs to get well."

"So you don't intend to marry BJ?"

"No," Katie Rose gingerly revealed. "I'm…I'm already married in the heart to Garrison…in fact, we went through an Indian marriage ceremony at the Reservation.""That…so that's why you went to the Reservation. I wondered about that when Samuel told me you were going there to visit your father's grave…"

"I did go there to visit daddy's grave. I was torn at that time about my feelings for Garrison and BJ. But I'm not anymore. When Garrison and I got married at the Reservation, I realized he is the only man I love…the only man I'll ever love. I denied it for as long as I could. But I won't deny it anymore."

"So when do you intend to tell BJ? He still thinks everything is fine between the two of you. He loves you a great deal. This is going to crush him," Jackie Lynn spoke her thoughts aloud. Her heart was aching for BJ. She cared about him a lot. She already thought of him as her son-in-law.

"Yes, it will. That is why I haven't told him. I don't want him to give up. I want him to totally recover. And he is. The dream of standing at the front of church and walking me out the door is helping him to heal. He's learning how to walk normally again, despite his injury. I can't take that away from him, mom. I may not be in love with BJ, but I do love him as a friend. I'm going to miss him a great deal."

"I can't believe all this is happening," Jackie Lynn honestly declared. She sounded a little beside herself.

"I didn't plan it this way, mom. If I could go back in time and change things...make it so BJ and I only stayed friends...I would. But I can't."

"So how long do you intend to keep up this farce? What are you going to do? Not show up for the wedding on your wedding day? It's getting down to the wire."

"I know, mom. This is all a huge mess! But BJ is getting better and better each day. I *will* tell him before the wedding. When...before the wedding...I'm not sure."

"Well...in the meantime, you better be much, much more discrete. What if BJ was the one who saw you kissing Garrison? The truth is going to be hard enough for him to accept. Don't make him find out by witnessing a physical exchange between you and Garrison."

"You're absolutely right, mom," Katie Rose agreed. "Garrison and I will be more careful. Do you want me to talk to Samuel?"

"No. I'll talk to Samuel. I'll find some way to explain things, without revealing the truth."

"I'm sorry, mom. I detest making you lie to Samuel. I despise *all* the lies. I'll be glad when I can finally be truthful. It will be so incredible when Garrison and I can at last be together and not have to hide anything. He can hardly wait for this to come to pass either. We have so much in common, mom. Accepting Garrison and I together is going to be hard, but once you get to know him...once you see us together...you'll see we were made for each other."

Jackie Lynn could hear the mirth in her daughter's voice as she talked about Garrison. It reminded her of the way she used to talk about Long Wolf when they had first fallen in love. *She is in love with Garrison Parker. I want her to be with the man she truly loves.* "Honey, your happiness is what is most important to me. Don't worry about my feelings for BJ," Jackie Lynn told her.

Katie Rose was so touched by her mother's caring words she felt like crying. "I love you, mom," Katie Rose stated. "Thanks for always standing by me no matter what."

"I'm sorry you have to go through all this anguish, Katie Rose. I feel partially to blame. I'm the one that encouraged you to pursue your feelings for BJ in the first place. I wish I hadn't done that. Maybe then the two of you would have stayed friends, like you should have."

"Don't blame yourself, mom. I thought I was in love with BJ until Garrison came along. I didn't have anything to compare my feelings to. But now I know what being in love is supposed to feel like. I think about Garrison constantly. I'm not only attracted to him and love him physically, but in so many other ways – our similar business backgrounds, our Indian heritage, just to name a few.

"I felt the same way about your father," Jackie Lynn confessed with a bittersweet mixture of reminiscent happiness and sadness. "This kind of deep love does not come along every day, so you need to hang onto it with everything you've got. Don't let anything, or *anyone*, get in the way. I'm here for you, Katie Rose. Let me know what I can do to help."

"There's nothing you can do, mom," she said a little despondently. "Other than keep my secret. I'll tell BJ soon."

"When you do, I'll be here to support you," Jackie Lynn reiterated one final time.

"Thanks, mom," Katie Rose said again. She felt incredibly blessed to have such a loving, understanding parent.

Chapter 30

Eye-openers

Callie was still in the bedroom, lying in the bed, when Mason came back into the room Sunday afternoon. She had eaten neither breakfast nor lunch. She was not hungry. Callie only wished to hide from the world, and she was afraid to leave the bedroom, for fear she would hide through drinking and drugs again. The temptation was much too great right now.

"Callie, we need to talk," Mason told her. He took a seat on the end of the bed.

Callie slowly scrambled to a sitting position in the bed. She silently studied Mason for a few moments. His shoulders were hunched, as if he had the weight of the world on them, and he was staring at the wall and not looking at her. *He doesn't even want to look at me. I've hurt him. But he hurt me too. I just want to erase last night. I don't want to lose him.* "What do you want to talk about?" she asked. Her voice was devoid of emotion. She felt numb.

"I talked to the bus driver. We'll be driving through Atlanta today. He's going to stop at the airport there. I want you to catch a flight home."

"You...you're sending me away?" Callie asked in alarm, hurt. Her stomach flip-flopped, and she thought she might be sick again, even though she had nothing on her stomach to expel. She was tasting stomach acid in her mouth.

"Yes, I'm sending you away," Mason replied with regret. "It's for your own good..."

"For *my* own good? Or for *yours*? If you get rid of me, it clears the path to be with Fawn, right?" she meanly accused.

Mason glanced back at her and shook his head in disapproval. He stood up from the end of the bed. "That hurts every time I hear it, Callie. But if you believe that, I can't do anything to change it. If you don't have faith in us, I can't make you. I don't know where we go from here. I need time alone to think. You do too. Moreover, you need to be away from the bad influences you are exposed to here. I probably should have thought about that before I brought you along. I never in a million years thought you would turn back to alcohol and drugs. That was one more thing I was wrong about."

"What other things have you been wrong about?" she inquired, studying him as he ambled along with his head down. He looked as if he had been whipped. The last time Callie had seen him so downtrodden was when his father died.

"I think I've been wrong about *us*," he began.

Callie sat up straighter in the bed. Her worst fear was about to come true. *He's about to break up with me. He's moving on with Fawn.* She unconsciously grabbed the blanket and wadded it up in her hands leaning her chin against it, like a frightened little girl. She wanted to dispute Mason, but she could not make herself speak.

"You see, I believed our love was great enough to conquer anything," Mason continued, looking at her with pained eyes. "But true love has trust combined with it. You believe in the other person. But you don't trust or believe in me at all. So it makes me wonder if you love me at all."

"That isn't so," Callie managed to utter. "I do love you, but it's hard to trust you with all the lies…"

"The only lies have been the ones Mark told you last night. I haven't cheated on you, Callie. You can't say the same. If I hadn't of come in last night…I don't even want to think about it. I want you to go home. We need a few days apart. I'll be home next weekend, and we'll talk everything over and see where we go from there. I hope there is a future for us, Callie. I really do. I love you so much…" Mason's voice broke then. He was actually fighting tears. "Just pack. You have a few hours. I'll make sure you get off okay at the airport."

He turned and darted from the room, accidentally slamming the door behind him. Callie jumped. As she stared forlornly at the closed door, she broke down and cried. *What have I done? Could Mason be telling me the truth? I don't want to leave, but I need to give him a few days. I need a few days to think about what I need to do to make things right between us. I can't lose Mason.*

She sat and cried for several more moments. Callie eventually forced herself to rise from the bed. She crept out of the bedroom. *I could really use a drink,* her mind told her. She scurried past the downstairs lounge. *Don't even look at the bar. You need to stay clearheaded.* Callie rushed up the stairs. *I need to pack. I'll do what Mason is asking. I'll find a way to make things right between us. I have to. I love him too much to let things end.*

* * * *

Callie's plane touched down about 8:00 p.m. Sunday evening. Her mom was waiting for her when she when she got off the plane. Her mother's presence came as no surprise to Callie. Mason had called her mom from the Atlanta airport and asked her to meet Callie when she got off the plane at home and give her a ride to the apartment. He was afraid Callie might end up in one of the airport bars otherwise. Truth be told, Callie was afraid of this occurring herself, so she was glad Mason had asked her mom to be there. She had continually fought the impulse not to order a drink while she was on the plane.

As soon as Callie saw her mother, she threw herself into her arms and broke into sobs. "Callie…what…!?" Mary Julia questioned in alarm, as she held her daughter with secure arms.

"I screwed up, mom," Callie said, when she could manage to talk.

Mary Julia led Callie over to some chairs. Her daughter was pale and shaking. Mary Julia feared Callie's legs might buckle. "Sit. Tell me what's wrong," she directed.

Callie sat down in a chair and her mom sat in the one right beside her. She took Callie's small, cold hand into hers, patted it, and said, "You can tell me anything, sweetheart. Tell mommie."

Callie hated that her mom always reverted into talking to her as if she was a child. But she greatly needed to talk to someone, so she chose to ignore this irritating habit. "I need to go to an AA meeting, mom. I got drunk last night and smoked some weed…"

"You..you what? Why? Where was Mason? He hasn't been drinking and using drugs in front of you, has he?"

True to form, her mother always blamed Mason. "Mom, please don't do that," Callie pleaded.

"Do what?" her mother asked with confusion.

"Don't blame Mason. Mason doesn't drink much, and he *never* uses drugs. I don't want to have to defend him. I just need an ear right now. Please don't blame Mason for anything. I've already done that. That's why I slipped up and turned back to old habits. Can you listen and not judge? Can you do that for me?"

"Okay," Mary Julia agreed with some hesitation. Regardless, she was wondering, *What has Mason done to my baby?* "Talk to me. Mommie will listen."

She won't be able to just listen. She'll only make things worse. She'll say I'm right about Mason cheating, because she has never trusted him anyway, Callie swiftly concluded. "Can you drive me to BJ's apartment? I need to talk to Katie Rose." *Katie Rose won't believe Mason has cheated on me, but she will listen to what I have to say. She can help me get my head together – much better than my mom can.*

"I thought you wanted to talk, honey. I'll listen."

"I know you would, mom. But I need to talk to Katie Rose."

"What about the AA meeting? Shouldn't I try to find you one of those?"

"I'll go to one tomorrow. I might call the rehab center tonight and talk to a counselor. They are there twenty-four hours. I'll be okay. Can you take me to Katie Rose's, so I can talk to my best friend?" she asked again.

Mary Julia felt hurt that Callie wished to confide in a friend instead of her, but the main thing she wanted was to help her daughter. *If talking to Katie Rose will help, I'll take Callie there.* "Okay, let's go," Mary Julia said, standing up.

Callie stood and her mom put her arm around her. The two walked away. "Thanks for being here for me, mom," Callie said. Her mom wanted her to talk, and Callie did not want to hurt her, but she needed Katie Rose's mature head and not her mom's emotional one.

"I'm here, baby doll. I'll always be here for you," Mary Julia said, and planted an affirming kiss on Callie's temple. They walked off through the airport side by side.

* * * *

In her mom's car, Callie's called BJ's apartment from her cell phone. Katie Rose answered the phone. She was alarmed to hear Callie was back in town, without Mason. *Both she* and Mason *were supposed to be back this weekend.*

Katie Rose could hear the distress in Callie's voice. *Something's wrong.* Callie quickly assured Katie Rose that Mason was okay, but she alluded to the fact that there was some problem between the two of them. When Callie asked if she could come over to the apartment and talk, Katie Rose told her to come right away. She wanted to be there for her friend.

When Katie Rose opened the apartment door, both Mary Julia and Callie were standing in the hallway. "I wanted to make sure she got in okay," Mary Julia strangely stated. She gave Callie a kiss on the cheek and told her to call if she needed anything.

"I will, mom," Callie assured her. "Thanks for picking me up at the airport and bringing me over here. I'll talk to you tomorrow."

Mary Julia left reluctantly. Katie Rose ushered Callie into BJ's apartment and shut the door. The two friends walked over to the couch and had a seat. "How is BJ doing?" Callie asked first.

Katie Rose had called Mason and Callie when BJ had lost his leg. Callie had offered to come home and lend her support, but Katie Rose had assured both her and Mason there was nothing either of them could do. Callie had called a few times since, and Katie Rose had told her BJ was healing and progressing well. She had been glad to hear that BJ was doing well. Callie liked BJ a great deal. She hated that he had lost his leg in a freak accident.

"BJ is doing fantastic!" Katie Rose answered with enthusiasm. "He's in the bedroom watching television." They had moved BJ's nineteen-inch television to the bedroom when he first came home for the hospital. They had not moved it back to the living room yet. "BJ went there to give us some privacy."

"He's a great guy," Callie professed with fondness.

"Yes, he is," Katie Rose replied, feeling a tinge of guilt. Callie was one more person she would have to break the news to about Garrison. "So tell me what you wanted to talk with me about. Why are you home…without Mason?"

"Because I screwed up," Callie said with remorse.

"How so?" Katie Rose asked.

"I got drunk and high last night," Callie confessed.

"You what...why?!" Katie Rose asked in astonishment. Callie had been clean and sober for years. *Something really bad must have occurred to trigger this response.*

"Mason lied to me. Or rather he tried to have Mark lie for him. Mark was supposed to tell me Mason went out with one of the guys. Instead he went off with Fawn. Mark refused to lie for Mason. He said Mason and Fawn have been having an affair all along. Mason confessed to being in Fawn's bedroom once..."

"Wait a minute...whoa...slow down, Callie," Katie Rose requested, taking a second to ingest all Callie had spurted out thus far. "So are you saying Mason confessed to having an affair with Fawn?"

"No. He said he was only in her hotel room to call me. That she *only* offered him a phone to use. But Katie Rose, this is the second time I've caught him lying about Fawn. Why should I believe he isn't having an affair with her?"

"I guess my question is...why should you believe Mark over Mason? Mason has told some little white lies about his time with Fawn but... he does that because you are jealous. I'm not defending his lies, but Mason is head over heels in love with you, Callie. I know what being head over heels in love looks like." *I feel the same way about Garrison.* "I don't think Mason would take a chance on ruining things between the two of you by having an affair with Fawn."

"Everyone cheats, Katie Rose. Look at my mom and dad. And when I was on the street living as a prostitute, most of the men I slept with were married men."

The proclamation about 'everyone cheating' made Katie Rose feel very uncomfortable – considering she was currently cheating on BJ. "Callie, your past was painful. As to your mom and dad, your mom had an addiction to sex. You have an addiction to drugs and alcohol, so you should be able to relate. She reverted back to an addiction when your dad walked out on her. And your dad did *not* cheat on your mom. He only shared a kiss with Flora. Granted, this kiss was not right either, but it wasn't as if your dad was sleeping around. Your dad and mom were faithful to each other for many years. Have you forgotten that? I'm sure your past has jaded you. But I don't believe *everyone* cheats. I don't think it's fair to lump Mason into the class of men you were dealing with on the street either. You once said to me that trust was very important. You are right. You have got to trust Mason. Look at your mom and dad. Your mom would not trust your dad to be around you. She thought because she was abused as a child that *all* men abuse. That wasn't true, but her fear and belief that all men abuse eventually broke up their marriage, and it kept you from having a father while you were growing up. Don't let your fears and false beliefs spoil what you and Mason have," Katie Rose warned.

Callie had not thought about it in this light. *Isn't that exactly what I am doing? I have no proof Mason and Fawn are having an affair. I'm condemning him because of my past.* "Oh, my God, Katie Rose, you are right," she said with confidence. "I've been a real fool. I need to tell Mason this. I'll go home and call him. I've got to find a way to get my jealousy and fears under control. I can't treat Mason like my mom treated my dad. I don't want to blow things between us."

"I know you don't," Katie Rose said and gave Callie an encouraging smile for the first time.

Callie put her arms around Katie Rose and gave her an appreciative embrace. She was thankful she and Katie Rose were such close friends. She had almost thrown away this friendship at one time because of her foolishness. "Thank you for talking with me, Katie Rose. I knew you'd be able to help me. You've always had such a level head."

Don't be so sure of that, Katie Rose was thinking. *I hope Callie doesn't feel differently about me when my affair with Garrison is brought to light.*

"I'll drive you home, and you can call Mason," Katie Rose offered. She stood to go and tell BJ where she was going, and to get her car keys.

Callie got up and followed Katie Rose. "I'll say a few words to BJ," she said.

"Oh…okay," Katie Rose said with slight distraction.

Katie Rose led Callie back to the bedroom and Callie stood in the doorway to say hello to BJ. She tried not to look at his leg. He had it hidden under the blanket, and he was not making the effort to get out of bed. Callie did not expect him to. Katie Rose felt another twinge of guilt as Callie and BJ talked like old friends.

She retrieved her purse. It was sitting on the floor beside the dresser. Katie Rose bent to give BJ a small peck on the side of the mouth. Then she started from the room with Callie.

"Callie, it was good seeing you. See you in a few, Katie Rose. I love you," BJ said.

"I love you too," Katie Rose mumbled, without looking at him. She scampered from the room.

Callie said goodbye to BJ. She turned and followed Katie Rose out of the room. She had sensed some tension. *Wedding jitters?* she could not help but wonder. Katie Rose and BJ's wedding was less than a month away. *Or is it tension over dealing with BJ's injury. I have talked Katie Rose's ear off about Mason and me. I'll see if I can get her to talk some about her and BJ in the car. I want her to know the support goes both ways.*

Callie followed Katie Rose from the apartment. They walked to her Mustang and hopped in. As Katie Rose backed the car out and pulled out onto the street, Callie broached the subject of her and BJ. "So is everything okay between you and BJ?"

"Sure. Why wouldn't it be?" Katie Rose rather evasively replied.

"I don't know. He's been through a lot. And then there's the stress of the wedding in less than a month. I'm here to listen and talk to as well. You certainly were here for me tonight. If there is anything you need to talk about, I'm an ear for you too."

"I know," Katie Rose answered. She seemed preoccupied.

"And..." Callie prodded. "I sense something is up."

"You know me too well. That's all," Katie Rose told her. She glanced at Callie with a nervous chuckle.

"Something's wrong, isn't it?" Callie probed. "Come on, Katie Rose. You can tell me anything."

"Callie, I...BJ and I may not be getting married," she began with hesitation, staring back out the windshield. *Why'd I say may not? We will not be getting married. I'm already married in my heart to Garrison.*

"Why? Has his injury put a strain on your relationship?"

"No. It has nothing to do with that. If anything, that's kept us together."

"What on earth is wrong?" Callie asked in alarm and shock.

"I'm not in love with BJ," Katie Rose broke the news, giving Callie another peek. *I wasn't going to tell her yet. But why hold back the truth? She'll find out soon enough anyway.*

"You're…what do you mean you're not in love with him. What's happened between you guys?"

"Nothing. I never was *in love* with him. I've made a terrible mistake, Callie. BJ and I should never have become lovers. We should have just stayed friends. That's all he is to me – a friend. That's all he's ever been." Katie Rose gripped the top of the steering wheel with both hands.

"What? Where is all this craziness coming from?!" Callie asked in astonishment. Her friend was supposed to be marrying this man in less than a month, and now she was saying she did not love him. *Maybe they put something in that weed I smoked last night and I'm hallucinating*, she could not help but speculate.

"It's true, Callie. I told you about kissing and fantasizing about Garrison Parker…"

"Oh my God! Don't tell me the two of you…"

"I'm in love with him, Callie. I've never felt about BJ the way I do about Garrison. Don't get me wrong. I care about BJ a great deal…"

"Then what are you doing? Why are you still engaged to him? You are playing him for a fool, running around with this Garrison guy behind his back," Callie unkindly accused.

"I planned to tell BJ on…of all days…Valentine's Day. But that was the day of his accident…"

"So you are staying with him, pretending to be in love with him, and saying you intend to marry him, out of pity? That's not fair to him, Katie Rose. BJ deserves better!"

"He does deserve better. He deserves a woman who loves him with all her heart, as I do Garrison. I'm not staying with BJ out of pity, Callie. I'm staying with him and still pretending to be his fiancé, because it gives him the incentive to get better – to walk again."

"Oh my God!" Callie proclaimed again, shaking her head in disbelief. "I can't believe this. Why didn't you tell him about Garrison all those months ago when you talked to me about fantasizing about him?"

"Believe me, I wish I had. I was determined to be true to BJ back then. I cut all ties with Garrison and was trying everything to get him out of my mind. But nothing worked. Then we were thrown together in California. One thing led to another…"

"And you slept together," Callie stated with distaste. She would have never thought Katie Rose capable of such an atrocity.

"Don't make it sound like some illicit affair, Callie," Katie Rose requested, momentarily looking into Callie's judgmental eyes. "I feel the same thing for Garrison as you do for Mason. I couldn't fight it any longer. Garrison and I actually got married at the Indian Reservation."

"You're married to this man?!" Callie repeated with incredulity.

"In the heart. Not legally…not yet. That's why I was going to leave BJ on Valentine's Day. His injury changed all that. Believe me, Callie. I hate the lies. Samuel saw Garrison and me kissing Friday. He told mom. So she knows the truth now too. I have to tell BJ soon, or he is likely to find out from someone else, and I don't want that. Finding out about Garrison and me is going to break his heart. I can hardly bear it. If I could rewind time and do things differently, I would. But I can't."

Callie was silent for several long moments. She was trying fiercely to digest all that Katie Rose had shared. Her friend was caught in an awful dilemma. *I could chastise her for allowing Garrison in, but is this what I want to do? Mason and I knew BJ and Katie Rose relationship was pretty one-sided for a long time – BJ loved Katie Rose, but Katie Rose did not seem to return his feelings. She* should *have merely stayed friends with him. But she didn't. Can I condemn her for finding true love?*

"Callie, I understand if you are upset with me. Please don't file Garrison and me under your 'everyone cheats' list. I should have been honest about my attraction to Garrison from the start. If I had told BJ, maybe he would have backed out of the relationship then. Maybe we still could have salvaged some friendship, and I could be helping him through this terrible time as a friend. We'll never know, because I didn't tell him. It's been mistake after mistake with BJ…"

"You must feel miserable," Callie commented with compassion.

"I do," Katie Rose admitted. Her eyes looked remorseful.

Callie reached over and squeezed Katie Rose's hand. "I bet Garrison makes you very happy, doesn't he?"

"He does," Katie Rose confirmed, and smiled for the first time.

"Then that's all that matters. I'm not going to condemn you, Katie Rose. You didn't condemn me when I did all those awful things so long ago. Your love has been unconditional. Mine will be too. I'm here for you. If Garrison makes you happy, you should be with Garrison. You should be with the man you love."

Callie's kind, understanding words moved Katie Rose. She felt tears sting her eyes all at once. "BJ and I are going to need all the support we can get to get through this horrible mess," she revealed, choking up. "It breaks my heart to have to hurt him. It's totally unfair to him, and I despise all this." She was crying now.

She pulled the car over to the side of the road because she was being blinded by her tears. Callie released her seatbelt and slid over to place her arms around her friend. "It will all work out, Katie Rose. We will all be behind you. And I'll be a friend to BJ as well."

Katie Rose laid her head on Callie's shoulder and allowed her friend to comfort her for several moments. She had been holding back the tears for so long. It felt good to be comforted by her best friend and to be told she was staunchly in her corner. It also felt terrific to come clean with one other person. Katie Rose would be so relieved when all of the truth was out in the open to everyone.

"Thanks, Cal," she said with appreciation, when her tears finally subsided.

"What are best friends for?" Callie asked and gave her friend an encouraging smile.

Callie released Katie Rose from her arms and slid back over to her side of the car. She snapped her seatbelt back on as Katie Rose put the car back in drive. The two women were headed out again. They were both elated to have the friendship of one another to help them overcome the trials in their lives.

Chapter 31

Truth

Callie called Mason's cell phone several times Sunday evening. After the third unanswered call, she left him a message. "Um…Mas…you know who's been calling, because you have caller ID. So I guess you don't want to talk to me. That's okay. You said you needed some time to think. I've already thought some things through, and I wanted to let you know I'm sorry. I'll leave it at that. I hope to hear from you soon. I love you. I *really* do."

Callie did not go to bed until after midnight Sunday. She waited and waited for Mason's return call to come. *Maybe he'll call tomorrow*, she was hopeful. However, there was this nagging fear in the back of her mind. *What if I've pushed him into Fawn's arms? What if he's decided it's over?* Callie fell into a restless sleep, worrying over this very thing.

* * * *

Katie Rose called Garrison first thing Monday morning. She asked him to meet her at his house at 11:00 a.m. She told him they needed to talk.

Garrison's car was in the driveway, under the carport, when Katie Rose pulled up at 10:50 a.m. *Good! He's early*, she thought with satisfaction. She vacated her car.

Katie Rose took a second to admire the azalea bushes. They were beginning their spring bloom. Garrison had planted white, pink and red bushes up by the house. They looked very pretty. It was obvious he enjoyed landscaping. Katie Rose enjoyed growing things as well. She had picked this love up from her father. *One more thing Garrison and I have in common*, she thought.

She gave him a smile when she saw him standing in his doorway waiting for her. He had already discarded his suit jacket and tie, and he had his sleeves and top button to his dress shirt unfastened. Garrison opened up the storm door and did not waste any time gathering Katie Rose in his arms and giving her an admiring kiss.

They had not seen each other since Friday. They had been unable to sneak away that weekend. Garrison clung to Katie Rose as if it had been eons since they had been together.

"So how's my lovely Kate today?" he asked with a satisfied grin. He took the leisure of giving her another, long, exhaustive kiss.

"I'm fine," she said with a jovial snigger.

Each and every moment in Garrison's presence brought her such joy. Since she had revealed their secret love to two more people, Katie Rose was feeling even more serene. She stepped into the house with Garrison and watched as he closed the door.

"You said we needed to talk, and you sounded very serious on the phone. Is something wrong?" he asked.

"Not really," Katie Rose said. Then she informed him, "You and I need to be more careful when we are out in public."

Garrison had taken her hand and began walking her through the house. They meandered through the living room and past the kitchen. Garrison was leading her to his bedroom. *We'll have to make this a fast conversation.* She wanted him as badly as he wanted her. Her strong physical desire for him never waned.

He turned the corner and pulled Katie Rose into his bedroom. As usual, his scent hung in the air. It was the first thing Katie Rose had noticed the very first time she had stowed away with Garrison to his house. Katie Rose loved his smell, so the aroma of his bedroom only served to whet her appetite for him more.

She tried to ignore it, and the pleasurable tingles in her body, as she focused on the conversation at hand. "We need to keep the physical exchanges between us behind closed doors. Samuel saw us kissing in your car Friday."

"Oh, oh…you're kidding," he said, but he knew she was not. "So I take it he confronted you about what he saw."

"No, actually my mom did. I told her the truth about us, Garrison," Katie Rose revealed.

"And? Was she upset?"

"A little. She likes BJ a great deal, but she said my happiness was what was most important."

"Good," he said with a pleased grin. "She should know the truth. Everyone should. I could not wait for this weekend to be over, so I could see you again. Each day without you seems like an eternity. So when do you tell BJ?" He had one arm hooked around her waist. He had reached to unbutton a few buttons of her blouse, and he was softly caressing the cleft between her breasts.

Katie Rose fought to ignore the delightful shivers his warm, tormenting touch was causing. Focusing on their talk, she argued, "That's just the point. *I* want to be the one to tell BJ. Not someone else. And if the wrong person happens to see us, he could find out a really horrible way. I don't want him to find out about us this way. We need to be much more cautious."

"We could go with the plan I suggested before. You move out of BJ's apartment and pretend to move back in with your mom, but you stay with me instead. How's that for cautious? Since your mom knows about us, she would cover for you, wouldn't she?"

"No…maybe…I wouldn't ask her to do that. Don't change the subject," she rebuked, bending away from the kiss he was trying to bestow. When Garrison kissed her, it turned Katie Rose's brain to mush. His touch was already making it hard enough for her to concentrate. "Garrison, stop. You need to listen to me. Alright?"

"I am listening," he said and bent to steal a couple of pecks – two to each side of her mouth and one in the center. "I wish you would stop pushing away from me. I've waited all weekend to touch you. You're making me crazy."

Katie Rose was going to tell him about Callie knowing about them as well. But this fact was beginning to seem less and less important. The more he kissed and stroked her, the less Katie Rose wanted to talk. *I need to calm him before we talk. I need to calm us* both.

The only way to elicit calm was to stop resisting him. She did not want to resist Garrison anyway. She had missed him tremendously. "Okay, you win," she chirped with longing eyes. "I missed you too."

Katie Rose put her arms around his neck and pulled her body in close to his. "We're behind closed doors now, so let's *not* be cautious." She began kissing Garrison with uninhibited passion. *We'll talk later*, she thought, losing herself to intense hunger for this man.

* * * *

When Mason went onstage Monday night with Savage Pride, the first thing he did was look for Callie's beaming face in the audience. She had been at the foot of the stage, cheering him and Savage Pride on, for weeks, but now she was gone. His heart felt heavy. He missed her enormously, and his mind was not on playing his music.

For the first time since Savage Pride's music career had taken off, Mason was glad when they had finished their portion of the show. The screaming, frantic overzealousness of thousands of energized fans did not even rouse him. Callie engulfed his thoughts. The concert seemed empty without her there to share the excitement.

Fawn was waiting backstage for him when he vacated the stage. She did not have a happy expression on her face. "What's up?" Mason asked as she approached him.

"That's kind of what I was wondering," she replied. "Can we go someplace and talk?"

"Sure. What better have I got to do?" Mason asked glumly.

Normally, Callie would be waiting for him. But since she was not there, Mason dreaded going back to the bus and being alone. He would be tempted beyond reason to return her call. He had gotten her message. But right now, Mason felt it was best if they did not talk. Callie might be sorry, but her apology did not mean she miraculously trusted him, and Mason could not take hearing any more of her hurtful accusations. It tore him apart, and it shook the very roots of their relationship.

Fawn led the way out the exit door. As usual, they hopped in her car and she speeded away. "Where are we going?" Mason asked.

"No place in specific. We can just drive around. I wanted to talk to you about Callie," she got right to the point.

"What about her?" Mason asked. There was a defensive edge to his voice.

"I heard from the bus driver that he had to make an uncharted stop yesterday…at the airport in Atlanta. He said he dropped Callie off there, per your request. Why'd you send her home, Mason? You fought tooth and nail to keep her with you. What occurred to change your mind? You may think I'm being nosy, but tonight was not your best performance. Something's bothering you, and I figure it has something to do with Callie. So that makes it somewhat my business. Plus, I consider myself to be your friend."

"You *are* a friend, Fawn," Mason affirmed. He decided to confide in her. "Callie had some trouble with drugs and alcohol years ago. When I got back from our meeting last night, I found her drunk and stoned and locked in a lip lock with Mark…with the rest of the guys cheering them on to do more. Callie's excuse for behaving this way was that Mark told her all about the affair you and I have been having. And Callie believed what he said. Simply because I went off with you last night and stretched the truth about where I was going…"

"Yeah, I heard you ask Mark to tell Callie you were going out with one of the guys. I wondered why you said that. I figured it was because of Callie's jealousy toward me. But, Mason, telling lies only throws fuel on sparks. Callie has a significant jealous streak, not just with me but with any other woman. She doesn't need your lies about what you are doing on top of this jealousy."

"Are you defending Callie's actions?" Mason asked with annoyance.

"Not exactly," Fawn clarified, giving him a glance and then focusing back on the road. "Because as the saying goes, two wrongs don't make a right."

"So, in other words, you think I was wrong too…"

"Yes, I do," Fawn declared without hesitation. "Men like to avoid problems. And you figured telling a little lie was the lesser of two evils. But you need to…pardon my French…get some balls. Face Callie's jealousy problem head on, instead of running from it by telling lies and sneaking around."

"Well, that's certainly laying it on the line," Mason stated with an apprehensive chuckle. "So I suppose you also think I was wrong to send her away. That's avoiding the problem too, right?"

"Somewhat," Fawn agreed. "But if Callie was getting wrapped back up in drinking and drugs, it was wise to send her away. Plus, sending her away gives you a few days to get your head together. The two of you will have a month to work this all out before you are on the road again. But for the next few days, I want you still focused on your music. Have you got that?"

"It's all work with you. Isn't it, Fawn?" Mason questioned. "Is that why there is no one special in your life?"

"That...and I tend to be very blunt...as in the statement about you getting some balls. I do have relationships when I'm not on the road though."

"Oh...you never mentioned anyone," Mason pointed out. "I shouldn't have assumed there wasn't someone..."

"My love life is private," Fawn told him. She paused; then she fleetingly looked him in the eye and said, "I'm going to share something with you in confidence, Mason. Because I do consider you a friend, and I trust you. You can share this information with Callie. It won't solve her jealousy problem...but it might help where I am concerned..."

"I don't know if anything will help," Mason disagreed. "She'll say it's easy for you to cheat on your special someone while you are on the road too..."

"That might be true. But it wouldn't be with you. It would more likely be with Callie."

It took a second for Fawn's words to sink in and for Mason to fully understand them. "Are you telling me..."

"That I'm a lesbian...yes," Fawn answered, stealing a look at Mason's shocked face. They were on a city street with ample streetlights, so it was easy to clearly see his expression. "Not many people know this fact, because as I said, my private life is *private*. But I'm the last person Callie needs to be jealous of. All you and I will ever be is friends."

Mason put his hand up to his jaw to make sure his mouth was not gaping open. To say he was shocked would have been an extreme understatement. He was flabbergasted. He never would have guessed in a million years that Fawn was gay. It was almost laughable, considering how convinced Callie was he was having an affair with her.

"Are you okay?" Fawn asked with an icebreaking laugh. She reached to touch his other hand which rested against the leather seat. "It's not a terminal illness, you know? It's only an alternative lifestyle."

"I'm sorry. I'm not trying to be offensive with my silence. It's just…I'm shocked," he confessed. He looked away from her, out the windshield, because he did not wish to stare.

"Good. You're supposed to be shocked. I like 'being in the closet' as they say. I'm not big on flaunting that side of my life. I only told you because it might help in your relationship with Callie. It's still important you be honest with her about what you are doing, Mason. Whether she throws a jealous fit or not. That is part of who Callie is, and if you love her, you will accept it."

"I *do* love her, Fawn," Mason pledged. "I can deal with Callie's tantrums. It's only her distrust I have a problem with. You can't have love without trust."

"Precisely. So don't give her any reason at all to distrust you. Be honest with her in everything you do. If she still refuses to believe in you, you cross that bridge too."

"Thanks for the advice," Mason said. He grew silent again. He was still reeling over her bizarre proclamation.

"Any time," Fawn said. "Do you want to go get a bite to eat?"

"Sure. Why not?" Mason said. He still did not wish to go back to the bus and be without Callie. She would not like him going out with Fawn, but Callie had no reason to worry now. *I'll share this info with her soon. I wonder if she will believe it. This time, I could understand if she doesn't. I'm still having a hard time accepting that Fawn is gay.*

As Fawn drove on, he was thinking over everything else Fawn had said to him. *I do owe Callie an apology for trying to have Mark lie for me. Fawn is right. I was trying to avoid dealing with Callie's jealous tirades.*

Fawn was very quiet as well. She only hoped her conversation with Mason helped. She did not like to talk about her private life, but she felt the truth might help Mason with Callie. She hated to see his relationship with Callie end. She still felt it was very grounding for Mason. *You're a friend as well as a business associate, Mason. I want to see it all work out for you. I'll help you in any way that I can.*

Chapter 32

Progress

Callie called Mason again Tuesday afternoon. She had struggled to wait this long. Ultimately, her overpowering desire to hear his voice had won out. She was relieved when he answered the phone. He gave a simple, "Hello". Callie was so thankful to hear Mason's voice, she was struck dumb. "Hey. How are you doing?" she eventually uttered, trying to sound mollifying.

"Don't you mean 'what' am I doing?" he responded with an antagonistic question. Mason regretted the words almost as soon as they were out of his mouth. *Why am I trying to pick a fight?*

"If you mean…did I call to check up on you? The answer is *no*. I missed hearing your voice; that's all. I miss you *period*. If you still don't want to talk to me, that's fine. As the song goes, I just called to say I love you. I'll see in a few days, right?"

Her voice sounded a little panicked – almost as if Callie was not certain if Mason would be coming home to her. *What does she think? That I'm going to run away with Fawn and never be seen or heard from again?*

Mason was disappointed in Callie's lack of faith once more. He was sitting in the front of the bus, beholding the scenery as it passed him by, through the darkened windows. He stood and walked through the bus with the phone. "Where else would I be going in a few days but home?" he asked. His vocal tone was harsh once again.

"I wasn't too sure after the dumb stunt I pulled. I realize I hurt you, Mason. I really am sorry. I got in touch with a counselor at the rehab center. I went for a session last night. We discussed my recent actions and the fears

301

that led me to behave this way. I want you to know I'm working to do better, Mason."

Callie's voice broke, and Mason guessed she was crying. It twisted his heart. He did not want for her to be in pain. He had never wanted to hurt her.

"That's good to hear, Callie," he said, softening his voice. He pulled out a chair in the kitchen and sat down. He was through with his agitated hike. He had a private spot, at least for now. All of the other guys were scattered throughout the bus, passing the time in different ways. Some were watching television; some played video games; and some slept. "I intend to change some things too. You were right; I shouldn't have tried to have Mark lie to you. I should have been honest with you about what I was doing. You would have been upset, because of your jealousy over Fawn, but I shouldn't have tried to avoid your feelings. I'm sorry. I'll be glad when these next few days are over, so we can talk face to face. I can't stand that you are crying and I'm hundreds of miles away, so I can't hold you in my arms. We'll work it all out, baby. It will be okay."

Hearing Mason call her *baby* again lightened Callie's dismal mood. His words of apology did as well. *He* isn't *having an affair with Fawn. He loves me. I can hear it in his voice. I can tell by his words. It was all lies, as he said. I've got to learn to trust Mason, to believe only what he says, and not listen to all the other rumors.*

"Callie, baby, are you okay?" Mason asked, after a few more moments of strained silence.

"I am now," she told him. She was on a cordless phone, so she could also move about. She walked to the bathroom to get a tissue.

Mason heard her blowing her nose. Her crying was subsiding. "I shouldn't have sent you home…"

"No. Sending me home was a good thing," Callie disagreed, heading back to the living room with the box of tissues in hand. "Going to counseling is helping me get my head back together."

"Was being around all the drinking and drugs again too much of a temptation?" Mason inquired.

"No. I didn't like that atmosphere. It brought back all kinds of bad memories. But it was my fear of losing you that threw me over the edge. I need to get my fears under control. I don't intend to do to you what my mom did to my dad, Mason," Callie stated with determination.

"What your mom did to your dad?"

"Yeah. Her fears and distrust, due to her past, destroyed their marriage. I'm not going to let *my* past destroy *our* future."

"I'm very glad to hear that," Mason said. "I'm glad I answered the phone tonight, Callie. I'm glad we talked. I love you, baby. All I want is to have a future with you. The concert last night seemed empty without you there. You're number one in my life, Callie. Without you, nothing…including my musical career…means anything."

"Same here," Callie concurred, choking back another sob. She pulled another tissue from the box and dabbed at the tears that had formed in her eyes. Mason's words of devotion stirred her emotions – especially him putting her first over his music. She knew how important his musical career was to him. Callie had feared she might have pushed him away. She was grateful Mason loved her in spite of everything, and he wanted a future with her above all else. "I can't wait until you come home."

"Me either. The rest of this week is going to be long. How about I call you each day like I did when I was on the road without you before?"

"That would be great!" Callie chirped with joyful enthusiasm.

"I have some bizarre news to share with you…it's nothing bad," he was quick to assure her. *At least not where* we *are concerned.* "I'll wait until I get home to tell you. You're not going to believe what I found out."

"I have some news of my own to share," Callie said, thinking of what Katie Rose had confided. "You won't believe what I found out either."

"You've peaked my curiosity," Mason said, a prying edge to his voice.

"Same here, but let's wait." *I don't want to tell him about Katie Rose and Garrison over the phone. But I don't want to keep it secret from him either. I don't want any more secrets between the two of us. It's won't be like I'm betraying Katie Rose's confidence. The truth will be out to everyone in a week or two anyway.*

"Okay," Mason conceded. He was pleased that they had worked through some of their issues. He was delighted that the wall between him and Callie had been torn down. He was looking forward to seeing her again.

He was overjoyed that he had reason to have faith in their love again. "I love you, baby," he said.

"I love you too, Mason," Callie responded. She said a silent prayer of thanksgiving. *From now on, I'll do whatever I need to do to make sure nothing comes between Mason and me. I will not let petty fears from my past come between us. I'll find a way to make them disappear. All that matters is Mason and I – together forever.*

* * * *

Jackie Lynn and Samuel went out to dinner Wednesday night. They went to a popular Italian eatery in the downtown area. On the weekends, there were lines of people waiting out the door to be seated. The name of the restaurant was Antonio's. Antonio's served some of the best pizza in town. They also had good spaghetti. Their choice of sandwiches and salads was great as well.

Antonio's was in a brick building, but the inner walls had been painted, in detail, by talented, local artists, to illustrate scenes from the city. One wall showcased the waterfront, complete with couples, bicyclists, kids throwing Frisbees, and people walking dogs. The other wall depicted the city skyline at night, including the city's railroad bridge, with a lighted train going across, and the other two illuminated bridges, with cars driving across them as well. The ceilings were exposed. Enormous, black, heating pipes and vents could be seen overhead. The waiters and waitresses wore tie-dyed shirts, with the name *Antonio's* in a circle on the front and a picture of a steaming pizza on the back.

Samuel enjoyed checking out different places to eat each week, and Jackie Lynn was game to try them. She and Long Wolf had rarely dined out. They mostly ate at home, as a family, whenever possible. When they had taken the rare opportunity to go out to dinner, they had frequented only a few favorite restaurants – like Cornucopia.

Jackie Lynn and Samuel were overdressed for Antonio's, since they had come straight from work. Samuel was wearing a custom-made grey suit, a baby-blue dress shirt with gold personalized cufflinks, and a solid navy tie. He dressed conservatively for work. Otherwise, he wore bold colors. Jackie Lynn was in a teal pantsuit, with a white blouse that had greenish blue diamonds all throughout it. Her hair had been gathered into a short and attractive ponytail – not a hair was out of place. She looked professional, yet also pretty. Samuel rarely saw her with her hair up. He liked this look, because he could see her exquisite face and eyes even better.

Samuel talked Jackie Lynn into splitting a medium, pepperoni and sausage pizza. He also ordered a pitcher of Miller Lite for them. *Pizza and beer* – Jackie Lynn felt like a college student again. She liked spending time with Samuel. They had a lot of fun, and he always made her feel younger than she was.

The waiter put in their pizza order and brought their pitcher of beer out to them. Since it was early evening, and it was during the week, the restaurant was not overly crowded. Regardless, the mouthwatering smell of Italian spices, fresh baked crusts and breadsticks, and pizza hung in the air. The waiter told them their dinner would be out in about fifteen minutes. Jackie Lynn could hardly wait. She was suddenly starving.

Samuel poured two mugs of beer, passing one to Jackie Lynn. As he took a drink of his, he asked Jackie Lynn, "So how is Katie Rose doing? She's been a little reserved with me this week, and I'm presuming she is acting this way because you told her what I saw."

"Yes, I did," Jackie Lynn confirmed, taking a sip of her beer as well.

"So what's up with her? Or would you rather not say? I don't want you to break any confidences you might have with your daughter."

"Let's just say all is not right with her world right now," Jackie Lynn replied and took another drink.

"That much I already figured out," Samuel acknowledged, noting that Jackie Lynn's eyes looked distraught. "If you want me to drop the subject, that's fine. But I know how much you love your kids. So if you want to talk about anything…anything at all…I'm always ready to listen. I won't judge. I'll merely listen."

Jackie Lynn toyed with the handle to her mug. *Should I tell him what is going on in Katie Rose's life?* She had not told Flora and Mary Julia yet. She would have to tell them soon. She was going to need their help in canceling everything for the wedding at the last minute.

"I'm sorry, Jackie Lynn," Samuel apologized, taking her silence for a sign she did not wish to talk. "Let's change the subject."

"No…it's okay, Samuel," Jackie Lynn surprised him by saying. She did desire to talk to someone about Katie Rose. "Katie Rose will *not* be marrying BJ," she announced, taking another swig of beer.

"So I take it she and Garrison *are* an item?" he inquired. "Garrison is the reason she won't be marrying BJ?"

"Right," Jackie Lynn confirmed. She was fiddling with the handle of her mug again and seeming to study the foam in her beer.

"Are you alright with this change?" Samuel questioned. He could tell by Jackie Lynn's rigid body language she was troubled. *Maybe I shouldn't have brought up Katie Rose.*

"It doesn't matter how I feel. What's important is Katie Rose's happiness."

"Katie Rose's happiness *is* important," Samuel agreed. "But so is how you feel. At least it is where I'm concerned. Talk to me, Jackie Lynn. Tell me how you feel. I'm here to listen."

Samuel reached across the table and patted her hand. Jackie Lynn looked up at him and gave him a smile of gratitude. She was sincerely happy to have Samuel in her life. "Thanks," she said. "It's good to have friends that care. I haven't told Flora or Mary Julia about what's taking place with Katie Rose yet."

Samuel was pleased that Jackie Lynn referred to him as a caring friend. He *was* her friend, and he definitely *did* care. He still hoped for more between them at some point, but for now, he was delighted Jackie Lynn considered him a friend she could confide in.

"It will all work out," Jackie Lynn said with more confidence than she felt. "I care about BJ a lot and hate to see him get hurt. But I don't want Katie Rose to marry someone she doesn't love. She loves Garrison."

"She told you this?"

"Yes, and she confirmed it by the joy I heard in her voice as she talked about him. She's got it bad for Garrison Parker. I should have realized she wasn't in love with BJ long before now. Katie Rose has never sounded so gleeful and full of love when talking about BJ. He's her friend. That's all he is, and that is all he can ever be. It's all so tragic, but it's the way it is."

"But if this is the case, why in the world hasn't Katie Rose called off the wedding to BJ before now?" Samuel sensibly questioned. The Katie Rose he knew was not into deception of any kind.

"Katie Rose still has not told BJ about Garrison. Nor has she called off the wedding," Jackie Lynn shared, further shocking Samuel. As she saw the perplexed look on his face, Jackie Lynn went on to explain, "The reason she hasn't told BJ is because of his injury. The wedding is giving him reason to fully recover. Katie Rose does not want to take this inducement away from him. She cares about BJ a great deal, even if she is not in love with him. When she does tell BJ, Katie Rose's heart will be broken as well."

"For sure," Samuel agreed, but was disturbed. "I'd like to be there for both of you if I can."

"I greatly appreciate that, Samuel," Jackie Lynn declared. She gave him another heartwarming smile.

After a few moments of silence, Samuel purposely changed the subject. He began to talk about other, *happier*, things. Jackie Lynn was amazed by how natural confiding in Samuel about Katie Rose had felt. He had managed to lighten her load a bit by letting her talk about it. Samuel would be there to support her and Katie Rose as well. This knowledge brought Jackie Lynn immense comfort.

Chapter 33

Heartbreak

It was the first day of April. Katie Rose came home from work to find BJ taking refuge in the bedroom. He had his legs under a sheet and was watching the evening news. He was still dressed. He had on a printed T-shirt, and Katie Rose could see the top of his jeans and the slight imprint of the end of his prosthesis. Normally, BJ took his prosthesis off when he laid in bed.

What's up? she anxiously wondered. "BJ, is everything okay?" she asked him. She stepped into the room. She had been standing in the doorway.

BJ looked up at Katie Rose with a downcast expression on his face and answered, "No." "What's wrong?" she inquired with distress.

"My therapy has come to an end," he proclaimed in a gruff voice.

"Your therapy? Why?" she questioned. Her eyes looked concerned.

"Because I can't go any further," he disclosed.

"Did you have a bad day? I'm sure things will get better, BJ," Katie Rose tried to encourage him.

"No, they won't," he argued. He slid his legs out from under the sheet and sat up on the side of the bed. "You know why?"

"Why?" she inquired with apprehension.

"Because you can't get better than perfection!" he exclaimed. BJ beamed at Katie Rose as he stood and walked past her. He proceeded to walk across the room. He turned and walked back to Katie Rose as well. "How was that?"

"Oh my gosh, BJ!" Katie Rose shrieked with excitement, smiling as well. "I can't even tell you are wearing a prosthesis. Your walk is perfect! Why in the world were you acting so depressed when I first walked in?"

"April Fools!" he declared with a mischievous chuckle. He pulled Katie Rose into a snug, delighted embrace. "I can't wait until the next fourteen days have passed, so I can *perfectly* walk my new wife out of church."

"I'm so proud of you, BJ!" Katie Rose proclaimed. However, when BJ silenced her with a hungry kiss, despair replaced her joy. Before she could think about what she was doing, Katie Rose scrambled out of BJ's arms.

"What?" he asked with bemusement. "Why'd you pull away like that?" BJ was studying her startled facial expression. *Why does she look as if she did something wrong? What's up with that?*

"I…I'm amazed! That's all," she lied, trying to recover. She placed more space between them. "Why don't you walk me into the living room?"

"Why the living room?" *She doesn't want to be in the bedroom with me. Why?*

"Because I want to see you show off some more. I'm very proud of you. You're two weeks ahead of schedule. All of your hard work has paid off, BJ. I knew you could do it." Katie Rose had a grin on her face, even though she felt like crying. *BJ can walk flawlessly. It's time to reveal the truth. I need to break his heart. I won't do it today. He's on cloud nine, and so he should be! I won't burst his bubble.*

"I'll walk you to the living room," BJ agreed, but his voice sounded strained. "Then we'll talk about what's really bothering you."

BJ started past Katie Rose, and she fell into pace beside him. She was astonished to see how normally BJ was walking. She was delighted for him. She wished they did not have to talk. She guessed BJ wanted to talk about more than her drawing away from him today. He more than likely wanted to talk about their total lack of intimacy. She did not want to have this discussion; it would lead her down a path she did not want to take today – the path that led to telling BJ the truth.

They had a seat on the couch. BJ noticed that Katie Rose was careful to put some space between them. He was even more uneasy. "Katie Rose, you've said me losing my leg doesn't bother you…that it doesn't turn you off…"

"It doesn't, BJ," she interrupted, to reassure him.

"Then why have you been sleeping on the couch? And why don't you want me to kiss you?"

Katie Rose's stomach churned. *He's leading me into a conversation I didn't want to have today.* "It *isn't* because of your leg, BJ," she insisted once more.

"Then why is it? I walked perfectly for you. So I've recovered from my injury. Why'd you pull away from me in the bedroom?"

"That's a fair question," she replied with a somber expression. "You deserve an honest answer…"

"And that honest answer is?" he pushed. He feared what her response might be. Regardless, he needed to know. Their intimacy had completely cooled since his injury.

Katie Rose's heart was beating in her mouth, and her stomach was whirling. She did not want to utter her next words, but it was essential she do so. The time for the truth was now. "BJ, I..I…" Tears came to her eyes and a sob closed her throat before she could finish.

"What? What is it, Katie Rose?" BJ asked in alarm, closing the distance between them. He threw his arm around her shoulder and pulled her staunchly against his side.

His close proximity and kindness tore Katie Rose's heart to shreds. She began to weep. BJ rubbed her shoulder and patiently waited. *She must have something awful to say,* BJ concluded. He dreaded hearing Katie Rose's next words.

Her emotions eventually settled, but Katie Rose was still having a terrible time saying what she needed. She looked away from BJ. Each time she saw his face, tears threatened to start again. BJ was not saying a word either. He was frightened about what could be upsetting Katie Rose so much. With baited breath, he waited for her to speak.

"B…BJ," she began once more, hesitant. "I've really screwed up…"

"Screwed up? How? What do you mean?" he blathered in anxious confusion.

"I…you…we've been such good friends…"

"*Been*?...friends?" BJ questioned. "What's that supposed to mean?" he asked with trepidation. "We *are incredible* friends. As well as lovers...or at least we used to be incredible lovers. What are you trying to get at? You are really starting to scare me, Katie Rose."

"This is so hard to say," she whined. "BJ, I...I'm in love...with...with another...man."

If Katie Rose had thrown a brick and hit him hard between the eyes, it could not have shook and disoriented him more. "You...you're what?!" he inquired, incredulous.

Katie Rose glanced over at BJ. She was unsettled to find all the color had drained from his face, his eyes were enormous with wonderment, and his mouth was standing open.

"W...who?" he managed to utter in a gasp.

"That doesn't matter, BJ," Katie Rose argued. "What does matter is...I can't marry you."

"H...how long have you been seeing another man?" he asked. "Why have you been pretending to love me?"

"I'm not pretending to love you, BJ," Katie Rose contradicted. "I do love you...It's just...I just recently found out that I only love you as a friend," she added insult to injury.

"Great!" he declared. His voice had an angry edge. "Well, old *friend*, why don't you answer my questions? How long have you been seeing this other man – whoever he is?! How long have you been lying to me – and why?! I need answers!" He had raised his voice a bit.

"I know," Katie Rose conceded. "It hasn't been long, BJ. Really, it hasn't," she rather evasively responded.

A light bulb all at once came on in BJ's mind. "Oh my God! It's Garrison, isn't it?!" he exclaimed. The time period fit.

Katie Rose chose not to lie. She was weary of all the dishonesty. "Yes...it is," she answered. She looked away sheepishly.

"I knew it! There was something going on between the two of you when he gave you those earrings," he accused.

"No, BJ. There was not. Not like you think. I was attracted to him, but that was all. I gave those earrings back. I tried to run from my attraction...uh...my feelings...for Garrison. I tried to close him out of my life entirely. But it was impossible. I've only realized my love for him recently. I haven't been keeping a secret from you for long. I swear."

"So are you sleeping with him?" BJ further grilled.

Katie Rose looked him in the eyes again. There was both pain and anger there. *Should I give him an honest answer? It will only hurt him more.*

"Never mind!" he snapped before Katie Rose could speak. "Your silence says it all!" *I've lost her! How could this have happened?* BJ was in agony.

"BJ, I'm *so* sorry," Katie Rose apologized. "I never meant for this to come about." She realized her words sounded empty.

"Then how *did* it happen?" he whined. The question was fruitless. "Katie Rose, do you have a clue how much I love you?"

"I do," she answered with grief. *Because it's the same way I feel about Garrison,* she thought, but mercifully did not add. "I've been dreading this talk so much. I never wanted to hurt you, BJ."

"We've got history, Katie Rose. You hardly know this man. How do you know Garrison truly loves you? What if it's all physical?" BJ argued.

"It isn't," she maintained with certainty. "I love Garrison, and Garrison loves me. What we have isn't a passing thing." *I want to spend the rest of my life with Garrison, and he feels the same way.*

BJ was silent for a moment as he let her last words since in. *There's no hope.* "Katie Rose, you are breaking my heart…do you know that?" he declared with eyes full of misery.

"I know. I'm going to miss having you in my life, BJ," Katie Rose replied, tears coming into her eyes.

"Not…not half as much as I'm going to…to miss *you*," BJ confessed. He was at his rope's end. Tears began to cloud his eyes as well.

When Katie Rose saw his tears, her heart felt like it was breaking in two. She was crying as she reached to embrace BJ – to comfort him. But BJ pushed her away. He stood and stumbled.

"Damn!" he cursed, as he attempted to hurry away. He was limping on his prosthesis again. His extreme mental anguish was deprogramming all he had learned about walking normally.

Katie Rose witnessed him hobbling out of the room. A few moments later, she heard the bedroom door slam. She was unsure what to do. *Should I go to him? No. BJ doesn't want to see me right now. Why should he? I need to leave him alone for a while. Why did it have to be this way?* She grappled with this question, but there was no good answer.

She stood and walked over to the kitchen counter. Her purse was sitting there. She picked it up. *I need Garrison,* she recognized with slight guilt.

She glanced with uncertainty toward the hallway that led to the bedroom, one last time. Then Katie Rose made her final decision. She headed for the front door. She was going to Garrison's house. She needed to feel his big, strong arms around her – to be assured everything would be okay.

* * * *

When Garrison opened his front door to Katie Rose, she collapsed in his arms, wailing. Garrison grabbed her and held her securely. He was frightened by her emotional meltdown. *What's happened?* "What's wrong, little beauty?" he questioned, planting soothing kisses on her forehead and along her cheeks. "Tell me, lovely Kate."

"Jus…just…ho…hold me…Garrison," she pleaded.

He did as asked. He also tenderly stroked her back and kissed away her tears from time to time. Garrison waited with tempered impatience for Katie Rose's tearful escapade to cease. It took several, long moments.

When Katie Rose's body stopped shuddering at last, Garrison led her over to his wrap around sofa in the living room. He carefully lowered them both to a sitting position. Giving her a prolonged kiss on her salty lips, he prodded, "Can you tell me what has you so upset? I want to be here for you, but I need to know what has happened. Can you talk about it yet, Kate? Take your time, beautiful, I've got all night."

"I…I did it, Garrison," she uttered.

"You did what?" he asked in bewilderment.

"I told BJ."

"Oh," he replied, nodding his head in understanding. He felt ashamed because he was glad. "I know how hard that must have been." He gave her another supportive hug and a kiss to her temple. His heart was pained for Katie Rose, because she was suffering. It was traumatizing for her to hurt BJ, and BJ was likely crushed. *I would be too if I lost my lovely*

Kate. "It will be okay, Kate – my Emerald Sea. Our deep love will help you through."

"I know," she agreed. "Being with you – seeing your face and feeling your arms around me – is the only way I could make it through. You should have seen BJ's face. He was shattered. He actually broke down and cried. And knowing I'm the one that hurt him is killing me." Katie Rose began to cry once more.

"I know. I know," Garrison consoled in a quiet voice. He kissed her forehead and massaged her shoulders. "Hurting someone you care about is a terrible thing for you. You have such a good and tender heart. It's one of the many things I love about you. I'll help you make it through this awful time, Kate. I wish I could do something to help BJ as well. I understand how he must feel. I'd be a basket case if I ever lost you."

"You never will," she assured him. She gave Garrison a devoted kiss on the lips and laid her head on his shoulder. The warmth of his body and the strength of his arms were so soothing. She whispered, "I can make it through anything with you by my side, Garrison."

Her words deeply touched his heart. Kate was all his now. He felt like the luckiest man alive. He could not wait for their life together to proceed. *I'll help you through the pain of hurting BJ, lovely Kate. I'll help you through everything in our lives now. It's the least I can do to show how much I appreciate having your love in my life.* Garrison gave her an affectionate squeeze. He continued to stroke her back and give her reassuring kisses from time to time, basking in their magnificent love for one another.

Chapter 34

The Switch

The alarm went off at 6:00 a.m. When Katie Rose first opened her eyes and saw Garrison lying beside her, she was blissful. But as she became more fully awake, heartrending thoughts of BJ began to snuff out her happiness. Almost as if he could sense her turmoil, Garrison slid Katie Rose into his comforting arms and asked in a voice groggy from sleep, "How are you doing this morning, Kate?"

They did not make love the night before. Garrison merely held Katie Rose until she fell into a safe and secure slumber. She was brokenhearted over BJ, and Garrison only wanted to be there to console *his* Kate. They would have many more nights to share their overwhelming passion for one another.

"Um...I'm happy and sad all at the same time. If that makes any sense," Katie Rose shared with him.

"It makes perfect sense," Garrison said and gave her a brief kiss. "I feel exactly the same way. I'm delighted you are here and you are all mine now. But I'm also unsettled, because you are hurting over BJ. I want to take that pain away, but I can't, and that is very frustrating for me."

"You *are* helping though," Katie Rose assured him, giving him another kiss of gratitude. "Thanks for holding me and rocking me to sleep last night. You treat me like a princess."

"As you should be treated, lovely Kate," Garrison professed. He kissed her again – this time a bit longer. As he began to grow aroused, he loosened his hold and wisely suggested, "We should get up and shower. Time marches on. I take it you are going into work today?"

315

"Yes. I have to. I have a videoconference with the McMillan brothers on the Anaheim project at 10:00 a.m.," she told him, as Garrison released her.

Garrison sat up on the side of the bed and turned on the small lamp on the nightstand. Katie Rose blinked, forcing her eyes to adjust. As she also sat up on the other side of the bed, she explained to Garrison, "I need to go to mom's this morning and catch her before she leaves for work. I want to go ahead and tell her she can begin canceling things for the wedding. Plus, I need to get a change of clothes, and borrow some of her makeup. Most of my things are at BJ's, but I still have some of my clothes and such at mom's."

"Yeah. I could give you my shirt to sleep in, but I can't exactly lend you one of my suits," Garrison stated with an amused snicker. He gave Kate an appraisal as they both rose to their feet. His T-shirt looked adorable on her. It was large and baggy, hanging almost to her knees. Once again, he found himself fighting his desire for this lady. "We don't have time to shower together?"

"No," Katie Rose answered with a slight grin. Garrison was pleased he could hear a bit of regret in her voice. They both desired one another a great deal.

"Okay. You can have the bathroom off the bedroom. I'll go shower in the bathroom in the hall. The first one out fixes the coffee."

"Deal," Katie Rose agreed. She approached him. She placed her arms around his neck and gave him a long, drawn out kiss. "I love you, Garrison Parker," she declared with a wide smile.

"I love you too, beautiful Kate," he concurred, beaming at her. "Off to the shower with you now. Or else!"

Katie Rose removed her arms from his neck and headed toward the bathroom. Garrison watched her walk across the room and disappear behind the bathroom door. He reluctantly started away to the other bathroom down the hall.

* * * *

Garrison was in the kitchen and Katie Rose could smell coffee beginning to brew. His hair was still wet, and all he had on was a pair of boxer shorts. Katie Rose, in contrast, was already dressed in her clothes from yesterday. She had combed and dried her long, straight hair. She planned to pull it back in a neat ponytail once she got to her mom's. She had not put on any makeup yet. She had a few items in her purse, but most everything of hers was still at BJ's.

"Can I fix you a bowl of Raisin Bran?" Garrison asked. "I don't have any eggs in the house. I usually eat a bowl of cereal to start my day."

"No thanks," Katie Rose replied. "Just a cup of coffee would be great. I'm not much on eating breakfast. I usually have some yogurt about 10:00 a.m. I have some in the refrigerator at work."

Garrison poured them both a cup of coffee and fixed himself a bowl of cereal. They had a seat in side-by-side chairs at his small, wooden kitchen table – it sat four. "Kate, I've been thinking," Garrison told her, as they both took a sip of their coffee, almost in unison. "I don't think you should have your mother cancel the wedding."

"What?" she asked, confused by this statement. "So have you changed your mind and you want me to marry BJ?" she asked, half teasing, taking another drink of the coffee.

"No, of course not," Garrison assured her. He took a bite of his cereal, chewed it up and swallowed it before he revealed, "What I was thinking..." he paused for another moment. "I was thinking *we* should get married instead? Your mom would have to send out notices to the guests on BJ's side, but otherwise, it's all planned. I don't care if I don't have a big crowd of friends there. I can invite my family and a few friends by phone call or word of mouth. So why have your mom go through the hassle of canceling everything? You still have a groom...just not the one you originally planned for."

"Garrison, do you realize what you are saying?" Katie Rose questioned.

"Very much so," he assured her. He took another bite of his cereal. Then he reached into the chair on the other side of him. "I haven't had a chance to go and buy an engagement ring, but these could serve as a sign. They are appropriate...considering we are already married on the Indian front anyway."

Garrison swept out a small box. The lid was off, and Katie Rose could see the pair of Dream Catcher earrings lying inside. She took the box from Garrison.

"I told you when you gave these back I would someday give these to you again. I'm giving them back now, Kate. So what do you say? Will you marry me, Emerald Sea? We're already spiritually married in the heart. I'd like for us to make it legal."

Katie Rose was awestruck. She had not anticipated Garrison's proposal – not this soon anyway. *Would it be right to do this?* Her mom, Mary Julia and Flora had gone to a great deal of trouble to plan her wedding, to the minutest of details. And more importantly, Katie Rose did love Garrison with all her being. As he said, they were already married in their hearts. It only made sense to make it legal as well. Katie Rose wanted to spend the rest of her life with this man.

She picked up the Dream Catcher earrings and slid one in each ear. These earrings meant more to her than an engagement ring would have. "Soars Like an Eagle, I would be delighted to legally become your wife," Katie Rose proclaimed. The gleeful smile that spread from ear to ear further confirmed Katie Rose's acceptance.

Garrison pulled her into a secure embrace and kissed her. Katie Rose could taste the Raisin Bran on his lips. "I love you so much, lovely Kate, my Emerald Sea. I'll spend the rest of my life showing you and everyone else this very thing. I'm the luckiest man in the world, and also the happiest."

"Well, I'm the luckiest and happiest *woman* in the world. Something else we have in common," Katie Rose joked, giving him excited kisses and savoring the overwhelming love that bound them.

* * * *

Katie Rose finished her cup of coffee, and she left to go to her mother's. Garrison finished his coffee and breakfast, got dressed, and left too. He was heading to BJ's. BJ often had physical therapy early in the morning. He wanted to catch him before he left the apartment. BJ would not want to see him, but Garrison did not care. He wanted to talk to BJ about Kate. Her happiness was the most important thing to him.

Garrison got to BJ's apartment about 7:35 a.m. He rang the doorbell and knocked loudly on the door. He stood and patiently waited. *It may take him awhile to get to the door. Depending on how well he walks first thing in the morning. Especially if I woke him.*

A few moments later, BJ opened the door. He was glaring at Garrison. "What do you want?! Did you come to rub salt in the wound? You already have everything that matters to me."

Garrison could not help but feel sorry for BJ. He was wearing pajama bottoms and no shirt, and he looked extremely tired. Garrison guessed he had gotten him out of bed, but he doubted if BJ had been sleeping. He looked as if he had not slept much. "I didn't come here to rub your face in the fact that Kate…um Katie Rose…has left you. I did come to talk about her though."

"What about her?" BJ asked with suspicion.

"Can I come in? I'd rather not stand in the doorway and talk."

BJ was hesitant to let Garrison into his apartment. He hated this man. He wanted to tear him apart limb by limb. But at the same time, he was worried about Katie Rose. If Garrison was here, whatever he had to say about Katie Rose must be important. BJ stepped back a few steps and allowed Garrison to enter his apartment. He shut the door and turned to face this man once more.

"BJ, I know how you feel," Garrison began.

"You don't have the foggiest notion how I feel," BJ contradicted. He instinctively balled his hands into fists.

"You're wrong. The one thing we have in common is our love for Kate," Garrison pointed out. "And I know I would be crushed if I lost her."

"Her name is *Katie Rose*. You said you wanted to talk about her. Start talking. I don't need your pity."

"Okay," Garrison agreed. "The fact is Kate…er…Katie Rose…" he hated using this name, but to appease BJ he would. "She is heartbroken as well. She never meant to hurt you, BJ. She loves you. It's just she *only* loves you as a *friend*. It's the only way she has *ever* loved you. She made a terrible mistake when she tried to take it to the next level. You both are suffering for that mistake now."

BJ thought a lot about these truths all night long. He fell in love with Katie Rose almost from the start, but she had only been his friend. He pushed her for more, but she put him off for a long while. He finally convinced her to take a chance on love with him. However, that was the problem. It was something he sold Katie Rose on – not something she actually felt.

"So what exactly is your point?" BJ asked. He wanted to get this man out of his apartment. He could not stand looking at him.

"My point is…you are in love with Katie Rose. So you must want her to be happy. Am I wrong?"

"Of course I do," BJ agreed. "So what do you want from me? My blessing?"

"*I* don't want your blessing. But Katie Rose could sure use it," Garrison pointed out. "You can choose to hurt her by holding her mistake against her. Or you can choose to give her your blessing and wish her happiness. You hold the power in your hands, BJ. Do you want to make Katie Rose suffer?"

The only person BJ wanted to make suffer was Garrison. He *did* love Katie Rose, and he did *not* want to see her in pain.

"I came to ask you to give it some thought. Katie Rose is coming by after work today to see how you are doing, and to get some of her things." She had told Garrison this plan, right before she had left his house that morning. "You can make her life hell, or you can show her you love her. That's all I have to say."

"Good. Does that mean you will be leaving?"

"Yes, it does," Garrison agreed. As he walked past BJ, Garrison could tell he was thinking over all he had said. *I've done all I could. I hope he'll give Kate a break. If he chooses not to, I'll still help her get through her turmoil. But BJ could make it easier.*

Garrison stepped out in the hall and BJ shut the door with a bang behind him. BJ leaned against the door, and he began to think. He had some important decisions to make before he saw Katie Rose later that day.

* * * *

As Garrison had told him, Katie Rose rang the doorbell about 5:30 p.m.

"Did you lose your key?" BJ asked, as he opened the door to her. He had showered, shaved and gotten dressed. He did not want to look as if he was not taking care of himself.

"N..no. I..I didn't think it was appropriate to use it," Katie Rose admitted.

"You are welcome here anytime," BJ assured Katie Rose. "We need to talk."

Katie Rose was elated when she witnessed him walking over to the couch. *He's walking normally again!* She had worried, after he hobbled off last evening, he would stop walking altogether. Katie Rose closed the door and walked over to the sofa too. BJ was already sitting, so she sat down beside him. "How are you doing?" she asked.

The concern BJ saw in her eyes confirmed the decisions he had made. "I'm doing as well as can be expected," he said. "I feel like someone I loved just died," he admitted. "It will take time."

"I know," Katie Rose agreed. "I'm so sorry, BJ. I never meant to hurt you. I've already said that, and I probably sound like a broken record. But...it's the truth."

"I know it is," she was surprised to hear him say. "In a way you are doing me a favor. You're not in love with me, and you never will be. I get that. So our marriage wouldn't have been a happy one. Better we admit that now, than after the fact. Right?"

Katie Rose was amazed by how rational BJ was being. "Right," she concurred, sounding ambivalent.

"Katie Rose, I love you. You were my first and only love. There will always be an extra special place in my heart for you. But *your* first and only love is *not* me. It's Garrison. Fortunately, he feels the same way about you. I saw and heard that for myself this morning."

"This morning?"

"Yeah. Garrison came by to talk to me about you."

"He..he did what?" Katie Rose asked in alarm.

"He pointed out that a man in love wants his woman to be happy above all else. And he's right. That is what I want for you, Katie Rose. I want for you to be happy. Garrison is the man who can make you happy – not me."

Katie Rose was having a hard time believing her ears. But then again, the thing that had made Katie Rose love BJ as a friend was his kindheartedness. "BJ, you are such a good man. You deserve a terrific woman. Someone who loves you with all her heart," Katie Rose professed, fighting tears. She wanted him to be happy as well.

"You're right. I do," he agreed. *I wish that woman was you. But it isn't.* His heart twisted with pain again. "I packed some of your stuff. It's sitting in the bedroom. I don't know if you want any of the apartment furnishings you bought – the comforter, the bedside tables…"

"N…no," Katie Rose told him. "You keep all that. All I'll take is my clothes and personal things. Along those same lines…" She unzipped her purse and reached into the tiny compartment in the back. She pulled forth her engagement ring. "I need to give this back to you. I forgot the diamond earrings…"

He took the ring from her and laid it on the side table, out of his view. He did not want to look at it. It hurt too badly. "Keep the earrings…please," BJ requested.

"Oh…that wouldn't be right…" Katie Rose started to argue.

"Let's just call it even…okay. You bought me furniture and nice clothes, and I bought you earrings in exchange. It's hard enough taking the ring back. I don't want the earrings."

"Okay," Katie Rose agreed. "I'll treasure them. I'm going to miss you, BJ," she honestly proclaimed.

"Well, remember, if you need me, I'm still here. You can always call."

His kind words caused Katie Rose to cry. She placed her arms around BJ's shoulders and gave him a final hug. Tears ran down her cheeks and dripped onto BJ's T-shirt.

BJ loved Katie Rose immensely and her happiness was what was most important to him. He was letting her go, so she could be happy, whether his heart broke or not. He squeezed her to him one final time and fought tears of his own.

* * * *

Katie Rose called Callie that night. She was slowly divulging to everyone the change in her wedding plans. Callie was glad to hear Katie Rose had told BJ the truth at last and was moving on with Garrison – the man she truly loved. She revealed she had already told Mason about her and Garrison. "In fact, Mason and I talked about your canceled wedding," Callie said. She sounded peculiar.

"And?" Katie Rose bid her to elaborate.

"Well…we sort of were going to see if we could stand in for you and BJ, rather than have your mom cancel everything. I had no idea Garrison was going to come up with the same idea. That's okay. Mason and I can arrange something else. We're tired of waiting. We're going to be home for the next two weeks. So we thought this opportunity would be the perfect time to finally tie the knot."

"That's a fantastic idea!" Katie Rose exclaimed with enthusiasm.

"What do you mean?" Callie asked, sounding puzzled.

"I mean, why don't you and Mason get married at the same time. We'll have a joint ceremony! We can't get married in the Catholic Church, because the priest won't let us. We'd all have to wait six months and go through classes to do that. So the church part of the wedding is out. Garrison and I are going to the Justice of the Peace. Why don't you and Mason join us? It will be an awesome day. There will be plenty of food at the reception, because there won't be as many people, with BJ's half of the invitees not being there. We can share the wedding cake, or you guys can order your own. Let's do it, Callie. It sounds like fun!" Katie Rose was very excited.

"Are you sure? Mason and I don't want to steal your thunder."

"Callie, I love you guys. It would be incredible to share this day with you. It will make it that much more special."

"You're the one who is special," Callie stated with genuine affection. Katie Rose was always willing to share everything. They had shared so many special days as children – all of their birthdays and Katie Rose's Indian name ceremony. It seemed fitting all at once to share another special day. "I'll talk to Mason about it, and if it's a go with him, then I'm game!"

"Yes!" Katie Rose cheered. Things seemed to be getting better and better. She could not wait for the next thirteen days to pass. Her life was almost perfect.

Chapter 35

The Wedding

Jackie Lynn was glowing as she appraised her daughter. Katie Rose looked absolutely lovely. She had on a traditional wedding gown – white satin, floor length, with an empire waist. Her heavy crinoline skirt gave the bottom of the dress its rounded fullness, so that, when Katie Rose moved, it appeared she was gliding. The entire top of the dress, front and back, to the waist, was ornamented with flower appliqués and tiny pearls. The V-neck front and back and the short sleeves were also lined with tiny elegant pearls. There were eight lace buttons up the back that ended at a bow with lace flowers. The flowers were also inlaid with pearls. As if these designs were not grand enough, the gown sported a train in excess of five foot.

Katie Rose's long hair had been curled and swept up. Small, flawless curls adorned the top of head, the band of her veil, and along the sides of her head. Her veil perfectly matched her gown. The band was aligned with small flowers and pearls. Three feet of crinoline lace was connected to this band and hung down her neck and back.

Katie Rose's wide smile and sparkling emerald eyes also added to her beauty. As a wedding gift, Jackie Lynn had given her daughter a string of pearls with a large emerald stone in the center. This necklace looked dazzling hanging around her neck. Naturally, she also wore Garrison's Dream Catcher earrings.

Jackie Lynn was delighted to see her daughter so delirious. Katie Rose was making the right decision marrying Garrison. All she wished for was her daughter's happiness, and Garrison brought her joy. Jackie Lynn still felt sorry for BJ. She hated that he had been hurt. She wished him happiness as well, and she hoped he found a special lady who would love him as he deserved to be loved.

Jackie Lynn was also thrilled Mason and Callie were getting married today. Callie, unlike Katie Rose, was not wearing a traditional wedding gown. She had chosen to wear a long, form-fitting, strapless, chiffon, periwinkle, formal gown. The dress complimented her stunning blue eyes and her naturally curvaceous body.

Callie's long, naturally curly, blond hair had also been painstakingly swept up off her neck. She left a few, loose curls dangling down just past her shoulders and also carefully freed a few wisps of hair to loosely frame her exquisite face.

Mason was dressed in a grey tuxedo with a white shirt and periwinkle cummerbund. His hair was no longer down his back. He had it cut short for the wedding. He had shaved off his mustache as well. The five o'clock shadow he often donned was also gone. He looked very handsome and reminded Jackie Lynn a great deal of his father.

Garrison was dressed in a black tuxedo with a white ruffled shirt and an emerald cummerbund. His cummerbund matched Kate's bouquet, which sported white and emerald flowers and white and emerald ribbons. Callie bouquet had periwinkle and white flowers with periwinkle ribbons.

Jackie Lynn thought it was terrific that her daughter, her son, and Katie Rose's best friend were sharing this special day. The only thing that would have made it idyllic was if Long Wolf could have been here to walk his daughter down the aisle and see his son marry Callie. Jackie Lynn felt a bit of an ache, but at least the pain was bearable now. Samuel was right. The pain of Long Wolf's absence was getting less and less as time went on.

* * * *

The wedding was performed at St. Peter's Episcopal Church. Carla, Katie Rose's secretary, had suggested St. Peter's as an alternative to a Justice of Peace. She and her husband had been married at this church, in their garden patio area, the previous spring. This church did not have the same stringent rules as the Catholic Church.

Katie Rose and Callie checked out the church and the garden patio area. They talked to the priest, and he said he would be honored to perform the marriage ceremonies. As another sign their decision to have an outdoor wedding was sound, their wedding day, April fifteenth, was an immaculate, bright, sun-drenched day with a temperature in the mid seventies.

The dogwood and red maple trees and spring flowers were all in bloom, so the patio area was naturally decorated with color and smelled outstanding. Jackie Lynn, Mary Julia and Flora decorated the wood gazebo, where both couples would exchange their vows, with white, periwinkle, and emerald material.

* * * *

As a lively rendition of "Canon in D" was played on Savage Pride's Clavinova, by Robert, the band's keyboardist, all the wedding guests arose from their white, wooden chairs. They watched with smiles on their faces as Katie Rose began to traverse along the white runner. Garrison was already waiting in the gazebo for her with the priest. His joyful, radiant face said it all.

As Mason walked Katie Rose through the garden, and up to Garrison, bit by bit, Jackie Lynn could not help but shed a few tears. Samuel squeezed her to his side, trying to provide comfort.

Mason gave his sister a kiss on the cheek and released Katie Rose. Katie Rose had a few tears of her own standing in her eyes. Even though she adored Mason and was grateful to him for filling in for their father, she missed not having her dad there to give her away. Mason stepped to the side to await his bride, and Garrison took Katie Rose's hand, giving it a gentle and reassuring squeeze.

A few moments later, the Clavinova rang out the traditional wedding march. Jonathan walked Callie down the aisle, kissed his daughter on the cheek, and gave her to a jubilant Mason. This time it was Mary Julia who shed a few tears. Flora gave her friend's hand a tender pat. She too had cried sentimental tears when both Katie Rose and Callie had come up the aisle.

Katie Rose and Garrison exchanged the same vows they had at the Indian Reservation. Mason and Callie exchanged traditional wedding vows. After both couples had uttered their pledges of love, the priest added a few words and prayers of his own. He then pronounced each of the couples husband and wife. Garrison and Katie Rose shared a long kiss, as did Mason and Callie. The select few who had been invited to the wedding ceremony clapped and cheered. There were many others who had been solely invited to the reception.

After having a ton of wedding pictures taken, both combined and separately, the two couples left at last for the reception hall – a nearby Knights of Columbus. Katie Rose could not seem to stop smiling. She had never felt so jovial in her entire life. She was thrilled to be Mrs. Garrison Parker.

Mason was ecstatic. He held Callie's hand as he drove them to the reception hall in their decorated car. All the guys in the band had thoughtfully decorated both Mason's and Garrison's cars. There was white writing on the side and rear windows – "Just Married" and "Another One Bites the Dust". There were balloons, streamers and condoms tied to the mirrors on both sides and to the antennae on the back. Tin cans, hanging from the bumper, also rattled and clanged as they drove down the road.

Everything seemed to be right in Mason's life now. He had everything he ever wanted – the love of his life, Callie, and a successful musical career. The only thing he could imagine that would make him happier was when he and Callie had their first child.

Callie saw Mason's cheery smile and returned it with one of her own. "I love you, Mason," she purred, feeling very contented.

"I love you too, Mrs. Greathouse," he replied, the smile on his face spreading even wider. "I can't wait for our new life as husband and wife to start."

"Me either. I have a little surprise for you," she told him.

"A surprise?" he questioned, glancing at her out of the corner of his eye.

"Yes," she replied with a snicker.

"Well, what is it? Or do I have to wait?" Mason asked.

"Well…you will have to wait. That is, almost eight months…"

"Eight months?" Mason repeated. "What would I have to wait that long for?" he inquired. But as soon as he asked the question, the answer dawned on him. Mason pulled the car over to the side of the road and brought it to an abrupt stop. "Callie, are you telling me…are you pregnant?"

"Yes!" she happily exclaimed.

Mason darted across the seat and tossed his arms around her, lifting her in the seat. "That is so cool!" he declared, giving her a few elated kisses. "When did you find out?"

"About a week ago. I skipped a month, so I took a home pregnancy test. It came back positive. Since it was so soon, and those things aren't always accurate, I made an appointment with my gynecologist. She confirmed it. I'm about six weeks pregnant."

"This is…it's *so* great! Let's announce it at the reception!" he suggested with merriment.

"No," Callie disagreed. "Let's just tell your mother, my mom and dad, and Katie Rose. It's still really soon, Mason. The doctor said everything should be fine, but…let's wait a little while to announce it to the entire free world. Okay?" She had worried about her slip-up with drugs and alcohol, but the doctor had assured her that this episode should pose no problem as long as she stayed clean. Callie fully intended to. She would not do anything so stupid again.

"Okay," he agreed. "Do you have any idea how happy you have just made me, Callie? I have it all now. Life can't get any better!"

"I feel the same way," she said and gave him an adoring, affirming kiss. "You better get us back on the road. Everyone will wonder what happened to us."

Mason gave her one final hug and kiss. Then he slid back across to the driver's side of the car and sent them moving along the highway again. He was the overjoyed. He felt extremely blessed.

* * * *

Jackie Lynn, Mary Julia and Flora were tickled with the way the reception hall turned out. They paid a local florist to decorate it. There were small trees with white lights at each corner. There was white, emerald, and periwinkle material draped along the walls, as well as papier-mâché wedding bells. The material and bells also hung down from the ceiling.

Each of the thirty round tables, which seated up to ten people, was covered by a white cloth tablecloth. A rectangular arrangement of flowers sat in the middle of each table. Half of the tables had white and periwinkle flower arrangements and half had white and emerald. There were also disposable cameras – for guests to snap candid pictures with – scattered to and fro.

Two, ten-foot, rectangular, receiving tables were set off by themselves along a far wall. These were for Katie Rose and Garrison, Mason and Callie, Jackie Lynn, Garrison's parents, Mary Julia and Jonathan, and Flora. These were skirted in white and covered by white cloth tablecloths. They had emerald and periwinkle material draped along the front of the tables. There were big round buckets of white, periwinkle and emerald flowers at each end of these tables.

The caterer's serving tables were at the back end of the hall. These were also skirted in white and covered by white cloth tablecloths. There was quite a spread of food – chicken fingers, Swedish meatballs, pasta, slaw, potato salad, ham and turkey finger sandwiches and a cheese and vegetable tray. Drinks were provided at the bar, which was across the room from the wedding party tables.

Savage Pride was set up in front. When they found out about Mason's wedding, they had wanted to play and DJ for it. Their roadies had set up a rather elaborate set, complete with large screen televisions on both sides, colored lights, and a raised stage.

They gave Mason the microphone and he sang "Baby" for Callie. The two danced their first dance as husband and wife to this song. It seemed very fitting, since Mason had written it just for her. Next, Katie Rose and Garrison danced to Savage Pride's "Love of My Life". Katie Rose loved having Mason's band play at the reception. She had always loved hearing her brother sing. He only sang these two songs, however. Then he went to join Callie again for the rest of the day.

Katie Rose and Garrison were making their rounds at the reception, after eating and sharing their first dance. They had just finished talking to Garrison's parents. Katie Rose had only met them the week before. She liked both Garrison's mom, who he had inherited his blue eyes from, and his stepfather, and they seemed to like her as well. She looked forward to getting to know them better.

As they walked away from Garrison's parents, Katie Rose was shocked to catch sight of BJ. He was walking toward her and Garrison – in perfect stride. He was wearing the khaki pants and brown shoes she had bought him for Christmas and also a solid-colored polo shirt she had bought him for his birthday. "Congratulations, Katie Rose," he said and slipped her into an easy embrace.

"B...BJ? What are you doing here?!" she asked in astonishment, with bewilderment and a little heartache. *How did he know I was marrying Garrison today?*

BJ pulled back from Katie Rose. He glanced over at Garrison and saw he was carefully studying him. *He's wondering if I'm going to make a scene. If I came to hurt Katie Rose.* "Your mom told me about the change in plans. She's called and talked to me a few times since...since we broke up." It was still hard for him to say these words. "I asked her if I could come to the reception. I only came to wish you *both* well. I..." he almost slipped and told Katie Rose he loved her. "I want you to be happy, Katie Rose. If this guy is the key to that, then so be it."

BJ offered his hand to Garrison. Garrison was amazed and pleased. He took BJ's hand and gave it a shake. He also gave BJ an approving nod and smile. *He* is *a great guy. That's why Katie Rose cared about him so much. Being here can't be easy for BJ, but he truly loves Katie Rose.* "We wish you all the best as well, BJ," Garrison told him. His statement was heartfelt and sincere.

"You take good care of her, Garrison, and you make her happy. Or I'll come after you," BJ threatened.

"You don't have to worry, BJ. I intend to do everything in my power to see Kate is the most content woman in the world," Garrison pledged.

BJ observed Katie Rose had tears standing in her eyes. "Hey, I didn't come here to make you sad. That's the last thing I want," he said, releasing Garrison's hand and giving Katie Rose another brief hug.

"You aren't making me sad," she lied, as he pulled away. "You're a very special man, BJ. I hope you find your special someone soon."

"Me too," he said with a bittersweet smile.

Savage Pride was calling for the two couples to go to the back to cut the cake. "I'm going to get out of here," BJ said. "I said all I came to say. Take care, Katie Rose. Call me if you ever need anything. I'm still your friend." *You'll always be my first love. You'll always have a special part of my heart.* "Garrison, you take care too." *You better take care of Katie Rose.*

"Bye, BJ," Katie Rose said as a few, stray tears escaped.

Garrison put his arm around her and pulled her close to his side. As BJ turned and walked away, Garrison turned Katie Rose in the other direction and walked her toward the wedding cake in the back. "No sadness today, Kate," he whispered in her ear and kissed her temple.

Before BJ walked out the door, he turned and watched Garrison walking Katie Rose away. He beheld him gathering her into an embrace and tenderly kissing her. *He loves her, and Katie Rose loves him. They'll be happy together. That's all I want for Katie Rose – to be happy.* BJ walked out the door. He was both sad and happy. He was sad because he had to let Katie Rose go, but he was happy because he truly loved her and believed she would be happy with Garrison.

* * * *

Awhile later, when Savage Pride played "Unchained Melody", Samuel asked Jackie Lynn if she cared to dance. Jackie Lynn accepted his invitation. She loved dancing with this man. He was a very good dancer, and truth be told, she liked the feel of his arms around her more and more.

As usual, Samuel found Jackie Lynn very becoming. She had on a tangerine, scooped necked evening gown. This dress brought out the brown sheen in her hair, and her green eyes also shone all the more. Of course, the contentment he finally saw in them made Jackie Lynn all the more lovely. Samuel was proud to be a part of that contentment. Jackie Lynn was getting more and more comfortable with him all the time. They would soon have a future as more than friends.

Katie Rose spied her mother and Samuel on the dance floor. Samuel was wearing a tailored navy suit, a white shirt and a navy tie with orange squares on it. She guessed he had deliberately picked this tie to coordinate with her mother's dress. They seemed so right together – not just in matching clothes, but their personalities also seemed to mesh.

Katie Rose took Garrison's hand and invited him to dance again. She also summoned Mason and Callie to join them. Carla and her husband, Flora and an unknown, older gentleman, and many other couples also joined in. When the song ended, Katie Rose left Garrison's side and went over to talk with her mother. Getting her alone for a few moments, she commented with an admiring smile, "You and Samuel make a nice couple."

Samuel had sensed Katie Rose wanted a private moment with Jackie Lynn. Thus he went back over to their table and sat down. He was watching Jackie Lynn and Katie Rose talk.

"Now don't tell me you are trying to match make too," Jackie Lynn said to Katie Rose with an amused smirk.

"Who else is trying to make you and Samuel a couple? Mary Julia? Flora? It appears Flora has an admirer."

"Yes, it does. His name is Timothy. He's a bailiff. They've gone to lunch a few times as well," Jackie Lynn shared with a conspiratorial grin.

"That's great. But let's not change the subject. We were talking about you and Samuel," Katie Rose reminded her.

"Samuel is a very nice man. I enjoy spending time with him. As far as anything romantic…"

"You won't allow it," Katie Rose finished her statement.

"I…I don't know that it's…I won't allow it. It's just…"

"Just what, mom? Samuel is a great guy. You deserve to be happy. Why not open yourself up to whatever might happen between the two of you. I almost lost Garrison because I tried to push him away…because I did not believe a relationship between the two of us would be right. I'm glad I finally made the decision to let him in. My indecision almost cost me *big* time. Don't make my mistake, mom. Daddy would want you to be happy."

"You are so wise, Katie Rose," Jackie Lynn stated with a proud smile. She pulled her daughter into a demonstrative, affirming embrace.

"Well…if you think so, then listen to my words. Okay? I want you to be happy too, mom."

"So do we," Mason said. He and Callie had approached from the side.

"Oh, great! My whole family is about to gang up on me," Jackie Lynn half teased.

"Huh?" Mason asked. He was not privy to the conversation Katie Rose had been having with their mom. He and Callie only came over to share their joyful news, since Katie Rose and his mom were off by themselves. "I didn't come over to 'gang up' on you, mom. I..uh..*we* came over to share some wonderful news with the two of you."

"What wonderful news?" Katie Rose and her mom said almost in unison.

"Do you want to tell them, Cal? Or should I?" Mason asked with an enormous grin, putting his arm around her waist and pulling her close.

"Why don't you let me go and get my mom and dad, and we'll tell them all?" she suggested. *She did not want her mom to find our secondhand. She would be hurt and angry.*

"Why don't we tell my mom and Katie Rose, since we already have them here? Then we'll all walk over and tell your mom and your dad," he countered.

"Tell us what?" Katie Rose demanded, growing impatient. She was always eager to hear wonderful news.

Callie nodded her approval of Mason's suggestion. Her mom was sitting on one side of the reception hall and her dad was sitting on the other, with a date. So Callie was not anxious to round the two of them up. This way they could tell them separately. She would make sure they told her mom next.

"Mom, you are going to be a grandmother. Katie Rose, you are about to become an aunt."

"I...Callie, you're pregnant?!" Jackie Lynn exclaimed a little too loudly. She grabbed her new daughter-in-law, hugged her, and kissed her.

Jackie Lynn had never been big on hugging Callie. She had been too much of a brat when she was small. When Jackie Lynn released Callie from the awkward embrace, Katie Rose was immediately in her face. "How long have you known? How far along are you?" Katie Rose demanded to know.

"I just found out for certain a few days ago. I told Mason today in the car on the way over to the reception. I'm only six weeks along."

"Congratulations! I'm so thrilled for you both!" Katie Rose exclaimed, giving Callie a hug. Katie Rose also embraced her brother.

"What's up?" they all heard Mary Julia ask. She had approached them when she heard all of their merriment. She figured they were celebrating something about Mason's musical career. She had not heard Jackie Lynn's proclamation.

"Mom," Callie addressed her, turning all of her attention to Mary Julia. "I'm pregnant."

"You...you're what?!" Mary Julia asked, unbelieving. A mixture of happiness and trepidation washed over her all at the same time. *What if Callie should have a girl? No! You can't think like that! You can't be fearful if Callie does have a girl. You have to trust that Mason will not abuse his child.*

"I'm pregnant," she repeated. "Six weeks along. Are you happy for us?" Callie was puzzled by the odd expression on her mom's face.

"Of course I am, sweetheart," Mary Julia finally proclaimed. She grabbed Callie and squeezed her a little too tightly. *It will* all *be okay*, she assured herself.

Callie was glad when her mom released her. She sensed some anxiety with her mother. Callie thought in despair, *She's probably fearful it will be a girl, and Mason will abuse her. I love you, mom. But I won't let your fears affect* our *child. I hope you can get it together, so you can be a part of his or* her *life.*

All of them took time to rejoice for a while. Eventually, Mason and Callie parted from the others. They went to tell her father the good news. He would be ecstatic. He would be able to spend the time with this grandchild that he had not been able to spend with Callie.

* * * *

Before Katie Rose and Garrison left for their honeymoon, Samuel approached Katie Rose. "I'm very happy for you, Katie Rose," he told her, giving her a departing hug.

"Thanks, Samuel. I know you will take good care of everything at Greathouse while we are away for our honeymoon."

They would be gone for two weeks. Not surprisingly, they were going back to California. Katie Rose was looking forward to sightseeing this time, and Garrison was looking forward to showing her around the state. He had been to California on several occasions.

Mason and Callie would not be as lucky. He and Savage Pride had to be back on tour in a few days. But Fawn, as her wedding present to them, had arranged it so they would have a hotel room each night for two weeks, instead of having to share their private time with the other members of Savage Pride, aboard the tour bus, even though it would be Savage Pride's tour couch this time.

Callie still was having a hard time accepting Fawn was gay, but regardless, she was working hard to contain her petty jealousies, and Mason was being completely truthful with her about whatever he did. They had jumped a serious hurdle, and they did not intend to let anything else come between them. Callie was, at last, starting to like, *and trust*, Fawn. She had even said a few kind words to her at the wedding reception.

"I will take the best care of Greathouse while you are away," Samuel pledged to Katie Rose. "But, Katie Rose, when you return, I will be retiring."

"Oh, don't say that, Samuel," Katie Rose began to argue.

"I have to say it, Katie Rose. It's time you took your rightful place, as President. It's what your father wanted. And I'm ready to step down. I've put in many wonderful years at Greathouse Construction, but now I want to spend my time doing things for leisure."

"Is some of that leisure time to be spent with my mother?" Katie Rose broached the subject.

"Would you like it if it were?" Samuel felt her out. Sometimes children – even adult ones – had a hard time with their parents moving on.

"Very much so," Katie Rose assured him with a welcoming smile. "You are a good man, Samuel. My mom deserves to be happy, and you can make her happy."

"Thank you," Samuel said in delight, grinning and giving Katie Rose another hug. "I've been very proud to work with you, Katie Rose. I can't wait to see you take over as President."

"You'll be sorely missed, Samuel," she assured him. "But if you want to retire, I won't stop you. You've certainly earned it."

"You can bend my ear anytime if you need to. But I doubt you'll need me much. You are very good at what you do, Katie Rose," Samuel praised.

"So are you, Samuel. And I'm sure I will be calling on you for advice from time to time. So your offer is appreciated," Katie Rose told him. She gave him a kiss on the cheek. She secretly hoped someday this man might become her stepfather. She held him in very high esteem.

* * * *

While Katie Rose was talking to Samuel, Garrison approached Jackie Lynn. He sat down at the table beside her and said, "Jackie Lynn, before I take your daughter away to begin our new life together, I wanted to take a second to talk to you."

"Me? About what?" She looked a bit puzzled.

"You hardly know me…and you've known BJ for years. He loves Kate a great deal; he's a great guy; and you care about him. I just want to set your mind at ease that I too love Kate a great deal. As to being a great guy, I had convinced myself that I was so much better than BJ. After all, BJ was just this skinny little oddball, who Kate had nothing in common with; right? Today, I was ashamed of myself for the things I've thought about BJ. I can see now why Kate loved him. He may be small in stature, but his gigantic, caring heart makes up for all of that. I realized I've been a jealous jerk, because he had something I wanted about all else – Kate's love."

"Well, you've certainly got that now," Jackie Lynn assured with a smile.

"I do, and you can't imagine how blessed I feel. It's a precious gift, and I'm going to do everything in my power to protect and strengthen it. I feel like I've been struck by lightening and lived to tell about it. Kate has absolutely knocked me for a loop. Before her, I was mostly married to my career and my painting. I had women pursue me from time to time, and I had purely physical relationships with them, but these women were never important to me and quickly left my mind. With Kate, it was all so different. She constantly consumed my mind from the first time I met her. I pursued her – even though I knew I shouldn't. I couldn't help myself. I am overwhelmingly attracted to her in the physical sense, but it's her kind heart, intelligence, loyalty and strength that have captured my heart. I've fallen hard, and I can't get up…no, make that…I don't ever *want* to get up. I know I'm rambling. Does any of this make any sense? I was only trying to put your mind at ease that Kate is *still* in good hands. I hope you'll someday come to care about me as much as you do BJ."

"You are certainly off to a good start," Jackie Lynn told him. She unexpectedly framed his face with her hands and planted a small kiss in the center of his forehead. As she released him, she said with a pleased grin, "There's only one thing you can do for me, Garrison."

"What's that?" he asked.

"Well, you are my son-in-law now. If it doesn't make you too uncomfortable, I'd like it if you would call me mom."

A knot formed in Garrison's throat. He swallowed hard and told Jackie Lynn, "I can certainly see where Kate gets her big, loving heart from."

Then, with a nervous chuckle, he added, "I would be extremely honored to call you mom. Thanks…mom."

"Welcome to the family, Garrison," Jackie Lynn said and gave him a warm embrace. *Daughters often fall in love with men who remind them of their fathers.* Jackie Lynn could certainly see the parallels. Long Wolf had fiercely pursued her. He, like Garrison, had been a strong-willed, self-confident man. His career had meant everything to him until she came along. Then he, like Garrison, had stopped at nothing to win her love. Jackie Lynn was grateful to Garrison for coming over and talking with her. She looked forward to having many, many more years to get to know this charming young man much better.

* * * *

Katie Rose gave her mother, her bother and Callie, Mary Julia and Flora one final hug in the parking lot before she and Garrison left. They traveled along the highway to his house – they would spend their first night as husband and wife there. Their plane for Anaheim left bright and early the next morning. Katie Rose was contemplating on her life and the lives of her family.

She was so blissful and relieved she made the right decision about Garrison and was now his wife. It touched her heart a great deal that BJ had come to her reception today to wish her and Garrison well. She would always have a soft place in her heart for BJ, and she hoped the two of them could someday be friends again.

Her thoughts turned to Mason and Callie. Katie Rose was elated for them – both in their marriage and their soon to be parenthood. She was glad Callie had finally come to terms with her jealousy problem and decided to trust in Mason and in their love. She saw a bright future for them.

Lastly, Katie Rose reflected on her mother. Samuel seemed to bring pleasure back into her mom's life. Katie Rose hoped her mother would eventually decide to take a chance on romance with this man. She thought they would make a very good couple.

"Hey, little beauty, why so quiet?" Garrison asked her.

"I was thinking," Katie Rose admitted with an easy smile.

"About what?"

"You and I, Mason and Callie, Mom and Samuel. I am so full of joy. I want the same for everyone I love and care about. It's all a matter of making the right decisions. I'm so grateful I decided to accept my love for you, and Callie has decided to trust in her love for Mason, and I hope mom will decide to give Samuel a chance to become more than a friend."

"I hope so too," Garrison said. He returned her smile and gave her hand a gentle squeeze. "The main thing is…we are happy, Mason and Callie are happy, and your mom is happy and has a chance to be even happier. In other words, things are pretty darn terrific!"

Katie Rose beamed at him. "Yes, they are," she agreed. They had all broken through the haze of indecision that held them paralyzed from true happiness. The future looked bright for all of them, and Katie Rose could not wait to begin hers with the man she so dearly loved.

The End

Continue the journey....

You have just completed **Sissy Marlyn's** first trilogy of books. Don't despair! There will be more engrossing novels to lose yourself in from **Sissy Marlyn**.

Planned for 2006: *Jury Pool* – a murder mystery, with a touch of romance and The *Bluegrass* Series, beginning with book number one entitled: *Bardstown*.

Don't be surprised if you find a character or two from **Sissy Marlyn's** first "*I*" trilogy popping up in *Jury Pool* and *Bardstown*. In fact, there will be a contest posted on **Sissy Marlyn's** website. The first reader to tell me the name of the character, from the "*I*" trilogy, and the page this character appears on, in *Jury Pool* and *Bardstown*, could win a special prize.

Check the **Sissy Marlyn** website www.sissymarlyn.com often for updates on upcoming novels and contest information.

Thank you!

Sissy Marlyn

Printed in the United States
45547LVS00001B/16-39